THE COTTAGE

THE COTTAGE

William Thon

Library of Congress Control Number:		2021911516
ISBN:	Hardcover	978-1-6641-7901-1
	Softcover	978-1-6641-7900-4
	eBook	978-1-6641-7899-1

Print information available on the last page.

Rev. date: 06/10/2021

To order additional copies of this book, contact:
Xlibris
844-714-8691
www.Xlibris.com
Orders@Xlibris.com
829536

CHAPTER 1

James of Molay was cornered. His pride had fallen, his strength had collapsed through the ongoing battles, his men and leagues of followers had been destroyed. The Templars had turned against James of Molay and Geoffrey of Cherney. The two men were as one and had turned their allegiances against the pope. As wisps of submarine life in so much as infinitesimal human objects will be subject to burn in Paris for heresy this year of 1314, the giant malaise of battles raged across Europe and against pagans, against the families of witches, religions who constantly seem to be fighting each other and religions against freethinkers and the independent spirits along the coasts of Africa, England, Wales, Greece, Italy, and all Middle Eastern lands, Norway, Sweden, and other parts of the natural world. Religion and its defiant and aggressive armies were killing, destroying, robbing, defrauding, and plundering all the villages, turning hearts and minds from the old ways so as to yield and bend them in the mandatory direction of the church. Taverns across England speak in huddles on how to defend the old ways against sword, fire, and scorn. Villages still speaking in Saxon language still huddle in the masses outside the eye of many newly built churches, cathedrals, and monasteries to plan their defenses in keeping the old ways within some families and not giving 100 percent of all minds and bodies to the church. Many who fight against the bands of marching priests usually wearing bandoliers to hold their daggers and swords or large sticks inside black robes do not prevail. Many houses fall to the Christian armies that plunder cities from Geneva to Londinium to Robert the Bruce in Scotland. Some towns and villages ravaged to ashes were littered with poles holding the fate of many strewn about as examples with backs upon spike, nail, sword, and pious furry as they spread new religion across Europe while forest nymphs, water goblins, and other prehistoric residual life-forms creep and crawl among the woods, rivers, oceans, jungles, and deserts. The new multiplying races of men from Asia to Europe, Africa to Norway, which evolution set apart from the norm, the obvious and pious. Watching, yes always watching, unseen, protected by night, cloud, fog, and storm, hidden for many millennia to come, several conductors set to watch after these lonely and sought-after beings and creatures.

Porius is one such person. Well, mostly humans assist them in living among the mortal, soldering and empire building competitive humans. Porius is a keeper of the old ways, watcher and protector of the downtrodden, unusual, unearthly beings now fast reaching extinction as the human tribes obliterate nearly every dwelling, nest, treehouse, hole, burrow, or other shelter these creatures all need to exist in a once plentiful earth that was home for millions of years or just a stopping place for travelling species. Porius watches with the others as war, religion, and boundaries are set laid and patterned over the earth. Europeans experienced trial and tribulations during the past few years. The poor continued to suffer with their advocates, such as all freethinking and, of course, the mystical creature that hid with anxiety. Porius, one of the last remaining wizards or long lifers, as the ancients called them, continued to have his work cut out for him. Those touched or spawned from the blood of visiting travelers and occasional visitors to this beautiful planet made of carbon life-forms so amazing and beautiful. Forests of vast wildernesses, oceans of the bluest waters teeming with a millennium of species drawn together in their circles of perpetual life from atom to being, seed to tree, coal to diamond and faun to deer. Wisdom more than wizardry circles Porius; and in his mind, peace, communication, intelligence, caring, concern, and invention populate his world, with its wide range of species and fondest wishes into the final result of pleasure in all things great and small. Among many prolonged periods of exacerbated debacles such as were present between the fighting religions, fighting for territory and profit among economic listlessness among the many, the hardworking, and the weak.

Mass hysteria flourished in the blurred realism that was mentally decapitating its victims. Wales lay alone and surrounded by Philip of France in connection with Edward the Second of England, house of Plantagenet, the son of Edward Longshanks, Hammer of the Scotts. Reluctantly, Edward sent his armies to surround Melisende, Queen of

Magical Realms in her castle. Piers Gaveston marched with Edward as they were inseparable and Edward had been named Prince of Wales. Even though Edward showed no aptitude for the life of a soldier, being too frivolous and surrounded by luxury, Edward's desire and lust for Piers Gaveston made him follow Piers on his quest to release the magical families from Wales, saving many from execution, debauchery, and the constant pillaging and burning of pagan and druid villages. Piers's lust for power and wealth made him mad with envy so he could present the young kind Edward riches. Edward Longshanks despised the blooming relationship between Edward and Piers. Two men in battles and in desire for each other behind cloak and shield, blood and fire, they remained constant together as inseparable. Edward and Piers mystical learned from many young wizards including Porius who watched from afar, watching through a pensive of silver and liquid.

"All these battles for territories, dominion, lust, and greed, I shall watch over thee," said Porius as he stared into the milky water of the pensive from his nest in his cottage within the forests of Kent, an eye waiting to be fixed on any successful ambush, a crime, odious, compulsive of all the Old World families, tribes, civilizations, and those who the modern religious armies gathered in vast numbers. Italy, Central Europe, England amid all other countries feeling the rash pope armies and smaller priesthoods which are out capturing those idle-minded beings and insistent on interrogations from religious leaders, dioceses who become judges and juries and mark thee all well. Scurrying in the forests ran the elves, goblins, witches, dwarves, pagans, farmers with no religion, and those who just suffice with nature, making their homes far off the main paths, hidden among cities while others just falsely hang a cross on the door to avoid suspicion. Even harder still live the prostitutes, dancers, actors, slaves, gigolos, and seducers who, unlike the farmer, mason, or house builder, make their living entertaining and well relieving tension in thousands of parlors, taverns, dance halls, castles, alleyways across the planet. All must now be cautious and pay attention to the inquisitorial religions who with intent of wiping out the old ways take all these creatures and target as enemy if not agreeable to the new faiths.

On his way to Scotland, Longshanks turned to Edward and Piers who usually caught armies off guard with plundering as they were taking their small armies to Wales and said, "Edward and Piers, you whores' sons who will not give away lands to the French, together you will mission to Wales and destroy the mystical realms and take the lands and riches for Christendom."

Edward proclaimed, "Shall we indeed, Father? For this deed, together we will go forth. No scorn shall come upon us, and one-third of the riches we shall collect and be given. Piers and I will build our own castle and remove Melisende, Queen of Magical Realms."

So it came to pass, and thus the Melisende castle lay surrounded by fifty men wearing battle leathers, armored with swords and shields, boots, and horses. Some foolishly started up at the castle wall where Melisende waved her wand toward the sky, her wand resting on a large chunk of clear sapphire. As the sprinkling reflection of stars filled the jewel until at her command the skies filled with black-upon-black skies and the once-shining sapphire became as black as its reflective surroundings, lighting became frequent with large slashes of light puncturing the earth around the soldiers. But they stood steadfast waiting for orders from Edward dressed in battle armor.

"Melisende, thy magic shall not save thee. Break down that massive gate," Edward shouted while twenty men bombarded the door and entered the castle grounds. Elves, wizards, goblins, and trolls all attached the twenty royalist marauders.

Melisende stood on the highest wall with crystal in one hand and wand in the other, her long flowing black robes bejeweled with emeralds, rubies, diamonds, and sapphires. "Thy recruits shall not kill all who dwell within these walls," Melisende shouted as rain began to pour down from the blackness she had made above.

"Creatures old and new alike, fold within the underworld!" Melisende said aloud. All took pause from fighting as a long blue flame came from within her wand as she pointed the wand made of wood, wood molded by elves of the highest order. The beam penetrated the earth amid the fighting, and a passageway appeared, swirling wider and wider and revealing a dark hole. One by one, each elf jumped, dived, or ran to leap into the growing hole as the soldiers watched each one disappear into the earth as the soldiers stood in amazed petrification watching these unreal creatures disappear into the hole. Two goblins pointed at a row of five rats and raised their arms toward the approaching soldiers. The rats followed the goblins' commands and ran up the rushing legs, biting their nether regions. After a big painful bite, each rat is seen leaping to the ground and running off while laughing as the soldiers were riddled with paid and an uncomfortable urge to itch just long enough for the goblins to reach the now closing hole and escape to the underworld.

Melisende slays a soldier with her penknife she holds bound to her waist.

Meanwhile, France's James of Molay was tied to the stake back-to-back with Geoffrey of Cherney with flames being lit at their feet, the crowd chanting and pointing, waving flags of the pope and spitting. Caesarea Molay screamed at her brother dying next to Geoffrey. "I shall avenge thee, my brother, and I will remember and record your good deeds! My love forever shall remember both Geoffrey and James as one." Soldiers of the pope were in black hoods and dangling large wooden crosses around their necks. There was a small black group of clouds as it began to rain, but not hard enough to extinguish the fire. Crows, ravens, and squirrels attempted to penetrate the flames but run from quickly away from the sword-carrying figures in black.

"The church may be winning this battle," shouted Geoffrey as his feet caught fire, "but nature will win in the end." Geoffrey turned his neck in the direction of James. "Remember, our meeting in another place means more than all of this. I cannot feel the burning."

"'Tis the end, Geoffrey," James said with his dying breath.

James whispered through the flames, "I cannot feel the burn, I cannot feel the pain."

Smoldering ashes filled the skyline among the littered dead and dying. Bodies pinned to wheels on poles or tied to the occasional stake were set as an example to set fear among peasants and villagers. Villages were strewn across Europe with the exodus of pagan, magical, and Old World families that scurried and hid from the new church—astonishing surprises from the pope to once-peaceful villagers. Geoffrey and James afire was just the tip of the iceberg; and even though some priests had compassion in their hearts in the hope to make a difference by helping the poor, destitute, and the dying, the pope was ordering prisons opened in Italia and taking out the murderers, cutthroats, and thieves who would be ordained as ready-made priests. They would be distributed among the historical families of Italia to spread terror among all families who did not follow the pope's religion and who would be made to suffer by the sword, fire, or fist.

Caesarea pointed her wand toward the burning men and shouted, "Elysium apparentum!" A blue light came from the end of her wand. More rain began to fall from the sky as the crowd stopped and stared at Caesarea. Mouths opened and gasped as they watched her call for her horse Alice.

"Alice, take me to house of Fraun in Paris," Caesarea said as she mounted her horse named Alice. Alice was raised by the magical family in Paris called Fraun. The main wizard of Fraun was Alibastor. Alibastor Fraun was kin to Porius Saladin of England who was building a cottage in Devon. The cottage was neatly tucked away in the woods off the coast of Devon. Porius Saladin was one of the greatest wizards of the age. His spells included many of the spells written within the Malefactor Centorius. Other Malefactorian spells were produced from ages past and collected by Melisende in Wales.

Melisende's castle was now under assault by the so-called holy armies of France and England coming up against the gates. Jules Gaston, the protector of Melisende, had his small army of witches, elves, fairies, and centaurs. But they were not enough to hold off the arrows, the battle-axes, and the heat of battle that was thrust upon them. Magical creatures were struck down one by one then family by family. The raging crowds of black dressing gown–adorned priests had ordered the killing of elven, fairy, centaur, and nymph; for naked, they lived and only a few had escaped into the forests of England to hide from man for as many years as possible until the fever of religion in minds stopped their destructive methods of torture and extermination. The backrooms of taverns, houses full of men and women selling their good looks for cash, artists with a flair for the infinity and magical creatures were under attack from city to city and village to village across Europe and the slow-moving wave across the world.

"Thou greatest gift of peace hath forgotten us. Not even Porius can save us now," Melisende said, holding within her palm the Stone of Purity, which was carved thousands of years ago by Sitium, ancient lord of magical creatures. Against the backdrop of screaming victims and falling walls, Melisende reached out her hand to Thomas Beaufort, son of John of Gaunt.

Thomas learned of all the magical creatures and their ancient ways by falling in love with Melisende. Over twenty years, they had sung, laughed, played, fed their kin. Together they formed a bond of secrecy that held the magical realm together, mighty together even when great distances spread the old-way families apart. Great houses of Italy, France, the Middle East,

England, and Wales would all plant their old-way belief in their hearts and minds and hide from the new religion that takes with vengence all they own, including children, livestock, vegetable stocks, and houses, slaves, merrymakers, wizards, elves, fairies, pagans, witches, and water goblins. Many had left this world with the help of Porius and others of his kind like Melisende to transport magical creatures to other more friendly and accommodating planets.

Melisende was dressed in her silver gown, which was weaved by her friends and companions in the fairy kingdom, who were best dressmakers. Diamonds and pearls lined the long trail of silver silk draped by layers of exquisite design. Melisende's gown glistened and gleamed with sparking sunlight, which echoes of another time, a peaceful time.

"We foresaw the coming of this destruction upon our natural world years ago," she softly said to Thomas. "Take this stone to Porius Saladin in Devon and have him do what is necessary."

Thomas pleaded, "My lady, is it time? Will I not see you again?"

"My heart is breaking, Thomas, but our lands have fallen." She wept. "Bali Normatim," Melisende said the spell, and this beautiful purple stone that was decorated in millions of clear beams of light simply turned into an ordinary-looking piece of granite, as ordinary as a dull-gray sky that neither rains nor drizzles and useless in benefit to any. Here lay the end of an era. After living in fear for years, huge masses of elven families had come to the realization that magical creatures may not belong on earth any longer.

"My lady," Thomas said, watching the stone turn from beautiful perfection to abysmal mediocrity.

"You will travel through the purple petal road to Devon and take this to Porius." She handed him the stone and picked up her wand from the ground, looking around at the magnificent chamber. Melisende pointed her wand to her beautiful bed made of gold.

"Invisible Christianity." She flicked her wand. "This spell will only allow magical creatures and families to see the original beauty of these objects, Thomas."

Melisende pointed her wand around the room and repeated the spell "Bali Normatim," and all the detailed splendor in the objects became ordinary—the chairs, basins, closets, clothes, pet toys, objet d'arts. Even her crystal ball turned into a piece of charcoal and was flown into the smoldering fire pit.

"I don't see a change, my lady. Is it because I do not understand this Christianism?" Thomas asked.

"This is true, Thomas. Only Christians will not be able to see these things as they truly appear." Melisende started. "They are coming, they are near." She instructed Thomas to place the stone in his pocket.

Pointing her wand at Thomas, she said, "Bali Normatim."

Thomas shrugged his shoulders and felt nothing. He acted splendidly and, becoming invisible to anyone other than magical beings, began to walk toward the door, which is now being bombarded with incoming splinters. The door broke inward, and the hordes of soldiers entered screaming for the blood of Melisende. Thomas walked unnoticed by the soldiers. Dodging their every move, he shouted back at Melisende, "I love you, my lady!"

The soldiers stopped and looked at only baggage and flying clothes; they stood still.

Melisende faced the oncoming soldiers and raised her wand. "Alendo Maxoria!" she shouted, pointing her wand at herself.

Melisende shrank to the size of a pebble. The wand dropped to the floor and melted in front of the soldiers' eyes. The pebble floated to enter the Stone of Purity inside Thomas's pocket. Housed inside the Stone of Purity, Melisende gave up her human form and became one inside the Stone of Purity. Thomas, not being seen by all the soldiers, floated out of the castle unnoticed by most. Some who did not believe the story of Christendom were able to witness Thomas walking by, but those few were only going through the motions of this sojourn and were unconcerned with fleeing beings. Thomas walked outside while all the creatures fought with soldiers and battle enraged against all the houses of magic. Oddly enough, while Thomas walked by the tent outside, standing were Edward the Second, Prince of Wales, and Piers Galveston. They both saw Thomas for who he was, proving that they were only fighting this battle as blackmail for their love.

"My lords." Thomas bowed as he passed.

"Are you not staying to fight?" Edward stated to Thomas.

"The battle is won, my lord, and you have won the day," Thomas explained.

Piers interjected, "We shall call off the battle and spare all who remains."

Tempering frankness, Thomas replied, "Thank you, my lords."

Edward, with tears in his eyes, said, "Go in peace, enough of the killing. Has Melisende fallen?"

Thomas answered, "Yes, but she will not be produced."

Edward said, "Go quickly before I am taken for weak. Piers, call off this mindless siege."

Piers mounted his horse and drove out with the orders of the king. The battle slowed, and the remaining living mourned their dead and attended the wounded.

While leaving for the Purple Flower Road, William turned back to the king. "Thank you, King. There will be peace on the other side." Thomas disappeared into the forest on his way to Dorset, carrying the stone with the forest approaching and the battle sounds beginning to grow dim in the background. The smell of smoke and fury or lack of such completely astonished him as the tears in his eyes welled up, Thomas knowing the importance of the stone that he carried. Even the heart and soul of Melisende lay within it. The pink roses that the stone passed gave a special scent in it, the honor due to the connection the stone had with nature and all the carbon and geological forms that reside on this earth.

There was a sent in his nostrils as of grass upon which the sun had been shining so long that every particular blade and every root and fiber beneath the ground seemed cautious and peculiar. The magical lights that had shone for thousands of years were being put out. Once manufactured and used to cure the weak, help the sick, clothe the poor, and understand worry, the world of men was replacing these ancient cures and kindnesses with a new darkness that demanded attention and payment, Christianity. Cadmus Upton, the priest of Devon, was the most feared and evil admixture zealot who tortured and destroyed on a whim. Cadmus raged against the villagers and demanded their allegiance throughout the villages of Devon. Porius knew of the zealot and must protect the magical families as best as he was able.

Heading toward Devon, Thomas was warned by the forest centaurs. Through Barnstable to Bideford and eventually to his destination, the cottage outside Bideford, Porius awaited Thomas who carried the Stone of Purity. Within the Stone of Purity lived the fairy civilization, Melisende, and was soon to house the Devon Centaur Exeter.

Exeter appeared before Thomas in the woods outside of Barnstable. "Thomas, you must house me in your stone."

Thomas stopped his horse and came face-to-face with the forest centaur named Exeter. "What are you, and who hunts you?"

"I am Exeter," the large beast now out of breath explained.

Noise was heard from horse and men who were coming toward them from the forest behind. The small rock in Thomas's pocket gleamed and glistened with a vibration.

"What's this I can feel in my pocket?" Thomas reached for the stone. Inside the stone was a miniature form of Melisende waving her wand toward the centaur. No noise was heard, but Thomas's eyes went wide upon watching the stone in amazement as Exeter became a miniature and floated into the stone. The men appeared before Thomas, and Thomas raised his arms as if to surrender. The Knights Templar rode by two and twenty and side by side, riding right past Thomas with his arms raised and sweating. The knights were not able to see Thomas for in fact all they see was a bush in which they all steer their palfreys past and ride on to another part of the woods. The sound of horse and men vanished, and Thomas pulled out the stone from his pocket and stared into the stone.

"Melisende, I love you."

The scene became unbearable to Thomas so he wandered on and on until he happened upon a busy house called the Old Cock. Inside, Thomas noted a gathering of townsmen at the rear of the tavern shouting and screaming about a priest, Cadmus Upton.

"Cadmus is taking our herds!" shouted one man with gray hair and a pipe. "Cadmus is demanding taxes above the normal amount to pay for his church. Why should I pay him more money when he collects from all of us on Sunday as it stands?"

"Why indeed!" whispered an old woman behind the bar serving Thomas. Thomas's ears picked up, and he paid for his ale.

One large tortoise wandered outside the tavern with slow moves. Children watched, and their parents pulled them from the spectacle of the ancient world. This particular large tortoise must have been aged two hundred years or so, still taking his annual stroll through the village and soon to make his way to the riverbanks of the forest.

"Look at the big turtle, Mummy." The child pointed as his mother smiled, nodded, and holding a large bundle of wheat took the child down the road. Back inside the tavern were full of odds and ends townsfolk, villagers, farmers, the baker, blacksmith, candle maker mis with children, dogs and even the odd cat strolls through one of the three open doors, ale flowing and spirits high.

"Who is this Cadmus?" Thomas asked.

"Cadmus Upton is the priest out at the village church. He is bound to turning all the villagers into god-fearing Christians," she stated.

"Oh my stars."

"Yes," she went on. "My cousin Ben and his family have been working the land round 'ere for thirty years. Never had no trouble 'til now."

"They all seem to be in a terrible state," Thomas said to his interlocutor.

"Why cant's the church just plain leave us alone? We work for a living, jus' leave us alone."

"I will look out for this Cadmus priest indeed."

"What business you have round 'ere, sir?"

"I seek a man named Porius who lives in a cottage."

"Oh, you'll find him at the end of the narrow path toward the sea," she said. "Nice man is Porius, always a kind word, and I know he dislikes Cadmus Upton. Something about a pagan past that Cadmus won't stand for, no way."

"I see, any chance of a meal?"

"Oh, I will fix ye somut," she said, grinning. "A pleasant honorable man like you is welcome 'ere. I've some nice venison and pheasant 'til go down a treat."

"Thank ye kindly."

After Thomas finished his meal during which he heard the crowd plotting to hide, defraud, and trick this Cadmus Upton, he kept himself from dozing. He put his hand on the stone, which lay in his pocket safe and sound. He closed his eyes and dozed off for what must have been a good hour. Finally, the woman behind the bar woke him and showed him on his way.

Large dogs ran through the streets, chasing squirrels while children played with tortoises outside the tavern. Three well-dressed men with colorful silks and padded neck buffs and polished black leather boots, with one tall man with long black beard, hair tied into two stringing braids that fell down his back and reaching his waist, walked down the country road whistling the latest county folk tune. Laughing and gibbering away at some lyrics that none could agree upon, all three touched the large tortoise, which was bound for the woods and shelter there away from the gawking crowded streets of the village.

"Come away from those creatures," said a concerned mother of one of the young girls adoring the reptilian shelled beings, who anciently were about one hundred and fifty years old. Tortoises may live for eternity because no one in this world is able to have seen them all the way through life.

Thomas saw the scene outside and the mother pulling its child away from the tortoise. Three men walking in their finest silks in the most effeminate were all trying to sing in syncopation, which failed and turned into a threesome chortle as they changed directions and headed for the welcoming open doors of the tavern.

"They are wonderful creatures," Thomas said to the woman while poking his head out the door and shouting with beer in hand to the onlooking concerned mother, superfluous was his gesture to stop the humiliation of these ancient tortoises. He took his beer outside.

"Good day to thee." The mother grabbed the daughter, nudging her toward home.

Thomas pet the head of the large tortoise, and the tortoise spoke softly so only Thomas could hear.

"Hello, Thomas, I am Wren," said the tortoise.

"Aye, and a talkin' tortoise who knows thy name," Thomas said, walking on. "A pleasure to see you again, Wren." Thomas turned back to the tortoise. "Maybe I will see you at the cottage."

The forest was dark, but quiet and comforting in some ways. A cool breeze blew by, and it reminded him of running through the midsummer forest of Wales with Melisende by his side. The night could be worth one hundred consciences when the owls are upon us. The purple petals turn to fern, oak, pine, and nettles. The sky raged a wind so fierce that the owls swept the earth of heaven, men, wizards, and gods and blew them all like paper dolls. With the wind came sheets of rain, and the forest became filled with the splattering sound of billions of droplets bending and falling to repopulate the forest. It was late now, and with his cap pulled down over his ears, he felt a vibration in his pocket. The stone vibrated and glowed, so Thomas pulled it from safekeeping in his pocket and stared.

Melisende appeared as a tiny shining star within and pointed her wand to the darkest part of the forest. Thomas followed and came to the cliff with the ocean below, the waves crashing upon the cliffs and splashing the sky. A light could be seen along the coast to the south, and he hurried his pace. Now black with sky above, ocean on one side and forest on the other, he panicked. Was he lost? Where was Melisende guiding him, and where was the cottage of Porius? A large raven appeared before him then circled and made a cry, which was startling yet comforting just in the knowledge that he was no longer alone.

The portcullis of his brain came clanging down on the disturbing possibility that he was alone until after following the raven, a light on the edge of the forest became clear—a cottage.

Lupines, purple, yellow, red, pink lined his path; and the cottage stood before him surrounded by floral he had never seen. Pansies, buttercups, ferns, and rows upon rows of his good providence awaited him. A sense of joy filled his mind. The rain subsided, the half-moon shining through the clouds as they parted. The moonlight shining on the cottage revealed a thatched roof, covered windows, and three chimneys all billowing smoke. Hand-carved wooden doors held etchings of animals, grotesques, and many faces on every inch of wood. Some of the doors seemed to have carvings of scenes from battles, weddings, parties, and objects of magical power. The raven that led Thomas to the cottage circled once more and landed on the hatch above the front door. Then as the door opened toward Thomas now only a few feet away and puffing, the raven departed with a screeching cry that was almost musical. In fact, as the door opened toward Thomas and light shone from inside the cottage, music produced was by fairy machines that floated midair—an ornate trumpet, cello, floating keyboard, and a few violins that floated before Thomas circled. As he stared at the floating instruments, he squinted at each instrument; when the light hit fast, an image of a fairy appeared. Each fairy seemed made from light, clear, iridescent. On sitting at the floating piano, the fairy tipped his hat to Thomas and a tiny voice sang, "Welcome."

A large figure entered silhouetted in the doorway and in a low booming voice greeted Thomas.

"Welcome, Thomas. Welcome to your new home." Porius stood before him, hands on hips, wand at his side. "I hope you enjoyed my welcome fanfare!" Porius moved outside, holding out a welcoming arm around Thomas and showing him in to the cottage.

Thomas's eyes went wide with the mystical magical revue before him. The miniature fairy musicians played faster and louder, and all of them flew to a floating stage over the mantlepiece in the main room. Even though they were floating, it appeared as if they were on a bandstand with musical papers filled with notes, music stands, and a small chorus behind the setup for the orchestra.

"Welcome, Thomas, welcome home," they all sang.

Here today and here for tomorrow,
No longer to beg steal or borrow,
Peace be with you every day, and here is where we all will stay.
Romantic adventures await us all and together we will prevail.

The singers sang, the instruments played, and Porius held his finger while smiling, shushing Thomas from making any noise and watching with spectacles. Shushing Thomas from speaking, Porius waved his wand like a bandleader's baton, and Thomas began to sing along. Thomas turned away from Porius and with wide eyes enjoyed the musical spectacle, with loud applause at the end of the song. Grinning from ear to ear, Porius took out his wand, and the floating orchestra disappeared.

"Oh, they have been rehearsing that one for weeks. Nice to see you, Thomas."

"Porius?" Thomas asked.

"Indeed, my good man. Porius, Wizard of Devon, at your service and here to assist you in becoming our protector." Porius pointed his wand at an empty space in the room, and a table and chairs appeared, floating at first and then settling.

"Why don't you just have a table and chairs?" Thomas asked.

"Ah, that is the trick and the fun of its kind, sir. They are present, yet hidden. I only reveal beautiful objects to those who need see them. For instance"—Porius held his wand so that three chairs appeared—"hold these chairs as if thy bosom and doth have fire and cheerful sun as thy siteth upon them."

Melisende appeared as a ghostlike form seated at one of the chairs and pouring a cup of tea.

"Melisende," Thomas cried and ran toward her, arms outstretched.

Porius interjected, "I thought seeing Melisende once more you would feel more at home."

"Melisende, here now."

Thomas reached out his arms to hug her, and his arms slipped right through as was normal with ghosts. Thomas looked at Melisende.

"I cannot touch you," Thomas exclaimed. "Oh, I want to touch you."

Porius blushed as he witnessed the touching scene. Melisende handed the floating cup to Thomas. "With these tides, only the oysters are happy," Porius said as the wind blew swiftly all the shores around England, rolling in their perpetual motions. Crows, ravens, owls, and pigeons dotted the skies while Franklin the raven rested upon thatch.

"Your tea," she said. "Your journey here was difficult, and over the past three days, you have made me so proud of you. There are loads to discuss, but first you must eat and sleep."

"Yes, my good man," Porius interjected. "There is much to plan and discuss because we have enemies on all sides." Porius continued. "Land and sea may be on your dreams, and your future will be with thee. Not to worry, your training will be long and strenuous, but ye has been the right on for the task."

On the desk behind Thomas stood a book that was the first and only ancient volume of rather heavy, going ten-thousand-page edition of the famous Malefactor, which lay before them and only opened to the wand command of Porius or any other wizard to whom Porius allowed the ritual of opening this great book. Within the book and deep in its mysterious pages were orders, spells, potions, and herbal remedies, which were known to have originated from ancient civilizations that included Kent's Cavern even though humans began populating Europe over fifty thousand years ago and from Kostenki. Despite its proximity to Africa, modern humans still populated Europe, and with them came spells from Africa down to the farthest tips as the Border caves, Blombos Cave, and Letoli with Africa's great deserts and jungles. Some potions were said to have been made by visitors from other green zone planets and from Skhul, Israel, Saudi Arabia, and Asia's Teshik-Tash Province came herbal remedies; and the notes on farming and science, mathematics, biological sections, and musical remedies, which were used for just plain good living all reside within the writings of the Malefactor. Most of the above-mentioned cities were under turmoil and wars from the new religions to wipe out the entire Old World families who ruled these places and replace them with the currently incumbent religion of Christianity and not to Porius's liking or any other farmer or family who currently may have their farms, castles, grand houses, or businesses taken, destroyed, or confiscated by the church if one did not pay protection and bow to the church's will. Now only Athena, Porius, and other less-known beings' aid to protect the old ways and occasionally assist and train families how to pretend that they were on the side of the new religion while practicing the old ways during late-night secret meetings, small gatherings, clandestine parties, and even orgies, homosexual encounters, and the viewing of beautiful dancers to uplift any party. Houses were raided, parties interrupted, male and female sensual dancers arrested, tortured, caged, and abused by the church. Athena and her two guards of the eternal Elysium assisted throughout the Roman empire while Porius mainly was concerned with England, France, Sweden, and Gaul. Bound on the island of Crete 2500 BCE with one copy in Indus script where through the trade on Knossos, a Minoan civilization, gold has been mined in the volcano called Thera possibly from the invasion of Mycenaeans from mainland Greece. All these ancient places gave up their historical remedies and potions, spells and thought process, which one day may prove significant within the Malefactor.

"That is the Malefactor Centorias, and I see you have met Franklin," Porius said to Thomas, watching him eye the great book with its cover of thick layers of black leather and golden silk threads attaching its every important page. Within are sections, wizardry, armor, herbology, weather conditions, mathematics, astronomy, biology, ancient Rome, ancient Egypt, Asia, and Gaul represented throughout.

Melisende disappeared to a tiny dot of light and returned to the stone in Thomas's pocket. Franklin was circling and squawking loudly as he circled the area, landed on a bit of thatch room, circled again, and repeated as he was always on guard.

"Melisende." Thomas looked down, and Porius regained his attention. "Melisende is only able to be seen for short periods of time, but one day you will both be connubially linked."

"Will I be able to touch her?" Thomas asked.

"Indeed, kind sir. Now, a feast."

Porius flicked his wand behind him, and the orchestra appeared once more, playing a merry song. The doors toward the kitchen burst open, and out came two elderly women wearing aprons and caps and holding plates of food—venison; jenny fowl; vegetables, raw and cooked; wild mushrooms; and foaming ale. Small musicians floated in the air, and the sound of music filled the air.

"We must always promote the scientific world of Enlightenment," Porius grumbled.

Franklin, the large black raven, circled over the area, perpetually looking out for raiders, zealots, and those who may threaten the way of things amongst friends or Porius.

"This is Parthenia and Grendle. Both come in to serve, cook, clean, and assist in any way."

"Good evening to you, Thomas," said Grendle.

"Thank you."

"Mr. Porius pays us well and keeps our village safe. You have a good time," Parthenia stated.

"Porius, yes, more of plans to keeping us all safe tomorrow, but for now, please enjoy."

"You must be starved, young sir," stated Parthenia while setting the food in front of Thomas. Thomas was about to sit on the chair where once sat Melisende but decided against it and sat across from Porius.

A loud operatic female shrill voice came from the orchestra. Thomas and the others turned to the tiny stage, nodding their approvals. She took a tiny bow.

Porius stuffed some food in his mouth and began. "With this unbridled violence and extremely heavy-handed cruelty dealt out by Cadmus Upton, you will need all strength to defeat this brute. But never mind that now, let's eat and be merry."

Deer played in the meadows surrounding the cottage and between its thick forests that hold conifer, deciduous forests with every type of plant, ivy, herb, fruit and vegetable, flower and vine that was allowed to flourish in this English climate, soil worthy of the finest-tasting foods. Squirrels ran and played as rabbits only pause momentarily from grazing on the bunches of grasses growing from pockets here and there with the gardens. Butterfly, moth, and caterpillar flourish among the milkweed, flowers, and vegetation, which filled every inch of space. One short elf pulled out some garlic and raced off toward the woods.

Elves were becoming more and more rare, and Thomas always kept getting close to one for a conversation but finding it quite difficult as elves were very matter-of-fact and do not hesitate or hang around when completing a task. Elves popped in and popped out as Thomas liked to say, some dressed in the finest silks and some only sandals and a bit of cloth, but usually holding a wand or stick, which they can wave when the moon or spell was in the right conjunction to perfume the air with magic and have the elves travel among their realm. Elves originated on several other green zone planets not unsimilar to earth's splendors, atmosphere, temperature, and weight. Elves were first known to have worked alongside societies of the Eastern Mediterranean's collapsed pharaohs including Ramesses III, who was defeated by the invaders in the 1170s. Driven out of Egypt, the sea of peoples went on to conquer and settle the coast of the

Levant, the fertile land east of the Mediterranean called Canaan, where battles never slowed nor ceased and unrest was usually prevalent. The mix of peoples with different interpretations of the Old Testament were Levant, Hebrew, Assyrian, Babylonian, and Persian. Elves went through each of these civilizations, and after years of trying to bridge the gap and mend religious zealots to work out problems between them and attempt to have each race live beside another and coexist until finally elves gave up and migrated out of the region. Elven families left the region and came to England in small remaining numbers to hide among the forest that surround the cottage in Kent.

Thomas stopped chewing for a quick moment and then returned to his delicious meal, hands occasionally applauding for the musical orchestra playing at a feverish pace. Soon, Porius, Thomas, Grendle, and Parthenia were dancing and stomping their feet to the folk dance music that seemed to lighten the world.

"Oh, very good, very good indeed," Porius declared while sloshing a large gulp of ale.

From outside the cottage, Franklin the Raven circled and sneered at every sound around them. Franklin the raven had a routine in that he circled areas and reported to Porius. Porius had used the election spell, which gave Porius the ability to hear Franklin and use his eyes when needed once an enemy nears and becomes attracted to the area surrounding the cottage. Porius could follow Franklin from land and sea and view all the existing dangers. Because while Franklin nestled on the roof for some well-deserved rest and the party inside quieted down, bellies full and fall asleep, across the sea ran Caesarea Molay who had witnessed her brother and his partner's death at the stake.

Caesarea Moly knocked at a door within the thin windy Paris streets. The door was of old wood, splintery, and encrusted in metal designs that tend toward the French fleur-de-lis in designed bent iron, old brick walls, and a metal ironwork all around each window and balcony somewhere deep in the Bastille, a busy street with unescorted ladies, some wine merchants, and across the street a late-night bistro with music from inside. The door was old, and a hand reached from inside, pulling Caesarea inside then shutting the door behind her. A large man stood before Caesarea with a long black beard and long hair. He held a candle and wore only a pair of booties obviously prepared by caring hands and a nightcap. Otherwise, he stood naked as the day he was born. Beyond him were two other men covered in only skin, hair, and if you look closely, little spills of wine. The dark walls were painted with pictures of naked people and animals playing in some mystical land or some artist's fantastic imagination.

"Pense que vous viendriez jamais." Fraun, the large man with the black beard, stated. "Oh, excuse me, we thought you would never come."

Caesarea was red with nervousness and blushing at the three nude men before her. Fraun noticed and quickly took out his wand and pointed to the dresser. "Oh, excuse us." Clothes magically floated from the dresser to all three men, and they all stood and dressed before her.

"Tea?" Fraun stated with his face grinning. Caesarea wrapped her arms around him and broke down weeping. The bells of the cathedral ringing loud in the background and wind started to mix with rain dripping down.

"Oh my dear." Fraun patted her head and held her close. "You have been through a terrible ordeal. Come in and rest. We are here and vill protect ye. We will take you safely from Paris to meet Porius." His French accent was so dear that Caesarea could not help but smile a little.

"They burned my brother and his companion alive."

"And we are here to make sure they do not get you," Fraun stated.

One of the now clothed men from behind shouted, "Et j espere ne pas nous aussi!"

"Yes," Fraun replied. "And not us as well."

Below the ground and under the city of Paris lined an army of fairies, and occasionally, elves wandered through the underworld, seeking acceptance for everything they do. Not sure if you have known any elves, but as a preparation for this book, you must be aware that the realm of magical creatures and beings is all around us. In fact, you may become a magical being if in fact you are not already a magical being. Sources say that Porius, the High Wizard of Devon, controlled all elements and creatures. Franklin, his raven, was father to other mind-linking fowl, mammal, and beast. Insects were also known for their magical indulgence and what will strike you most of the insect kingdom were their easy, idle, careless, and almost frivolous look at life, possibly due to the lack of pain, extreme heat, dizziness, balance, and other senses that are not used within the insect world. The insects' migration and duplications over eons of evolution control in an atmosphere was called the Bios Realm. Within this realm repeated a constant energy that linked all things and protected them from their inward and outward realities.

Franklin nested on the roof, the souls inside sleeping. Thomas thought for sure that he had witnessed both Parthenia and Grendle place logs between their legs and fly off for home, but he could not be sure it wasn't the drink.

Caesarea slept next to Fraun in Paris. Once asleep in a cot, which appeared as she fell, her clothes floated from her body, leaving her naked on the cot, breasts bare. The men peered at her slightly, one adjusting his midsection. They all roll over grinning then fell asleep. Caesarea's clothes floated to the sink and washed themselves with soap and water, wringing themselves out in midair, flying across the room, and spinning to let the air lift and press. The clothes made their way to a few feet from the fire and stand there with an occasional turn. Once they had all dried, they folded themselves with the most manufactured perfection an object and led itself. The fact remained that surrounded by endless nothingness touching the clothes, they seem to be of an ability to think move and act just like a human. This was a spell that remained inside the Malefactor Centorias and was perfected by Porius around fifty years ago. Porius then taught this spell to many magical beings and on and on. The propulsion of spells was important for the magical communities to align and share best practices. Holding a wand was a simple, yet complicated position to take because for a spell to work using a wand, it usually must first be charged by a crystal, and second you must always touch the body somewhere with the handle or body part that may be affected if using medical spells.

Before you go to sleep
Everything in every way is getting better and better
Chances of olden ways
Be of no fear and be of no pain
Thy shalt find peace in the ways ahead
Join of cloth, silken, and gold
Follow thy heart to what is true
for thou shalt reap the happiness beyond this earth

Peasants, fishmongers, bakers, and ladies and lads malingered about in the rain-speckled streets of Paris. A fishmonger sets up his stall for the early morning trade. Ladies, men in leather, boys, butchers, bakers all milled about to either finish the night or start the next day. Paris' routine is home to many a brilliant scene, and its aromas of efficacious culinary designs are second to none.

The moon moves across the sky, keeping the balance of the tides in unison with the sea creatures that handle the other balance. Seaweed, flower, fish, crustacean, mammal and urchin rejoice nightly. The sleep of dreams, the swim of dreams, the thought of dreams, smell of dreams, and color of dreams connect us all in the ever-changing fiber of time and space. Billions of planets with billions of earthlike atmospheres house hundreds of millions of other civilizations, each in their own time and space and all connected by dreams, that timeless point in which all life, death, birth, and instinct reside. Here lies the responsibility of all creatures within these countless beings that connects the seeing. Thomas and other creatures have the ability to visit the counsel or summoned when the council demands.

The council of the three green zone planets Marion 1, Marion 2, and Marion 3, the heads of all three planets, occasionally summoned Porius through the light ship and ascension to Elysium. Teaching and filling with the powers that even Isaac Newton would appreciate. The ability to ride the light ray through the galaxy and other galaxies that had joined the vast ray of light, which has been connected to earth for fifteen thousand years and holds the key and knowledge of other worlds, worlds that had been through the overpopulation and wars that can decimate a planet. Porius was taught the ways of future planning to avoid pollution. So many worlds that once industrialized, poison their world until it is unsustainable and eventually die millions of years before the planet implodes in its own evolutionary track. Porius had seen the future and the way to a green earth versus an earth that was rotted with overpopulation, disease, pollution, and starvation.

To avoid this path for earth, Porius had been taught by the beings from these surviving green zone planets. Green zone planets were those close to the same distance from their suns as earth is to its sun, which are capable of building and sustaining life. Though there are hundreds of green zone planets, the three Marion planets hold the keys to scientific and environmental discoveries that can save any world and provide the technology to travel among them without the use of combustible technologies or fuel-filled ships. The technology of light, light ships, and the speed of light are known and utilized for thousands of years. Earth has its secrets and unknown to those who follow man-made religions and the controlling of minds to bend to the will of the church, synagogue, chief, Buddhist, or dictator. Science was all that mattered to Porius and those who unfortunately identified as magical beings, which always seemed absurd to Porius as his knowledge and bloodlines from his alien ancestors were simply different. Peaceful always, respectful at times, engaged, and always attempting to solve problems and situation with the most care as any being is able, Porius and now Thomas would endure to receive, assist, and engage others to the path of freethinking, self-learning, and open-mindedness to others.

Ravens croaking from beyond the woods soon formed a circle above the cottage, waking Franklin as he sneered and gave his comparatively isolated and unique croak. Inside, Porius opened one eye to the sound, sat up suddenly, stretched his arms out, and walked out to clean himself in his usual daily manner, waving his wand and saying, "Elven triumph and aqua entirioto." A magical spray of water poured over him while Franklin the attentive raven snickered and swooped down upon a large worm, swallowing the defenseless worm in one quick gulp. Porius flicked his wand again, and his clothes swooped from within the cottage and floated in midair before him. He dressed himself with care. A ring landed on his finger with the sign of the dragon. A beaded necklace floated around his head and placed itself gently upon his robes. Silken shoes ran out before him, and he stepped in each with a smile. Hearing the others inside waking and the two women Grendle and Parthenia begin cooking the breakfast and the aroma awakened Thomas. Thomas walked out with a towel around his shoulder.

"Morning." Thomas nodded to Porius as he walked down to the river to clean and freshen himself for the day.

"I hope your dreams were pleasant," Porius said to Thomas.

"More bewildering than pleasant. Be back shortly."

"In what way bewildering?" Porius said, eagerly wanting breakfast.

"A girl in the village is so beautiful that both sons of the highest-ranking families are enthralled. One has asked for her hand in marriage and the other is afraid his family will send him away for asking," Thomas said to Porius.

"And what has this to do with thee?"

"My heart has also fallen to thee, her bosom, legs, face, and neck appeal to me. Her hair is the darkest black from her Italian bloodlines, and she is not keen on the new religions and has a way of thinking unlike other pretty girls in the village," Thomas said, sitting down to eat.

"Invite her and let her find her way. Maybe here she can shed light upon her ordeal," Porius said. "Beauty is sometimes a curse because of how others perceive the beautiful, and she must be careful not to make the wrong choice."

Inside, the bread was baking, the ham grilling, eggs mixing, and table set with a green juice drink prepared by Parthenia while each process was a whispering emotion to each other, persuading the audacious Porius to come and eat. An elf appeared with bright light and snapped before Porius.

A large tortoise wandered behind the cottage, laying eggs that mostly would be eaten by squirrels. Fauns played in the meadow surrounded by wheat in the back of the cottage. Ponds with lizard, toad, lily, waterlily, and foliage of many sorts lined the ponds. These secure ponds would house different species of wandering elves, trolls, centaurs, wizards, witches, fairies, and many others too numerous to mention visited these ponds daily. Occasionally, one would enter the cottage and visit with Thomas or Porius. Leal can be found philandering beside the ponds on the happiest of occasions.

"Athena shall appear, Athena is coming," an elf shouted, and then just as quickly as he appeared, he disappeared in a puff of smoke.

Parthenia, Grendle, and Porius stopped to stare and were motionless. Porius then announced, "It appears we will have another for this morning meal," he stated to Grendle and Parthenia.

"Athena always brings guests. We had better get busy," said Grendle in a not-too-excited tone.

"Aye," replied Parthenia.

Porius walked out the front door and saw Thomas drying himself and looking up into the sky. Franklin croaked again and caught another large work down in one gulp. Above them swirled a glow that ascended upon them, plunging through the light; and in glowing detail, dressed in golden gowns and crowns laced with diamonds, appeared Athena beside her two beautiful and barely dressed women carrying swords or golden steel, wearing helmets with wings and lace that barely covered the usually hidden bits.

"Athena. Welcome," Porius said, hands held out wide. She landed in front of him. "He is all right, leave him," Porius announced to the two women who now hovered above Thomas. Thomas viewed the spectacle in a mild sense of amazement. Thomas's right hand was still holding the towel to dry his hair in place. The two women landed before Thomas and bowed. Thomas was now slightly aroused at their beauty, golden hair, and magical appearance.

"I am Thomas. Welcome, and who are you?"

"I am Alexandria," the shorter of the two announced and bowed again, planting her sword on a belt, which wrapped her barely nude body with see-through lace.

"My name is Gloria. We are here to protect Athena."

"No harm will come from me, I promise. Welcome," Thomas replied.

Gloria danced to a flute song that was being played by Alexandria, Gloria's thin waist swerving to the rotating flute.

Take thee champions of truth
Return to the fires of Elysium and the bodies of ritual
Jewels of past and present scattered over the flesh of now

Gloria sang while her body floated and her wardrobe of see-through thin mesh revealed every explorable place to adore upon her skin. Jewels appeared with the music and bounced lighting off Gloria's tight muscles and then fell to the floor but disappeared just before penetration until soon the dance stopped all applause and the meeting ensued.

"Please come in and join us for a morning meal," said Porius. "Nice to have a bit of music in the morning."

"Yes, I have always been partial myself," said Athena.

"Life without music is like, well, like seeing with no color," Porius said.

"Or like rain without clouds," Thomas joined in.

"Precisely, Thomas, yes," Athena said with delight, Alexandria and Gloria in agreement now, dressed and eating the stacks of food resting before them.

Parthenia and Grendle were at work in the kitchen coming in and out from the kitchen with fresh food and mead. Thomas helped in washing up and clearing a way until Porius brought us all back to the meeting at hand.

"We cannot, Porius. The mortals are awaiting at Dover for Caesarea led by Cadmus Upton and some townsfolk he has tortured into assisting him," Athena explained and took Porius aside and whispered to him. What she whispered could not be heard by the others. Porius stepped back from her and shouted, "Go and may peace go with you."

Athena flew in midair toward Thomas, stating, "Thomas, I will meet you another time. Please stay safe with Porius and guard the cottage at all costs. We will meet again soon. Come." She waved toward Gloria and Alexandria, and all three flew off toward the west out to sea.

Porius said to Thomas, "A witch is guarding the rune of Courage, and Cadmus's meaning to take it from Caesarea is in deepest concern."

"I am leaving Fauboug St. Martin for England Fraun."

"I will see to the boat, and my soul take with you. The deck shall be clean, and you will arrive stalely, Caesarea. Rue de Temple shall miss thee."

Porius waited with Thomas at the cottage in England while Athena, Gloria, and Alexandria flew to meet Caesarea on the boat skippered by a lonely skipper named Harry. Caesarea was fitted with horse by Fraun who waved her goodbye. Once at the English Channel, Caesarea boarded the boat alone with Harry. Harry watched a careful eye but crossed the channel in no time, with the cliffs of Dover off to the north. Athena landed in front of Caesarea, the water crashing into the side of the boat.

"Cadmus Upton awaits you with men to take you to the burning," Athena said to Caesarea, eyes burning as Gloria and Alexandria watched the coast and pointed toward Cadmus and ten men waiting for Caesarea.

"We shall outfox them, Caesarea. I enchant the deck broom to take you," Athena stated, pointing at the broom that lay at Caesarea's feet. "Take this broom and use it to reach Porius. Fly along the cliffs to the edge of the forest, and after a few miles, a raven called Franklin will meet you and show the way."

"I shall, but what of Cadmus and his men?" Caesarea asked.

"We have a friend waiting beneath the sea, my dear. A friend," Athena said, pointing her wand to the sea. "I call on the great Kraken. Come forth and protect us."

A sea creature came up from the depths toward the coast where Cadmus and his men stood in amazement. Men scattered, and those on horseback turned and ran while Cadmus cursed the charging beast.

"Witchery befalls us, men. Retreat, retreat!" Cadmus shouted while turning himself and running toward the forest.

"Thank you, Athena," shouted Caesarea. Whilst mounting the broom, she stated, "Cadmus's men are going to see this mounting of the broom, and that's how rumors start." She mounted the broom, flying for shore.

This particular occasion called for a broom to be a useful tool of flight and in most sincere harm shall come to the wizard or other magical creature who may use wood as a way of magical transportation. Many wizards aged quite quickly in their pursuit of this type of magic. One Henry Fielding was practicing with wood at the age of seventeen, and he became sixty overnight, or so the tale was told. Wood may be used because not only is it a living thing, but because it also can get rather bored being no other way to travel. All types of wood can be used for magical transportation devices. Wood also holds the power to transform its molecules within moments of its intermigration due to age, this being said it's always good to have wood.

"Your broom will become legend," Athena stated, arms outstretched toward the flying Caesarea and smiling. "Peace be with you, my child," she yelled. "We leave for Italia where others need saving."

"Farewell," Caesarea shouted back while exiting the ship and leaving Harry to tun his two-sail ship for home, billowing waves and images of frightened seamen and freezing participants of this amazing spectacle that many creatures only dreamed of, before I suppose, making the point of the fact that there is more in this world that needs showing and loving, befriending, supporting and rationalizing thoughts with.

The Kraken returned to the sea without actually harming anyone, but the frightful beast made Cadmus stop. His retreats could be heard and he could be seen looking back to his men to follow him after Caesarea. But none returned, and he stood indignant and alone as the ship faded into the fog in the distance. He said to himself, "Heathen treachery shall be banished from thy land, and all riches shall be mine. I shall follow ye, Caesarea, I shall follow the."

Cadmus mounted a horse and headed up the hill toward the cliffs and, cloak getting wet from the now falling rain, followed Caesarea.

"You will have to ride fast and hard to reach me, Cadmus," Caesarea said as she turned back to see the small ship sail back toward France and the Kraken retreat back to his watery world. Ivy, bramble, wild berries, and the edge of conifer trees pass under Caesarea while her magic broom carried her toward the edge of the forest and beyond toward Essex and Porius.

Looking below her, she noticed a small group of elven creatures working diligently to block the path of Cadmus. In the confusion, Cadmus's palfrey jerked and gets obviously spooked as the beast witnessed the creatures before them. The horse stopped abruptly in its tracks and, with eyes wide with fright at the elves, reared its front legs, knocking Cadmus Upton to the ground where he almost fell rolling down in mud and earth toward the cliffs.

"Come back here, you cowardly beast, come back here," Cadmus shouted at the fleeing palfrey and watched it ride away to safer and more known territory. Cadmus stood and decided that going alone in the forest may not be the brightest idea. He turned around and headed for home—alone, his small band of men deserted, and his horse gone. Cadmus was alone and angry as he retreated toward his home and church.

Porius awaited Caesarea, and after sending Thomas to meet her at the edge of the cliffs along the forest line, Porius opened a circle and called the elements as he prepared for an incantation, a usual practice usually in a room set aside for magic. Instead of drawing a circle, Porius had a circle drawn around the entire cottage, which encompassed rocks of many colors, many elven folk, troll, mouse, and other creatures who had worked with Porius from time to time.

Evidently somewhat dismayed by the storm brewing, Cadmus cursed the ground, cursed the sky, and shouted heretical and repellent remarks to the sky. Though miles away from Porius, Porius watched and heard ever word using a pensive, which now hovered on the small table filled with rainwater. Porius peered in the pensive. "Bring forth the scene of Cadmus Upton and reveal his actions," Porius stated while swooping his wand over the pensive. It revealed an image of Cadmus while he stumbled down a cliff drenched in rainwater, mud, bramble, and thicket. The onlooking elves giggled with laughter as Cadmus slipped, rolling down the hill toward shore.

"Witches on brooms flying. Now I have seen everything, and this must end," Cadmus shouted, fists smacking the muddy ground while the elves turn and head back toward the forest and safety.

Tiny elves began to play on their ancient instruments back at the cottage while Porius winked at the pensive, turning it off and preparing the cottage for his guests.

Caesarea's broom faltered, wiggled, shook, and splintered beneath her, hurling her to the ground at the edge of the forest. "Augh, we must be close. Prepare to dismount," she said as she leaped to the ground now a few feet away. The broom stopped and stood motionless for a few seconds while Caesarea wiped herself off and stood. "Thank you, my wooden friend."

The broom turned and flew off toward the sea to once again regain the comfort of its place on board the boat headed for France. Once a magic flying broom, it was now turned back to a useful tool among the crew. The captain witnessed the return of this independent-thinking item, shook his head, and smiled.

Franklin now circled. "Ho, Caesarea from France!" cried the black circling raven in a terrible screaking voice. "So you are here."

"You must be Franklin! I have heard rumors of ye."

"Oh, aye, me lady, that is I. Listen to the rain and follow my flight toward a nice, safe, and warm bed ye shall dwell in tonight."

Caesarea walked, following the raven as he circled and sang along the shore, leading her to Porius, Thomas, and the cottage. She stopped occasionally, exhausted and starting to perceive a kind of terror inside, the unknowing of what will come and what the future holds. To the right of her were the cliffs with waves crashing below. The left of her was a forest thick with overgrowth and a mix of every type of berry, conifer, deciduous trees, hedges, flowers, bluebells, and even the occasional elf popping its head out for a quick look at Caesarea. Now dripping in from head to toe, shoes squeaking, and her gown and cape growing heavy, she found the material difficult and removed her cloak. When she looked up for Franklin, she did not see him. She panicked and searched the sky.

"Franklin!" she shouted. No reply.

Franklin again appeared and swooped down close to her ear. "Time to consecrate, my lady."

Caesarea stopped and reached in a bag, revealing a bowl. "Let me see."

Caesarea began the incantation. "Sea salt, rose oil, springwater, and small thread of my cloak should do it." She tossed the ingredients to the bowl, and a light came from the bowl then vanished. Before her was an invisible curtain as if a giant sheet of glass waves before her, like waves on the sea; then it disappeared. Thomas was revealed at the edge of the forest beckoning to her.

"Come quickly before the barrier is closed, quickly!" Thomas shouted.

Caesarea stepped across the imaginary line, and as she does, a path was now visible through the forest. Tree, twig, bramble, and ivy all move aside as she walked. She stared down at the ground and around on all sides, and while walking, the forest moved itself step by step. She looked back, and the forest closed behind her, making the view back to the sea once again covered in thick forest and green.

"I have never seen such a spell, and you must be Thomas."

"Welcome, and yes, this is one of Porius's best spells, which keeps the cottage location hidden. No one may enter unless their heart is true. And my extreme pleasure to meet you, Caesarea."

"I have been longing to meet Porius again because I was only five when last we met."

"Yes, and what a wonderful warlock he is," said Thomas. "Like a father he has become, and his zest for life and freedom knows no bounds. I am looking forward to your stories and look ahead, the cottage."

As Thomas pointed ahead, the forest opened up; and along its path, hundreds of flowers rise and open. The sun peaked through the clouds, and birds, deer, toads, squirrels, grasshoppers, and all manners of magical creature including a few griffons. Grendle, elves, Parthenia, Franklin, and one centaur or half horse half man stood outside the cottage. The door opened, and first came out the floating band that played a fanfare. Then Porius stepped out from within, hands stretched out toward Caesarea.

"Princess of our world has come to visit. We are all your devoted protectors," Porius said and bowed down to her, and all followed his gesture. The deer even turned down their necks in reverence.

"Come in and be one with us all," Thomas said.

"I don't know what to say," Caesarea stated while tears of happiness dripped from her eyes. "Porius, thank you.

"I am sorry to hear of your brother and his mate," said Porius.

"They have passed to Elysium, my friends, and go with them a great passing," she wept and entered the cottage.

Inside, they eat and listen to Caesarea's story of France and the battles and the rescue of her brother's pain from the flames, her escape, meeting with Athena, the kraken, and the devilish Cadmus Upton. The music slowed down after several hours; and eventually all fell into their beds, cleaned, well fed, and rested. They all dreamed of another day, another battle, a future where magic lives equally and religious people of faiths do not gather and spread their hate. Other worlds, other civilizations, the bios of insects, the waves of the sea all occupied the dreams of the sleepers.

A noble gesture of defiance and desperation awoke Porius—the sounds of gulls, the morning flickers of flame that could be heard from the fireplace, which has been lit with a nice heat circulating among the visitors. Soon everyone was awake, washed, fed, and sorted outside where Porius revealed his plans to return Caesarea back to her realm in Wales. Traveling with very great speed was difficult and needed special preparations.

"The forest will not be able to sustain the spell which guards us here, my friends, and there are at least a dozen Cadmus Uptons between here and Wales. Caesarea must return to her home and save her realm from further destruction. She will go there and have all magical and independent-thinking individuals hide from the Christians and show the pagans, witches, Jews, elves, and our friends in the animal kingdom how to live among them." Porius looked out over his gathering.

Thomas interjected, "Why don't we fight?"

"No, my dear boy, we must show everyone how not to fight. There are too many of them, and they will destroy the natural world and the order of things. Even as we speak, offshoots of the Knights Templar, the pope, are predestined to take over the intellectual world and kill everything in their path. No, we must not fight. If we do fight, then we will die, and there will be even fewer of us to secure the far future. My dear friends, it may be thousands of years until we are free from these religious zealots." Porius sighed.

The small crowd was quiet and still as a breeze, and the smells of lavender passed them. Geranium, iris, daffodil lay beneath it.

"These flowers are as much a part of our world as toad and man. Our keeping safe together is the plan to secure our future. Books as the Malefactor Centorius must stay hidden from public view. The ruins will be populated, and within the ruins are doorways to other worlds built on a stream of light. The other planets to whom we speak must be kept secret. No religious people shall enter their world or know of the ruins. Even if the ruins are captured, they will turn to stone in the hands of those not worthy. The stones will last thousands of years until the worthy open them and free the creatures, kingdoms, and doorways to other planetary civilizations.

"Powers rocked the pyramids as they were being built. Man, slave, woman, child, and all pilgrims were used in the building of these massive pyramids, dirt filling the slave's mouths throughout the long working hours of the day, taste of the whip occasionally skimming the flesh, delivering a burn that the memory cannot diminish. The religions of ancient Egypt also believed that the suffering of others is necessary for the success of religion.

"Behold," Porius said while lifting a bright blue rune before them. Everyone stared in amazement.

"From the smoldering fire consumed within this rune, I call upon the to protect Caesarea within."

Porius aimed his wand toward Caesara, and a light came out from the tip, covering her in gold-like medallions. The rune stone hovered beside her and shook in several shuddering spasms, and joy overcame her face. She waved to the crowd while she shrank in size. The circling gold medallions covered her and pulled her toward the stone, shrinking to microscopic size and becoming one with the rune. The stone floated down into Porius's hand, the light fading until its appearance was nothing more but a piece of granite.

"This stone reveals nothing to all, but within its shell lies worlds within worlds, and these worlds will protect Caesarea until she reached Wales. Franklin, please call the falcon."

Franklin cried out in a birdcall that only ravens seemed to have the ability to produce. A moment's silence, and then a large falcon appeared in the western sky above the tree line.

"Take them to Wales," Porius said, holding the rune high so that the falcon fixed its aim and plucked it from his hand. All the creatures witnessed the spectacle, and Thomas sat back on a tree stump that held toadstools of several different species as Thomas wiped them from his hand.

"Be safe, Caesarea, and travel with the falcon's protection," Porius shouted to the carried stone.

Below Porius walked a large tortoise that must have been two hundred years old, slowly walking, not noticing the events surrounding him.

"My good tortoise, a pleasure as always," Porius said, stopping for a moment to bow slightly to the tortoise.

King Edward the Second missed his Gaveston and married Isabella, daughter of Phillip the Fourth of France, and produced four children, two of which practiced many of the herbalist remedies of the times and helped spread the antireligious cause to villagers, townsfolk, and others who did not believe or take up this rising fear called Christianity. King Edward offered a glass of wine to Porius during one of the king's many secret and resourceful visits to the cottage. Their friendship, though secret, flourished into herbal training, knowledge, and studied items that some might call magic. These men called it opening up the mystery of life one item at a time—astrology, alchemy, geology, and most of all, cooking.

From the cottage garden came items planted from all over the world; and the occasional African, Italian, French, and northern European persons of notoriety frequented the cottage. People who believed in science, mathematics, herbology, seminarian wonders of thought, even trickery and cunning, needed to be taught about one another if the future will hold any remnants of the past races. Parts of the world were watching out for one another, the Christians coming in force.

"Once the religion has burned its hole in their minds, you will witness blank stares, mindless control, and power which sickens individuality and weakens simple-minded will," Porius said to King Edward.

"Agreed. I have seen it, Porius," Edward stated. "I have seen it in the eyes, in the angry voices, in the raging speeches to helpless crowds."

"I am afraid they believe it," Porius replied.

"Simple minds, indeed, and all lies."

"Deep down they know they are lies, but these lies come with power, lies come with danger," Porius stated, head shaking in his hands, the fire burning under the hearth. The magical band played a low sad song. King Edward turned toward the little floating band and smiled.

"How do you do it, Porius?" Edward said, pointing to the tiny musicians. "They seem so real."

"We are real," the band director shouted in a musical way befitting to the melody.

"They exist."

Porius leaned back, hands on hips, white gown getting hot by the fire. "They play because they are the last of their kind," he said. "Musical elves come when they want, where they know it is safe, and perform the future of music. I know not which far-off galaxy sent them."

Porius said, looking up and pointing, "But the band loves to play, and we are delighted at their chorus."

"Amazing," King Edward said and stood up, putting on his cloak. "I must go, the new bishop arrives from Italy tomorrow and I must put on a good show."

"Watch him, Edward, and listen to those around him. Plant an eye close to him," Porius stated while opening the carved wood door. On the outside of the door stood two beautiful guards in full armor, both with muscular build and keen eye. Edward exited for Londinium.

A few moments after, the hooves of Edward's horses were heard no longer. Already in the dining room were Thomas, a couple of dwarves,

Parthenia, and a table of stuffed pheasant, fish cakes, and green runner beans from the garden.

"Let's eat," Thomas said while digging in and pouring apple brandy. "He seems nice."

Later that night, within the Purity Rune, Daphne called out for Melisende. "Alexa Maxoria," Melisende, Queen of Wales and Houses of Fairies, appeared before Daphne's tiny figure.

"Melisende, our tiny form and strength are not enough to stand wait to the force or mortals who are coming into our lands," Daphne pleaded to Melisende.

"Daphne, you are leader of the northern fairies from Dunmow, Suffolk, Essex, and as far north as Lavenham. I grant that you leave scouts to stay watch over your lands, and they will remain over centuries until freedom comes back to the magical world," Melisende replied, dressed in solid white and floating before Daphne within a white glowing ring of misty light. "Forward you will fly back to your lands. Carry this stone to all, and the Alexa Maxoria spell will bring them through the gateway. The travel is tough to stand for the wings of fairies, but for now, you must retreat into the inner worlds. Take this rune stone to all thirteen remaining fairy families, and within the stone they will find a new home. For within the stone is the gateway."

Two ducks walked through the bushes between the spotted ponds, the female quacking as she was apparently full of eggs. The male duck flew off, leaving her stranded to build a nest and make ready for the ducklings, which will surely hatch in thirty days or so. Franklin rolled his eyes from the rooftop, thinking to himself, "I am sure we will be missing a few nights' sleep once she starts quacking in the middle of the night."

"Elysium?" Daphne said softly and looking down. "I have heard of this place, but have heard it is a difficult crossing for fairies. Difficult."

"My dear, I will be there in spirit to assist all with their crossing," Melisende replied and waved her wand above Daphne. Before them stood Porius out of invisibility and in another glowing circle.

"You called, Melisende? Oh hello, Daphne." Porius quivered to the ground in exhaustion. "You could have given me some warning, Melisende. I was just talking to Thomas at the cottage."

Back at the cottage while talking to Porius and Porius disappeared before him, Thomas was dumbfounded at the unexpected disappearance. Thomas heard the echoing voice of Porius. "I was called away unexpectedly, Thomas. I'll be back for dinner."

"Porius," Thomas said while looking around for the ethereal voice of his good friend. Thomas shrugged his shoulders and got on with his morning.

"Now, Melisende, how may I be of assistance?" Porius said while he and Melisende were floating in circles of misty light. Daphne now rested on a tree branch in the forest. Passing was a large tortoise that strolled by ever so slowly and stopped to graze on some delicious grass piled up on the side of one path.

"Nice to see you, dearest tortoise," Melisende said quickly then told Porius the difficulty that the fairy kingdom was encountering while the churches were being built town by town and village by village. "You see, Porius, fairy families are having a tough time of it."

Daphne spoke up to defend her honor. "When people convert to this new religion, they lose sight of us," Daphne stated, now flying up close to their faces. "An uneasy look if becoming common among the farmers, bakers, and townsfolk who always worked side by side with us. Then they go to church on Sunday and after a few weeks they can no longer see us. Fairies have stated that mortals are calling us fairy tales and starting to believe that we don't exist."

"Now calm down, Daphne," Porius said. "Melisende's way is what we will have to do. Follow me and we will visit all thirteen families and assist them with safe passage."

Porius waved his wand, and the three were off in a blink and reappeared twenty-three miles north in front of the first fairy family. Porius shouted the spell and circled the family with his wand. "Alendo Maxoria."

The earth shook, the wind blew harder through the trees while the family was ionized, made invisible, and sent through a tunnel of change where bright lights, wind, and pressure consumed them all, their wings pulling from them in the force as they grabbed on to their wings, pressing them to their bodies. Their tiny clothes all got destroyed and blown away before them. The whole family floated naked in the maelstrom. Porius and Melisende hovered over the spinning stone as worlds transported beneath its shell. Within the rune was a gateway. A stationary point of light sent a stream to other worlds, to friendly worlds who had partnered with magical creatures for over five thousand years. The Incas, Aztecs, Egyptians, and Chinese have all been familiar with the ancient other world planets' races. Elysium was its general name, which was actually a combination of many words. Each of the thirteen families traveled by evening, and soon Porius was back with Thomas and Melisende returned to Wales. Following this display, it became clear to Porius that the world as he knew it was changing.

The old way would fade as a new chapter on this planet earth began. Not the world where once housed the families of magic, the centaurs, fairies, elves, witches, warlocks, pagans, and others. The sky would change, and only the constellations would remain constant in their moving skies. Insect kingdoms would rotate as the earth spun; science, chemistry, mathematics, and common knowledge would all start to walk behind the gulping greed of religion and the mind control of theocratic minds. Religion was coming, and preparation was in order. The doorways must be opened to the other worlds. And then they must be closed so the theocratic evils do not leak into the other worlds. Our disgrace was this plague of religion.

All this while ducks, deer, and all the other woodland families of creatures made nest and completed the circle of life with no thought or knowledge of what humans were perpetrating against one another across the globe.

The Romans began to fall family by family, and as they fell, temples were knocked to the ground, to be replaced by giant cathedrals. The freedoms of nudity, poetry, and knowledge were becoming encrypted in Rome, Florence, Venice. Priests opened the prisons and made the most vicious killers in charge of destroying the great family homes by estate and turned the families into slaves, torturing and oppressing them all into submission.

Wales families were caught up in the storm, and Catholic priests in many numerous points captured the non-Christians and impaled the resistors on wheels upon spikes. This became a deterrent. Within a year, hundreds of bodies lay upon the wheels that stood high on top of poles, allowing the crows and buzzards to peck the corpses until only bones remained. Then up went another in their place. Some priests killed even the converted if they did not give up their lands or crops to the church. Up on the spikes they all went. Havoc ran amok, stretching from Sicily to Ireland, and later Scotland became infected with the Christian germ of mental, torturous examples and greedy thoughts, all to enrich their churches and give an imposed importance on the Christian souls.

"I hoped this trip would make a difference. Right now, if someone asked my opinion based on pure logic, I would say this wave of religion will last a few thousand years," Porius said to Thomas back at the cottage, eating a lovely dinner with the tiny floating band playing in the background, their tiny bandstand floating. The conductor floated toward Porius, asking, "Will we be safe?"

"Oh yes," Porius said, "as long as you remain within these walls when you come to visit. This cottage will keep you safe." He stuffed his face with chicken cooked on the bone with ale.

"The ale is most fine this evening, Porius," Thomas said, gulping down a mouthful.

"Indeed, most agreeable," Porius replied. "I am turning in early today, what with the fairies' journey. I am plumb worn out."

"Will I ever be able to leave the cottage?" Thomas asked.

"You may, and I will train you on how to remain hidden and remain safe," Porius stated.

"I would also like to visit Caesarea and Athena and most possibly the women of Athena's guards."

Thomas's eyebrows rose as he remembered the beautiful women who guarded Athena, their golden skin and exquisite physiques.

"These times are filled with unsung heroes, Thomas," Porius said. "You have a purpose here, Thomas, to bring this world back once all the devastation is completed and the day of reckoning is at hand."

"People I know and have loved are changed. Even my mother is under the God-fearing Christian spell. She no longer recognizes friend from foe. Her hard-earned money goes weekly to the church. Myself now secondary to her new belief," Thomas said, shaking his head.

"'Tis true of many, my boy, but ye shall find peace."

Porius turned toward the band. "Play something uplifting and fun, a dance."

The band played, and the night sky came over the cottage. Owls played with Franklin out in the yard. The flowers closed to sleep from the sun, dreams filled the air, and a mouse rolled a lump of something unrecognizable to his hole. Inside, a family of mice—two babies, a few older mice, and the mother of his dependents—assisted as they all go toward this rolling object, pushing into the den. A few quick and eager ants took a bite or piece and walked back to their nests. Mice are like men when it comes down to it. Part of a man must be mouse-like. Franklin picked off one of the rats from the edge of the ivy, devouring the rat on the thatch of the cottage.

In Avignon, the Kingdom of the Arles, part of the holy Roman empire was now in France. Pope Clement V, even though he suppressed the Knights Templar and put several to their deaths, added his rule to association with Cadmus Upton in Essex and planned, plotted, and devised a new invasion on English soil. Without the alert of the king or any military forces, this invasion was done by stealth from village to village and home to innocent home. Half a dozen armed men would attack a village, or so went the plan. The dialogue would be short and concise. They would go to the villagers and ask them if they believed in the one god, and if they refused, then they would be tortured until they did believe. If they owned land, then one-fifth of their crop would be given to the church. So this plan went from Cadmus to his small army village by village they prowled, and if a church was not within walking distance, then one would be built. For this was the order of the day, and this was decreed by the church and their one god. Pope Clement would send men to collect the fees from the sold farm goods, fishing, armory, and anything else so mandated by the church. During this struggle, the families who did not want to comply would have the eldest taken and placed on a wheel raised to the sky until nature destroyed them. The stench of rotting flesh could be smelled throughout the forest where such displays prevailed. France was now littered with bodies on poles until most families caved in under pressure and submitted their goods to the church in the name of their god.

June in York among the influence were congregating a mass before the hillside at the mound of the castle. Mason Walters was informed of a traitor against the old ways and spoke quietly to his two mates. Both men were dressed in leather brown satchels around their waists, Cornish hats, and swords.

"Belay the notepaper in which you carry," said the dark-haired soldier standing beside Walters within the crowd of worshippers who were now humming a familiar song. The rain began to spit and spat, and small pieces of the crowd diminished into coverings and hats, and the crowd dissipated. Mason Walters stood, wand in hand, and the soldiers in leather faced away from him, watching the crowd slowly move away. The chief counsel spoke to Walters.

"You and your kind are welcome here, Walters. Your men may stay at the lodgings by the river or at the base of the castle."

"Thank you, Your Grace. We wish only well for all within this realm, for my family have lived here for 1,200 years."

"And I have known your fathers, Walters, and they have always served us well," the chief counsel replied.

The chief counsel in his robes and necklaces turned and walked toward the castle, turned toward Walters, and said, "Come with me, Walters. Come with me into the castle and show me some tricks."

"My lord," Walters stared, beseeched.

"These ways have always fascinated my deepest desires. I have heard much and would like to learn something," the chief counsel said, turning back toward the castle.

Walters and the two men one with raven-black hair, strong muscles, and protruding chest and buttocks followed Walters into the castle out of chains. The other soldier followed behind, looking back for an unfriendly foe who might jump out of the rain and attack. Once into the main chamber, a large fire in the giant hearth, the men removed their swords and went to the back rooms to clean themselves and freshen up. Over an hour passed, and the men reappeared in new clothes made of colored leathery materials, which were laced up the sides from hip to armpit. Leather-padded shoulder harnesses caressed their physiques, muscles bulging at every opening between the leather. They both moved to large sofas close to the fire. Th chief counsel entered the room, apparently blushing. He had changed into his dressing robe and called for wine and cheese. Platters were brought forth. The men devoured everything placed in front as they drank and laughed and occasionally sang. The conversation was fast and furious for a bit; then the chief counsel revealed his name—Norman Little. Walters told him of the Christian rule over their land.

"Taking our holidays like winter solstice and turning it into Christmas and spring to Easter. I see where this all could lead, and that is the end of our ways," Walters said.

"Not all infernal nightingales like you and your two men surely. I do fear for your kind and I sympathize, but as a politician and a member of the church, it is mandatory or I lose my head or burn at the stake. Not all is as brave as you and your men. Why, I could even be hanged for lodging with you," Little replied.

"Well, Mr. Little, kind of you to invite us."

"Are those men touching each other?"

"Well, you have heard of the ways of my people. These two lust often and hard."

"I say, this is quite something I am not sure I can watch, though it is difficult to stop watching," Little said and he gazed at the men who stopped petting each other and sat down like gentlemen.

"Thank you for the wine," the dark-haired man said.

"Most agreeable," said the other.

"You are both most welcome, and what are your names?"

"I am Leal, and my friend here is Simon. We come from Wales to defend the warlock Lord Walters."

"Devoted, I am sure."

Little turned. "Come to feast int the great hall," he said gleefully. "It is time you are all treated as friends. There is much to discuss."

Walters lifted his arm, pointing for the men to follow Little into the great chamber. The walls of stone were covered in hanging paintings, and Walters stopped at one. A beautiful woman standing in the wind looking over a field.

"It is Caesarea. It is my princess."

"Is it," Little replied in a bit of confusion.

Walters brought out his sword and asked Little, "Where has thee found this treasure, for it was painted by my father?"

"It was paid for by my father at Lavenham."

Walters sheathed his sword and pulled out his wand.

"Oh, a wand," Little stated in amazement as they both started to move toward the dining room once more, the men following and staring at the painting. One of the men stared closely and said, "I've had her Caesarea."

"Correct. But what is she doing here?" Walter said as he raised his wand back toward the painting. As he did so, the tapestries moaned, the fire howled, and a screaming could be heard throughout the castle. Guards at the ready, even outside the castle, people woke up from slumbering, ears perked up. Even the church bells were heard ringing in the distance.

A spirit appeared from the painting and hovered naked before them. He floated as a ghost over the table and completely naked. "Lithe am I, and I have heard your call, my lord Walters."

"Your beauty does you good service, but tell us of the painting, where has she traveled?"

"It was bought true by Little, and I know of another who hath who lies in his mind's perdition. Cadmus Upton is his name, and he stole it from

Caesarea's father at Hastings before he sent his pipistrelle bat out to follow the legacy. This is all I can say, I must leave."

He floated back into the panting, and another screech could be heard in the far-off distance. The fire roared once more.

"OH MY GOODNESS," said Little.

"No problem, let camaraderie prevail. In fact, MEN, THIS PAINTING IS HOME. LITTLE IS ONE OF US."

The night progressed, dinner was delightful, and later, the men were given a room in the back to rest. Because in the morning, Walters and his two men would begin a journey to Chelmsford and Hastings in search of my Cadmus Upton. More than words were in the minds of Walters and his two merry fellows.

Chapter 2

Romany, the language of the Gypsies, had been heard off in the distance; and Walters, Leal, and Simon were in tow ride on horses that were not strong, not large. In fact, they could barely hold the weight of these two large men. Every few hours they would stop, rest, eat, and let the horses rest. Their horses were Billy for Leal, Tuine for Simon, and Shadow for Walters. No one ever knew such happier horses because they knew that Leal and Simon would not bring them down. But once they reached Hastings, they would be set free to graze for this was their last journey.

"For years, Billy and Tuine have served us well," said Leal while he waded in a stream, washing himself. Bill and Tuine were splashing, drinking, and eating as much grain and wheat in the surrounding fields. Simon was off in the distance primping and cleansing in the stream in some private area. The sky became gray, and a flock of ravens flew out from a place in the woods before them.

"Simon, get dressed and come back here," Leal whispered loudly toward Simon. Simon grabbed his clothes and put them back on in the water, rushing back toward Walters and Leal.

"Prepare for battle, men. I smell them."

In front of them and out from the woods came ten men led by Cadmus Upton. They stopped across the river, and in formation, Cadmus shouted. "What is your business here?"

"We seek passage to Hastings, my lord. We seek Cadmus Upton."

In shock, Cadmus grabbed his swords. "C-Cadmus Upton, you say? What do you seek him for?"

"Do you know this man?" Walters shouted across the river.

"I am he."

"Then hold your sword and come forth up where the river narrows."

Both parties moved south along the river until the river narrowed, and Walter shouted, "Tell me if you know of Caesarea?"

"Know her? Haha, I have banished her from this kingdom."

"Then you are a fool, and I will make you regret that statement."

Cadmus drew his sword but remained on his side of the river. "There are only three of you and ten of my men," he said while his men prepared to charge through the shallow part of the river.

"Then come for us," shouted Walters, egging on the party.

"I will kill them all," said Leal, grabbing his sword and speaking softly so Walters and Simon may only hear.

"Let them go into the water first, Leal. Let them come for us."

Cadmus stood with his team of men behind them, and they slowly came into the river, wearing black and a large cross. Two of the other men looked like ex-soldiers who were probably salvaged from the Knights Templar.

Walters pulled out his wand and raised it toward them, shouting in Latin, "Sink Thee all but Cadmus Upton," waving his wand toward the oncoming group of thugs in black, cursing and waving their axe and sword, mace and wooden planks. Nine of the men's horses stopped and only Cadmus remained. The horses began to sink inch by inch and hair by drenched hair deeper into the river. Until they were each swallowed. Then horses empty of riders came forth to freedom from under the river. No men appeared for they were lost under the water, bubbling and now steaming river. Cadmus turned back toward the other side of the river.

"Shall I go after him, my Lord Walters?" Leal said, eager to pounce this foe.

"No, he will retreat for now, and we will catch up with him later."

"Those poor men," said Simon, watching Cadmus run his horse into the woods.

"Rise, men of the deep river, you need not die for this venture," said Walter, waving his wand over the river.

The nine men came out and floated in the air a bit before they were dropped into the river, coughing and swimming to the other shore, running now back into the woods—wet, disgraced, and just a bit humiliated.

"They will not be back," Simon said.

"Easy prey, my lord?"

"Easy prey," said Walters now surrounded by nine fresh horses. They befriend three new horses and set their friends free to graze as promised.

"Be thee well, my friends. we shall miss thee," Walters said to the horses as they turned on their way. All three horses bowed their necks toward the three men and, smiling, departed for a well-earned retirement.

Geese flew through Kent, and butterflies circled Lean. Giggling, they tottered off together. A mist appeared before them, and a shape in darkness spoke. "Walters, listen to me. Walk ten paces and pick up the stone." Walter turned left and quickly bent down and grabbed his sword.

"Porius, where art thou?"

Walters took ten steps, and beneath him was a stone of solid ore. Grabbing down, and as he touched it, all three men were cast into the stone—clothes, horses, saddles, skin, teeth, and eyes. Turning, spinning, floating, swirling, departing from this world. The three felt sick and opened their eyes to see each of their compadres backed by colors and swirling rays of light and soon a calm and a shiver. Then blacked out, they briefly gazed upward, or is it down, way down into the abyss of time?

Walter tried to reach out for Leal and Simon as their heads tilted back and legs rose and swirled. Here, the float for time was not mentioned and relayed; they were released to the other side.

Elysium was where they landed and touched and fell, smiling. There were rivers green and casts of shiny unfamiliar glass and gold. Hovering also were larger-than-life insects of unusual shape and size above them. The three seemed to be wearing clothes made of red and gold and made of old machinery. Only buzzing could be heard among the insects who immediately lost interest in three men who had arrived in Elysium, the future home of eternity, and a greeting was finally heard.

A manlike creature came forward, surrounded by several half-dog, half-cat creatures with somewhat human faces, grinning from ear to ear and sipping tea.

"Welcome, I am Glestone the Wise Keeper of Elysium, and you three are most welcome. Behold your world of waiting." His red silk scarf covered an odd figure.

"I am Walters. This is Leal and Simon," Walter stated while helping Leal and Simon to stand. Bent over and rubbing his head, Simon asked, "Water please."

"Yes, of course, my dearest fellow." Glestone clapped, and a plate floated before them. A house elf dressed in top hat and tails poured and floated to the other men, quenching their thirst.

"This is my elf Wopsie." He pointed to the black-and-white-dressed elf who seemed more than eager to please Leal, Simon, and Walters.

"My pleasure. Some mead?" Wopsie said, materializing goblets of wine before them, which was being handed to him from a smaller elf who seemed shy, but most attentive.

"Is this your first time traveling by light?" Glestone said as he motioned to the elves to take the coats and leather satchel of belongings. Leal kept a watchful eye on the parcel.

"Mind how you go with that bag. Ye may find the contents are most important for our quest," Leal said, adjusting his leather straps around his waist and upper body, black boots with silver buckle.

All three nodded in agreement, and sweat poured off their bodies.

"Feel free to take a swim in the river. It will cure your ailment, and here, you are welcome. I remember I felt quite poorly my first time I've flown the light," he said, sipping his tea at a large porcelain table. Three other people walked toward them.

"Franklin said he would find you three," a beautiful female voice said, walking toward them from the edge of the forest.

"Athena," said Simon.

"Yes, and welcome. Caesarea is here as are the elves and several of the thirteen fairy families."

"You are as beautiful as ever, my very sweet lady of elegance."

"The food here is exquisite, the place is free of crime, fault, religion, or attitude. Look, to the east is the forest of Longhorn and the west the Land of Lindly."

Athena hugged Walters.

Simon and Leal grabbed Walters, and all three embraced and walked to the river to bathe while Walters turned back and said, "Love will come, my dear, but the traveling by light has taken hold and into the river we must go."

She smiled and greeted Caesarea and then giggled while watching the three healthy specimens of fit men bathe, joke, and splash. Fools would never be bound, for this is Elysium. Creatures from the river came close to the men, watching, panting, slipping in and out of the water. One half dolphin half man swished by Leal. Leal was startled at first and then crazed with delight when he felt the playfulness of the creature.

"Walters, Simon, are you seeing this?"

Leal turned to the men as they stared in amazement.

"I have never seen such creatures," Walters said, his hands on his head, washing the light from his hair.

"Eel-like creatures mollusks, slugs, dolphin, water lilies of unusual shapes."

As they walk to the shore, they were greeted by Athena and Caesarea.

"These are all water species from other worlds as if you might not have guessed, my dear sirs," Athena said.

They will pretend to foray with you, but their attention span only lasts several minutes. The crowd gathered to meet them, and they were brought to a castle crossing a bridge over rushing white river, white like the river in Interlaken, blue like the turquoise seas of Bermuda, and at the peak of a rough bit are occasionally white like the cliffs of Dover.

That night, a meeting was held in a large chamber, which they called the Hall of Souls, named after all that went before them.

"My good people," Glestone said in a loud voice that echoed to the land.

"Earth is taken, and the seeding has begun."

Mormaers hiss's voices raised.

Many were saying, "I knew this would happen there." "You cannot stop religion once it has gotten ahold of a young civilization."

"Yes, my friends. We are bound to let it wear off, but it shall take centuries and mortals will war, overpopulate, poison, and throttle the beautiful earth."

Walters and the men looked down, remembering their families, their farms, and playmates.

"We will go back and keep order and save the old ways," Walter said, and the crowd silenced to hear.

"I too will go back and hold fast to the old ways?" bravely stated Simon.

"You may not help the earth, but we will try."

"You will try and fail, but you will have this place to use for eternity."

"Now let's eat," said Athena, holding a large plate of grapes, wine, fruit, and quail.

"Game, my favorite," said Leal.

Athena looked at his muscles and rolled her eyes while she bent over to offer him the plate. They dined, laughed, chatted, planned, sang, and occasionally ate more. The night rolled into late, and slowly, they retired to chambers to sleep, dream, and play. This castle city was of Elizabethan architecture and hilly green full of flowers, hedges, fruit trees, thatched room houses. Some of the creatures or animals were most horse, pig, and then somewhat chickens ran free around the village. The village was called Karnes, and it circled the castle, the world of worlds in Elysium. So many friendly civilizations from far-off distant galaxies visited Elysium through the light-traveling experience, fleeting visits for most as they were only allowed to stay in Elysium for a short while to occasionally escape a multitude of problems. On Elysium, it was often found that species practice exhibitionism with nudity, magical practices, and the sharing of spells and potions, healthy routines, and patterns. Liturgists were nowhere to be found on Elysium because religions were not welcome and religious people could not travel by light. The first and most important requirement for light travel was within the mind, and if some beliefs block will, then that could not be used. Well known to Apollo, Athena, and all the gods of distant worlds, their relatives and ancestors may be free, but they will understand the knowledge from birth. Porius, son of Ethon, brother of Gero, and king of the magical world in England, could travel freely, from earth to Elysium and from Elysium to many other worlds. Some trips had taken Porius as far as twelve galaxies from earth and lasted two years. In human years, Porius may be well over 2,000 years old and still able to transfix the most difficult animal into submission by his thought. Porius had knowledge of Walters, Leal, and Simon and wished them back from Elysium.

At his slumber, in the middle of the night, Walter awakened, the two moons of Elysium shining bright outside his Elizabethan windows. The moonlight shone on Leal's naked muscular back across the chamber. Next to Leal lay Simon and some woman of golden hair and pink flushed skin. They lay piled together dreaming. Walters fondled himself and heard the inner voice of Porius as he gazed up upon the wood-carved ceiling of the chamber.

"Time to return, Walters, and bring Simon and Leal," Porius said inside Walters's head.

Walters closed his eyes and fell fast asleep. The next morning after primping and feasting and saying fond farewells to all, the three walked to the portal. Standing on a white cement-like circle in the middle of the forest, Walters, Simon, and Leal with hands on swords departed, floating within flashing lights. In multidimensional movements, the three men started spinning, grabbing their clothes tight and their swords even tighter, circling and spinning for several moments in time. Walters looked at the two men as they twisted and turned and tried to cry out. Leal lost his top portion of clothing then his waist belt that anchored his sword, which flew off in another direction. The sword came loose and went flying around the men as they spun among the lights. Leal's trousers soon followed, and Simon held tight to his clothing, Walters doing the same. Leal went flying nude as the first day of his birth, clothes and sword flying around them all.

Finally, the ground was revealed and they landed. First, Walter landed on his side. "Augh!" he shouted. Simon next landed on his buttocks and bounced several times till he stood. Finally, the nude body of Leal landed on his feet, his clothes falling around him, the sword swirling above them. Simon shouted, "Look out!" pointing at the sword. Luckily, the sword fell fast and landed pointed to the ground two feet from Leal, from his muscular chest, his black chest hair two feet from the sword.

Before them stood Porius. "A fine landing, men. I could not have done it better." He waved to Thomas and Franklin to greet their guests.

"Thomas, this is Walters, Simon, and Leal," Porius said as he helped them to the river. "A nice dunk in water will relieve you all." Porius helped Walters and Simon while Thomas helped the leaning naked Leal.

"My clothes," said Leal.

"Have a swim, and I will fetch them for thee," Thomas said as he admired the perfect specimen of mortal male before him as they bathed, swam, splashed, and laughed.

Once out and all dressed, Walters said to Porius, "So this is the cottage."

"Welcome," Franklin said, circling the men.

"Franklin?" Walters asked Porius while pointing at the circling raven.

"Indeed, my dear Walters, and this is Thomas," Porius said as Walters and Thomas shook hands.

"Thomas, the one Porius has chosen. My extreme pleasure, Thomas."

"I am here to serve you all, Walters. Porius has told me of your adventures," Thomas said eagerly.

"We have important adventures at hand, Walters," said Porius.

"You must mean Cadmus Upton?" stated Walters. The men were still splashing and catching fish with their bare hands in the river behind them.

"You had an encounter?" Thomas interjected.

"Yes, I had their horses sink beneath them."

"And then you rode them off to Elysium," Porius said, smiling.

"It was quite an adventure," said Walters, Thomas just taking it all in.

"There shall be no need for horses on this venture," said Porius.

Simon and Leal came out of the river, refreshed and holding two trout in each hand.

"Ah, this will make a spending meal for us," said Porius. "Rather handy having them around?" he said to Walters.

"Handy and irreplaceable each, for they are my protectors, friends, mates, and good to have around for a party."

"Come, let's cook these trout and have a feast," Porius said. Thomas, Franklin, Walters, Simon, and Leal chatted and joked as they walked into the cottage.

At dinner, Thomas asked Porius, mouth half full of pheasant. "Where did the runes come from?"

Porius, looking a bit uncomfortable, washed his food down with ale, wrinkled his forehead, and began. "A few years ago, a great earthquake shook the lighthouse at Alexandria."

The band stopped playing in the background, and the house went quiet as they heard the mellow voice. Parthenia and Grendle came from the kitchen, and all eyes and ears were toward Porius. A mighty shaking was heard and felt as far as Spain. From this, thousands of folks died, some weaving baskets, some breastfeeding their young, some playing music. All shook, rattled, and rolled as their ceilings crashed down, which was indiscriminate because even the noble house of Ptolemy was either killed, injured, or made homeless by this tremendous earth shaking, which engulfed thousands and ruined villages.

During this crashing and bashing within the lighthouse of Alexandria lay within its great walls mole holes built by Porius's ancestors and the ancestors of magical families from South America, Nigeria, Greece, England, and Wales. The Stone of Purity that now held Melisende, the Mystical Stone now resting in the cottage's garden, fell from the wall. The Unity Stone and the Stone of Courage that housed Caesarea were all held within the walls within the lighthouse at Alexandria. Poseidon, lord of the seas, at the time happened to be dining with a few young undersea creatures with bodies like men but hands like fish; and as they were dining and the ground shook around them deep under the sea, Poseidon knew he must act. Poseidon and his men quickly swam up from the depths of the sea. As they expelled from the sea at a mighty force into the sky, a group of centaurs caught each of them and carried them to the lighthouse of Alexandria, the shaking now over and the four runes rolling down to the bead of the sea. Poseidon picked them up and rescued each stone, waving his pitchfork over each of them, and stated,

> Rune of magic, rune of life, within and without shall never be seen.
> Only those of plenty and the Bios (insect realm)
> Only thy hearts of magic and pure of thought
> May these runes appear and never to be witnessed by those who hold anger.
> Doorways within and without that open for thy pure souls
> Open and transport, close and hide, secure and support.

These lines were repeated over each stone and from hence previous the stones remained beautiful runes to all magical creatures and for those with no anger in their hearts. But to those who fueled anger, seek dissent, or anyone from within a diocese district may gaze upon their true images but instead will see a harmless piece of granite stone of gray.

Porius rested back in his chair. "These small creatures who come from out of nowhere and appear with instruments in hands and smiles on faces appear whenever they feel like practicing because sometimes on the other side of Elysium through the stone or Purity or the Mystical stone or any stone this merry band of fellows and madams between other worlds and this they travel." Accepting the hospitality, food, and kindness of Porius was an almost nightly journey from whichever stone they happened to be traveling that particular day.

Last night, the band was visiting Europa within the Mystical stone transport, and that was where they were housed, rested, washed, and farmed. Yes, some days, the little elfish creature or floating musicians came to Porius.

Porius explained each elfin-type musician to Thomas and the others. "This." He pointed to a bass cello-type instrument with strings of golden thread and wood of finest mahogany. "Well, meet Trop of Capricorn, bandleader and lover of grape wine and women." He pointed to TOC as he bowed and removed a tiny red cap and said, "We will take requests from any of the realms."

Thomas interrupted the introductions. "Play 'Harms Full of Wheels.'"

TOC replied, "Easy, and one of my newer favorites." TOC nodded his head to the band. "One, two, three, and..." The band played into "Harms Full of Wheels," a favorite among the villagers around Londinium. The band played louder and louder, and the guests began dancing as the wine and song poured into the night sky. Outside the windows of the cottage floated several fairies, who must have recently floated from within the Purity or other stones. The night moon swung over as the owls sat perched to watch the amusement. Small rats cropped up, and Franklin and a couple of his raven mates all gathered to laugh, joke, mingle, and well, whatever other amusement was at hand. The piano player went into a long solo then the drummer. Then the ancient horn instruments blew, tooting rock and roll, Porius waving his wand occasionally as light was spilling out, changing colors over several other fairies, goblins, elves, and dwarves, all appearing outside and inside as light came out of Porius's wand. Several other creatures flashed colors of light, rays of sunshine, and seemingly flying fish appeared, ostriches party crashers, many dodo birds, red robins, bluebirds, nighttime flowers begging to expand and give out amplifications of the music. Moles, a small family of hedgehogs, wolves, traveling otters, and even a few penguins waltzed by, asking directions from a fairy who pointed toward south.

Franklin the raven flew up high into the moonlit sky while the sound of the festivities below diminished, the forest becoming blacker and yet bluest with the murmuring where the moaning badgers and grunting wild boar and other mammals could be heard. Franklin swooped down close to shore, and waves could be heard crashing against the cliffs. Two of Franklin's fellow ravens close behind circled the church only several miles from the cottage, smoke billowing out several chimneys from within a small dwelling that stood beside the church. Inside was Cadmus Upton, reading his scriptures, preparing for tomorrow morning's weekly assault on the villagers, instilling fear in their hearts and panic in their minds while feeding them the writings of long ago and collected in a book. The name of this book is the Book—not very inventive, Franklin was thinking to himself and landing on the windowsill. Cadmus could be heard inside reciting something from Matthew, also known as a reliable source of Jewish tales and more recently Christian or, as Porius regarded it, part 2 of the Book.

Franklin was sitting on the rooftop with his other two friends who had rather just come along for the ride to dig worms from the ground and swallow them whole. Franklin removed something from beneath his wing and looking basically like some type of arachnid as it walked gently down the wall inside Cadmus's home.

"So when you give to the needy, do not announce it with trumpets," Cadmus said as the small spider walked across the table to his goblet of wine and dropped in a medicine prepared by Porius. Cadmus fell into a deep sleep, and the ravens came into his home. All three walked around pecking and squawking as fully audible to be heard as an older maiden walked in with a straw-like broom, swishing at the fowls.

Franklin said, "Well then, not even Porius thinks you could." She stood, still fraught with fear.

"Doth thy speak what magic is this?" she said.

"Tentative as always, madam," Franklin shouted, grabbing Cadmus's ring from his hand.

"Why, she's here within this raven and in that ring. She's here," the woman shouted as the spider climbed on board and the descent toward home, leaving behind a snoring Cadmus and a wide-eyed staring blank-faced woman whose morbid receptivity made her a dedicated target for such a shock. Franklin, ring in talons and smiling, turned back to his partners. "That was fun."

As they circled the house and church higher and higher, an owl swooped by. "Hey, watch it!"

In the morning, the river was filled with naked figures, splashing, gesticulating, clinging to each other, bouncing off one another, swimming back and forth, and just generally having a good time all 'round.

Clothes banged themselves against the rocks and splashing in the water then fly to wind dry themselves. Shirts, hats, undergarments, veils, scarves, cloaks, platoons, even the odd handmade shoe may step into the river then wipe clean on the moss alongshore. Yes, back at the cottage, the party spilled out into the morn; and after feasting on bread, cheese, and other concoctions, the crowd, dispirited from such an event having to end, all headed for their homes.

"I thought I would ask you now. So whatever you do or say, it means that no matter what, you will survive," Porius said to Thomas while they dried and dressed along the shore of the river, the sun beating down upon them.

"My lord, please, what is your demand?"

"To ensure my recognition and thus would not like to force upon thee, child of beauty as you are and such an interested party of my magical world. Will thou allow me the resistance potion and spell? Which is to say a spell and potion that mixed together will allow you to live on for centuries and become the caretaker and watcher over the cottage."

"Centuries, you mean?"

"Yes, my dear boy. You will remain here as guardian." Porius sighed.

"I, well yes... I—"

"The items of change that you will be witness to are foretold, the industry coming and the evils that will endure."

"I-I, well, Lord Porius, my heart is here, why would thine need to ask?"

"Because, dear boy, time is infinite, but time is time. You will remain in this form in this planet to keep the transport doors open and to keep the ruins protected, for within them lies the pathway to all the other worlds. Phasing into oblivion daily is no way to live if you decide that the magical transports are easy to navigate even for magical."

General liabilities may occasionally fall upon Thomas as he spent his centuries guarding the cottage, guarding the bios, the winged creatures, animals, trees, bushes, and shrubs. Atom upon infinitesimal atom of living both past, present, and future needed a guardian. People who longed for others and had no means to transport and arrive safely for visits all knew this to be true.

"Our hearts are with each other, but our physical being is not present. Our memories hold us to each other within billions of pinpoint lights of energy to reimagine each other as they are. Memory finds the evolutionary graph between worlds and takes the everlasting images of light. This light is said to have a fundamental reality, and upon it may we travel and rearrange molecules for space travel and portal transporting. Magical creatures have this in bread, but humans must learn this ability because their stage in the evolutionary progress is not ready. Only civilizations from far-off galaxies that have evolved without the pause of discrimination or civilizations to whom place intellect and science, creativity, and imagination above all other thoughts will evolve with the automatic knowledge of disintegration of one's molecules to transport and reconnect on the other side. Machines made of plant life living beings feed amongst all rays of light which assist in the evolution of all magical creatures.

"Thomas, tonight we will have pheasant, roasted with a red wine reduction sauce."

"Shall I copy the chef who visited from Calais?" Thomas replied to Porius.

"Eager as always to please, my dear boy."

"Maybe you will perform your spell upon me, my Lord."

"Yes, tonight, the moon is full, and my potion is ready."

Two butterflies floated by Porius's head and flew into the open window of the cottage then out again through the back windows. One butterfly, huge and purple, landed on Porius.

"My stars, Thomas! Will you look at this beautiful creature."

Standing on his shoulder, slowly opening and closing his wings, it began its descent and circled Thomas three times. Porius got out his wand and pointed toward Thomas. "Acrealite and once more around, Thomas, my friend."

Thomas witnessed the beautiful butterfly of purple dark blue and touches of gold antennae circles Thomas once more and fly off into the forest away from the cottage.

"Augh, Thomas, you are wearing your pointed shoes."

"Yes, the elven queen Thias made thine from mythrial," Thomas replied.

"Mythrial is used in my undergarments," Porius said, showing Thomas the inner lining of his draped button-up breasted clothing, woven from fabrics spanning from Italy to France and the mines of Cornwall. Twelve wooden buttons with golden thread line the lace-embroidered clothing under the long flowing cape of Porius. Tiny faces were sewn into green-and-lavender-colored fabrics with scenes engraved of battles, scenes of rejoicing, all interwoven among the clothing of each garment. The stockings made of a silk-like material in lavender color and green pantaloons hand laced lined above black bootlace upon boots of dark-brown leather, revealing embroidered animals—a hare, a pig, a dodo bird.

Speaking of dodo birds, dodo birds, pheasant, quail, peacock, chickens, crows, and other fowl ran through, flew through, feasted, walked, pecked among the flowers of the cottage gardens.

The night sky was filled with dark ominous clouds as a storm covered the area, and soon, lightning and rain upon rain chucked down in every direction. The church had to cancel Sunday's meeting as the church got overrun with floods. The townspeople locked themselves indoors; even Cadmus Upton stayed in his cottage next to the church. Three men visited him from the village, all wearing swords and bearing the cross hanging around their necks. Cadmus spoke to them of a coven in Brighton that had flared up and was raging its voice against the church of Brighton. Cadmus paid the men four gold pieces to go and "crush the pocket of infidels," said Cadmus.

"I want the leaders of the families beheaded and their heads mounted on the road alongshore which leads into Brighton!" Cadmus shouted.

"Thee shall be done," one man replied. They took their coins and exited.

The next day, the three men found a family of nonbelievers and did what was asked of them, terrifying the families of Brighton one by one. They all bought crosses to wear around their necks, placed crosses on their walls, and begging willingly attending church as to avoid the murdering affiliates ordered by Cadmus Upton to kill all who do not attend church and pay money to the church.

In small meetings, it has been heard that there were complaints of villagers wondering why they needed pay taxes and on top of that money to the church on Sunday. Unfair and unwanted, most people thought about it but dared not speak it, or their fate would lie upon the poles for all to see or the noose, axe, or horse whatever demise was set upon them. Within weeks, the road to Brighton lay strewn with heads on poles with expressions of terror, bodies piled high on poles, their stench surrounding the cities. Women were afraid to even cry openly for their butchered families for fear of being killed or tortured themselves and not having the power or will to defend themselves. They all must conform to the church. England folded, town after town and village after village. France began to fold, the Germanic countries. Magical families were killed, hunted, tortured so they folded one by one. Secretly, a few covens remained under cloak of Christianity and under the dark of night by secret code in letters and not in Latin. In the new English, the writer with an occasional letter was intercepted, traced, and the authors destroyed. Only fools were said to betray the church across many lands and across many countries. This idea ate away at Porius from within.

"How, how, how, Thomas? That is the question. We can't stop it, we cannot fight against it. So the only way is to wait and let the future unfold. When knowledge becomes more important than belief, when the human mind creates on its own again and does not need the faith of another, only then may we return," Porius said.

The river could be heard in the background as the sunset disappeared behind the wall of forest that surrounded the cottage. Lights of fairies soon appeared among the garden's surroundings. Porius turned toward his interlocutor, dressed in the finest clothes and shining black pointed boots, stood Thomas.

"My lord, I am here to assist you with my life and goodwill," Thomas stated, facing Porius's wand in hand.

"Drink this potion and become one with the magical world." Porius handed Thomas a vial of glowing blue.

Once the potion within was fully down into Thomas's stomach, Thomas reacted, fists clenching he went down on his knees, mind bending and visions appearing. Thomas lay on his back, feeling a breeze go through him and spreading to his fingertips, toes, hair on his head, waist, and palms.

"Porius," Thomas said, eyes shining and skin quivering.

"Porius, my lord." Then he stood.

"This feeling running through my veins and wrapping around my mind." Thomas hugged himself in fascination and sexual arousable endorsement into his loins.

"I may have used a bit too much mushroom, but enjoy, my boy, enjoy." Porius backed toward the cottage in full spectacle and grinning as he watched Thomas and the magical creatures around him embrace.

"Thomas," Porius said while raising his wand, "we all thank you and will stand by you through the centuries, protecting the cottage and the runes."

"My lord," said Thomas while kneeling and bowing before Porius. Butterflies circled and a large caterpillar quickly walked over his shoe. He smiled. "You must teach me this potion." He was resting now on the ground with hand on hips.

"I am afraid your first task comes tomorrow, Thomas."

"What? So soon. Surely."

"Tomorrow, three men are coming to meet back at Cadmus Upton's home, and Franklin has been watching and listening by placing a spy within his walls. You must go with us and destroy these men. They have killed, tortured, and made others suffer far too long."

"Yes, my lord Porius."

"Two families only remain, and one of the last tortured parties mentioned their names, and we must destroy these men before they get a chance to kill again."

"I understand," said Thomas, upright and smiling.

"We leave at dawn. And this potion will protect you from injury but give you the will and cunning needed for such an event."

Walters, Simon, and Leal after their adventures in Elysium. Miles from the pond of Porius, they come to a small barnlike dwelling, the evening sky now becoming dark with fawn and pigeon disappearing into the edges of the forest and crows flying from the barn. Walters witnessed a light inside.

"Maybe someone within will offer us refreshment," Walters said, knocking at the half-made door of broken wood and moss. "Hello, anyone at home?"

The door swung open inward and revealed a well-dressed man in cloak, French furniture, a piano-type instrument in the back, smoke coming from within over the three travelers.

"Ah, you must be Walters, Leal, and Simon," the elderly gentleman said, grinning as they stand back in surprise.

"But, my lord, how did you—" began Leal.

"Porius told me through telekinesis that you may be arriving. It appears he follows you by pensive. Allow me to introduce myself. I am Foalon," he said, ushering them in and bowing. A woman scantily dressed in silks left the room and bowed out in the back toward a dark passage leading to other rooms.

"Foalon? Foalon the Mystical?" Walters said as the three entered this surprisingly civilized room, which from the outside barn-looking hovel one would not expect such a beautiful exhibition—metal and gold chairs with red embroidered cushions, swivel bar, and a roaring fireplace.

"Hungry, my good fellows?" Foalon asked.

While Foalon swept his wand over the table, two thin young men dressed in elven clothes of green velvet, gold, and skintight leather vests placed plates of a feast before them. There were two large turtles and a black cat sleeping on his back with his legs in the air up against the leaded windows. Dust and smoke filled the air; the smoke had a sweet smell of that type of skunk that could only be transmitted through a pipe.

"Wine?"

Foalon waved his wand, and a girl of blond hair and naked to the waist but wearing a veil of golden mesh that covered her from head to toe poured from a silver etched pitcher wine that filled each large goblet to the brim.

"My lords." The beautiful blond wine purer bowed facing them and vanished as did the other elven-type men in green.

"Leal, Simon, and I are quite hungry. Thank you, my lord Foalon."

"A pleasure, thank you kindly," said Simon as he threw his cloak, belt of sword, and shield down beside his chair. They all sat and feasted, ate, and were merry. Foalon told them the stories of his past and Londinium and the fall of Wales, Exeter, Canterbury, and parts of France that he had witnessed from the past ten years of the new wave of Christianity.

"Yes, my friends in Saint Michael's Mount in France. I have even been taken out and sent packing to the woods or worse. Betting on those inside the lower streets of Paris behind the wood piles set up by woodcutters, laborers, and anyone else who needs the funds to make it in Paris," Foalon continued. "Under the floorboards of the Le Corbeau, or zi Crow, tavern you would find the entrance to Madam Foalon's brothel, now hidden and moved to the woods for safekeeping."

"My lord, what are you doing here in this wood?" Walter asked while the other two men finished eating and witnessed the reappearance of green-clothed elven men appear before them, taking away the empty plates and disappearing again into the unknown, elven men in green clothes with skirt, helmet and metal gloves on their tiny hands, marching pillaging, extorting, and plotting to do what they must to survive.

One elven male in green velvet and draped golden chains said to Walters, "There is not much work for elves since the world of Christianity has turned its back on the elven population, calling us 'Uncommon and far too different,' the usual arguments that keeps different types of peoples from mingling.

"Good day to thee," he said, only standing about four feet tall and wobbling a bit as he ventured deep into the forest with the other elves as they quickly vanished among the thickets of wood and leaf.

"They don't hang about," Leal said, wiping his mouth as the disappearing green elf took his handkerchief from Leal's hand, grinning and looking at Leal from head to toe slowly. With ease, he vanished.

"No, no they don't, Leal," Foalon stated as the other green waiter took his handkerchief. The girl reappeared, and Foalon said, "You may leave the wine, and please, a refill."

They all put out their goblets toward her, and the request was granted. Walters's eyes swayed, as her large pendulous breasts dangled and bounced around like independent bodies.

"My dearest Walters," Foalon continued to his interlocutors, "we have a plan that would need some guarding, and you three men are somewhat magic, responsible, daring, and quite fetching, I am bound to say."

Foalon licked his lips and had the slightest blush as he gazed upon Leal's muscular form, sparkling eyes, perfect white teeth as Leal adjusted his battle leathers.

Further on in the forest, the noise was heard from the tavern deep in the woods called Le Corbeau, "THE CROW." Two young men wearing the most feminine attire entered, followed by Leal, Foalon, Walters, and Simon. Inside the tavern, a harpsichord was being played by an elderly, yet stately woman, broad in shoulder and wearing cooking clothing as if she had just left a kitchen to play a few tunes for the onlooking crowd. An elf walked by, arguing with a young man who seemed qualified to take a drink. Walters ordered several large goblets of ale.

'This is the finest ale from the hops of Kent," said the man behind the bar dressed in puffy trousers, white full sleeves, open front shirt bound with white leather laces. "I have a lovely steak and ale pie."

"That sounds most pleasing," Walters said, handing Leal the pints.

"Take a seat, and I'll have Robert bring it out to you," said the barman, running back to the kitchen and whispering into Robert's ear, pushing him back toward the kitchen. Soon, Robert came back with a large tray that held a mixture of ale pies, cheeses, and bits of apples.

"Thank you," said Leal as he placed the items on the table. Harpsicord was playing in the background, the people coming and going, all in all a lively place. Leal took a few pebbles from his inside pocket and placed them before Foalon sitting next to Leal. "I have been a puzzler for quite some time, and I have discovered a correlation between the puzzling pebbles given to me by Thoth, god of Egypt, and a weapon we may use. For you see, if I puzzle together the face of a dragon, then I may be able to bring this dragon to life."

"Amazing," said Walters, Foalon, and Simon in agreement as they watch the pebbles roll onto the table.

"Yes, but my hope is to have this dragon help destroy the army being assembled in Hastings by Cadmus Upton."

"Good plan," said Leal, Simon agreeing and Walter nodding approval.

"Well, that's just it. You see, I am not sure I will be able to contain the dragon once I've unleashed the spell," Foalon stated as he walked to a bag of colored pebbles and dumped them on the table before them. For hours, they all placed the pebbles around the center table.

Leal made the teeth. "Teeth strong enough to pierce metal," Leal said.

Walters created the eyes. "Eyes with vision like a hawk," Walters said.

Foalon formed the skull bones and circumference or outline of the dragon's head. Simon added color here and there and filled in spots left untouched. Finally, a fierce-looking dragon made of colored pebbles, its mouth open and fangs gleaming, stood before them.

"Now the spell," Foalon said.

"Wait please, my lord. Simon, Leal, and I have traveled out and need rest before such an adventure," Walters stated, putting his arm to hold down the book Foalon was trying to open.

"Yes, yes of course, a good night's rest and in the morning, we produce the spell which will bring our creation to life."

The next morning as the rain subsided and the wind slowed to a slight breeze, the men dressed and walked to the nearby stream and bathed, joked, frolicked, and feasted on another meal brought from the elves and girl with the golden hair in mesh see-through clothing, subtly caressing her every curve and crevasse of her milky-white skin. Leal adored her beauty and slowly reached for her, but his hand slid right through as she was not actually before him. This ubiquitous female perfection only of ghostly powers smiles at Leal, bowed to Simon, filled their goblets, and disappeared. They all sat around the puzzle they had previously worked in a team tight group to produce.

Foalon the Mystical began his incantation, wand held out toward the pebbled face of the dragon.

"Temporized fragrant size and sight, bring forth the dragon to fight." Foalon waved his wand over the puzzle table, the three men surrounding clutching swords in their belts and with eyes wide.

Before them was unleashed a mass of light and sound, a blowing of power of lightning, thunder, and growing mass. The growing flesh of a dragon swiftly grew before them. Knocking over chairs and men crashing through wood and quivering through cushions came forth this mass. The men fell and crawled as splintered walls, tables, and each other flew in every direction. The creature grew and twisted and turned, bending, quivering, and growing in size, the head bursting out of the roof of the barn. Wood and splinter flew like an army of fowl. Two-foot-size nostrils blew smoke and fire, the wood of the barn scorched in circular patterns. Simon's clothes got burned as Leal padded them out. Walters grabbed his sword and crawled toward the stream. Foalon followed and soon Leal and Simon crawled within inches of the stream, coughing and gasping as the beast grew and grew. The men were now splashing in the water. Fire and smoke filled the barn as it burned to cinders. The dragon stood full before them, knocking over trees and hedges and billowing forth huge puffs of smoke, and as the dragon started to look over itself and see what it has become, it sneezed a bit of flame on its own foot. Patting out the flames, the dragon regained a bit of control, staring at the four men now washing in the stream.

"Thy will be done," the dragon said toward the men as he turned toward Dover.

"No, wait, my pet," Foalon shouted but to no avail.

The dragon bounced on its legs, shaking the earth as the men tried to stand rock and roll against the ground once more.

"Thy will be done," again the dragon said, now seeming to smile and bouncing as if trying to fly.

"Thy will be done," the dragon said in a loud booming voice that quivered the trees, and it bounced once more.

The clumsy dragon was now walking toward Dover and bouncing once twenty feet, again one hundred feet again, and it is lifted while knocking down the occasional fur tree and maple top.

"Angus of the Young will know of this. I should not have made such a beast," said Foalon in desperation. "Angus was too caught up with the Bruce to mid us in the southern Hebrides to know."

"We must concoct another beast to destroy it," said Simon.

"Good idea, Simon," said Foalon. "Come all of you back to what's left of the barn. We must hurry and find those colored stones." They searched, hid, planned, and made sure ancient articles were left safe from the prying eyes of collectors or being offered to the general public.

A song was sung by Foalon, accompanied by his miniature lyre, which he hid under his cloak.

Music is the way to happiness
Join hands to sing
Guide each other to Elysium and together they shall be free.

Back in the destroyed area of the barn where once stood a dwelling now stood a few bits of smoldering wood and tree, bits of goblet and mirror and glass but the colored stones were visible. They all gathered quickly and with haste. They collected and moved to the area least burning.

"Get the table," said Simon to Leal.

Hovering over the table, they all began to place again: Simon the eyes, Leal the teeth, Walters the head, and Foalon filling in the bits. He then stood, turned away, and thought. He thought that the last dragon would go on, so this one must be limited, this one must be timed.

Foalon repeated the end of the spell, the men watching on.

"For once the dragon is defeated, there shall exist no more." He waved his wand.

As before, the beast formed out of smoke and flame, but this time, they watched from a distance. The twisting, expanding, and forming creature before them this time not as clumsy when formed and turned toward the men.

"Thy will be done."

CHAPTER 3

There is magic for all seasons and celebrations from fireworks to lovemaking. A faery ring when one runs three times counterclockwise around the faery ring, then three times clockwise, and then three times counterclockwise again will bring luck and long life, which is one of the reasons dancers occasionally fall into that pattern while they prance, although some lazier wizards were known to have left crystals or beads in the center and walk just once clockwise around the circle, reciting, "Will it bring, faery folk, my wish can't wait, for I know it's not too late and so I make my offering."

Porius recited the spell, and before him came his small floating band, rested and willing to entertain. The music began as Thomas feasted with Porius in the cottage. No doubt a prudent critic would abstain from eating anything that was not made from cleverness and below the ground of the cabin. The bios of ants, caterpillars, worms, and slugs create their own creations of expression that line the earth below the thoughts and wishes of mortal men and women.

"Porius, teach me a new spell," Thomas said while leaning back in his chair.

"Oh, my dear boy, I have just the thing. The Dalmatian spell of spots will work," Porius stated while he retrieved the Malefactor from the mantel, placing it on the table between them, and began.

"Fowl and water, desert and sand, pale and black come from my hand," Porius said, facing Thomas and pointing.

Thomas glowed and itched speckles and spats of white and black; looking at his hands, he saw them change from white to black. Soon, the black shrank in spots, revealing white; and a grin came on his face as he opened his trousers and, looking down, said, "And white to black."

Porius and Thomas roared with laughter, and the band began to play a happy tune. Parthenia came out of the kitchen. Both men were still laughing, and we leave this joyous gathering. Parthenia, hands on hips, stared at Thomas and shook her head. Thomas laughed hysterically at his newly spotted body.

Outside the cottage, Franklin sat on the roof and grunted, groaned, and leaped into the air. Flapping his black raven wings, he swirled around the cottage once for due inspection then circled a bit wider for more inspection and then circled wider still before coming back to the cottage, entering the front door and perching in the warm of the room, enjoying the spectacle. Parthenia gave Franklin a cup of water. Porius and Thomas went through a few more hysterical spells changing each other from lion to bear, snake and leopard, before finally settling down and having their final cup of wine. The band disappeared, the house got quiet, and all slept, dreaming happy times in the fog of the wine.

At midnight, the cottage was dark with splinters of moonlight cutting through the windows. Porius in his bedchamber was soaring in his dreams and snoring in his sheets, Thomas in his smaller back bedroom slash storage room. The kitchen was still with moonlight coming through the windows. A far-off crash was heard, and the sound got closer, now pounding sounds of earth and pressure. Porius awakened and flicked his wand to his clothes, which swirled around him quickly and dressed him completely. Porius pointed his wand toward Thomas, and the same occurred. The crashing out in the garden sounded only hundreds of feet away in the forest.

A sound of heavy breathing and a flicker of light was seen and heard out in the forest, and as they went outside, Porius stated, "A dragon!"

"A dragon?" Thomas said, wiping his eyes as they both stared toward the forest.

"Foalon has done his job," Porius said to Thomas.

"Foalon the Mystical?" Thomas asked Porius.

"The same, I believe you met him in Wales," Porius replied.

"Why, he was a pleasant wizard, why would he create a dragon?" Thomas asked.

"This dragon is to defeat the small army Cadmus has engaged at Dover."

Porius told him of the take of Cadmus Upton and what Franklin had discovered by spying an army of seventy men waiting to pillage the countryside and seek out all the pagan and faery people and bend them to the Christian way. The sound of the dragon could be heard stumbling through the woods toward Dover. Porius and Thomas boarded their horses and followed through the woods until the morning rose and the dragon finally could be seen through a clearing above the cliffs of Dover.

"It appears Foalon's creation was successful, and in not failing, this beast may do us a great good." Immediately, the two follow the dragon slowly as the dragon walked on the ground instead of flying. It looked back and noticed Porius and Thomas and winked.

"It knows we are here and are not foe. It also knows its mission," Porius said.

The men walked their horses toward the dragon as it gained speed, flew over the cliffs, and headed toward Dover Castle. Circling the castle, the dragon disappeared in the forest behind Dover Castle in the area where Cadmus's church and barracks of his men started to scramble. The dragon swept down upon them and burned part of the barracks. Men rustled and dressed, mounting their horses and beginning to ride. The dragon caught one in its mouth and gulped him down, the horse that held him flying off into the ground and rolling until it stood and ran off toward the forest. Soon, many men started running for the forest as the dragon caught one more then headed toward the church.

"Thomas, look out!" yelled Porius as the second dragon moved swiftly past them and headed for the other dragon. A battle ensued between the two fighting dragons of smoke and fire, blood and screeching, trees tumbling and men running off toward their homes. Cadmus Upton was now outside his church, dressing and in shock at the spectacle of two dragons crushing several more men's barracks and horses. One dragon bit hard on the neck of the other. They rolled together in a melee of smoke and fire. Cadmus fell to the ground because of a tree branch that was hurled in the air by the fighting dragons. Porius and Thomas watched from afar as Porius stopped Thomas.

"There is nothing we can do here," Thomas said to Porius as they both watched the spectacle. Running men disappeared one by one as they fled into the woods or got crushed by the fighting dragons. Cadmus was now unconscious and lying at the front of the church. Porius raised his wand and pointed it to Cadmus. Cadmus's body levitated and went into the church by Porius's spell.

The second dragon bit hard on the neck once more with a clench that killed the dragon. They both disappeared into a pitch of powder and smoke, and all was quiet with only the sound of the running men in the distance and behind Thomas and Porius on horseback ride then followed by Leal, then Walters, Foalon, and Simon.

"Foalon, this is quite something," Porius said calmly.

"Men, let's bury their dead and head for home," said Foalon, dismounting his horse and taking a sip from his flagon. Systematically, they dig the three holes for the dead and bury everyone before Cadmus awakened, and they all turned home. Foalon descended back to the sea were a boat awaited him for his return to France. Margaret of France, the second wife of King Edward, consulted with Foalon occasionally in secret and under guise. Walters, Leal, and Simon headed north toward York where Roger Mortimer had been driving back raiders to the north of Ireland. By the time the men returned to York, their Edward the Second and Piers Gaveston, while attempting to obey the ordinances of 1311, still visited each other in York on occasion.

Walters, Leal, Simon, and other friends prepared large feasts with wine and song. The days were merry. Isabella, queen and wife of Edward, despised these outrageous parties that consisted of nude dancers, flashy shows of comedy, and attempts at historical fictional theater. The theater went down very well at these splendid gatherings. Edward II wished to take a journey to Castle Caernarfon in Wales in early October of 1318, but then Edward and Isabelle would later reside in Berkeley castle in Gloucester Castle. Once Gaveston was due to the house Plantagenet, rumors of misconduct between Edward and other men of his guard rose. Isabelle turned a blind eye, and Leal was currently the object of Edward's truest desire. So onward Walters, Leal, and every bolt of electricity from Simon on his feet and ready for any alar. Walking past the first village, the blacksmith heard beating metal with tingling unequivocal piercing; the smoke in the distant waste burnings could be seen and smelled. Two teenage girls showed leg to the threesome and were smiling as they passed.

Soon, they unmounted and walked their horses up to the Black Cap tavern. Inside, the crowd was noisy and rowdy. Walter set the men at a table and gathered three ales. Two women spotted the men from the other side of the bar. One woman smacked the other on the shoulder and turned her neck in the direction of Walters's table. The other woman wearing a red dress with white embroidery-lined sleeves slowly sashayed across the noisy place. Simon grinned as they approached, but they were stopped by Walters carrying his load of ale. "We are just passing through, my dears."

"Such a shame," the buxom leader and most straightforward of the two said.

"If you need a place to stay—" the other began. Simon and Leal grabbed for the goblets of ale.

"Thank you for the offer, and let me by you both a drink."

"Most kind of you, sir," she said, looking him up and down and licking her lips.

"My friends and I are seeking the way to Exeter and will be most glad of direction."

"Not far, my dear. Just follow this road until it heads a bit farther north, past the mine where the workers are, out past Pointer's Field."

Simon dropped his pendant suddenly; it clattered away and fell into a corner under the table. He propelled himself down on his knees and crawled for the pendant while the woman in red raised her eyebrows and stated, "Too bad you not stopping."

After the meal and ales, Walters, Leal, and Simon remounted the freshened horses and headed for Exeter. Eyes of the villagers were all keen and full of wonder. Soon it became an awful night full of thunder and lightning, rain, and the occasional gust of freezing wind, then a calm as they rode on further toward Exeter.

Finally, the inclement weather stopped, and Exeter lay just ahead a small row of spikes lining the road, seventeen in all, which held severed skulls and bits of clothes and hair. Not freshly beheaded but off-putting to say the least. The men tried hard not to look at the heads and focus more on the road ahead although used to such sights. "There must be a church near us. These heads look like a pagan slaughter to me," Walters said.

"I am bound to agree, sir. The sickness of it all," Leal said, riding quickly toward the edge of the city.

"Caerwys was once home to Isca Dumnoniorum, and Romans have trampled these grounds as well."

Following the river along the edge of the buildings, they came to a three-story building with light coming from inside and windows. After posting the horses around the back and leaving them with a short man named Hilda who will feed, brush, reshoe, and bed the horses, the men entered this quite lush interior with its oak paneling carved of faces, cupids, dragons, and royalty. The wood carvings covered most of the exposed wood, and shiny brass-looking railings surrounded a staircase of peculiar beauty. There were velvet cushions upon lace-trimmed lay couches, chairs, and purples, greens, and golds. Three well-dressed men sat at one table playing some form of piquet card game, laughing and drinking, barely raising an eyebrow. The table of fun-loving cardplayers barely acknowledged the men as they entered with bags and sweat, the three basically unnoticed. A beautiful woman appeared behind a curtain. "Walters, welcome and so good to see you."

The men greeted her and were taken upstairs where they were given a large room with four beds and tables, wardrobes, and beautifully lined walls. Shaken by a stir in the corner of the room, they beheld a man lying and snoring who had the appearance of a mystic wearing black, pointed shoes up toward the ceiling, his white beard ruffling below his open mouth.

"Looks like we will be sharing a room with Foalon the Mystical," Simon said to the startled friends.

"They seem to boss magical beings in the same rooms, I'm afraid," Walters said as he disrobed and lay to dream—to dream of the tomorrow when they would be saving Alfie, the elven prisoner, who was being transported to Exeter for execution from Cadmus Upton. Foalon must have heard the news from Franklin, who had been sent by Porius and was resting on the roof outside, always aware, one eye open, talons resting. Soon, Franklin's loneliness ended while at post above the tavern. A female raven landed next to him, studying him with her clear eyes as her legs crossed femininely, making that well-known gesture toward a male. Franklin nodded his head, and she rubbed him once with her neck against his, their feathers mixing with the mild wind and the moonlight gleaming their black forms while stars twinkled in the heavens.

The morning sun peaked over the seas, and from the east, hooves and wheels could be heard with men grumbling of a long terrible night, ten in all, Cadmus at the front of the team. All ten men dismounted and used the river to wash. Outside, tents were quickly set up and the wood-wheeled cage holding Alfie who trembled in the corner. Naked and dark from mud patches and bruised, Alfie shivered, encaged in the wood frame. One of the ten men brought him water in a copper cup, and he drank enthusiastically. The man also slipped him some cooked meat, which Alfie swallowed in one gulp.

"You see, my poor magical friend, we are not all bad," the soldier said.

"Th-thank, thank you, Jeremy is it?" Alfie replied, smiling.

"How did you know? Oh, you're magical," the soldier replied.

"No, you are telling me, but cannot hear. Like a pigeon with eyes seeing more than mortal."

The soldier paused. "I have nothing to do with this lot. My allegiance is to the king, and I have no wish to see you executed, please believe me."

"No cause for worries. Something is stirring," Alfie said as a crash from the front door began and out jump Walters, Simon, and then Leal, who was still naked from the waist up, only a strap across his waist with his sword. The others had swords drawn, pointing at the picnicking men surrounding a campfire with Cadmus standing over them in morning prayer. Cadmus saw them and shouted, "To arms men, to arms!"

With redoubtable aggression, the three men surrounded the ten soldiers, and Simon grabbed four of the men's swords who were over by the fire as they were preparing for food. The element of surprise tenured the three men, and all the other six still not holding swords stood frozen for a moment then all moved toward their steel. Walters took out two men, one a cut to the arm and other to the leg both kneeling in pain.

"Fight, you fools!" shrieked Cadmus while running for his sword. In doing so, Simon ran his sword under Cadmus's neck, cutting the leather that held his large cross of gold. Simon reached for the ground quickly and stood with cross in hand, sword still pointing toward Cadmus.

"You want it?" Simon said. "Fetch it." He was smiling at the large golden shining cross in his hand. Cadmus slowly watched the cross in Simon's hands.

"No, no, please give me that cross," Cadmus pleaded, now on his knees, hands outstretched toward Simon.

Simon said, "Set Alfie free." He waved his sword toward the cage. Cadmus bellowed to all the men to stop fighting.

"Set him free," Cadmus said as he pointed toward Jeremy still by the cage.

"Gladly," said Jeremy as he opened the cage. Only the crackling fire could be heard as the dust settled and several deer and birds stared at the cage. Jeremy opened the cage, and Alfie slowly stood in the morning sun, limping and wearing only rags. He stepped out onto the pathway toward the river. Limping, he walked toward the water with all eyes on his sad figure. Walters, Leal, and Simon retreated with swords sheathed. All the other men stood and faced the sad figure of Alfie stepping into the river. Looking back at everyone, he went down under the water and was gone. Under the surface of the river, Alfie washed and, yet not floating, grew gills, fins, and a tail and swam with the current. Unknown to all who thought they knew elves, elves have the power to become or not become called the changeling. But for our purposes, the eyes of all watching and seeing Alfie disappear under the water stood mystified.

"I have heard rumors of water sustaining life. He is well," Walter said. "Now this cross which Simon holds, do you want it back?"

Cadmus stood. "It is my property and unless you wish to be called thieves."

"Give it back to him," Walters said to Simon who gave it to Cadmus gladly.

"I was only going to chuck it in the river and watch him swim for it, my lord."

Cadmus grabbed the cross and placed it neatly. Foalon stepped out of the tavern. "What have I missed?" Foalon said, placing his black pointed hat on his head.

"The elf has been set free," Simon said aloud.

"Well, that is fine news, indeed," Foalon said, walking up to Walters. "I heard you were close, Walters. I knew you would save the day."

Cadmus grabbed for his horse, mounting to ride back east. "You will all see someday, believe me. You will all see." In anger, Cadmus rode alone back to the east. Several of his men regained their mounts and others, excluding Jeremy, who remained.

"You other men, do you not wish to follow your priest?" Foalon said to all the men now regrouping toward their breakfast on the fire.

"Most men here are not that eager," Jeremy said as the others just grunted, groaned, and filled their bellies with food, ignoring the scene and mostly just being fed up with the idea of cleansing in the word of God.

The sun shone from above as Franklin and his friend departed from the roof after witnessing the morning amusement and excitement. With one last rub of the neck, the ravens departed, each in opposite directions, Franklin heading back east toward the cottage and she on whatever familiar nest awaited, circling overhead black of wing and feather watching the wounded and winning retreat to the inn. Franklin circled and headed back toward Hastings and the cottage. His friends Porius and Thomas waited his return as they played stone toss out in the garden. Franklin, scouring over the forest, over the green meadows and streams, wafting, whirling as he fluttered, almost hitting the treetops and hearing the sounds of nestling creatures and forest beings coming and going beneath his flapping wings, still a long way from Catsfield, Crowhurst, and finally the forest outside of Hastings where the cottage awaited. Gusts of wind slowed his flight, and a familiar tree ahead beckoned Franklin's tired wings. Age seemed a distant memory to Franklin, but his age was older than most ravens seen wandering without flock or friend. Landing on the familiar oak tree, Franklin landed on a large branch next to a larger hole, which revealed an owl, Pristine. The owl winked acknowledgment toward Franklin and lazily sidestepped his bulk and gray, giving just enough room for Franklin to stand next to the owl and sleep. The owl turned toward Franklin. "Nice to see you, Franklin."

"And you, Sir Oak," Franklin replied.

"On your way to Porius, I imagine," said the owl.

"Indeed," Franklin replied.

"Wish I was younger and in better health as I would take the next jaunt with ye," the owl said, scratching his beak with his talon.

"I should be back in Hastings by the morrow," Franklin said.

The owl turned his head around and grabbed a bit of meat of unrecognizable features.

"Here, have something to eat." He threw the mass of red in front of Franklin.

"Thank ye, Sir Oak," Franklin said while tucking in. "I am too tired to think of hunting, most obliged indeed."

Franklin ate, slept, and was off before dawn. When he awakened, Sir Oak had already departed, most likely to rebuild his stock of food.

Franklin first flew down to the stream, and after splashing about and picking a few choice earthworms, most likely colloquially gaining some energy, he was off, on to Catsfield, then finally before him and beyond a misty cloud barrier and thick forest outside of Hastings, the ocean could be heard in the beyond as wind and high waves splashed against the cliffs. Oak, aspen, cottonwood, and other deciduous trees with conifers and breaking through a thick cloud, he saw a minstrel beneath his final flight path. Too tired to stop, he landed on the cottage. Porius and Matthew were outside planting something in the yard while the noise of the muse came from beyond.

"Welcome home, Franklin," Porius stated gleefully, wearing his suspended golden-laced silken gardening clothes. Thomas waved while he wiped his brow toward Franklin.

"There is food for you on the ledge, Franklin, and I think you may like it. Something to pick you up."

Thomas faced the music coming from the edge of the wood, and it stopped. Porius stood facing the music. There was some silence, and Porius turned to Thomas.

"It seems to be Byron Fortly the minstrel," Porius said.

"Today is a nice day for music, Porius. Allow him to enter."

Porius waved his hand toward the muse, and now exposed from the woods beyond came Byron. Black hair and knobby-kneed Bryon was just the picture of the 1300th-century character you find wandering and playing tunes for pennies—green star cut material with grab bags and tights of silk, flat leather shoes, and a smile from ear to ear.

"Hello, Porius," Byron said, holding his flute and drum handing at his side. "Allow me to play Your Grace a melody."

"Byron, welcome, help yourself to some mead." Porius waved his wand, and an outdoor dining set appeared as another smaller band appeared before them and played on ancient instruments.

"Thank ye, Porius. It's funny I don't usually find this place, but I am glad I did."

The table held glasses of mead, meat pies, and cakes of fruits held open wax like table. All three chomped and laughed as the band of three tiny floating musicians played a lyrical song. One bearded gentleman about two inches tall stood on a magenta bandstand playing a gittern, and a citole was held by another who floated on the same majestic-colored bandstand, rather like a piece of large floating ruby, gleaming and spiraling beneath them as the sunlight shone through its clear magenta mass. The men danced and sang.

"Come dance with us. Come and dance, dance all in one."

They giggled and only stopped to have a sip of mead occasionally, Franklin fast asleep on the rooftop among the musical noise and Byron playing drum. Be it also seen by bluebirds, dragonflies, butterflies, insects, mice, squirrels, foxes who hid behind the wooden pile due for chopping. Deer poked their heads from the forest's edge, and two fawns circled each other beyond in playful delight among the music, flower petals, and wasps who even seemed to dance and possibly even buzz in rhythm and tune to the song.

"Come dance with us, come and dance, dance all in one."

Time, as always, was the enemy of the happiness that flowed as if wanting eternity; a dark cloud came overhead, and it began to rain.

"Come in and join us for a meal and a rest, Byron," Thomas said, walking toward the door and waving inside.

The small band disappeared, the animals returned to their daily routine, and Porius waved his wand and put away the table, food, and finished planting the berry bush he had started a few hours ago. Soon the night fell, the storm gathered, and a fierce howling could be heard. Inside, the fire was lit, and the three men sat around talking of what they had recently seen and where they most recently had been.

Byron said seriously, "I did see Cadmus Upton on my way through the forest the other day. His men almost ran me off the road."

"Not really the music lover you would expect in the forest, I am afraid, Byron," Thomas stated while stretching his arms and taking his shirt off to rinse in the outside storm.

We have a few roasted ducks if you would like to stay for a meal," shirtless Thomas said, wet from standing out in the storm and removing his trousers and undergarments to hand on the area beside the fire. Thomas redressed himself in a silken avocado-green nightshirt and resumed his place by the fire. Byron looked down at his own filthy clothes and body and excused himself for a few moments.

Byron left for about twenty minutes, and when he returned, he was also naked with his clothes hanging from his arm, and he hung them by the fire to dry.

Porius, looking at naked and shivering Byron, held out his wand; and Parthenia and Grendle appeared before them, staring at Byron and blushing.

"Well, that is a lovely sight," said Parthenia, now holding out a bit of cloth toward Byron. He used it and wiped himself down his tight skin bouncing with youth and muscle. Grendle handed Byron another, a blue kirtle made from Grendle's own hand and laced in white. Once fitted, you could see the thin muscular ripples beneath the clothes.

"Wine," Porius said as Grendle retrieved some lovely red wine goblets made of some stone material. All three men sat comfortably sipping their wine, and Parthenia laughed with Grendle in the background, making a racket in the far-off food preparation area.

Grendle could be heard whispering. "Did you see that body? I know what I'll be dreaming of tonight," Grendle said as they were heard giggling louder in the background. Rain splashed down hard on the cottage. Thomas, Porius, and Byron were sitting by the fire while Franklin came in out of the storm to sleep in the window box by the front door.

"Cadmus Upton is a problem," said Byron in desperation.

"We know of his deeds and what will be coming," said Thomas.

"All we can do is act peaceful and try not to get in their way," Porius interjected to his interlocutors while lighting a long pipe full of something sweet smelling and filling the air. He passed the pipe to Thomas, who in turn passed it to Byron.

"Nice," Byron said, blowing out the smoke.

Franklin flapped his wings and floated out of the top window, which was always open for his coming and going.

"I prefer the rain to the smoke, thank you," Franklin said and flew outside to rest on the rooftop by the chimney, which was warm and where a ledge hung over a bit, which kept him dry, the smoke billowing above him into the storm.

"The raven spoke," Byron said in amazement and pointing up to the window where Franklin departed.

"Indeed, I trained him from a youngling," replied Porius.

Thomas giggled. "More wine?"

"Thank you kindly," Bryon continued. "Do you feel the Christians will start punishing the rest of the pagans around here, Porius?"

"Yes, I am afraid it is inevitable, dear boy. We will all need to be on guard, and if you must play along, play along."

"You mean lie," Byron asked.

"Yes, if you must—anything to protect yourself from harm."

"What if they ask me if I go to service?" asked Byron.

"It is mad that we have to, to these extremes," Thomas interjected in an angry manner and slapped his leg.

"We must protect the living and the ones who believe in magic and nature. Danger and hate will follow these churchgoing pontifical zealots I know. Where will they stop?" Porius said.

"Are we powerless to stop them?" asked Byron.

"No, but it may take centuries," Porius answered.

"Centuries," Thomas whispered.

"We are working with robin, hawk, pigeon, and other woodland creatures to prevent the natural world from being completely destroyed, but Christian greed in their own belief will bring pain everywhere," Porius began.

"The earth will bend, and man will be plagued by the onslaught of believers, and nothing will stand in their way—not family, not friend, not freethinking being. Things will be hidden."

Hidden from behind the wall appeared the Malefactor Centorias floating in the air toward Porius and finally resting in his lap.

"The Malefactor Centorias here rests on my lap and holds the key to the future," Porius continued. "Spells and potions and dialects not muttered for centuries and only wizards, witch, and pure of heart may use. This book must be hidden."

The men looked at the book lit by flickering flame light and outer skin carved leather, old and beaten.

"Before I tell you more, I need to inform you both of Dr. Milleni from the Republic of Venice. Currently, Venice is the most since they began building the Doge's Palace in Venice. Dr. Milleni needed to relocate his offices, for he is not a doctor of science, physiology, but of music. His teachings have been the constant pleasure of many a student including magical families, elves, fairies, and even our occasional visitors here at the college, who play in such fanciful delight."

Back in Venice, Athena assisted Dr. Milleni as he was cast out of his home by crusaders, builders, and architects all in brotherhood to build the great Doge's palace.

Porius back at the cottage continued his story to Byron and Thomas as soon as the kitchen staff, floating musicians, Franklin, and some outside deer were leaning in toward the conversation. Porius took his wand and opened the great book, and in it appeared the image of Dr. Milleni, crawling on the cobblestone bath with a large sack full of belongings that included a music stand, harp, writings of musical notations, and clothing, weeping and dragging along the canal while passersby seemed unconcerned by his weeping self-image. Porius waved his wand over the book.

"Athena, bring him to me," Porius said while the light of the image glowed against his face. The crowd witnessed the event in consumed passion.

Smoke appeared beyond in the courtyard among the bluebells and light rain.

"Come forth with all my power." Porius stood, wand out facing the yard, and walked slowly to the center garden. Swirling smoke and mild wind swirled in front of him.

Parthenia and Grendle put their hands over their mouths to keep the smoke from outside infecting their lungs as others followed.

"Come forth, my good doctor, come forth."

Within the powdery black and stinking smoke, which poured out more and more, the garden a vast thick cloud, unable to see inside, Porius's figure disappeared into the thickness.

Thomas cried out, "Porius!" His hands were stretched to the disappearing Porius.

"Stay back, Thomas, I am here. Be not afraid," Porius said from inside the cloud. Animals ran toward the forest as blackness fell all around them, the sound of rain now beginning to fall. But the thickness of smoke and cloud revealed nothing but black.

"Byron, come toward my voice. Stand and be not afraid," Porius shouted as Byron stood and walked toward where Porius was last seen.

"Reach for my hand," Porius shouted back.

Byron obeyed and grabbed hold of his hand. Porius whispered into his ear, "You will walk between worlds, but your musical being is important and why I brought you here."

"But I don't understand, Porius," Byron said while grabbing hold of his hand. Porius tossed Byron with all of his might into the blackest part of the cloud. Screams of other worlds cried through the night among the cloud, and soon all was clear.

Beyond Porius lay nothing now but rain on flowers and confused participants.

"My pure suppliant of the mortal may have been a bit tricky," Porius stated to the onlookers, and Thomas stared with a confused look on his face.

"Be still all because Byron is between worlds right now, and he will know what to do."

"But, Porius, you could have told him or warned him," said Thomas.

"I needed him fresh to follow his musical instincts. Thank you, Franklin, for bringing him to me," Porius said to Franklin, who was licking and flapping his wings to remove the dust as the raven looked back at Porius, also amazed at the quick instruction and surprising turn of events.

"Unfamiliar places reaching now, and here they come, back to us."

Porius fell to the ground tired and aged, his wand falling from his hand as Thomas ran to his side.

"Porius, my lord," Thomas wept of worry as he held Porius's weak figure dressed in the finest white lace in his arms.

"Water," Porius shouted, and Grendle handed Thomas a goblet full of water, which he held for Porius to his lips. Porius fell fast asleep.

Thomas was confused, but before them another cloud appeared. This time, it is white, blue, green, and red, swilling Thomas's eyes and before him appeared crossing the bluebells. Dr. Milleni, Byron, Athena, and her two mistresses. Only Athena wore clothing; everyone else was naked and shivering. Clothes had been lost during the transfer, and bare-naked shivering Byron was on his knees holding old Dr. Milleni. Athena stood by Thomas.

"Get them clothes and food, quickly before they catch their deaths. I will deal with Porius." Athena knelt to Porius and held his head within her hands glowing with life, and she disappeared within moments as well as her beautiful golden-skinned mistresses wearing the golden mesh armor and flying up and far off to the west. The three depart.

"Athena," Thomas shouted toward her, "wait, please wait!"

"She doesn't hang around," Porius said, sitting in the garden, now holding himself up by the arms and wand in his lap, smiling toward Thomas.

"Porius," Thomas said with glee while dressing Byron and Milleni.

Byron, Milleni, Parthenia, Grendle, Porius, and Thomas rejoiced as the music floating band appeared. They all stood and walked into the cottage.

"What a night," Porius said as they went inside.

Rain was pouring harder and harder while waves crashed the cliffs beyond the forest. Fairies, elves, woodland fox, deer, squirrel, dove, and pigeon appeared outside the windows of the cottage and slowly disappeared into the forest. Parthenia supplied food, mead, and wine to the group of still surprised Dr. Mellini, who began. "Gratzie, Portiuos Gratzie mio amico. Two preachers from the diocese visited me with threats and hammer. Uccidere," Mellini said while heavily breathing and trying desperately to compose himself.

"*Uccidere* means death, those fiends," Byron gasped.

"The horror of it after all these years you lived peacefully in Venice. What, has it been fifty years since you began teaching music in Venice?" Porius said.

"Fifty long wonderful years, Porius," Mellini continued. "Falling stars of music my gift hath been spreadeth."

"Many will come and visit you in England, Doctor," Porius said, upbeat, clear, and standing proud.

"Yes, Doctor, I have prepared a place for you in Dunmow amongst witch family, forest fairies, Dutch, African, and other herbalist and freethinking individuals within Essex and Suffolk. Many families you will be able to teach English students just as well as Italiano," Porius continued.

"Bold times these are for musical player, herbalist, farmer, alchemist, and mystic. We must be bold to settle what is left between the infested areas. There are some parts of English even the Catholic church may not penetrate. No tortures, stalking, posting, or setting up on wheels here."

"Gratzie, Porius, fomu gratzie, I am old and wish to be still, thank you all," the doctor said as he fell asleep in his chair.

Porius put him to bed in one of the back rooms, which was usually used for storing goods and food. Porius closed the door behind as he exited. The doctor's snoring could be heard in the background.

All was quiet, and all was still. Thomas, Byron, and Porius undressed for bed and dreamed. Dream of places and peoples, creatures, and faun. Below the ground, the worms created dangle and drill, preparing themselves for the most likely possibility of one day rising to the top of the tectonic plates to the crust of the earth, taken away in flight to high dimensions, being dissected into other molecular portions, rejuvenating the escorts of infinity and breaching all time and space. Bird is fed and is regrooming the constant layers and futures called life.

CHAPTER 4

Richard of Bordeaux, King of England, was deposed in 1399; and Porius, though elderly now, was still with Thomas, Franklin, the cottage, and all its creatures. Cadmus Upton was still serving over the local church, and on this cold winter morning came calls from villagers to the cottage.

Jules Mitrakovitch and his family were down with an incredible sickness that seemed to be spreading. The ironmonger, the cabinet maker Spinetti, and the wife of Jules Mitrakovitch came to the cottage. Thomas ushered them in to see Porius one by one. Weeps of sorrow from each of them and the tears of Porius flowed. For the last visitor Mrs. Mitrakovitch, Porius stated, "My dear, for what is a wizard his worth unless I can assist in attempting to make the sick well?"

"Thank you, my lord, what shall I do?" she asked Thomas, watching off to the side while adding logs to the fire.

"First, my dear, take this potion of garlic and ground citrus." Porius handed her a jar and packet.

"Then boil a lot of water and have him breathe the rising fog." Porius acted out the directions.

"Thomas will go with you, and I will work on a mustard plaster and tour the other ill ones," Porius said while grabbing several packets of garlic and citrus mixtures.

Porius visited six separate colleges and ended back at the cottage just after midnight. Even several parishioners greeted Porius with thankful and open arms. Franklin followed his trail, through occasional rain and sleet they had traveled, and finally resting in the cottage with a goblet full of mead.

"Did you see some of the villagers, Thomas? Scary. I am glad they came to see me because any longer and we would have had widows and widowers around the village."

"indeed," Thomas replied.

"Foul weather this winter, and since Richard has been deposed and since he took his revenge on the appellants and John Gaunt's dead, this is bad for England," Porius stated while drinking his mead and falling asleep. "Henry Bolingbroke as king, this may be too much."

"Richard, our beautiful king," Thomas stated while staring up at the flame shadows on the ceiling.

"Henry of Monmouth will come into his prime soon and replace him, you mark my words," Porius stated. "You mark my words."

The men fell fast asleep and fell into the world of dreams. Dreams of soldiers, battles, avarice, villains, traitors, the Tower of London where Richard was held before Henry Bolingbroke who took over Richard's reign. England was in turmoil; the French had infiltrated throughout the western villages and as far north and Scotland. Henry Monmouth, later to be known as Henry the Fifth, awaited in the wings with battles on his mind. Henry, Duke of Cornwall and Duke of Aquitaine.

"I have faith that Henry's thirst for war will not be satisfied as he engages as sheriff," Porius said.

"Parading around as sheriff, but his eye is on the prize. In many ways," Thomas said.

"Yes, he will amount to a good king as soon as he removes his uncle from the throne." They giggled themselves to sleep.

The winter passed, and spring turned to summer, to fall, and on until April 9, 1413. The windy day awoke Porius as Franklin flew outside screeching in his usual manner. Porius exited the cottage wearing his fine jewels and silk wardrobe.

"Henry the Fifth is king of England." Franklin circled above while a few other ravens joined in the chant.

"Well, this is a fine day," Porius said, turning back to Thomas who came out tucking his shirt into his belt.

"We have a new king," Thomas said gleefully.

All this excitement and what was really on Porius's mind were two water goblins. These two somewhat friendly water goblins were the last remaining out of the vast number of water goblins who evacuated to lyceum to escape the raid on magical creatures. Porius assured them that for the time being, they may drill on the side of the river just beyond the grounds of the cottage. Most of the times water goblins were good at keeping out of sight. Water goblins always believe that they are infallible and never mistaken. When Porius asked them a few months prior to escape this world and descend on another more welcoming planet, they both stood firm. Harold and Clarice were the last two remaining water goblins that at least were known to Porius and other members of the magical council. Harold the water goblin's age would have it over two hundred, and water goblins, or so legend is told, seem to never age. They are as is the lobster in their nervous and regenerative systems, rejuvenating continuously and always remaining at the height and weight that best suits them. Clarice had the skin of the color of avocado with long fingers and quite an extended forehead, which is most common amongst the royal families of water goblins who dwell around Europe and England, Scotland, and Wales. Once, at least three hundred water goblins lived along all the river and ocean shores, mainly in western Europe and scattered about, usually very difficult to keep track of due to their quick speed and agility. The main diet is fish and tree bark, which is one of the favorite meals. Harold and Clarice were blessed with perfect teeth, so strong that when they bite into bark, it would be like biting into a piece of cheese.

Harold is furious deep down inside when he and Clarice did not like or agree with the new religious humans who had been attacking magical creatures or, basically in their minds, creatures that Christians just don't understand.

Water goblins are not filled with magical powers other than quick speed and rejuvenation to keep young and fit, able to breathe underwater, which is where they sleep, live, and even in winter below the ice if need be due to the fact that water goblins do not feel cold or heat. Hairless, elongated, and exaggerated features make them seem most frightening to the inquisitive human who may on very rare occasions see in the wild.

Porius and Thomas were walking down to the river one morning to seek the nesting couple. Once they reached the river, Porius whistled a high steady note.

A pause and nothing, Porius tried again. Still nothing. "This usually brings them up," Porius said to Thomas.

"Whistling again, possibly a high C." Thomas joined in, and the sound was long and soft in the morning air. Finally from below the edge of the river, two heads appeared. Slowly came the eyes, both staring at Porius and Thomas. Then finally, they rose and stepped out of the river, dripping naked and with webbed feet, elongated bodily parts.

"Hello, good Porius and Thomas," said Harold warmly. Both Clarice and Harold bowed with wide grins.

"Good morrow, my friends, and how are thee settling in?" Thomas said, bowing back to them.

"We have never had it better," Clarice said. "We were wondering if we would have the pleasure of making your acquaintance."

"I just want to see if everything is all right with the arrangements," Porius said calmly.

"Or did you wish to see if we are still here and not out making mischief?" Harold said, giggling, and Clarice joined in with a chuckle.

"Well, to be honest, it has crossed my brow," Porius replied.

"We do have some hard feelings about the rest of our species, Porius," Harold continued. "Clarice, as you know, is more shy than I and will not admit to what she feels so easily."

"Yes, I know Clarice is the sole discretion," Porius said.

"Please let me tell you that we may be paying visits to Cadmus Upton or others of his fanatical followers, but we will not harm them or lead them back here," Harold said.

"That's good, then we are of agreement. I don't mind if you pull the odd prank, and I believe that they deserve an occasional scare or fright."

"Well, you two could do it," Thomas said mischievously.

"Hmm, well, I agree goblins are quick and we do tend to frighten the odd human, but we will be basically good," Clarise said, turning to look at Harold up and down and grabbing his arm, pulling him back under the river.

"Wait, my friends, wait, please, I have a job for you and would like to ask a question," Porius said, leaning toward the couple as they disappeared under the river quickly.

"Oh well," said Porius, "maybe next time. I had forgotten that you must speaking quickly to water goblins because they tend not to hang about long."

"Yes," Thomas said. "A bit of them go a long way."

Thomas and Porius headed back to the cottage where breakfast waited and a new day began, with the birds singing, deer running and playing as they chased each other through the woods and around the cottage.

"A lively morning, Thomas. A lively morn." Porius felt uneasy and strangely unsure of what actual plans Harold and Clarice could they have in mind, mischief at the least.

Meanwhile, under the river between moss and fish, flotsam and plant life waving against their skins, Clarice pointed downstream and quickly they both swam, never coming up for air until they reach the sea, then out past the waves catching bags full of cod while Dover Castle sat high in the background, the cloudy sky overhead. Ten, twenty, thirty cod and quickly back they travel. Miles up the river to the forest beyond the cottage, piling up fish by the front door and quickly back into the river unnoticed by human or creature. Water goblins are so quick that they may hardly be seen once in the fast-paced motion, which gives them the purest joy.

Later that morning, Porius and Thomas noticed the huge pile of fish.

"I see Harold and Clarice have been busy," Porius said, looking at the pile of fish.

"We shan't go hungry, my lord," said Thomas.

Parthenia came out and grabbed the fish to smoke fillet and store, grinning from ear to ear. The small floating band appeared in the background, and all was well with the world.

Porius grabbed a walking stick and explained to Thomas that he needed to go to the village to fulfill an urgent request from Walters, Simon, and Leal to take the few remaining stones and hide them at Canterbury Cathedral. Arriving at the village, Walters and the men drank mead and argued with the villagers about whatever comes up for fun. The Black Bull pub was out along the country road and usually filled with good folk and lively music, decent food, and occasional sellers of mystical charms, cures, and whatever may be held to bring a profit. Simon held two dead pheasants and placed each feathers and all in a sack obviously purchased for a different time and location.

"Porius, my lord, how are thee?" Walter said, wiping the food from his mouth. Porius entered the Black Bull with Thomas in tow.

"Thomas," Simon said and bowed to greet them.

"Those look tasty," Thomas said "Try this as well Simon, some Cod freshly caught this morning."

Thomas placed five large cods on the table in front of Leal, Simon, and Walters.

"Very nice," Walter said. "Surely you did not want to meet us to give us fish. What's the game, Porius? There is always something afoot if I knew thee."

"Well yes, come outside with me for a moment." Porius took him out while Thomas ordered a couple of goblets of ale. Leal smacked his bum and laughed as Thomas passed him on the way to the bar. An elderly gray-bearded man pours him a couple large goblets foaming over and dripping. Thomas dipping his head to not waste a drop.

"I'll take one of those cods, and the drinks are on the house," said the bartender. Thomas slapped one large cod on the bar.

"Very nice." The bearded tender grabbed the cod and laid it behind the bar.

A woman came from the kitchen, went to a blackboard, and with a piece of jimson writes,

COD Fresh

SPECIAL Price

Outside, Walters and Porius were sitting away from the crowd whispering.

"Walters, here in this leather satchel are three rune stones that need storage. You know the east passage below Canterbury Cathedral?"

"Yes, you mean twenty-one steps down and eight stones up?"

"What a wonderful memory you have, Walters, indeed just the place. Would you mind placing these runes there? We are fearful that raiders may come through now that the Christians are starting to convert pagans and, well, it's only a matter of time, you know."

"I understand, Lord Porius. We will deliver them by morning and seal the stone as before."

"Thank ye, my good man, thank ye. I am sure Thomas has a large flagon of ale inside, and my mouth is ready."

"I hadn't a clue you had more magical items on you, my lord. Anything I can do always."

Meanwhile that night while Walters and his men delivered the runes to Canterbury, HAROLD THE WATER GOBLIN went with Clarice to the church of the newly ordained priest Cadmus Upton. They circled the priory and inside where the candle flickering. Franklin circled overhead, and shaking his feathered head finally came to rest on the apex of the priory. Cadmus inside was rehearsing a speech for his next transmission or just blurting out something to offend and shock the unexpected victims, which he will most assuredly call sinners. The water goblins stuck their long stretching unhuman faces in and gave a scream. Cadmus leaped from his chair in fright, spilling an inkwell and screaming, "Satan, beasts, Satan!"

The two water goblins ran back to the forest giggling and laughing, prancing and then finally splashing into the river, and Franklin shook his head and ascended toward home to report the mischief to Porius.

Walters, Leal, and Simon went to Canterbury and hid the stones for future generations, which was uneventful because there were no guards or resistance of any kind. Over the next year, Walters, Leal, and Simon traveled about doing odd jobs and getting paid then home in deepest Essex. On Walters's estate, they toiled and lived among the peaceful villagers, occasionally visited by Dr. Milleni, Athena, and her two women protectors, Porius and Thomas. Grendle and Parthenia came to cook and clean for Porius daily and afterward went home to their own families in the village to take care of their own.

In 1402, Charles the Sixth of France, still repentant over killing his brother Louis the First in Brittany, had some trouble with two water goblins. Yes, by all accounts it was Harold and Clarice due to their love of haunting castles at night, sneaking in to royalty bedchambers, and scaring the life out of folks for fun. It is their little way of revenge, which makes them laugh still for over the past year. Once a week, they would bring a large pile of fish for Porius and Thomas and greet them occasionally in the garden of the cottage. August of 1402 was extremely warm, and a party was set up by Thomas to celebrate his love for Elena, the cobbler's daughter.

Elena was heavy in size compared to most other girls in the village, but Thomas loved her all the same. Thomas, on whom Porius had cast the spell over in which he would never grow old, had promised to love Elena in her lifetime, and Elena was pleased with that but had vowed Thomas never to marry in case she decided that his everlasting youth may compromise her good nature at some point in her life.

August mail was sent to Athena, Walters, Leal, Simon, and Dr. Milleni. The water goblins were invited but not likely that they would hang around for long. Jeremy the soldier who actually had deep passion for Thomas and was mildly upset with Thomas for his pledge to Elena still was coming to the summer party. Even Byron was coming as extra tents were built out back for several to collapse after luxurious entertainment, song, and food.

The sky was clear of cloud, and the guests started arriving. Athena appeared out front of the garden on a large flying golden ship led by reindeer, four to be precise, covered in gold mesh thin white clinging silk rolling from her neck around her bosom, thinly stretched around her waist and tied, a short golden skirt covering her front and buttocks but revealing her beautiful thighs all muscular and golden brown followed by golden laced shoes that wrapped around her leg almost to her knee. Athena's shoes were plastered with jewels of many colors like emerald green, ruby red, topaz, among others. Gloria and Alexandria were flying in midair beside her with swords sheathed and spears by their sides, following her every move and floating between any who came too close unless specifically ushered by Athena, like Porius who greeted her handsomely. Porius was standing in his whitest robes draped in grape leaves and golden lace.

"Welcome, Athena, Gloria, and Alexandria. Thomas, the first of our guests have arrived," Porius shouted back at the cottage while Thomas came out with Elena by his side, stumbling and gazing up at the beauty of Athena and her two beautiful soldiers. Elena grabbed Thomas's wrist, noticing his arousal at the beautiful three before him.

Entering from the edge of the wood was Walters, shouting, "Athena!" Walters ran toward her and grabbed her waist, the two soldiers drawing their swords in anger.

"It is okay, ladies. It's Walters," Athena said as they retreated.

Leal and Simon came in from the hedge followed by Bryon wearing little but a loincloth and strap for his guitar, Leal taking notice of the young, thin, and handsome musician.

"This party is showing great promise," Leal said, looking around and grabbing a goblet of mead.

"Music," Porius said, waving his wand as the small floating musicians appeared above them, playing an amplified melody of grace and honor, a waltz in nature and movable in style.

"Athena, your beauty knows no bounds," Walters said, grinning and bowing before her, Simon, Leal, Thomas following suit. Thomas was still holding the hand of Elena while he bowed; she was pulling him up.

Athena floated toward Thomas and looked down from her position of floating in the air, the breeze moving through her white silk and gold lace.

"You must be the Elena I have heard of," Athena asked.

"Yes, my lady," Elena said, caught up in the spectacle.

"Nice to see you, my lady, and your lovely companions," Thomas said. Porius was just looking on and drinking down some mead. They all were standing around in the garden. Butterflies were moving through, deer in the background playing, rabbits, squirrels, birds, and Franklin high circling above the grounds.

"You must forgive me, Athena. I have not been circled by magical people before," Elena stated.

"Yes, but Thomas has told me of your keen interest, and I hear your father and mother were from sorcerers' stock."

"Yes, I am keen on learning the way of the pagan, and I have no interest in the new religion that is sweeping through the villages of England."

"More than England, dearest Elena."

"True, we have much to talk about," said Porius, intruding on the conversation. Everyone else were mingling while sipping the mead and enjoying Porius's most excellent flowered garden.

In the middle of all this merriment, a huge crash occurred just outside the trealing. They all ran toward a large puff of black smoke, and there appeared Dr. Mellini, all covered in smoke and dust.

"Mellini, my good friend. Welcome," said Porius, greeting him into the garden beyond the forest.

"Practicing the transport spell," Walters stated while waving his hand below his nose and laughing. Others giggled at the attempt of magic transportation by Mellini.

"Perfected. I think you will find perfected, for I am here amongst you," Mellini said in his most Italian accent. "Athena, my lady, good to see you."

"And you, Dr. Mellini, nice to see you indeed. Love from Italia," Athena said.

"How is the old country? Still ravaged?" Mellini asked her.

"Yes, I am afraid most of the royal and magical families have been taken from their palaces and replaced by preachers and evildoers claiming the so-called love from their new god. Don't get me started," Athena said, drinking her mead and starting to weep.

"Now, let's keep it light, everyone. We are here to rejoice in each other being alive and well," Thomas said and everyone agreed.

"A dance, a dance," said Athena, grabbing Walters, Leal grabbing Simon, Thomas with Elena, Mellini with Byron. Even the two guards stepped lightly on the earth and placed down their spears to dance with each other. Byron joined in playing his lute. Jeremy watched the muscles of Simon and Leal. They waved to him to join them, and in a circle around the fountain danced Simon, Leal, Gloria, Alexandrea, Porius, and Jeremy occasionally switching partners and laughing. Below them and below the grass, the underwater wells and water pockets, the bios, the ant kingdom, the worms, snails, and beetles all danced to the swirling music of the floating band. Even beyond the woods on the edge of the river danced our water goblins arm in arm and waist deep, swirling to the melodies.

Food was prepared, meals eaten, laughs and jokes abounded with good nature.

"Everyone, what is orange and sounds like a parrot?" Thomas asked the crowd in the evening and answered, "A carrot."

"Thomas, that is an awful joke," Leal said while hugging Gloria in a slow dance around the fountain, their bodies flowing in circles, elevating occasionally from the ground as if weightless and filled with some helium substance.

"Time for an evening meal," said Parthenia from inside the cottage. A large table was laid out in the garden; and turkey, venison, fruits, freshly cooked vegetables, wine, grapes, and large loaves of bread were laid out in plenty.

The smells alerted a few insects, but everyone ate while occasionally whipping away any intermittent fly, bee, or wasp. What a joyous day in August this has been. One to remember for all time and the dinner talk.

"You know, Porius?" Walters began, sitting across the table from Porius with the others looking on. "The night we hid you know what, down the stairs, we noticed peculiar beetles."

"Yes, they will guard the cache inside the walls for centuries. Insects guard the cache and relay anything suspicious to fowl and deer. The message is passed and relayed to Franklin's group and then heard here. It is a nice arrangement which can never be broken. You see," Porius continued, everyone eagerly listening to his wisdom.

"Insects are easily spoken with and will apply themselves and millions of future generations by the cast of the simplest spells."

"Is that true, Porius?" Athena asked.

"Yes, indeed. Easy," Porius replied while everyone else around the table sat back and were taking puffs from a small wooden pipe, which circulated the table, attached to a water hookah-type appliance.

"Good smoke, Porius. Very good indeed," said Leal while breathing in the sativa, the odor of which flowed through the air like clouds of sweet reminders.

The band in the background played a jazz-type slow music, the sound of a dragging saxophone type or horn, which is made by Byron on some wind instrument he carried in his strap.

The crowd was quiet and still; deer and pheasant walked around the table. One squirrel hopped up and grabbed a handful of nuts in front of Simon.

"Hahaha," Simon said while he slowly waved at the smiling squirrel as it scurried home with its nuts. Simon's slow swipe toward the playful squirrel was a million times too slow for the inquisitive creature.

"Oh good, I like it when our garden friends enjoy a bit of food," said Thomas, taking his turn on the pipe, coughing a bit and passing it on.

"Nice music," said Alexandria to Leal.

"And a beautiful evening," Simon said before taking his turn on the pipe.

Then without warning, there came a sprinkle, then a drop, followed by bigger drops. Porius stood, and everyone got up and grabbed something from the table and headed into the cottage. Animals were running to take the leavings behind them, both of the water goblins also grabbing turkey and vegetables and stuffing them in their mouths while heading back to the river.

"Yes, everyone inside," said Porius.

Inside, the wet clothes were removed and lighter clothes replaced. Leal was staring at Byron and Jeremy as they stood naked wiping the water from themselves and reclothing in light robes. Wine was poured places found, and Athena sang.

Fowl and faun—whistle and cheer.
Love with friends and tidings are here
Swing and bitter, wild and far
Take each other as we are
Falling stones from years gone by
Whilst away the tears we cry
All this and much more to all
Here we stand yes one and all
Here we stand yes one and all.

The musicians began playing this melody, and the others joined in.

Fowl and faun—whistle and cheer.
Love with friends and tidings are here
Swing and bitter, wild and far
Take each other as we are
Falling stones from years gone by
All this and much more to all
Here we stand yes one and all
Here we sing yes one and all

"Here we love, yea one and all," Leal sang solo after the song.

Many years of fighting a toil
Many tears of loss and need
Bolder fears will come in years
For now we love without those fears
And for now there are no tears
Love will flow throughout this night
All will take their own special flight.

Leal finished and Gloria began.

Mountain sink into nothing
Your lips begin to whisper
Everyone shalt know this war
Castles fall and tumble
Palaces may crumble
We will all defend the old world
We shall all defend our world.

Gloria finished and Porius began.

All together here we love
Futures will go on and on and on
Another life another song
It will remind of this time together
Through the hot and sticky weather

No more tears shalt fall to the ground
And to us all our bond
The love that lies inside us all
The world without war
One and on and on

"Another life, another song," Porius finished.
"I can't sing," said Elena.
"Nor can I," whispered Dr. Mellini.

They all laughed and raised their goblets, some rolling on the floor. Leal stood and walked out of doors to remove his robe and hang them inside. Naked, he walked to the river to bathe and take care of any other bodily functions that may arise.

Once he returned, the others followed one by one, cleaning and primping in the river's shallows. Occasionally, a water Goblin swam by, their naked bodies among the fish, plant, and other water creatures that swirled in the deep.

The cottage had no need for fire this warm evening, just room for another cot in the hearth. All four rooms were covered with bodies later that night, Leal and Byron going out together for a late-night walk since the rain had stopped earlier. Gloria wandered the perimeter with Alexandria making sure no nighttime spies were watching. Franklin was at his post atop the cottage.

Owls flew around the garden once the sun went down and midnight approached. They were still awake indoors, the chatter never seeming to end, the wine never seeming to stop pouring, and the laughs and music keeping on coming.

The tortoise resting in the garden grazed by morning, evening, and most usually minding its own business not knowing or caring if he was one hundred or two hundred years of age. Two smaller tortoises stood grazing beside him, looking like the eggs had finally hatched and this tortoise would leave its relatives once he moved on to another place or shelter of garden of delights to live.

Franklin fluttered his feathers on the rooftop, eyeing the ground mice, rats, and wormlike creatures that slowly or quickly ran across the grounds.

Thomas was holding Elena on his bed in his back room, and on Thomas's floor was Alexandria and Simon who lay facing each other in fascination. Not in any sexual nature but a curious one at the least.

Alexandria placed her hand on his full hard muscular chest covered in thick blond hair like wings of a hawk, spanned out across his bosom. He was returning the gesture and touching her subtle breast and kissing her red full lips.

Porius was alone in his bedroom, and outside in the center room, Athena was staring at Walters and leading him outdoors to a tent covered in silk canvas. Athena was covered in a new sensation of panic, and she led him, excited, through the curtain doors, disrobing him. Inside, the curtain closed, and all was quiet except for the sound of the loon and other nighttime creatures.

The precocious insiders were either touching or sleeping with dreams of such a nature. The bios below the surface of the earth was in sleeplike mode except those restless nighttime insects that roamed and crawled, slithered, and swayed. Owls flew close to Franklin, waking him, and he barely put up his neck for a moment and grumbles back to sleep at his post when sleep came over them. Andromeda in the far horizon dipped under the curve of the earth and slipped beyond the horizon. Meritorious creatures like Athena and Walters were enjoying the moments from midnight to one in the morning until deep in their own sleep and dreaming. Walters dreamed of being wedded to Athena and dressed in golden garments, flying with her to adventures beyond.

Gloria and Alexandria dreamed of flying about with Athena and protecting her from evil and from the new religious zealots of the day.

Porius was dreaming of Henry the Fifth on his Crusades and hoping he was lenient with his victims.

Leal dreamed of his usual intimate behavior with different peoples at different times and places.

Thomas was dreaming of Elena, and Elena was having some spooky thoughts and dreams about the future. Elena's past had been witness to many atrocities from the new wave of Christian folk who had been entering the villages and some outsiders from France and Spain who had taken up residence in the English villages and set up churches to preach this new religion with fables of evil and sinners.

Though all may occasionally through the night dream of such evils that are apparent around them, they all awakened in the best of moods and happiest of natures. This was the departing and the party over the memories shared, the function of delight. Hopes and brave days lay ahead of them all.

Porius waved goodbye that morning to Walters followed by Leal and Simon as they looked back. Leal threw a kiss to Athena. Byron was playing his lute while walking out away from the cottage grounds, only to disappear into the woods. Franklin was reaching for worms he had collected and set aside for later on the rooftop. Thomas and Elena waved to their friends as they all departed. Athena rode her golden chariot led by four deer, which flew off into the distance, the mild sound of ringing bells in their wake. Jeremy was heading back to the service of the king as he guarded his post at Dover castle.

Thomas and Elena were alone on the garden, deer grazing, bird flying.

"What a splendid time. What a splendid time in the extreme," Porius said, watching everyone depart.

"What excellent friends you both have," Elena said, giving a final wave.

"I wish they would never leave," Thomas said.

"My thoughts exactly," said Porius, "but things must be done and homes still must be kept secure."

"Where is Dr. Milleni?" said Porius.

Back at the cottage, the door opened and out walked Mellini. "What have I missed?"

They all began to laugh.

"Where has everyone gone?"

"Come on back inside, Doctor," Thomas said. "Time for breakfast."

John of Burgundy investigated the murder of Louis in France and the conflict that generated a civil war in France between the Burgundians and the Armagnacs, both having relatives and ties to the English royal family. Turmoil once again ensued, and while Henry the Fifth was beginning his campaign called his Crusade in his mind now, the sheriff of Cornwall and in 1403 was stabbed in the face by an arrow at Shrewsbury while fighting the Welsh. Porius was sent for and gave Henry the best possible care, which is the only way Henry were to survive. Henry paid Porius handsomely for his efforts once cured, and Henry vowed to Porius that he may keep his pagan ways afloat, and they may coincide with the new religion that even though Henry used Christianity to defeat many a foe, he still has a place in his heart for the old ways of England and the druids, witches, pagans, sorcerers, and alchemists.

Owain Glyndrwy of Wales defeated and not to the liking of Porius or other mystics in England, but progress was starting, and Henry the Fifth led the way. Riches of all kind awaited Henry as he followed his armies to terrorize and pillage, and even though it is to the wealth of England, time will tell what repercussions occur. Maybe not in this century or the next, but peoples of many cultures can wait generations for revenge. Porius knew this and worried about many generations in the future and places of modern destruction and servitude.

Years passed at the cottage—1405, 1406, and again in August 1407, another party ensued, and everyone met at the cottage for one fun-filled night. On this occasion, Athena rode horses that flew and had hooves of fire. Once again, they all sang, told stories of the past year and terrible changes among the villages and cities of Europe. Cathedrals were built for the new god and prayers now by once normal families to the unknown god. Porius and the others were a little more concerned during this event, but again, they all departed and in the winter of 1407, a strange thing occurred.

Midnight brought with it a strange odor among the grounds of the cottage like moss or grass wet from fresh rain yet mixed with a fragrance of wine. Porius was awakened by this peculiar smell as was Thomas, and they both met by the front door.

"I heard Franklin squeak," Porius said, opening the door.

"And this smell, so strange," Thomas replied as they exited the cottage.

Winds slowly blew cold up their nighttime robes and between their sandal straps. A shadow appeared moving, yet not in coordination with the moonlight. The shadow appeared before Porius, the light at the end of his staff now glowing. Thomas stood behind Porius while Franklin flew away from the scene. This ominous strange shadow was almost lifelike with an odor unlike any other.

"Stand firm, Thomas," Porius shouted behind him, the wind picking up.

The shadow grew and shrank, moving and wisping around the garden until finally it was still and the smell subsided.

"My dear friends, Canterbury needs you, my dear friends," the voice came from the now-still shadow.

"Thomas, hail Franklin and send for Walters to meet us at Canterbury," Porius said, turning back to go inside.

"We must prepare for battle," Porius said to nervous Thomas.

"Battle? I am not familiar, Porius," Thomas frettingly stated.

"No need to worry, just bring your knife strapped on your waist," Porius said, grabbing his wand and a sword.

"And call the horses," he said to Thomas.

"Porius, the voice, what of this voice?" Thomas asked.

"It was Dr. Mellini using the method I taught him for messaging."

"We have no time to lose, lives are at stake and most probably on a stake."

They packed small bags and mounted two horses in the garden, which piques the interest of the water goblins and a wild boar that was startled by the event.

They rode over hill and valley toward Canterbury, Franklin sending word to Walters by many a fowl friend. The wind kicked up, and the riders rode through wood as the water goblins followed a safe distance hiding behind the occasional rock or shrub, tree, or mound. After an hour or so, they came out of the forest and saw the cathedral in the distance. Lights reflected against the sky, and there was the sound of an angry mob out in the front area of the cathedral with several men in black coats with a few, possibly twelve soldiers around them, the soldiers holding back an angry mob.

"They are no ye kin, thay be ours!" one villager screamed, raising a garden instrument toward the soldiers.

"Devils, these beings are devils," one of the highly priests shouted to the angry crowd.

"Get him on the wheel," the priest shouted, pointing down. A young man strapped naked and kicking was being held down by three soldiers bearing the red cross and tying him to the wheel.

"Now, raise his devilish soul up toward God," the priest shouted, holding a whip and flicking it toward the angered crowd.

"Leave him be, you villains," the mob yelled.

Porius and Thomas rode their horses up to the crowd and dismounted. Porius ran toward the man being placed on a wheel, slashing his sword in the air toward the soldiers holding him down and begging to raise his naked body up toward the sky on top of the pole, the wheel loose and turning.

"Yield, this insane attempt," Porius shouted.

Cadmus Upton appeared from behind the other priest, also dressed in black, a large wooden cross dangling from his necklace.

"Kill him!" Cadmus shouted to the soldiers and pointed toward Porius.

The crowd quieted down and moaned with fear, stepping back. Whispers could be heard among them.

"It is Porius, the great protector of the people and sorcerer." The crowd moved back.

Several soldiers circled Porius and Thomas, and Porius raised his staff as the light penetrated the sky. The water goblins appeared and moved through the soldiers, knocking their heads together, tripping them from behind, moving in and out. Porius fought with one while Thomas held one back, staring frozen his knife pointed to the soldier. Cadmus retreated and left the scene, the other priest engaged in battle. The fight continued, and Porius's white robe was slashed by one sword and he turned and knocked the soldier back against the pole. The naked victim was still struggling, hands tied behind his back and only one leg free. Porius maneuvered closer to him, and one of the larger two priest tried to grab Porius, but he outmoved him.

"Oh no, nothing from you," Porius said while sliding his sword under the leg of the priest and down he went. The crowd cheered for Porius, watching the scene from only feet away in the glowing bonfire light. Walters, Leal, and Simon came riding up and dismounting, discouraging any further fighting as the soldiers disbanded and fled away back to the woods. Porius was holding one priest down. He grabbed his large wooden cross, removed it from his necklace, and threw it into the bonfire. The crowd cheered as two men freed the nude captive and wrapped him in a warm robe.

"Good timing, Walters," said Thomas, never more thrilled to see anyone in his life.

"My pleasure, Thomas, I did not know ye can fight," Leal shouted.

"Well done, Thomas," said Simon as he ran at the second priest and knocked him to the ground. Simon also removed the cross from around the neck of the second priest and threw it into the bonfire. The crowd cheered and came closer to Porius, cheering the men.

"Canterbury is once again safe, my friends," Porius shouted to the crowd. They all came toward Porius cheering. Then a wagon came up, and the crowd picked up Thomas and Porius's cheering. They placed them on top of a mountain of hay and brought him through Canterbury cheering.

"Porius has saved our kin and rid the village of these evil priests," the crowd screamed. Soon Porius and Thomas got down from the fan-filled ride through the village and ascended on the pub called the "Black Crow Pub" where they were bought ale and local food. Music plays and singing was heard. The man once naked and tied to the wheel came up to Porius.

"I am not a devil, I just don't follow their religion," the man said.

"No one deserves treatment like that for any reason," Porius said.

"These unpredictable days we are in," Walters continued to Porius by a fire in the Black Crow.

"Times indeed, my good friend, and what can get into the minds of these zealots to torture, kill, rob, steal?"

"What indeed," Leal intruded, overhearing the conversation.

"This power of hate is getting far worse," Porius said. "I am afraid for the future, I fear that all freethinking wise people may be in danger to this cause."

"Where will it all end?" Walters asked.

"It may not end, my friends. It may not end at all." Porius drank.

Everyone disbanded and returned to their horse's whistle, grin, and chatter. Porius and Thomas returned home, the water goblins already far ahead, traveling through the waterways toward Hastings and passing the nighttime creatures circling above, lining their path or crawling through tunnels beneath the hooves as they head toward home. Cocoons were preparing for a winter release from frost moths, which in vast numbers fill the chilly air searching for food and mates. While Porius rode, a nighttime fairy flying by his side caught his eye, the fairy's miniature body waving while going the same speed. Porius squinted and winked at the passerby. His mount was not so calm, but after a quick nervous tick, the poufy white horse remained on course.

Walters and his pals rode to their estate, and they reached their homes at close to or about the same time. The water goblins rested down below the river and among the flowing moss and plant life with some pockets of ice collected in small gatherings where the depth was unmoving and shallow.

Thomas undressed and hung his clothes out to dry. Porius changed to his night robe and then turn in. Both retired and thought of the mission and what a success it had been. Outside the black of night, the moon disappeared around the earth and even Franklin slept indoors tonight, away from the cold, black, frosty early morning. Sleep brought the most special dreams, especially after being heroes in mind and body.

Morning was a spectacularly bright day, almost springlike in many ways. Byron was heard singing out in the garden and cooking on a small outdoor stove or comet as it was called in this time. Pork lean bacon, eggs, toasted bread, and hot warmed milk with spices awaited Porius and Thomas as they walked out into the garden.

"Morning, Byron, what is this a morning feast I see?" Porius said, bending down to grab a piece of bacon that looked cooked to perfection.

"Yes, my lord, I have been working for the farmer at the end of Green Close, Milner," Byron said.

"I did not know you could cook," said Thomas, entering the garden and sitting at the outdoor table set up for just such occasions.

"Well, my lords, since you have always been so kind to me, I wanted to repay the favor. And since the farmer has lavished me with food, my first thought is to share with ye."

"And very kind of you just the same. Thank you, Byron," Porius said.

"Plus, I have heard tale of what happened at Canterbury last night."

"What, news travels quickly in winter." Porius chuckled.

"The whole village and Hastings are all talking of it."

"I hope in a positive way."

"Oh yes, indeed, even the Christians are pleased because even they do not approve of torture of the innocent."

"My thought is bent on what will be coming next," Porius said.

"This should be quite the call to arms for the people who still follow the old ways," Thomas said, adding egg to his plate with bacon and toast.

"The people are all as one on this, Porius. You were a hero last night," Byron continued. "I wish I would have been there."

"Don't worry, the way things are going, you will be called in many different ways," Thomas said.

"We all need to be on guard at all times. What I cannot understand is what gets into these zealots' heads which makes them so pious. To torture and kill, steal from the poor," Porius said, gulping the warm milk.

"Cadmus Upton has not yet returned," Byron said.

"I can only wonder what he is up to now," Porius said.

"What can we do without raising too much suspicion?" Byron asked.

"Do nothing," Porius said. "Do nothing and don't say anything to anyone you do not know."

The air was still, the deer grazing behind them, and Franklin eating his morning meal on top of the roof.

"Several men in black robes and monks have been circulating the villages. They know at the front door and tell the insiders that they must go to church and follow their one true god," Byron explained.

"This is worse than I would have imagined," stated Porius.

"The men force themselves inside the homes, and several tales have been told of the men taking favors," Byron said.

"Yes, got one," Porius said in his most inspecting voice to his interlocutor.

"The men have raped young ones in front of their parents and even the farmer's daughter," Bryon said.

Porius interrupted Byron, "Yes, Milner's daughter is quite beautiful, but so young."

"The farmer is mad as you can imagine and ready to kill Cadmus Upton for sending these beasts to torment his daughter," Byron continued. "They also take food without payment and have made threats to Milner that if he does not visit the church on Sunday, they will burn his farm and take his land."

"Byron, tomorrow is Sunday. Please make sure you go back to Milner and his family and tell them all to go tomorrow to the church and pretend to be faithful."

"Pretend?" Byron asked inquisitively.

"Yes. Tell them Porius said to pretend. Once they leave the church, place this at the back of the church," Porius said, handing a small box to Byron. "Within this box is a watcher and keen asset to us. Once the box is placed at the back of the church, tell Milner and his family they will not need to visit church again. And no harm shall come to them from any priest or other zealot of Christianity now or in future times.

"May I ask what is in it, my lord Porius?" Byron asked.

Thomas was all ears and eager to hear of the contents within.

"It is a friend to us all. Our eyes and our ears, our hopes and our fears lie within. Please ask them to open the box a small bit and leave it open when they leave for home.

"I will fulfill your wish, Porius."

"Byron, make sure they do not open the box until they leave it at the back of the church."

"Yes, my lord Porius," Byron said. "Back of the church."

CHAPTER 5

Sunday morning after church, Farmer Milner greeted the priest Upton on his way out.

"I am so pleased you were able to join us, Milner," Upton said, staring into Milner's eyes.

"It was an offer I could not refuse," Milner said.

"Your family in tow I see, welcome," Upton said.

"My family does not speak Latin or understand what is being said most of the time," Milner stated.

"It is the word of god, and your trust is in me to know what is best for thee," Cadmus said abruptly.

"Good day," Milner said and quickly walked out, his wife, son, and two daughters quickly walking past Upton and heading for home.

Turning back, Milner let the others go ahead, and he turned toward the back of the church unseen. Close to a brick at the back and between a grave's headstone and brick, he placed the box and opened about the width of a finger. He stood there watching for something of what was within. Nothing happened so he left quickly so as to not raise suspicion and joined his family. They all turned back to make sure no one noticed their father's visit to the back of the church.

"What a terrible speech the man made inside the church. Are we all sinners, Father?" one of the daughters said. "I don't consider myself a sinner in the slightest, where do they get off?"

"No, thee are not sinners. Take no head to what was said in that place of worship," Milner said and they all quietly walked home. "Surely the church must be doing good deeds somewhere, like feeding the starving or helpin' the sick."

"We have Porius and his men for that task. But what will the people do when Porius has gone?" said the daughter as the sky filled with cloud and rain began, mud piling up around the mounds alongside the road as rain glistened on the farm crops, houses, and animals that dotted the fields of whey, spinach, onions, and leeks.

The thoughts that were conveyed during the sermon Cadmus Upton set upon the village this morning was the basic—putting fear into each other. But what Cadmus did not realize was that while he was expressing types of evils done by one man, none of the villagers here would ever be susceptible to any such evils. Rape, incest, murder, theft was all mentioned in the sermon; but none of these ideas exist for most of these peaceful villagers. The Milners especially were taken aback by the evil thoughts that came from the preachers' mouths. Fueled by zealot thinking, Cadmus pressured villagers to give them their coin as he threatened them with eternity of pain in his fictional hell.

"We would never hear of such evils," said Milner's second daughter.

"Unless we went to hear a sermon," said Milner's wife when they finally reached their home among the wheat fields of Kent.

"NONE OF YOU WILL HAVE TO ENDURE THAT AGAIN," Mrs. Milner said, weeping a bit.

"Yes, we follow the old ways here, and may the green man bless our fields and may our hearts stay true to each other."

"I love you, Papa," Milner's son said.

That night when the midnight hour passed and the moonlight flew over the box left by Milner behind the church, fingers on a tiny hand, nails on edge of each finger and hand, but no being, crawled out of the box a spiderlike hand with no body. Hand out of the box spell was something Porius learned from the malefactor book, which was incidentally first performed by Thoth, god of Egypt over 1,100 years ago. This spell was difficult to manage because what happens is this. The reflection of one's own hand is copied, copied in wish and mind and once planted will crawl and remove the memory. The actual hand was a copy of Lord Porius's hand and the memory and thought to be erased.

Back at the cottage, Porius dwelled on the box and stared at his hand in the moonlight. Thomas was looking on and Franklin on top of the roof looking down.

"Hand wave the o protects," Porius said.

Jewel of the north, east and west protects.
Milner here but not here.
Milner here forever, my hand protect thee.
Dwelling of this box, thee within shall not target Milner
Dwelling of this box, thee within shall not target Milner
Shall not follow or plague Milner.

Porius stared at his hand; and back at the church, the hand crawled up the back wall and finally reached the roof, crawling in the moonlight, each finger grabbing hold. It circled once the roof's perimeter then circled twice, the hand crawling in the moonlight. Porius closed his eyes, and the hand disappeared from the roof in the moonlight. Even the box still lying outside the church had vanished.

The Pines of Rome

Athena was fighting in Roma for her families of sacred ages being taken from their homes imprisoned and some tortured upon rock and wheel. The prisons were opened by the churches, and the men out of prisons, jails, and fort holds had become priests and monks as they had been chosen and released by the church. The churches and priests wanted to use the criminals to do their bidding and grab all the greatly homes and royalists, taking their fortunes all around Roma and placing them in the pockets of priests. Flowing out from the prisons were murderers, thieves, and worse all with this new forgiveness, which was placed on them by churches and the greedy zealots within. Great house after great house had fallen to the Christians, men once knightly and true not imprisoned and some on spike. Their lands were taken from them and sold for profit, once temples and some palaces of pleasures now in ruin. The dancing male slaves were bound and shackled together from one house, their landlord being dragged behind while the fearless men in black whipped horse and cart. One cart that went by the coliseum was full of naked men in a pile, dead and rotting.

Athena watched the cart go by as tears welled in her eyes, and her maidens filled with anger. The battle began, and Athena attacked the forces from the prison in Roma with the rest of the families still alive enough to fight. One spear that Athena threw went through six men in black, and the shackled men were released by her women, the men running back to the homes where fighting still continued. Some families beat the Christians, and twenty-two houses had fallen while fourteen houses remained. Athena helped all the houses of Italy, and finally after three days of fire and war, the fourteen houses remained intact.

The wounded were taken in and assisted; the fourteen houses all had melancholy, and even though they had survived this day, what of the future and what of their sons and daughters and the Christians' rape and pillage across Roma?

Athena was at rest within the house of Rinaldi among pillars of white, the burn marks of war surrounding, many statues having fallen and broken, but few beauties of nude Apollo Detra and Prometheus remaining among the water where Athena bathes in splendor while the limping slaves were happy to still be working knowing of other families who had fallen. The slaves had been murdered and raped or worse. Athena stayed at the house of Rinaldi for ten years, and several of these houses were treated by Porius and his crawling hand, being one of the main bits of magic that will save these artifacts for future generations to come.

The beautiful art of Italy, many disfigured and destroyed by the Christians, would never give pleasure to future generations, the tedious and brilliant artists, stone chiselers, craftsmen, painters, all the best of any generation, their work destroyed, moved aside for the thought of a new false religion. Porius and Athena spent ten years traveling from England to Italy, France, Wales, Scotland many times per year. Always new places to secure, as soon as someone was secure, another church was built and out came the zealots one by one. Once screams were heard by Porius, he would quickly react and either he or Athena, Walters, or Dr. Mellini would rescue those in need. Yes, the churches may take most of the hearts and minds of unsuspecting villagers around Europe, but never all. There will always be ways to keep the few unfaithful and freethinking peoples from enslavement. But it was a long, hard ten years, and traveling was not so easy for an aging sorcerer and Athena, the last of the Greek gods.

The pope and magistrates of the Catholic church circled Roma and were planning the expansion and assault on England, France, Spain, Wales, and Germany. Over the Alps and across the channel, through Paris and Londinium, all the plans were being made. Pope Gabriele Condulmer, better known as Eugene the Fourth, currently held the seat of pope but by no means steady in his plight. Eugene the Fourth opened the gates of the prison outside his hometown of Venice with prisoners now escaped and some beholden to Eugene, the latest pope in a long line of bloody popes speaking in Latin to a group of murderers and thieves.

"All seven of you shall rise, and with the power vested in me, I now pronounce and declare all the servants crimeless and redeemed by our Lord," Eugene said to the bowing men in the great cathedral of Roma as they knelt before him.

"For the love of God, ye shalt all prevail in your destruction of the pagans. You will first go to the families on the hills to the west, greet them, and ask for their allegiance; and if they refuse, first come to me and bring the head of each household. Bind the women and children and remove the slaves. If slaves resist, you have the permission to restrain and bring them as well. Each of you will receive five men each."

Other prisoners dressed in loincloth and shackles still not completely removed walked up from behind and joined each newly appointed killer of the pope. These newly made priests would be used to terrorize the final great families of Roma. Unless they turned their riches to the church, they would die and even worse. The heads of the families would watch the torture of their young before them until they confided in the pope. The band of empty faces and with knives to their backs joined and bowed toward the pope. The pope dispatched the bands of men, and as they left, he had his own slaves surrounding him bow their heads as he passed, dressed in bright red silken gowns, jewels, and large golden rings, which every newly appointed priest kissed before they exited with the small band of men each. Then the pope turned, and with him he took three male slaves and two female slaves into the private chambers. There he dropped his robes and made his slaves perform sexual acts as they treated him with unspeakable tasks. Soon this pope will meet his end by just one of these male slaves who refuses to comply with his advances, and in 1409, a new and even more terrible pope will take his place. But for now, Eugene is pope, bishop of Cinnea and cardinal of San Clemente. Roma shook at the thought of him.

Hot weather struck Roma as the great houses were emptied and great men and women were murdered and piled in the streets, their homes and estates gradually engulfed by the church. Athena occasionally fought, and several families on the north of Roma stood without giving in. Those families would last, but there were only a few, two of which Athena had given dragons to protect as she only had the power for several.

Acula Domina was one priest who was given the septumus curse and was sent bursting with worms back to the pope, stating as he stood naked and expanding in front of the pope, "Do not come near the Astrella palace or all will be cursed."

"What does he mean?" asked the pope. As he got closer to the man, worms were falling from the man's mouth.

"What spell is upon him?" the pope cried out.

At that moment, the man exploded, guts and skin covering the pope from head to foot in the explosion of his body from within—a spell that Porius had taught Walters who in turn had taught Athena.

"Dear god!" the pope screamed, looking down at his robes now drenched in filth. The pope ran out of the room, screaming into his chambers where he descended into a pool of water while his slaves washed him and took his clothes.

"Burn them," the pope said, pointing to the disgraced linen. Quickly moving, the pope returned to his chamber. Two nude young men held in their palms candles with melting beeswax and dripping down their arms for they feared the torture if they moved.

"You may leave," the pope said to one youth who quickly ran to the kitchen to remove the burning wax from his shoulders and arms. In the kitchen, the cook pulled long wax threads from his waist and legs, some even reaching his toes. The young man dressed and then tied a small black belt around his waist and, wearing a short skirt made of white silken material, put on his sandals and left the pope's home to join his friends in the city. Roman men, boys, and two black-haired women, Celia and Auria, walked with him as he told the story of his paid job of standing naked in the pope's chamber and holding his lights. Other favors requested by the pope were unmentioned, but his friends knew what went on in the home or palace of the pope, a palace that once belonged to the Maltobano family, a family that was held hostage, tortured, and eventually murdered one by one. Athena knew of this pope and had pledged revenge and would seek revenge from whatever pope lived in the Maltobano home.

That night after visiting Venice, Athena, Alexandria, and Gloria flew to Rome to deal with this pope. At the same time, from across the miles, Porius and Thomas decided to go into the village. Upon entering the village, the baker and his wife saw Porius and Thomas.

"Hello, Porius, and thank you for the seeds. My wheat crop is most wonderful this year," the farmer shouted.

"My pleasure to eating your delicious bread this year, thank ye."

"Porius, did you see who went into the inn?" Thomas asked inquisitively.

"I was not paying attention. What miraculous creature hath gone into our watering hole? I am looking forward to a pint."

"Looks like one of those priests in black," Thomas said as he grimaced.

"Well, hopefully he is a quiet priest. I am not in the mood to hear the prophecies this day," Porius said, looking vexed. Porius was wearing his long white robes with the encrusted golden embroidery work that featured animals, vines, and other pictures all done by the elves and villagers of Kent.

"Morning, Porius, mornin', Thomas," said the grain grocer setting up his stalls.

"Porius, the lavender seeds were spiffing this season. Thank thee," said the woman, setting up her perfumes to sell at her stall.

"You are welcome, Minerva," Porius said, bowing as he passed. "Your stall smells delightful, Minerva."

Thomas talked to her and bought a small vial of lavender for Elena, the cobbler's daughter. Most of the people in the hamlet came out or waved to Porius, his white robes flowing in the breeze. Thomas placed the vial of lavender in his green waistcoat pocket. The cobbler came out to meet Thomas and Porius in the road while the crowd grew.

"Thomas, thank you for the fish you gave Elena last week. I made you these new shoes with no buckle as a gift," the cobbler said, wearing his leather pants and white puff-sleeved shirt.

"Porius," the butcher said, carrying two fresh pheasant and handing the two prize birds to Porius, all cleaned and ready for cooking. "These are my two finest, and I must say you were correct in planning those wild mixture of seeds. I have never seen a healthier season for birds." The butcher stated his thanks for Porius coming into the village to bring seeds to plant the varying types of wildflower that the quail and pheasant enjoyed.

"Yes, I noticed my flocks have been growing since I have been planting more barley, rye, and other grasses," Porius said while hanging the free pheasants over his shoulder.

After an hour or so in the village, Porius and Thomas walked back. "Well, there you see, Porius, it's all about as you say the science of nature," Thomas said, arms filled with bags of supplies and most not costing a penny.

"Villagers just want someone to look out for them and they need steering in the right direction," Porius continued as the walk. "Instead of reading spiritual books, they need to research all the evidence that is laid out here before us." Porius passed his free hand over the countryside. "The more I research and the more I discover, Thomas, I feel the more we are on the brink of great things. Though my time is getting shorter, I find that there is more and more coming that will change the world."

"What do you thing will be the most significant science?" Thomas asked.

"I believe the electronic impulses that come from lightning and current of this force will be tamed and run through many a future device. I also hope that this and the use of the sun will be used for energy because the alternative may be machines using the minerals of the earth. Yes, I don't see how the race of men will utilize energies for dirty sources. Let's hope that the men will grasp the clean energy-building sciences over those sciences that may pollute and disrupt nature. No, I don't see that happening," Porius stated.

"I wouldn't put anything past our mortal race, Porius," Thomas said inquisitively.

Clouds and wind came up as they arrived at the garden, bluebells waxing and deer scampering about the fawns circling in joyful merriment Porius and Thomas. A large buck appeared at the tree line, and the fawns stopped in obedience and slowly walked out of the garden looking back with beautiful eyes to Porius and Thomas and gracefully leave the garden into the woods, escorted by the buck and doe. Entering the cottage, Porius noticed a small pile of cod by the doorstep, which Thomas gathered for the kitchen.

"Looks like the water goblins had brought us another pile of fish," said Porius gleefully.

"Yes, most agreeable indeed," Thomas replied.

Inside the cottage, Franklin circled and landed on the windowsill, peering in at the evening meal prepared and waiting on the table by Parthenia. Porius hung the pheasants in the pantry and swallowed a large gulp of mead before resting at the table on the wood-carved chair. Squirrels and rabbits were carved into the arms, and the chairs were bought of gold and steel yet wood they were made.

Doth winter creep in the middle of summer,
Must religion and fire burn in the coming hearts of man?
Shall kinsman and friend turn into foe in this mist of Latin words which soar above us?

Porius explained.

Thomas swallowed some ale and turned with a tear in his eye to Porius in the candlelight. "My lord, the eve which comes on the marrow and the will of sick witches and pagan de fuel amongst the new religions, as they come in ceremony and fright. Cadmus Upton plots, schemes, plans, and is never contented as the cause he has set upon the world. Italy, France, Persia and most likely the east await the ends of what has been," Thomas said in an unusually and uncommon statement.

"And what of Elena, Thomas? Will thee make her a wife? Make her merry to thee, behold to her in always, Thomas," Porius pleaded.

"Nay, Porius, nay. It is not for me wholly, it is not for me." Thomas paused then continued. "My eye is cast by others, and I cannot be true of one. My head is turned by Athena, my eyes filled with love for Leal and Byron."

"This I understand good, Thomas," Porius said, smiling and turning toward the crackling fire. "Thomas, my Thomas. These thoughts are natural, and it is not meant to always be enchanted by one thy may be still betrothed, but glance toward others. Be not in despair because all humans have such feelings. Those which are keen to question it and respect it within themselves shall be true to themselves and better serve the common good of mankind."

"Yes, you speak the truth and maybe I shall proclaim my betrothal to Elena, but not yet. I have spells to learn and journeys to travel."

"More than you know, Thomas. More than you know." Porius poked the fire. "By chance, tomorrow will come. Byron, Walters, Leal, and Simon and the five of you are going on a quest."

"A quest?" Thomas, astounded, said.

"Yes, well, something of a quest indeed," Porius said, reaching for the Malefactor. "Within this book lies a spell which of vine and flower, bird and wing calls for a beast." Porius opened then closed the book and placed it back on the special holder made of gold for the great book.

"A beast," Thomas said, now sounding a bit worried.

"A large beast which guards the last flowers of Burgundy," Porius continued.

"Porius, are you sending me to France?" Thomas asked.

"Yes, dear boy. To Calais and the forest beyond is a cave which has the flowers, and you must retrieve them and bring them to me here at the cottage."

"Your will is my duty, Porius," Thomas said as they both fell asleep in the flickering light.

Franklin circled the cottage as the rain softened and moonlight shone through the blackness. Badgers and owls hunted, crossing the gardens and the night life of the forest boldly. The water goblins left a new stack of fish and ran about, peering in the windows of the cottage, and grinned as they viewed Porius and Thomas falling asleep in their chairs. The water goblins now on the window awakened Porius as they stretched and sleepwalked to their beds and fell into a deep sleep, Thomas dreaming of the adventures ahead and Porius dreaming of a future fraught with danger and unpredictability.

The morning had winds from the east, winds like never before, blustering, blowing, bellowing, storming dry and fast. Thatched roofs went flying, sand and dirt swiftly moving through the grounds of the cottage, through Hastings, through even the infantry of Richard, his lionheart waving goodbye to England as they set off to France. The wind blew around Londinium; the lonely and the long lost would forget their loneliness in such a wind. Porius went out of doors, his robes blowing, and saw tree branches falling around him. Even down in Cornwall, the wind blew at such magnificent force as never seen before, pub signs falling and ripping from their posts, animals scurrying for shelter. Wind, yes, the mighty blow came crashing.

Porius could not help but think that malevolent forces must be behind these gales. Powerful winds had been traditionally greeted with ambivalence, but not this oppressive blow. Porius knew that some wizards occasionally use wind as a spiritual cleansing force, and this did not seem to be an exception. Thomas stepped out into the yard, screaming, "Porius, come back in, come back!"

"I must try something," Porius yelled back as he held a knife covered in cloth. Porius walked to the peach trees, and surrounding them, he pointed the knife covered in cloth toward the blow, circling the area or circumference of the tree. Then he went to the apple trees and performed the same ritual, tree after tree chewing up the dirt in his teeth from the wind and continuing until each tree had been protected. Then he walked toward the cottage.

"Franklin!" Porius yelled toward the cottage as Franklin flew out from the cottage while struggling against the gale.

Franklin grabbed the knife and flew above Thomas and around the cottage facing the covered blade to the wind.

"Good, now back inside." Thomas ushered Franklin and Porius back inside, Franklin getting blown against the far side of the cottage. "There, now let's wait and see if this ancient wind spell works."

Watching outside through the leaded windows, Porius and Thomas waited and watched. "The fruit will get ruined if this doesn't work."

A knock at the door, and Porius was greeted by a small group of farmhands.

"Aye, Porius, our masters have sent us in pleading assistance. The orchards are faltering due to this unbelievable wind," stated the spokesperson of this small band of merry men who dusted off their clothes, leaving a small fog hovering within and without the cottage. Thomas waved at the air and stated, "Couldn't you have done this before entering?" fussing, Thomas said.

"My Lord Porius," said the man wearing red woven clothes, baggy trousers, and a hat of blue.

"Yes, I can assist you, my friends," Porius stated with his kindest grin. "A mug of ale for you all?" Porius said, waving his wand, and all the men held chalices filled with ale as their eyes filled with the magic performed in their presence.

"My word, thank you," one man said, gulping in amazement.

"It is magic," another said, gulping. "And right in front of us."

"Thank you, my lord, the pleasure is all mine," said Porius. The wind seemed to slow around the cottage; the fruit trees seemed calm. The spell had worked.

"Now listen to me, all of ye gentle farmers. Take this cloth and divide it amongst you in pieces of about this size." He held up a small rag. "Wrap the end of each blade as I have done here." Porius revealed his blade.

"Yes, my lord," the spokesperson said inquisitively and gulped the ale, wiping his mouth.

"Then point the blade toward the wind and circle the outside area of each tree and house, cowshed, and haybale," Porius finished.

"Will it work?" the leader stated while he drank down his ale in two gulps.

"Please look beyond in my garden." Porius opened his door. The wind did not come into the cottage, the trees stood still, yet the wind carried branches, leaves, and other forms of debris over the cottage and around all the garden's sides.

"It works," the leader stated.

The men took their rags and ripped them into pieces, and all took them in different directions toward their farmlands. Each farm, plant, and tree got the treatment prescribed by Porius, tree after tree and farm after farm, calming the storm. Meanwhile, the church bells rang in the forms of the wind. Cadmus's trees withered in the wind, and days passed before it subsided.

Days later, Porius discovered a pause in the wind and then a hush, which came over England. Soldiers came back out from the tents in which they were hiding. Dover castle once again opened its doors, Richard began his plotting against France, Cornwall regained its fishing, and the farms sent men out once again to work in the fields.

Flowers, fruits, vegetables, and meats were brought to the cottage by farmers one by one. Porius opened the door and saw the bags and piles of food.

"We cannot possibly eat all of this food, Thomas," he said to Thomas, rushing outside. "A party. Yes, a party is in order."

Franklin flew once more and invited Leal, Walters, Simon, the villagers, and even Athena, Dr. Mellini, Caesarea from Wales, two elves, and a few fairies while birds, deer, squirrels, and hedgehogs watched on from the tree line. The party continued for a day and a night, and musicians played. Parthenia and Grendle cooked and cleaned with the help of many a farmhand and their wives. Children played sack races in the garden. It was a party to be remembered for years to come. Finally, at noon the following day, the crowd dispersed and all who were left were Porius, Athena, Walters, Thomas, Simon, Leal, and Athena's two golden-covered female guards. Sitting around the outside tables and half dozing, Athena asked, "So, my dear Porius, do you believe there was any malevolent force behind the wind storm? It did seem a bit ferocious."

"My dear Athena, you are suspicious. What makes you think?"

Porius interrupted by Thomas. "Porius, I know you had doubts."

"Yes, I predict though I am not in confirmation of this fact that Alibastor Fraun from France sent us the gale. It seems to have his mark upon it, and I know he was dabbling with such a spell years ago."

"Why he in particular?" Athena asked. Walters, Simon, and Leal listened with interest.

"Well, Alibastor is not happy with Richard and his plight against the French of late," Porius continued. "It has occurred to me that maybe he was trying to slow the progression of Richard while the French king builds his defenses. This seems logical, and I must say that it has slowed the cause from Richard. In fact, I believe they are all still in Dover and along the English coast."

"Maybe true and seems most understandable," said Walters.

"Alibastor does not particularly like the Catholic king of France, but to stop bloodshed of the innocent, I can see it as a possibility," Porius said.

"Why don't we try to contact Alibastor?" Thomas asked.

"Bring my the pensive and I will need honey, molasses, and a rune stone."

Thomas set the pensive on the table, and all watched as Porius added the molasses, honey, and stone to the pensive. Waving his wand, he called out, "Alibastor, Alibastor." Nothing.

The quiet was calming, and the bluebirds flew overhead while all watched them fly, tweet, and play. Finally, a voice from within the pensive rang out into the garden.

"Porius, is that you?"

"Yes, my friend. How are you?" Porius replied back into the sticky mess in the pensive.

"Well, my lord, I had a notion you would be calling me soon."

"Ah, then it was you?"

"Well, I hope you protected your trees."

"Yes, but it was quite a terrible blow against us, Alibastor."

"Was it, indeed. Sorry 'bout that."

Everyone rolled their eyes and shook their heads.

"Yes, Alibastor, you must be careful with such a high gale."

"My apologies, but I heard Henry was heading our way with army and sword and you know."

"Well yes, I took that to be the case, and I have asked Henry to mind his way. He said he will be merciful, and I assume he may be somewhat merciful."

"Lord Porius, listen," Athena said, hand on her head.

"I hear it," Porius said while standing on his feet, ears cupped by hands bejeweled with emerald and ruby rings. "I can use these for a spell." Porius contemplated the issues of Old World diseases, including diphtheria, measles, influenza, and smallpox as they were carried to the Americas by infected Spanish colonists. His mind wandered on spells he may send the tribal peoples before they were torn apart and destroyed by disease.

"Quick, my staff." He gestured to Thomas who went in and brought out a long staff of polished wood encrusted with jewels. The top of the staff glowed with burning colors. To wind to the Native Americans, he threw out a hand, and silver sparks flowed to America, up and up, through the several layers of atmospheric influences as this power had been given to Porius from ancestral bloodlines, which reached back to other worlds and different atmospheric conditions. Sick to his stomach slightly, Porius's mind was on the dust that flowed over oceans and rivers, streams, lakes, and mountain peaks to the Indian civilizations, one particle of dust to each, the Navajo, Apache, Cherokee, Sioux, Paiute, and Cheyenne people's leaders. Each particle ascended up the nostril of a few chiefs and both male and female tribespeople who, shall we say, had a special tent for sexual encounters as a form of pleasure and a cheap price. This way, Porius understood that through these prostitutional beings, life would be given and the saving of many thousands of natives shall be saved. It had come to pass of late that 90 percent of all Native Americans have already died from the diseases brought mostly by Catholic ships.

"The Centari peoples of the third green planet are calling us," Porius said. "Ready and make yourself set for the journey. Take clothes for warm weather, and meet me here in one hour."

Athena and her two girl guardians dispersed. Walters, Leal, and Simon refreshed themselves in the river; and all met redressed with the situation, swords at their sides.

Leal wore his high black leather boots and short trousers that were met with leather straps that wrapped his muscular figure. Simon followed suit, and the men returned in one hour to the garden.

Porius held the rune as a light appeared above. Thomas was wrapped in mesh, leather, and a smaller sword by his side. He also carried the wand given to him and transfigured, and even the water goblins watched from the edge of the forest. Athena and her two maidens, Walters, Simon, Leal, Thomas, and Porius stood tall as the light engulfed them.

"Transporting," a voice said as they were extracted from the earth and circled in light.

"Level two second green zone planet," the voice said within moments.

"Level three second outer rim," the voice said.

Porius explained to the others while they all stood frozen. "Hang on, my friends."

The voice rang out around them as they all stood shrouded in lights, "Transportation complete. Welcome to Centari Planet of Gower."

"Well, all of you please sit and drink," a voice called out to them all from another garden not unlike Porius's, only the plants were slightly altered with more fluorescence added to the pinks, reds, turning them to magenta, while he also pondered the biological exchanges across the globe; for with the advent of long-distance navigation of the fifteenth century, explorers covered more of the world than ever before, leaving their seeds and diseases with the innocent tribal people from Africa to the North Pole. No place was too far to land, seed, and populate, but to Porius's mind, overpopulate. Porius worked over his mathematical calculations and, with Thomas in tow, multiplying the seeds of sailors with the number of ports, ships, and travelers will attack each country from all sides; and in, say, one hundred years, each country would hold several races in each. Then America, hit from all sides, Porius saw, would fill up with Asians on the west, Spanish and African on the south, and European and Scandinavian on the east and north.

CHAPTER 6

A short man of about five feet tall ran toward Porius while the others sat on benches to catch their breath and sip water that was flowing from fountains surrounding the wooden double-seated benches, fruit trees, ivy, cornstalks, and primitive-looking gardens surrounding them. Flowers were of plenty. Elves hovered at the edge of the garden.

"Lord Gower, nice to see you again," Porius said, shaking the palm of Lord Gower. Gower wore another similar white bejeweled robe as Porius.

"I hope you appreciated my garden, Lord Porius."

"Yes, indeed it looks quite similar to mine," Porius replied.

"I followed your garden plan to the letter and copied down to the last shrub," Gower stated while looking around and rubbing his hands together in excitement.

"Let me introduce you, Lord Gower, to my friends, Athena."

"Lord Gower, a pleasure, and my ladies, Gloria and Alexandria, my faithful soldiers and companions." Athena allowed the two ladies to bow toward Lord Gower.

"I have heard of your great exploits, and thank you for coming."

Porius continued. "Leal, Simon, Thomas, and Walters."

"Yes, men, thank you all for coming, and I know you will all have a pleasant stay and will help us attend to this untidiness at hand."

"Porius, this was very sudden, what has taken place?" Walters asked, now standing flush, still with red skin from the quick light journey to Centari Gower.

"My Lord Porius and friends," Gower continued, "WE HAVE BEEN INVADED."

"Oh dear," said Athena, the rest showing grave interest.

114

"Yes, invaded, and we have no defenses from these types of villains. We are friending farmers, scientists, educators, musicians and artists, and the like. We have no knowledge of battle or fighting or competition, and we are being killed."

"Killed?" said Walters, eager to defend.

"Yes, you see, they landed about forty kilometers from where we stand. They are wearing black and appeared several weeks ago in the city of Carolina just north of us. They bear the sign of a crucifix about their necks, and they have killed over forty creatures, ten elves, three men, two women whom they called witches, and several other creatures who have recently come here from earth for refuge. I cannot understand it. I-I assume they are from earth."

"Hold on and how did they travel here?" asked Porius.

"Well, I believe they found an elven with knowledge of the transportation device, tortured him in England or Spain since those are the only two transport areas. Then they tricked him into coming here."

"They have followed us," Walters said.

"It is not possible," said Athena, alarmed.

"To my knowledge, it is possible," said Thomas. "Torture methods of Christians is quite effective, and if they were placed on a rack and their body stretched, they will speak of what is requested. The pain would be so terrible that nothing could be held back."

"Well, we have work to do. We must find these villains at once," Porius said.

"Thank you, my lord, I knew you would come. We have since stopped any being from using the transport unless invited," Lord Gower stated.

"Very well," Porius said. "We rest tonight and leave first thing in the morning."

"Yes, rest, come with me, and my castle is not unlike your castle at Dover. I have ordered food, wine, and song for entertainment tonight, and thank you all for coming." Gower took them all through a path in the forest.

On the other side of the forest stood a castle at the edge of an ocean and from the north could be seen valleys and hills with smoke billowing up in the distance. As they all stood on the wall of Gower castle staring north to Carolina, Gower pointed to a village in the distance.

"It does look like a battle," Leal stated to Simon and the others.

"I am ready to fight at first light," Simon said, and the others confirmed.

"I may follow at a safe distance behind, but we will rid you of this cursed mess," Thomas said as the others turned and headed into the brilliantly colored castle.

"Lord Gower, you have outdone yourself," Athena said while looking from the top stairs at the beautifully decorated food hall, where there were piles of apricot, mango, fish, fowl, and drinks. Large flowing curtains draped the walls, and elongated tables of wood were carved with images of small animals, squirrel, chipmunk, chicken, and fox. Music played from the small stage, and a few elves played harmoniously together almost a transient style of music to match the finest composers of earth.

Electric lights of blue and green circled the walls.

"Ah, you have worked out the electricity rules, I see," Porius said.

"Yes, my scientists are most advanced and in fact the same brilliant mind who worked out the electricity and solar energy poser also invented the light transport, which was done about twenty-three years ago. His name is—"

"George Handle?" Porius interrupted what Gower said.

"Yes, my lord George, I have forgotten you met prior."

"I would like to meet this brilliant scientist Lord Gower," Athena said while holding a goblet of wine to her lips and sipping.

"Yes, he is currently working on a flying machine that uses balloons filled with helium 3 but will be here in a few days and is eager to meet you all as well. We have removed all the scientific minds from Carolina as to keep them far from the marauding Christians who are, as we speak, taking minds and lives amongst the innocent."

"Let's discuss our approach," Walters said as they all sat around the elongated table eating and drinking.

Leal removed his sword and vest as the occasional eye glimpsed his beauty. Gloria and Alexandria giggled at the far end.

"The very best and easiest way for you all to travel is the northern road by horse, which we have at the ready. I have five horses," Gower said while others came in to meet the travelers.

Together they sit and planned, ate, and occasionally danced. Thomas not having a horse to ride out would stay behind with Porius tomorrow and monitor the siege from a pensive in Gower Castle.

That night in Carolina, people stayed locked inside their homes as the noise off in the distance of chanting and knocking about could be heard. Ten men in black robes cut down trees in the middle of Carolina and built a large crucifix at the center of the city. Most of the architecture surprisingly matched that of England in the twelfth century, thatched roof and stone walled. Two homes were overtaken, and the family was killed for its use. The one child who did not refuse was now serving the two men tea.

"Tomorrow we will go after the farm I noticed at the south side of the city," said a man dressed in black stinking of sweat as his robes were far too thick for the current climate in Carolina. "Tell the other men attending to stop for the night and rest. We have caused enough disturbance for one day. I fear no assault, and soon this area will be ours and by the grace of God soon the planet."

The man put down his team. The young boy serving ran to the back room and pulled covers over his head, shaking in fear, and with one eye on the door attempted to sleep. His mind was filled with images of his mother and father raped and then burned alive out for all to see. The smell still haunted the city, and the screams still carved firmly into his memory—another night with these brutes. In the young boy's mind, he regretted the future being all this. Two weeks ago, they had all lived in peace.

The next morning, the boy was awakened by shouting.

"Where is that boy?" a loud voice yelled, and the boy jumped to his feet.

"Come here, boy," the man screamed at him, shaking the boy standing before him. "Bring me some tea and bread."

"We have no bread left, sir. We would need to bake it, and my mother is—"

"Well then, go and get some and be back quick," the man shouted, scratching his greasy black hair.

Other men were stirring outside and sleeping along the outside of the cottage. The body odor wafted around the area from the uncleaned and unwashed man, who had now awakened and was binge eating their food, which they have pillaged from other citizens of Carolina. The boy returned with breads and jams for the two obvious leaders who currently ruled his once simple and peaceful home.

Once these beastly men were fed, they would begin knocking on doors and asking, "Have you heard the work of Christ, you heathen? Open up!" they would say as they kicked in each door and searched the cottages. The cottages with the most jewels, useful belongings, and skilled participants would be their next victims. The people who were simple and not strategically located may find themselves lucky as they were of no need to these pillaging Christians.

Back at their castle, Porius and the others ready themselves. Porius upstairs with Thomas would keep an eye on the fighting through the pensive. Walters, Simon, and Leal would ride with Gloria and Alexandria behind. Athena would stay at the castle and greeting the wounded and suffering with kin from the city. Already several people were sick or injured. One man was half burned with burn marks all down his body as he tried to save his wife from the burning. All the victims of the men in black. Athena attended to them one by one. Athena's healing power was that of a highly skilled nurse with antiseptic knowledge and bandaging skills; plus her kindness and reassurance did not go amiss among the thankful.

Gower, though never married and ruler of this planet, had several friends who also assisted Athena.

Leal and Walters were in front, Simon behind, Gloria and Alexandria cautiously behind. A black cloak moved quickly to the right of Leal.

"Who goes there?" Leal shouted as birds flew from the bushes.

"And who are thee?" a booming voice came from behind the verge, sword drawn and he racing toward the horses.

"We have come to clean this world of filth like ye," Simon answered, dismounting and meeting the force of three men in black cloaks, metal meets metal, and the others stay on horses. Simon cut one in the leg, and down he went; then another in the stomach in and out cleanly, down he went. The third man witnessed the swiftness of Simon's skill and began to run. Walters rode up alongside the running cloak and swept his sword toward the man.

"Heathens!" the man in black screamed as his decapitated head rolled to the bush, mouth still open and blood flowing from its gapping lips.

Walters rode back to his position. Simon stabbed the man with wounded leg.

"No survivors," Leal stated.

Simon watched the man die under him, arms outstretched toward the sky until breathless.

Then there came the sound of horses coming from Carolina, the large one leading in front who was recently ordering about his young slave.

"Quick, Simon, Leal, flank," Walters said as they widened the area and begging a battle of twelve against the five. Gloria and Alexandria killed their fair share with blood and honor. Swords wielding, Simon was on foot attacking the horsemen all wearing back. One, two, three went down now surrounding Simon. Even the small boy once ordered about by the leader came out with knife raised. Leal stabbed the leader in the heart, and off his horse he fell. The small boy knelt above his head and stabbed the fallen leader through his mouth.

"That is for my mum and pop and all the horrible evil words you shouted." The knife went through his once-shouting skull.

Leal dismounted as did all the others, and the battle was misted by the rising dust, sweat, blood as the air was filled with shouting. After fifteen more minutes, Walters and his band of men stood the victor.

Back at the castle, Porius watched the fighting through the pensive and grabbed Thomas by the shoulders. "We have won, we have won!"

Thomas shouted down the castle hallway, "Lord Gower, it is over, we have won!" Thomas turned and saw Gower running toward him as a large black man wearing black cloak and wielding a large knife ran after the running Lord Gower.

"Porius," Thomas yelled as he saw the man in black about to stab Gowers.

"Disarm!" Porius shouted, startling the knife-wielding thug.

The raised arm froze, and Gower ran behind Porius.

"How did you get in here?" Porius asked.

"Never mind how, but I shall kill thee." The black mass rushed Porius and tackled him to the ground.

Blood spilled and flowed on the marble floor around Porius and the fallen man who lay on top of Porius. With tears in his eyes, Gower shouted, "Porius, no!"

Gower's face was covered by trembling hands. He looked down at Porius under the large black figure.

"Porius?" cried Gower.

"Get off me, you bloodthirsty Christian," Porius said from below the lifeless figure, pushing the dead carcass off him, and his black body rolled over to reveal the tip of Porius's staff now covered in blood and planted deeply int the figure's chest.

"I told you I needed my staff," Porius said with nervous glee.

"Porius, I thought you were killed," Thomas said in happy triumph.

"My dear Lord Porius," Gower said, assisting him to regain his stance.

The blood stopped gushing; Gowers had several elves clean up the mess along with Walters, Simon, Leal, Gloria, and Alexandria.

"Take all of these bodies back to earth, Porius. We do not wish to dispose of them here," said Gower.

———

'Let's not show humans how to travel in this way for many millennia," said Gower.

"Agreed," said Porius.

"Until every man has the thought of war out of his or her minds, at least," said Gower.

"That may be very a long time with humans," said Thomas.

A few hours passed, and the entire crew with a pile of dead bodies wrapped in silken fabric stood at the transporter; as the distance and time was spent eventually, the group ended up back at the cottage.

"Load the wagon with these bodies and take then to the church where Cadmus Upton lives and have him give them peace." Walters agreed, and the three men stacked the bodies and headed out toward Hastings.

Athena, Gloria, and Alexandria said their goodbyes and evaporated while waving to Thomas and Porius.

"Ah, peace and quiet, Porius. This is what I desire, peace and quiet," Thomas said, heading into the cottage.

"I wonder what comes next, Thomas. I am full of wonder." Porius walked into the cottage changing rooms and washing himself in his stream-fueled water shed, which he heats the running water using coals alight.

That evening, Porius wore a black gown, simply cut to hug tight his skin and no jewels, no lace just black.

"It feels very empty, this black," Porius said to Thomas as Grendle brought some food to the table.

"It really isn't you, Porius," Thomas said.

"Too dark by any means, my lord," Grendle remarked as she went back to the kitchen.

All the mothers toting babies back at Centari celebrated the taking of their distressing torturers and unwelcomed guests. Gowers raised goblets at a large feast for all the heads of cities. "We raise a toast to Porius and his friends for saving our planet from these fierce men," Gowers said.

Porius sensed his name being toasted, and his workings sensed rejoicing on the far-off world, drinking his evening ale and toasting Thomas.

"To a world saved from our possible invasion." He raised his goblet toward Thomas.

"A world saved. Now let's save ours," Thomas replied.

Franklin was nesting on the rooftop by the warmth of the chimney. As the moon shone above them, the nightingale sang, the foxes played around the garden. Deer wandered about aimlessly, nipping on plant and bush.

Ants slowed their working day chores in the bios. Slug, snail, caterpillar, and more ease into their evening.

The water goblins slowly crept outside piling up fish for the household for fun, peering into the leaded windows of the cottage, startling Thomas a bit. Once Thomas recognized the two water goblins, he said, "Water goblins always watching."

"They are keen. I am sure there is a large pile of fish outside I can almost taste it," Porius said, swallowing a large sip of ale.

Clouds drifted by as Walters, Leal, and Simon unloaded the pile of bodies dressed in black. Simon ripped each necklace and cross from the marauders, and holding the bunch in his hands, he knocked on the vicarage's door loudly.

"Cadmus, are you in there?" Simon yelled through the door.

Cadmus appeared, wearing his black robes and holding a candle. "Who is it at this time of night? Oh, Simon," Cadmus said.

"Yours, I believe," Simon said, holding out his hand full of crosses and dropping them at Cadmus's feet, the moonlight shining in the reflected silver crosses amongst most made by wood.

"Mine?" Cadmus said, looking at the large mound of dead men, now starting to smell.

"We found them and want to return them to you with all our love," Simon said as he left the doorway, mounted his horse, and drove off with Walters and Leal.

Cadmus stood, mouth gaping and eyes wide. He slammed the door, and a shout could be heard from outside of Cadmus's disappointment.

The three men drove back to Walters's estate, stopping on the way at the village pub in Hastings. The name of the pub had recently changed to the Woodman's Axe. The men inside drank and made merry. Byron was there playing a lute for some villagers, a few girls were dancing in the center of the room, people were talking, dogs were running through, and dirty children giving the occasional scream of adventure.

"Nice to be home, boys," Walter said, Simon and Leal sitting across the table from Walters.

"It is very nice to be home," said Leal as he leered at Byron, golden hair flowing about his lute. Simon downed one goblet of ale and returned to the bar for seconds.

"Don't be stingy!" shouted Walters to Simon at the bar while downing his first drink.

"Make that two, no, make it three," Simon said to the woman behind the bar, witnessing Leal raising his arm for another, eyes still fixed on Byron and his lute.

A light rain outside the frosty mist appeared close to the earth as the moon shone high above the Woodman's Axe. Sounds from outside could be heard.

"You should have seen Cadmus's face," Walters's voice echoed, and he told the story to all the publicans and villagers.

The wind started to ease in and cover the sounds coming from the pub. The village was quiet, and even the ironmonger closed shop for the night. The farmers were at their homes eating with their families. Geese honked as they landed for the night, deer rustled through the bushes, foxes circled and played. All was right with England.

On March 22, 1421, Thomas of Lancaster, brother to Henry the Fifth, laid siege to France; and war went across France until after Henry captured Dreux and the siege of Meaux. Henry died suddenly on August 31 at the Chateau de Vincennes, sick with dysentery and possible survey. He died in the arms of his latest friend at arms.

Porius now getting on in years, and Thomas reaching middle age, Walters, Leal, and Simon still living together on the estate of Walters in Kent. Athena less frequently visited, but the angry mobs still laid siege to many a villager and occasional small battles continued. Porius occasionally called out the forces of Athena and Walters to save families and protect villagers and farmers, and those who tried to keep the old ways in their homes found it harder as time marched on around England. Ships continued exploring new continents.

Henry the Navigator was a Portuguese naval explorer who discovered the Madeira Island, and though he did not actually sail and was sent Joao Zarco and his men were on board ship and sailing back from Africa when out at sea, the last sighting of a large sea serpent was seen and listed as a magical sighting. Joao and his crew were rocked back and forth by the huge beast, its long sixty-foot body smashing up against the sides of the ship. Mouth wide and leaping from the waves, the beast caught two men in its jowls, leaving only their shoes behind on deck. The large scaly beast holding its victims went down into the sea and was never sighted again. Cautiously, Henry and his crew made for Portugal to tell their tale, paintings were made of the event, stories turned into legend, and soon became the stories pf myth and legend.

Porius knew of the beast, and while hearing the story in the Woodman's Axe, Porius thought to himself, *I would have liked to have seen this creature.*

Cadmus's church grew stronger. Canterbury Cathedral became much more hospitable and loaded with people to hear the word of god. The Old World ways slowly took a backseat to the new religions of Christian and Muslim, Judaism, while Porius grew older and time began to swiftly move by.

CHAPTER 7

June of the following year, Porius taught Byron, Thomas, and a few other villagers interested in the old ways some spells, including the wind spell, which may come in handy at some point in their lives.

"Remember, my friends, that you must know the spell to relieve the wind once it's stopped." Porius dismissed everyone from the garden, and as they began to leave, he made a statement.

"My friends, I am getting on in years and would like you all to know that this may be our final visit of this nature."

"No, my lord," Byron yelled at Porius, and the others stood dumbfounded including Thomas.

"Yes, my friends. I need to take a journey to the south sea. I need to view the final creature of the sea, and the only way is to board a Portuguese ship, which leaves Wednesday week from Dover. I will be gone at least three months, but home and rested by September."

Porius stood tall as the people came close to him, giving him hugs, wiping the tears from their eyes, whispering good blessings in his ears before they left the garden.

Porius was alone with Thomas as Thomas walked up to Porius. "I knew this day was soon to come."

"Dear Thomas, I will return. And you must keep watch over Franklin and the cottage."

"My heart will not be sound without you near, Porius, my lord."

"How about having Byron stay with you or Walters, Simon, and Leal. Surely they will come and visit."

"Porius, they may already be on their way," Thomas said.

Time passed and the next morning as if by clockwork magic rode in Walters, Leal, and Simon, rushing into the cottage.

"Porius, we have heard the news," Walters said, panting and out of breath.

"Porius, you cannot take a sea journey," Leal said, running to Porius as he sat at the Malefactor.

"The Malefactor shall be hidden within these walls, the runes hidden at Canterbury," Porius stated to their bewildered faces. Walters and the others sadly faced Porius. Simon and Leal had a hand each on Porius's shoulders.

"Thank you all for coming, and this is something that I must do."

"What protection are you to have?" asked Simon.

"None, I shall leave Thomas here to protect the cottage and assist any troubled farmer or visitor. Athena will keep watch over the journey from a pensive in Italia. I will survive the journey."

"Porius, how old are you, and what feeble man can stand a sea journey at your age?" Simon said the, others in agreement.

"Now, now my fellows, I will survive."

"Then I shall accompany ye and watch over your every step," said Leal.

"I insist," said Walter, and Simon agreed.

"I shall keep ye safe as these journeys can be fraught with many an obstacle, my lord," Leal pleaded.

"Well, all right, Leal, your protection and company will be most welcome," Porius agreed.

"Thank you, my lord, I have always wanted to witness the sea creature."

"Plus my Portuguese is not up to par. Latin is fine, but I believe the captain Joao may only speak Portuguese, a tongue I may not be that familiar with."

"Portuguese?" said Leal.

"Yes, Leal, because there are no English ships at present to go through the current to African coast, which is where the sea serpent resides."

"Have they accepted you, and will they allow me to join the crew?" Leal said eagerly.

"They will do my bidding, but please remember this will be a Christian ship and you will have to hold thy tongue on occasion because they may have strange rituals and most likely on Sundays."

"I see and agree," Leal said.

"When are you off then?" Walters asked.

"Monday night we board ship from Dover and leave early Tuesday," Porius said, pouring the men ale into solver goblets.

"MY LORD PORIUS," Thomas cried as the others viewed his despair.

"Thomas, my greatest protégé on earth," Porius said, wrapping his long arms around Thomas while he wept.

"Thomas, I will stay with you as often as needed," Simon said.

Walters went to the window and, moving the curtains aside, shouted to the men, "Something is lurking beyond the forest, Porius."

Porius went to the window, leaving the pitcher of ale on the table.

"I wonder how the protection will last with me gone," Porius inquired.

"Porius, will it stay strong?" Thomas said in anticipation of what evil men may find their way to the cottage with Porius away.

"This will be a good test, I'm sure," Porius said.

"A test?" Thomas said.

"Yes, I am getting on in years now, and at some point, I will be gone. I have made the cottage protected for all time. The seal will not break, and if it does, I will show you, Walters, and the others the protective circle chants and spells before Tuesday."

"Not to worry, Thomas, Simon and I can be here within two hours, and we have an eye on you. Plus, Franklin's always keen at watch."

"Franklin is in his hundredth year and still going strong," Porius said.

"Hundredth year?" Thomas said.

"Yes, it is a long story, but Franklin will watch over this cottage as will you for many millennia to come," Porius continued. "Far be it for me to explain, but we are here for the duration of time. We will watch the grounds and keep watch over the earth."

"Walters and Leal seem to be aging a bit, Porius. Do you have any spells for them?" Simon asked.

"I am afraid not, Simon. You see, I only have the power to make one soul immortal, and it will be Thomas, but all of your energies will join me in Elysium in the future. Green grass, golden buildings, and vast experiences await you all long after this life on earth ends."

"Wisdom and knowledge," Walters said. "That is all we seek."

"I look forward to the journey, Porius, and for the next few days I will study my Latin and prepare for the sea," Leal said.

"Dress warm, Leal," Porius said as they all sat down to a nice supper.

Parthenia and Grendle filled the table with food. The band played floating on its bandstand, and the water goblins watched with glee through the windows, mounting up fish by the front door.

A song ensues and all the men sing
Misty Misty Mountaintop
Sea upon enchanted sea
Travel with my friend and foe
Is the life for me
Channeled wills and hearts delight
Sea upon enchanted sea
Travel with my friend and foe
Is the life for me
Misty Misty Mountaintop
Sea upon enchanted sea
Taking each other by the hand (Porius's and Leal's eyes meet}
Is the life for me

Another few songs and flagons of ale, and they all finally lie about the room and fall asleep—Thomas in an armchair, Leal and Simon entangled on the rug by the fire, Porius snoring in the back room, Walters still awake and staring at the now dying fire as he slowly fell asleep.

The next morning, the deer were out playing around in the garden, Franklin eating his morning worms, and tulips opening up in multicolored glory.

"Morning," Simon said as he walked back from the river dripping in water and his nakedness for all to see, shaking the drops from his body. Leal followed with his wet, thick black chest hair like a bird shining in the morning sun. They dressed and grabbed Walters and their well-nourished horses two black and one beautifully painted white and brown horse under Walters as they ride off back to Walters' estate.

Monday morning arrived, and Thomas sat with Porius and Franklin eating his worm on the roof.

"I will miss you, my lord," Thomas said, manning up. "But I shall keep the grounds safe"

"I know you will, Thomas, and I too will miss ye."

"There may be not much time, but when Leal gets here, may I ask a favor of you?"

"Yes, my good man, what is it?"

"Can I wear the emerald ring, which you keep on the mantle?" Thomas asked as they both looked at the small wooden tree long since dead that held a green sparkling ring of emerald.

"Yes, yes indeed you may." Porius went toward the ring and placed it on his finger. "There is no magic in this ring, but it suits you and gives you the stature deserved by watching over the cottage," Porius said gleefully.

"Blast this weather," Porius said as he finished packing his leather satchel in preparation for the long sea voyage that awaited him. Leal arrived, knocking hard at the door, his long black hair falling around his chiseled features turned up toward a sky, which though showed a few rays of sunlight beaming down around the garden, black clouds cracked with dry occasional bursts of lightning. The door opened.

"Leal, welcome, Porius is almost ready," Thomas said gleefully, holding his hand out to make sure that Leal caught a glimpse of emerald now resting upon his finger.

"Oh, I see Porius has made you a present! And a fine one as well," Leal said, stepping into the cottage, his small black leather satchel packed so the sides were bulging. Leal wore leather pants with black high boots, a tight mesh black metallic blouse covered in part by a black leather vest, his arms exposed from the shoulder down his large muscular arms showing signs of movement as he dropped the satchel. His belt held two daggers, and a small sword hung at his side.

"Leal." Porius stood before him smiling. "You look well, my protector." Porius grabbed his satchel and was wearing his usual white long gown with gold-trimmed lace, arm coverings of delicate lime green, and avocado-green intertwined needlework of dragons, trees, elves, and deer.

When they stepped outside into the garden, Parthenia and Grendle were waving to Porius in the window, both revealing tears running down their faces as they waved him farewell. Good journey their lips said to him as he waved back. Deer stepped out behind the forest and bowed their elegant heads toward Porius and Leal as they strolled toward their awaiting horses. The journey to Dover was quick under the lightning and cloudy day.

"Ah, the ship," Leal said as they approached a three-sail mast schooner. The *Bend* was the name of this vessel, and the captain greeted them as they approached. Dismounting from the horses, Leal shouted to the horses, "Home!" The horse turned and ran toward Walters where they would arrive in a couple of hours.

"Captain Joao, I presume," said Porius as he reached out to shake Joao's hand.

"Si, senior. Oh, Lord Porius en dis must be Leal," Joao said, smiling and leading them onboard. Joao was wearing the usual working captain uniform, nothing fancy—leggings, cap, blue-and-red-colored plumage. The men all nodded as they passed, some fixing the riggings, others handling the ropes. Soon the tide came in, and they were off, songs of joy and fresh air out on the sea toward Morocco. The sun beat down on the men, most half naked as they manned their posts, Leal pitching in to sweep the deck and follow other men as he mimicked their trade. First Leal climbed the ropes to join a man who was fixing a sail. Leal watched and then relieved him as he finished the needle workings. The other men appreciated Leal's outstanding assistance and eagerness to all types of work.

Later that day, Captain Joao said to Porius, "Leal, he is acessivel, Senior Porius."

"Oh handy, yes, most handy," Porius said as he tried hard to understand the Portuguese captain.

"Si, handddeeee, un a muscular," Joao said as he imitated a strong man.

"Oh yes," Porius said, also mimicking a muscle man. "Tre muscular, indeed." Porius sipped a warm mug of brandy, and the sea rolled out around them.

Soon they passed through the Bay of Biscay, and off to the left they saw Belle Ile until Bayone lay in the distance and the night began to fall. Sounds of snoring rumbled through the underdeck rooms, the galley smelling of liquor, roasted meat, and vegetables. Porius Leal, Joao, and Michael Fennigan, the ship's first mate sat around a table discussing the journey, the sea, the weather, women, dogs, and the world around them. Turtles and dolphin splashed in the moonlight in the waters outside as waves rolled and below underneath the *Bend*, a hardy ship built for speed and luxury, containing cargo usually food from Spain like satsumas and lemons of which on board were plenty.

"Well, how did you enjoy your first day at sea?" Michael asked in his most-hackneyed accent toward Porius and Leal as they feasted on roasted chicken and vegetables.

"The grub is glorious," Leal said, smiling, with chicken falling from the edge of his mouth.

"Well, this is hardly my first time at sea. In fact, I took this course twenty year ago at least, went to Morocco on another expedition to watch some whales."

"Whales?" Joao asked.

"Yes, indeed, I was with Athena, a lady friend of mine who is quite interested in whales. We watched them all the way from Morocco to the Canary islands and round back close to Portugal. It was an exciting journey, and the ship was called the *Pike* under Captain Jouarhi from Africa."

"Oh si, I know the captain, very good, veree good," Joao said, smiling.

Soon the calm of the sea engulfed them all in a deep sleep. Porius shared the cabin with Joao, and Leal shared with Michael. All was quiet and calm until morning arrived and another day of sailing.

Shouts from on deck could be heard with the captain commanding, the sailors behaving, and Leal pitching in here and there. Porius stood staring out to sea at the front of the ship. The waves came stronger, and the days passed quickly. Soon they landed in Africa. Outside of Casablanca, they anchored and waited as the supply ship reloaded the vessel and they were off again, this time farther out to Mogador Island where they waited all night. Then circling the island, Porius asked the captain, "Circle the island three more times and then head north."

Captain Joao followed, and after three days of fishing and circling the island, they headed north, but this time a little farther out to sea and heading back for England.

One night while the rain was chucking down all around them and the waves were high and tossing the ship, a loud scream was heard out at sea. Porius, Leal, and Joao investigated. Hardly being able to see, Leal pointed out to sea. "There, my lord." They all headed toward the bow of the ship, Michael steering steadily through the storm.

"I see it, I see it!" Porius shouted with glee.

Before them, the large serpent raised its twelve-foot-long and at least eight-feet-wide head and a long neck that rose above the ship. It let out a scream. All the men on the ship covered their ears and shivered in fright. Some brave enough came on board to witness the mighty creature as it postured and gleamed in the moonlight; then Porius stood tall with his arms stretched wide, staff in one hand.

"Greetings!" he shouted to the creature.

The vast being was not all in visibility, just a huge neck, and it crashed down into the sea once more.

"Oh-ho," shouted Joao as he ran to watch the giant beast as it went beneath the waves and out of sight, Leal rushing close to them, Michael still staring out toward sea and keeping the ship safe through the storm. There was applause from all the men and shouts of joy all around.

"Well, that was an amazing sight. Make no mistake," Leal said.

"Outstanding," Porius said, smiling and scanning the surface of the sea for another glimpse.

"Behold," Porius shouted and raised his staff toward the sky.

The serpent raised erect from the sea at an amazing force, all water and scales, teeth, and a long purple fin that ran down his long neck raising high then splashing down next to the ship. The water from the splash soaked Porius and the others as they all shouted, "Hoorah, hoorah!" Again, the mighty beast rose from the depths and then plunged down into the sea with the force of a hundred horses.

CHAPTER 8

Below the surface of the water, seals, sharks, whales, and other fish types scattered to remove themselves from the underwater vibrations. Small elven-type people wearing seashell and breathing devices lined the floor of the sea, looking up to watch the creature race the ship, watching the whales laugh as the interested parties aboard the ship found it all so exciting. Sharks circled in wait of a hopefully not so careful sailor who may lean a bit too far over the side and supply them with a fresh meal for the day. Odd that no one aboard ship would ever know that the elven peoples were watching them from below.

Clashing waves pelted the ship. Until finally, the serpent could be seen no more and into the vast ocean it went toward another adventure and toward another awaiting vessel.

"This has been a special day indeed," Porius said later on as Leal, Joao, and Porius sat around the table enjoying the visions that were presented to them on this day.

"Yes, I will be able to tell my grandchildren about this day, my lord," Leal said.

"But I have been in these waters many times, and I have never seen the beast except once before. How did we make it appear?" Captain Joao asked Porius.

"The thing about serpents, which was written by Egyptians over one thousand years ago is that they like things in threes," Porius explained.

"Ah, three circles of island," Joao said inquisitively.

"Si, Senior Joao, tres circles," Porius replied.

"The size of it and so rare to be sure," Leal said.

"So glad you came, Leal, not sure anyone would believe me without a witness," Porius said.

"They might think you an old fool indeed."

"But where, how do say, hidden, the beast?" Joao asked.

"That is a question indeed, a beast that size sure must have a home and other serpent, but this is the only recorded serpent to my knowledge," Porius stated. "Worrying that the best will have no mate, will this be the last?"

A silence fell as they all sat sipping brandy and eating a potato dish made especially for them by the ship's cook.

"Very tasty this potato morsel," said Porius, licking his fingers.

"Yes, Alejandro my chef, it is called tortilla."

"Nice, Joao, thank you and I would like to meet this Alejandro."

"Come." Joao led them to the galley.

"Alejandro, come and meet Porius and they like your tortilla," Joao explained in Portuguese.

Alejandro, pleased with the compliment, smiled and mimed out the ingredients to Porius.

"Oh, I see. Very well, potatoes, flour, egg, very good. Your humble servant," Porius said, applauding lightly toward the Alejandro who accepts the compliment graciously.

Later that night close to midnight, Porius and Leal sat up on deck watching the waves of black-and-purple blue swiftly pass. The few night crew men tended to the midnight chores, and they began to walk toward their cabins.

"I believe there is more than meets the eye when it comes to Mogador island," said Porius.

"Que," Joao said.

"I thought I have noticed a gleam in your eye, Porius," Leal said as he sipped some hot chocolate made by Alejandro so eager to please a beauty like Leal.

"Fortune awaits I feel, and the serpent guards what is hidden there," Porius said.

"Any clues to back up your suspicious mind, Porius?" Leal asked.

"Possibly, I will know more tomorrow. Captain Joao, can I beg your indulgence one day to wait here as I try a few finding spells?" Porius said in Portuguese.

"Si, Senior Porius. Si."

The next morning, the waves were still pretty tall with whitecaps. The captain ordered Michael to come about and circle the island three more times as Porius suggested. After the third circle again, the beast serpent came from the deep, rising and crashing back to the sea.

"A name," Porius said to Leal while they watched the beast rising and splashing for the second time.

"Aneon! Amemasu!" Porius shouted toward the rising beast. "Amemasu."

Nothing.

"Repun Kamui!" Porius shouted. "Repun Kamui!"

The serpent rose. This time, the giant head of the serpent seemed to turn toward Porius, hearing the call to Repun Kamui, Lord of the Sea.

"Repun Kamui!" Porius shouted again. The serpent splashed down to the sea, and this time, instead of raging up into the air and breach with a mighty force, the beast landed horizontal on the ocean waves, floating, floating, the large beast lying longer than the ship called the *Bend*.

"Ah, we have tamed the beast," Porius said as he stood along the side of the ship's head over the serpent who lay as if awaiting another call from Porius. "Repun Kamui," said Porius in a much calmer tone.

All hands crowded to the edge of the *Bend*, watching the spectacle unfold as the serpent rose with the waves and fell with the lowing water, now swishing along the surface of the ocean, circling the ship and creating a whirlpool of waves.

Time seemed to stop. The sky became blue, the ocean became still and flaccid except for the circling whirlpool the beast had created surrounding the ship. Some of the men fell back from the edge of the ship while others watched in amazement.

"Hang on to something!" Porius screamed to all onboard.

"Segure-se em algo!" Joao screamed in Portuguese to the men not understanding Porius's command.

All grabbed ropes, and as the ship began to turn and twist, the sails failed and one became lost as men tried to hold them still.

Finally, all was calm and quiet. The serpent disappeared, and Leal stood leaning over the edge searching for the beast then pointed. "There."

The beast came up to the ship, its large mouth wide open toward Porius. Behind his large teeth like fangs shining within lay a crown made of gold and jewels. The mouth open, Porius grabbed the crown quickly and took it aboard.

"Most obliged," Porius said to the serpent who seemingly smiled back toward Porius then circled the ship one last time and disappeared under the waves. Again, the sea began. It waved in its natural state, but the winds picked up the crown at Porius's feet and all eyes were upon it.

"Behold," Porius said to all and raised the crown for all to witness its magical glory and beauty.

"Ecce," Joao said in Latin so all may understand.

"Ecce," Leal said as they all stared at the crown shining in the sunlight.

Porius put the crown upon his head, and all cheered, yelled, bellowed, and screamed. "Hoorah, hoorah," the screams of joy could be heard a mile away, the happy crew and ship's captain beholden to a miracle like never before seen. The serpent who gave a crown to Porius will be told for many years to come, a tale of man and animal, sea and friendship in one partnership, in one victorious moment.

"It is the crown of Thebes," Porius said to all. "Long lost and forgotten."

"This is something even I have heard tell of Porius," Leal said.

"Yes, Athena will be arriving soon," Porius said, the men on crew all in attention.

"Men," Porius began while Joao repeated everything in Latin and Portuguese to the men after every line.

"You have all witnessed magic and were pleased of the opportunity. Many of you have new religions and belong to families where such things are not possible. I promise you all to share in riches from this journey and soon you will witness other magical goings-on," Porius paused while Joao repeated every word.

"I hope," Porius continued, "this is a special day and remember it well. You can still believe in your gods and go about your cultures in peace, but please remember this day. You all were a part of history and the end of times where spectacles as these are fewer and fewer."

Joao repeated, the men cheered, and Leal watched their faces and weeps for joy of the moment and for what he had just witnessed.

"In a few moments, you will witness another spectacle. The golden god Athena will arrive with her two mates." As Porius said this, Athena nodded, and her two beautiful golden maidens appeared before them. In shock of the arrival from midair, Athena stood before Porius.

"Porius, you have found the crown. Only you could have performed such a task," she said as Porius handed the crown to Athena.

Athena placed it on her head and floated above the ship. All hands cheered and cried and howled in joy as Athena flew up higher and higher.

"Thank you, Porius. Your journey has saved many and repaired another world," Athena said, rising and rising and her two maidens accented beside her, up higher and higher.

Athena paused while Gloria floated down to Leal, kissing him for a few moments.

"Come, Gloria," Athena shouted.

"Oh, Gloria, the unity rune," Porius said, pulling out a stone from within his robe and handing it to Gloria.

Finally, the three flying goddesses were up and out of sight.

"They do not stay for long," Joao said, still amazed at the beauty of the three visions of loveliness, which were recently and for only a few moments before him.

"No, not for long," Leal said.

All the men on board the ship cheered and sang, laughed, and cheered some more. Porius walked to sit at the bench on the deck as the men came to bow before him and went about their business, some whistling, some humming, and some just discussing the spectacle, which they were all a part of.

This day ended in sleep-filled bliss for all aboard ship. Soon they landed in Dover, and Porius reward everyone on board with riches presented to him from Athena. Thomas was amazed to be greeting Porius and Leal so soon after their journey began and they were home safe and sound.

Meanwhile, back in the sea below the bubbling waves and deep below the caverns and canyons, far under the sharks and whales, where the fish swam with lights glowing from their body, surrounded by black and only the occasional extended ray of sunlight that reflected through the deep, rested the serpent. Alone and lifeless, its energy spent, Porius and Athena felt its desperation within their hearts, and together they felt the thoughts of the serpent. Eyes of pink revealed a stairway to another inner function.

"Athena on a far-off world, stop to hear me," Porius thought as he sat at the table, Parthenia bringing him mead.

"Porius, are you not well?" Thomas asked, sitting beside him.

"It is the serpent. Athena and I have thought and our will is bent upon his anguish," Porius stated gravely.

Serpent of time and Serpent of glory,
Make this thy final story
Thou hast done good deeds throughout thy many a year
I feel you and shed my tears
To thy place of rest and your essence shall finally rest.

Athena stated as Porius heard her through the miles in his mind as they were linked.

The serpent lay upon the bottom of the sea as the final breath escaped its enormous body, and it dreamed of times past, of glories won. The serpent remembered its kin and species once thousands of years ago when others existed before the hunter and before the ship.

"Centuries of even Aetius the Roman general had seen such wonders," Porius mumbled.

"Mind of fury and mind of flame, help us to salvage all creatures who flee from the groups that offend them," Athena said, her golden hair draping around her sumptuous cream-colored physique, bubbling down upon groups of bubbles, air pockets and the occasional group of squids, jellyfishes, dolphins, and sea spiders.

The dust floated as the fish of lights—yes, the anglerfish—squids of giant size with bioluminescence including giant crabs, worms, and other large-size animals come to watch his passing. The fluorescence of the undersea creatures collectively lit the mighty serpent as he drew his final breath.

The multicolored glow surrounded the peaceful beast, and a tear fell from Athena at the same time as a tear dropped from Porius; the last sea serpent was no more. Six-gill sharks, giant vampire squids, and other deep-sea creatures utilized his remains, and his spirit spread throughout the undersea kingdom.

"Thomas, I have been traveling, and I have seen the future of earth. The future will need our kind. I foresee the future as not the beauty of the natural world around us."

"What is it that you foresee, Porius?" Thomas asked.

"The many races of people growing and growing with no control and possibly overpopulating the continents with no restraint and the need for more, which I see in people's eyes and deeds. I see this small planet, centuries from now, overpopulated with angry humans, polluted and filled with war," Porius confessed, angry by their different religions, races, and greed.

"What can we do?" Thomas asked.

"Do?" Porius is silent.

"Yes, Porius, surely with your wisdom to spread."

"But who shall listen, Thomas?" Porius said sadly. "The mind of men is captivated by other books now and tales of men performing miracles, but the way shall lead them wrong. It is not miracles that people need. It is common sense. It is working with nature and not against it. It is not competition and greed for being the best. It is being equal to each other and being kind and living side by side with nature."

"What brings this on, Porius?" Thomas asked.

"Oh, just an old man with visions of the future. I see the old ways fading away and the filling of minds with sin, deceit, and separation of civilizations, and mind you, I am talking about civilizations upon earth."

"Why must they all be so different?" Thomas stated.

"Precisely, my dear boy, precisely. We have the Christians and all of their many different interpretations. We have the Islam, Judaism, how can they possibly live together? Well, they cannot."

"You are correct, Porius, indeed."

"We just have to stay, and you, my friend, will need to hold this place for a very long time. Are you willing?"

"I-I am not sure I am worthy," Thomas said, not knowing what was being asked.

"Thomas, the purity stone is before you and will become a part of you. This will make you unique among men. Are you willing?"

"Well, my lord, I assume I . . .," Thomas strayed his thoughts and tried to speak.

"You will be labored with staying here for thousands of years to come, Thomas. Yes, your body will die in fifty or sixty years, but after that, are you willing?"

"But I want to see Elysium."

"You will, Thomas, you will be able to depart from earth to Elysium," Porius continued. "Over the next few months, I will show you and teach you how to travel the light from Elysium to earth. I will teach you how to keep the cottage safe."

"My lord, why will you not stay?" Thomas asked.

"I am not able to stay. You see, a wizard has used his magic, and his time is short. The only way for me to return is by thought," Porius said as he stood and waved his wand.

"A pensive." Porius created a clear floating pensive before them, and within showed the future. Cities of light, masses of transportation vehicles all polluting, noise ridden and people shouting, large piles of garbage along sides of the roadways. "You see, the future."

"Oh my." Thomas stared eyes wide into the pensive.

"Enough." Porius waved his wand, and the large floating glass pensive disappeared. He flicked toward the mantle, and the small floating band appeared, playing a somber tune.

"Well, Thomas, now do you understand?"

"I will do it," Thomas said, sitting back down and taking a large gulp of mead.

"Something a bit livelier," Porius said to the floating band. They stopped the somber song and played something more light and bouncy almost Elizabethan in quality.

The door from outside swung open, and Leal stood naked from head to toe, dripping in water. He entered and dressed in a new robe provided by Porius. Parthenia, sticking her head from the kitchen and looking Leal up and down, licked her lips then went back inside the kitchen to prepare the meal long awaited by Porius and Leal.

Leal's gown was tight fitting, and every muscle and crevasse was visually apparent. They all sat and begging to eat when Walters and Simon both burst in.

"Porius, welcome back," Walters said.

"Ah, Walters, do we have a story to tell you!" Porius said as he led them to the table.

Franklin tapped on the outside wing, flapping and screeching in a facetious manner and making such a ruckus that before Walters, Leal, and Simon got settled, Porius went out the front door. "What is it, Franklin?" he said while exiting the cottage in the evening air. Voices were heard in the background just beyond the woods.

A crowd of villagers with pitchforks, clubs, and other possible weapons walked in a circle around the cottage and back and forth. Walters and the men went with Porius while Thomas stayed behind with Franklin and the safety of the cottage. Porius and the men stepped out into the road in front of the villagers.

"My friends, what is it, how can we help?"

"Lord Porius, our village is being ravaged by the Christians," one villager and obviously the leader said.

"Well, come, Walters, Leal, and Simon," Porius said, holding his staff, and the men followed.

The raging crowd exploded into a cheer and then all were talking at once. "They have taken my farm," one farmer shouted.

"My bakery is taken over by men in black cloaks, my home, my children have been taken," another woman shouted wearing an apron and green silk dress.

"My friends, we will all go together and confront these villains," Simon shouted as he unbuckled his sword. Leal was quick in line behind him dressed in his usual leather of black.

"To the village," Porius led on with the crowd, and as they approached Hastings, many birds and animals of all kinds ran toward the forest. Other villagers were heard screaming in the distance while defending their homes. The light of several small fires, and smoke could be seen just beyond the tree line.

At the edge of Hastings by the canyon and at the base of the hill, Porius, Walters, Sam, and Leal led the villagers into the first burning home.

"Flame of evil thought and mind, put this fire far behind and cast on to those who lit this ember soon to them may sit," Porius said the incantation, and the house fire went down to embers. A few embers flew in the air, and Porius pointed at the floating embers.

"Walters, follow those embers and they will lead us to the culprits," Porius shouted, pointing ahead. The villagers heard and followed the floating embers until sure enough, one ember flew low and struck a priest on his backside before he fell to the ground and went cold. The other embers did the same, leading Leal, Simon, and Walters to begin the sword fight of each. One priest bent over and tried to remove clothes from a young man, his mother trying to fight him of her son's attacker. The ember hit the priest's backside, and as he turned to pat out the fire now starting on his black cloak, Simon drew his sword and stated, "No, you don't, you villain." Simon swept his sword down upon the priest clean through his arm just below the elbow and it fell to the ground.

Porius went to each burning building with the same spell, and the houses distinguished the flying embers, which went toward their pyromaniacs. The villagers followed as the battle raged from one home to the next, the stores, and for a quarter of an hour until finally the villagers begged, taking back their homes.

"Round them up," Porius shouted as Walters, Simon, and Leal held four priests in the center of the village at sword point.

"Where is the man responsible for this rage against these good folks?" Porius shouted at them

"Ve hav been commissioned to make way for ze pope," the broken English poured from the priest as he pointed to the shore.

"Kill them!" Walter shouted, and Leal raised his sword, his face badly cut and bleeding.

"No, spare these last few and bury the dead," Porius said while stopping Leal's fatal blow.

"Simon, see to Leal's face wound. You men with your new religion must leave this village, never to return," Porius shouted at them, and they began to leave.

"Wait," Simon said as he went to each of the four men and removed their crosses from their necks. Then Simon saw to Leal.

The villagers hugged their wives, sons, and daughters and consoled in Porius, thanking him for saving them from the ransacking that was sent upon them.

Leal lay down, and Simon took large ants from a bag and placed them face-first on the wound. The ants bit and injected an antibiotic as well as numb the area of the wound. Simon removed the ants' bodies and discarded them, leaving a long row of ant heads on the wound.

"Well done, Simon," Leal said. "Thank you."

The priests left toward the sea, their cloaks still smoldering from the coals that had recently singed them. Porius went to the first villager that seemed to be the leader and removes a stone from his pocket.

"You see my friend, I slipped the stone of courage into your pocket." Porius smiled.

"My Lord Porius, Hastings is restored, and we all are grateful to ye. My pub has been changed to be entitled the Unicorn in your honor. Please come as my guest, and your men are welcome. Drinks on the house," the publican stated while they all go to the Unicorn and drank while two women washed Leal's face, making sure not to disrupt the line of ants holding his injury together.

Porius, Walters, and Simon sat around a table chatting.

"These attacks are getting more and more frequent, my lord," said Simon.

"Indeed, and if the pope is close by and arranging a visit, we must be prepared," Porius said.

"Where do you think he will land, Dover?" Walter asked.

"I do not believe he will come to Dover. I more think he will sit offshore here at Hastings, but I will meet him and send him back to France or Spain or Italy or wherever he ascends from and beg him to leave this island alone. Not that it will do any good."

"They are coming," Simon said.

"They are here, Simon," Porius insisted.

"London, the Cotswold, York, Wales, we cannot stop them, but we can slow them and stop them from taking all," Porius said.

"Minds and ways will change from fear or persuasion. Either way, we are in the middle of it," Walters said.

"I have seen men's hearts and minds change from the peace-loving mortals we admire to the poppas and arrogant, biased and ridiculous ways of religion, yes we have a battle on our hands and it will last for centuries," Porius said.

"Centuries?" Simon said.

"Yes, I am afraid so," Porius answered. "But look at Leal, fatigued and injured and still the happiest of them all, another ale," He shouted while pointing at Leal.

Two women tickling his muscular form along the back wall, Leal grabbing them and kissing and joking while they blush. One woman is blond and quite beautiful puts her hands around his biceps blushing'

"Oh, Leal, you are so strong," she said.

"And beautiful," the red-haired girl said after cleaning his face and walking back to the bar.

The people in the pub raise their goblets to Porius and he saviors

"Hail our heroes!" shouted the man behind the bar.

"Hail!" the crowd yelled out.

One woman brought bread and hives to Porius. "Thank you, very kind of you," Porius said, placing the bread before him as he ripped a piece and handed it to Walters, and soon Simon followed.

Another well-dressed man came to Porius and handed him a ruby from his pocket. "For the cause," he said, handing it to Porius.

"Oh, indeed nice and will come in handy, I assure you." Porius handed the ruby to Simon. "Simon, this will buy some loyalties of those being persecuted currently."

"I shall guard it," Simon replied, placing the ruby in his satchel.

The front door opened, and a moth hovered around Porius. Porius heard the moth and shouted to the others. "Come, children are in trouble." They ran up the hill at Hastings flats, and six children were there crying and wearing dark brown robes and cloaks standing around in the center of the road. Walters went up to the three boys and asked, "What is it, my children?"

There were three boys with dirty faces, and there were three girls, one blond haired with blue dress and two with red hair and brown dingy cloaks smelling of smoke.

One of the girls pointed up the hill toward the smoldering embers of a house. "Our parents are dead," she said with eyes full of tears, the others crying and reaching out to Leal, Simon, and Walters.

"Come to the Unicorn, and you three boys must be the baker's sons. Come, we shall restore you to your families," Porius stated, and they walked the children back down to the Unicorn public house.

"Not so fast," a voice called from the road beyond by the edge of the sea where a boat stood tied.

"The pope! Take the children back quickly," Porius shouted to Walters, Leal, and Simon, and they took the children back to safety. Meanwhile, the pope wearing black and bejeweled with large rings, was surrounded by three large men. These men looked frightfully large and equipped to fight.

"You must be Porius, the wizard, I presume." The pope waved his hand toward Porius. "Take him and bring him to the ship," the pope said as the three men grabbed Porius and bound him with rope while he struggled.

The baker and Leal came running back to the scene and about to pounce the three men as the pope shouted, "Touch them and he dies!"

"Stand back, Leal," Porius shouted, the pope taking his staff and pointing toward the ship. "Take him, take him."

Leal and the baker stood watching as the pope held a knife to Porius's ribs and they lead him to the ship the next road over.

"Unbound the ropes, we set sail," the pope was heard shouting.

Leal jumped onboard and fought a few men but was captured and bound.

"You men will not be much good trying to sail in those ridiculous robes," Leal shouted. Porius heard him and turned toward Leal.

"Leal, what are you doing here?" Porius shouted.

"He wants to be with you, Lord Porius," the pope shouted as he waved his arms to his men.

"Take them both to the galley below." The pope followed them while they were tied and positioned in the galley.

"Porius, believe it or not, we need your help."

"Our help?" Porius said, still struggling to break free.

"Yes, do not worry. Once you help us, we will set you free and your pretty boy as well," the pope said.

"What is this help you desire?"

"Well, the Isle of Wight has two of my priests held prisoner in some sort of magic. You release them, and I let you all go."

"How do I know to trust thee," Porius said.

"You don't, but I promise and ye shall be set free once the priests are set free."

"What binds them, Porius?" Leal asked, now calming himself in resolute that the three large men who had bound him were far too muscular to allow any escape.

"You knew not to invade the Isle of Wight, Senior Pope," Porius said.

"What spell you have on the island must be released for you to be set free," the pope sneered.

The boat rocked back and forth and was soon out to sea.

"Unbind me and I promise no attempt to escape," Leal said to the closest brute who still bound him.

"Let him go free," said the pope, waving his hand.

"And I am frightfully tired, let me go and we will assist you in your cause," Porius said, smiling at the pope.

They were both set free and walked up to the top of the ship, seeing Hastings disappear in the mist behind them as they went out to the channel and was soon on course toward the Isle of Wight, the last refuge from any religion. The isle stood as a testament to all that of the old ways, and only nature resided there in peace.

Porius and Leal found a place in a corner of the first floor and rested until morning. Sleeping and snoring, the morning came quickly. Porius was tired from his past dealings the previous night between saving children and wondering what Thomas must be thinking. Porius woke before the others and whistled in the air as a pigeon appeared in the distance and landed on his shoulder, Leal waking and with one eye open watching Porius say something to the pigeon and it flew back toward Hastings.

"What was that pigeon saying to you, Lord Porius?" Leal asked, now waking and standing beside Porius, watching the crew awake or asleep at their posts.

"Pigeons are a good way to communicate with Franklin. I want to let Walters, Thomas, and Leal know we are safe."

Soon the pigeon relayed the message to Franklin; and back at the cottage, Walters, Simon, and Thomas were filled with relief as they woke to Parthenia and Grendle's breakfast, the large pile of fish outside in the garden, no doubt left behind the previous night by the water goblins.

Leal stood stretching and exercising his arms with large pools of rope as a young monk blushingly handed him a jug of water and some morning fruit.

"You will never be able to clime the ropes safely wearing those robes," Leal said to the young blond monk, who really must only be in his early twenties and not speaking a word of English. He shrugged to Leal.

"You don't understand me, but here let me show you," Leal said, waving the boy toward him as he walked to the ropes and climbed a few steps up and then down.

"Never in those robes," Leal repeated, pointing to the young monk's robes.

"Que?" the monk said.

Leal grabbed the monk, strips him of his robe, leaving him standing there naked except for his sandals and a small band, which is basically a string around his waist with a bag covering his genitals, buttocks exposed. Other crew members saw what Leal was trying to explain to the young monk. And the young monk climbed the robes shivering.

"There, you see, isn't that much easier?" Leal said, laughing.

The shivering monk agreed by nodding his head then quickly placing his robe back over his head. Leal grabbed the boy again, tied a short piece of rope around his tiny waist and cut off the robe's extra length.

"Here try this, I bet that will be much easier for you," Leal said to him, and the boy monk nodded in agreement.

"I think they all understand you now," Porius said, shaking his head.

The other monks on the crew tied their waists and cut off the lower part of the robe and cheered, obviously making this arrangement of their attire easier to maneuver among the ropes.

"Look, land ho!" one of the men said who was steering the ship.

"Salazar Winters," Leal said as he noticed that the captain was an old friend.

"Leal?" Captain Winters said in shock.

"What are you doing on this tub?" Leal said after he ran up to greet his old chum.

"Well, Leal my good fellow, my last position did not go well with the mischief back in Spain," Captain Winters said.

"A living is a living, one must find work where one is mostly accommodated," Porius said, coming up to greet Winters.

"Lord Porius, this is an honor. Why are thee both on this journey?"

"Well, not by choice truly. We were commissioned late last night. And we are here to free a couple of men from the isle."

"I see, well, I sure know nothin' 'bout the mission. I just deliver us safely, and then it's back to France with the pope."

"I hope by way of England," Leal said.

"Not to my knowledge," Winters said while heading into some fog.

"Hmm," Porius said, turning to greet the pope who had joined the group.

"We shall be there shortly, if I am not mistaken," the pope said.

"Yes, we saw the isle a few moments ago, but this fog, there, land ho," Captain Winters said as they saw a clear landing before them.

"Do not land, Winters. Take it to the north shore," the pope commanded.

"Sure, your will is my duty."

"Through another mist, I see," said Leal as they banked into another fog.

Just as they reached the north shore, the fog cleared, and they were anchored. Porius, Leal, and the pope entered a small row boat. Leal rowed them to shore. Standing on the shore were two men in black robes, both bending and both apparently frozen to the spot.

"You see, you see, Porius, black magic," the pope said.

"Not black magic at all, Your Grace," Porius said as he called for his staff. Leal reached down and picked up Porius's staff and handed it to him while the boat slid up on the sand. The pope began to exit the rowboat.

"I would not be so quick to step on land here, Your Grace," Porius said, stopping the pope.

"What do you mean?"

"Well, if you will allow me, I won't get frozen like your men. You see, this island is protected by nature and no religious man is allowed to move upon it."

"Something the elves placed on the island," said Leal.

"Correct, Leal, how did you know?" Porius asked.

"We were told this story at my father's table when the elves used to visit us in Hampton," Leal replied.

"Elves, magic, just release my men, Lord Porius," the pope stated in agitation.

"Release them," Porius said, now standing firm on the shore, his robe just getting slightly wet along the bottom. The row of white-laced flowers turned a slight brown color.

"Free them!" the pope shouted.

"They will become free shortly. Hang on, Your Grace," Porius said.

The men wiggled free and then stood, eyes wide, and quickly turned toward the boat and jumped in, Porius following behind.

"Well, I said I would set you free." The pope pulled out a dagger from under his cloak and pointed it at Leal.

"Exit this boat as well, Leal, and join your master," the pope said, pointing the sharp dagger toward Leal.

"All right, I will obey," Leal said and calmly joined Porius on the shore.

The pope and his men rowed back toward the ship, leaving Porius and Leal far behind.

"It appears we may be stranded here, my lord," Leal said, shaking his head as they both watched the rowboat get increasingly smaller in size until finally reaching the ship. The pope waved from the boat and shouted something back to Porius.

"Have a nice time, Porius. I will not be seeing you again," the pope shouted, and the ship turned toward France and disappeared in the foggy film, which lined the outer rim of the ocean.

Back on shore, Porius and Leal stood there wondering what to do. But Porius had a plan, and what a plan it was too.

"First, we must get some grass from over there." They walked to grab a few handfuls of grass.

"Then," Porius continued, "we will need a little assistance from a creature I know who haunts this island."

"Not the griffin?" Leal asked in excitement.

"Yes, Leal, I am impressed that you know your historical facts about the isle," Porius said as he pointed his staff toward the air.

Come one with wing and claw
Come one who reaches tall,
Come one who impress all
The mighty griffin

Porius repeated the chant a few times, and a roar was heard in the distance. The huge beast appeared before them, circling with his mighty wings and birdlike face, black feathers meshed with black hair, claws of yellow, and eyes large and brown.

"Greetings to you, oh, griffin of time."

"And to you, Lord Porius." The griffin was speaking in a low voice, which sounded like as if it were underwater.

Leal was amazed. "I did not know a griffin can talk."

"Yes, talk and sing," Porius said.

"I shall carry thee, Lord Porius and friend," the griffin said while they boarded his backside between his mighty wings.

The griffin ran and jumped, wings expanded. Then mightily, its flapping began, and Leal was smiling behind Porius as they flew above the fog toward home. Below, the pope's ship was spotted.

"Shall we?" the mighty griffin asked.

"Oh, let's do," Porius said, smirking.

The griffin swooped down upon the ship and, with his mighty claw, ripped off the main sail. It fell to the top deck, luckily injuring none of the poor monks following the pope's command.

"What is going on up here?" the pope was heard, and then as the pope dressed in black looked up, he saw Leal and Porius flying above and out into the fog.

"Dear Christ protect us," he said, shaking an angry fist at the exiting creature.

Porius and Leal arrived back at the garden. Walters, Thomas, and Simon greeted the griffin, fed it, and allowed it to rest among the deer, rabbits, fowl, and of course, Franklin who really didn't like the sight of the huge beast so he kept his distance by remaining on the rooftop safe and sound.

CHAPTER 9

"Welcome home, Porius," Thomas said. "Welcome home."

The prodigy was finally home for the summer holidays. At the cottage and then at the garden and forest, they'd learned a genial contempt for their fellowman. Yet they continued to sing songs, to play the floating band, to mix with deer, caterpillar, flower, and bird. Incorporated into mud and dust from the earth we rise, and all things must until once again they die or go farther thus.

"Streams of bios lie underground," Porius said as they ate breakfast out of doors the next morning, Leal mostly naked in the morning sun as he swayed back from the river, Thomas eating heartily while looking up and seeing Athena descend from the sky, her two beauties in gold and lace flowing down beside her. Byron was playing his lute in the sun while Simon petted and pranced around the garden with deer, squirrel, faun, bluebird, raven, and fox. Franklin circled the garden over head as the occasional cloud weeps in the far-off distant forest.

Thomas had arranged a celebration with bottles of local ale provided by the farmers who had new children to raise under the protection of the old ways as they will long remember what horrors the church had brought to their lives and what occurrences vividly were set in the children's memories of parents being raped, tortured, killed, or turned into slaves.

"Farming, pottery, sculpture, masonry, and many other wonders will now fill the children's futures," Porius said to Athena while telling the tale of the past few days, and she listened in almost disbelief.

"My dear Porius, it's happening all over Spain, Roma, Venice, Paris, Athens," Athena said.

"We must keep up the good fight," Gloria said as she interrupted the interlocutor and nestled with Alexandria on the grass beside the long table, which was dressed with food of all types.

"An excellent spread, Thomas," Athena said.

"Thank you, Your Highness, and you are looking as ravishing as ever," Thomas said, blushing.

"We have traveled much, and if it were not for Alexandria and Gloria protecting me daily, not sure what fate may have befallen us."

"Leal is looking as beautiful as ever," Gloria said as she put up her hand toward the dripping wet Leal who'd dried himself and slipped on his leather sort trousers, waistcoat of leather, and boots of black. Walters was sitting with Gloria and Simon was coming to rest next to Byron's lute.

Clouds rolled overhead, wind slightly awakened, leaves falling all around, but the heat was enough to warm the chilliest of thoughts. As the deer descended once more to the edge of the forest, Porius stood in robes of white and lace of pearl.

"To being together and safe from harm."

"Cheers," they all said, raising goblets and enjoying the coming afternoon.

Winter 1430 was extremely cold, and while the wind blew ice from the north, Porius, Walters, Simon, Leal, and Thomas gathered at the Unicorn in Hastings to folly a farewell to Thomas's never to bride. Thomas said his farewell to Elena. The marriage was never to be as Thomas went from Love to many a cool-off period, which mainly consisted of longing for others besides Elena. Elena resigned herself to the fact long ago and decided to marry the baker since his wife had left him several years ago and was never seen from again. The story went that the baker's wife met up with a knight who took her to Londinium and never returned. As Elena and the baker exited the Unicorn, Thomas turned to Simon and Leal. "Ah, free once more," Thomas said as he raised his goblet to toast the others.

Henry the Sixth was reigning and was visiting Dover this day, and though Henry had very few dealings with Porius and his kind on this occasion, Henry needed some help with the king of France. Knowing that Porius was difficult to track down, he sent out nightly scouts to the Unicorn to see if Porius was present and in good cheer. Once the scout—a small man, scared, blond, and of feeble walk—rode back to let the king know Porius was present, the door of the pub flew open; and as the icy wind sprinkled its winter delight on the happy dwellers within, a voice called out.

"Ye must be Porius," King Henry stated.

"Your Highness, a pleasure," Porius said as all stood and bowed to his grace. "Come and join our table, my lord," Porius said as the man behind the bar ran a goblet to his Royal Highness. Henry sipped a large gulp.

"Excellent Kentish brew, it appears," Henry said, grinning from ear to ear and satisfied with a state of pure joy and fulfillment on his face. His bejeweled gown and garb was sparkling in the fire's reflections.

"Simon, Leal, and Walters, I would venture to guess." All the men bowed and drank after his excellent recital of all their names.

"Thomas as well."

"I see you are well informed of my team of fellows," Porius said glowingly.

"Indeed, I have always been impressed by the stories of your escapades. You see, a good king knows how his friends are; and, Porius, I count thee amongst them."

Porius bowed and then they all sat, following Henry's example.

"There are divines amongst the nobility and families of France of late as you may have been instructed," Henry stated.

"Yes, I am aware."

"Did you allow knowing that I shall be named king of France soon, and we want to make sure it's an easy transition?"

"Well, no, but I thought it may come to this," Porius replied as the others watched and listed.

"The economic problems of France are severe, and I am not the most, well robust of Kings to rule. I know Charles before me was tougher and ruled by the occasional fear tactic where I as well."

"I believe I understand, Your Majesty," Porius said. "Your timid nature toward war does you a great credit. Also, your kindness to the old ways, pagans, and people—well, people like us—is most appreciated and we will stand behind you all the way."

"There are many factions and quarrelsome nobles which are numerous and far too many for me to keep straight in my head."

"This would concern my thoughts as well."

"With Humphry the Defender of the Realm and sitting upon the Council, I want to get some thoughts from you, Porius. John Somerset has taught me well, but seems to suffocate me and has not made me tough."

"I see well."

"I can teach you to fight," Leal said.

"I may teach you to trick," Thomas interrupted.

"Thank you, but I don't want to fight," Henry replied.

"So be it, Your Highness. I have just the thing for you."

"Porius, I knew you would happen upon my meaning."

"We will all meet you at Dover Castle tomorrow night. There are things I must prepare."

"Until tomorrow." Henry stood, and they all stood and bowed as he exited.

There were cheers all around the pub as the king rode back to Dover.

"And in my pub, live is grand," the man behind the bar said while holding the king's goblet and after rubbing it clean places it up on the highest shelf.

"Come, men, to home and a good night's rest."

They all followed Porius and headed back to the cottage. The rows of thick woods and hedge seemed to open and close as they passed until they come to the garden while deer, owl, and mouse run by the five of them. Then they go inside, and Walters quickly got the fire going and poured them all some ale. Porius opened the Malefactor and read some passages then went out again to the back of the frozen herb garden.

"I will need this. Oh and this," Porius said as he picked several species of dried plants from the earth and carried them back inside.

"I am so cold my knees are knocking," said Thomas. They all laughed and lounged until each one fell into the land of dreams, protecting the realm and feeling most secure that King Henry knew them all by name.

The next night at Dover were Henry's half brothers Edmund and Jasper, both wearing jackets of deep black and collars bejeweled with many sapphires, emeralds, and rubies and laced with gold around their tightly fitted wrists. Walters, Simon, and Leal stood near the entranceway to the largest meeting room within the castle.

Edmund glanced up and down at Porius, and Jasper sat watching Thomas. Porius entered and spoke with King Henry while he sat on a golden and leather cushioned chair, which rather resembled a simple throne.

"Very impressive," Porius stated to Henry in admiration of the furniture, drapes, tapestries, and long hanging bars of iron.

"Porius, my good man, what has thy brought to cure me?"

"Your Highness, first off, let me see," Porius said, pointing to Thomas.

"Yes, Lord Porius," Thomas said and handed a bundle of cloth-wrapped articles to Porius.

"Come and stand before me, Your Highness," he said, moving into position as Henry obeyed.

"Should I be wary?" Henry asked in hesitation.

"Oh, good gracious, no, just stand here," Porius said while grabbing the king's shoulders and positioning him directly in front of him.

"Thomas, the first bundle." He reached out to Porius, unwrapped a small porcelain dog black in color, and revealed a ferocious stance in its frozen position.

"Quite a bite on this doglike stature you hold before me," Henry said, staring eyes wide at the porcelain dog of black.

"Behold," Porius said. "Stand firm, Your Highness, and fear not what cometh." Porius placed the statue in front of the king on the stone floor before him. The room was silent, and all eyes were watching as Porius raised his foot high and brought with all power in him down upon the small porcelain dog, crushing it to tiny bits. The king faltered, but Porius motioned for him to remain still.

"Lilacs," Henry said, wiggling his nose. "It smells of lilacs."

"Yes, the color of the French, no, be still," Porius said as he swept the pile of rubble and broken porcelain into a pile.

"Guard thee and show thee power within thee." Porius waved to Simon.

"Come, you may clean all this up now."

Thomas handed Porius the second bundle, and Porius unwrapped it, which revealed another porcelain figure of a stout, muscular man and somewhat revealing Leal in face.

"Why, it's . . .," Henry began to say while pointing to Leal.

"Well, I needed a model, and I wondered when this would come in handy," Porius said, smiling, performing the same routine of breaking the figure under his foot, saying another citation.

"Strong is thee who is presented and fearless heart now is thy royal highness." Porius again had Simon and Leal pick up the pieces and bag them.

A couple of women entered the chamber, wearing robes of white and gold and sipping some wine.

"Come on," the woman said as she motioned to servants to set table, and a procession of men, women, children came bringing multiple types of meat pies, ale, vegetable plates. Musicians came in and began playing some beautiful sweet music.

"It is done," Porius said and bowed to Henry.

"Very well, now join us for a feast." Henry summoned all to eat. Never had Thomas seen such a wonderful spread of food, beautiful women, and men dressed in the finest apparel join.

"A pleasure to meet you," Leal said to one strong strapping lad wearing the sign of the dragon and sipping wine. Leal knew this knight and had fought beside him recently in France.

"I remember thee," Leal said.

"Girard, and I remember thee, Leal." Girard bowed. "The pleasure is all mine."

Thomas rolled his eyes and moved to let Leal and Girard swoon each other in private. Porius chatted with the king and wife, mother and daughters. Walters was eating meat pie and discussing war maneuvers with Jasper while Thomas spoke with Edmund.

"Have ye been shown many ways by Lord Porius?" Edmund asked.

"Yes, it is quite interesting to say the least."

"You are most fortunate to live with such a well-known and powerful mystic," Edmund, sipping his wine, replied.

"You have heard of his heroics?"

"Many a memorable evening has been spent listening of the exploits of the great Lord Porius, saving villagers, fighting the church, protecting farms."

"I am pleased the royals are so well informed."

"We royals, as you say, do know that the old ways have protected and made happy many who request assistance," Edmund replied.

"I am so glad of it," Thomas replied.

"The sea journey is surely to become legend, and the pope makes me laugh."

"Well, no harm came to him."

"That is just it, you see, even though we royals watch and see most what goes on amongst the peoples of our land. Even though the church has much power and wars are waged in its name, we do not always side with the church. In fact, it's mostly politics. Most kings would much rather have the older ways back in the fold."

"It is sad what has happened. I suppose the only real good is that the countries afar and England may be speckled with beautifully built buildings to decorate the landscape."

"Yes, many are quite nice," Edmund replied.

"Canterbury for one," Thomas said.

"Oh, and Windsor."

"Beautiful indeed."

"What is Porius's estate like, grand?" Edmund asked.

"Ha, oh no, not at all. In fact, it's only a quaint cottage in the forest," Thomas said, laughing.

"A cottage," Edmund said while stuffing meat pie in his mouth and giggling with Thomas. "A cottage."

Porius heard the word *cottage* revealed and quickly moved to Thomas and peered at his eyes, hoping for the location of the cottage not to be revealed by Thomas.

"Edmond, a pleasure to see you, my lord," Porius quickly said while interrupting the conversation.

"Thomas was just telling me of your quaint cottage in the woods."

"Yes, it is very small and not much to look at, but we like it and its home. My garden flourishes and, well, it's home."

"Essex?"

"The location would not concern you, Lord Edmund," Porius said.

"In the woods?" Edmond asked.

"Well, there are many woods in Essex. Yes, yes, it's out that way."

"This wine is lovely," Thomas quickly said, changing the subject and making sure that Porius got his drift.

"Yes, quite lovely, and what a pleasant bouquet," Porius said.

"I am glad you enjoy it, we just brought this batch from Bordeaux Lord Porius," Edmund stated while eyeing Leal and Girard who had come to join the conversation.

"You must be Lord Porius, and I must say I have always wanted to meet you," Girard said, bowing to Porius.

"Girard, yes, Leal often speaks of you. France, wasn't it? Were you two—" Porius was quickly interrupted by Leal.

"Yes, Lord Porius and Edmund, Your Grace, we fought alongside each other twice and are glad for this reunion. Many were lost in the last battle," Leal said.

"Many indeed. We were drenched in blood from head to toe, never a scratch on Leal though. His craft of fighting is met by no one, and I am always pleased to have him close."

"Porius, a toast," King Henry said, raising his goblet.

"Friends and country, this is what makes us strong, and may health be ours for years to come." Henry drank and all followed.

Icy wind blew outside the castle as night became black, moonless, windy, wet. Two large yeomen announced the arrival of other guests, which included the French ambassador and his wife, a few business associates from the aria, and others to join the celebration. Meeting Porius and his men was cause for celebration due to the celebrity status and acclaimed reputation as one of England's most prized possessions.

"Good Porius, here is my ambassador of France," Henry introduced Porius to the Duke of Burgundy and liaison to Charles the Seventh of France."

"Charles is not a bad man, make no mistake," the duke replied, bowing to Porius.

"Yes, I am sure the pressure is a heavy weight on King Charles's shoulders as it is our good Henry here," Porius said.

"It is not all fun and games being on the throne. Let no man tell you otherwise. Surely, goodness and mercy are both in our hearts. It's the politics, which gets under my skin. As a tick annoys the common dog, so does politics annoy the realm. You can never win, and there is always some higher goal. My father Henry was good at getting what was expected and had the strength and stamina for all this quibbling and squabbling. Can't see it myself. France has enough of what it needs. England has enough, and the trade can be repaired."

"But, Your Majesty, the church," said the Duke of Burgundy, interrupting Henry.

"Oh yes, cannot forget the church. Always wanting and prying, showing their strength. Will it never end, and will they always want more, never satisfied is this pope?" Henry stated.

"I am afraid this is the course which has been chosen. Money is of high importance," Porius commented.

"The hearts and minds are following as the church gets more and more powerful," Henry continued. "Now all we can do is act in support."

"It is a good idea to be as political as possible these days," Burgundy said.

"What of your people who do not belong to the church?" Henry said to Porius.

"Yes, there are a great many families who still want the pre-Christian days to return, and they have been warned to not rise against but at least may pleasantries and appear to join in, but hopefully their bloodlines will remain true, and we hope they will go unnoticed when it comes to undue pressure from the pope or the many local priests, which numbers are growing daily," Porius replied.

"Athena and her two companions," the yeomen announced as silence fell over the room. In walked Athena dressed in lavish white embroidered gown and her two maidens of rare beauty as all eyes watched the graceful walk of Athena.

"Henry, a pleasure to meet you once again." Athena bowed.

"Athena, what a rarest of all treats," Henry said, blushing and kissing her extended hand. "And your beautiful maidens, welcome."

Athena, Alexandria, and Gloria walked, appearing to be human and in full outfits, not the usual seductive gold mesh, which revealed a bit more flesh than appropriate for this event.

"My Lord Porius," Anthea whispered into Porius's ear. "I came with warning that Edmund plans to follow thee to the cottage and attempt to gain knowledge of its location."

"Thank you for this information, Athena," Porius replied.

Walters grabbed Athena from behind in surprise, and they embraced. Walters then showed Athena around the castle, Gloria in tow with Simon and Thomas mingling with Edmund and the others. The party ensued for several more hours, and great tales were told, bellies filled. Dancing maidens performed; high-kicking men performed several dances of extreme athletic ability. Even a tamed leopard was brought in to be admired and petted by those brave enough to approach.

"Nice leopard," Porius said while stroking the animal's head behind its ears.

"I am so pleased that you are in full admiration as we have raised him since he came as a cub with his wounded mother. Once the mother died, the cub took my wife to be his own, and we have enjoyed him ever since. Ortha is its name," Henry said.

"Ortha, a pleasure to meet you," Porius said as the large leopard was walked back out of doors with the game keeper.

Leal and Girard mingled with Athena, Gloria, and Alexandria.

"Athena is infallible, we know," said Girard. "So there must be a reason for your visit to Dover."

"Yes indeed, Sir Girard. We come bringing a warning to Porius."

"Warning?" Leal said.

"Yes, please keep an eye on Porius when he turns for home and watch out for those who follow," Athena said to Girard and Leal, gazing at them with a possible touch of desire.

"Girard looks most suitable for you, Leal," Gloria said while Thomas pulled her back to the crowd to mingle and be by his side.

"This is Gloria, protector to Athena," Thomas said to a few others with which his recent acquaintance has been made. The party ended with the dawn of morning, and all retired to separate chambers around the walls of the castle. Most slept until noon; and when Porius, Walters, Leal, Simon, and Thomas awakened, they noticed that Athena, Gloria, and Alexandria had long departed. King Henry still slept, and they mounted the freshly fed horses outside the castle and leave for home. No followers seemed to be present, but just in case, they took a special path through the woods, which though mazelike, eventually happened upon the garden. Franklin circled with gleeful song, Parthenia and Grendle busy in the kitchen baking breads and pies and feeding the men as they sat around the usual table. Leal and Simon were sitting close to the fire, and all was home safe and sound.

A heap of clothes soon appeared in a pile, and Parthenia cleaned, scrubbed, and dried each bit of clothing as the men sat in the heated sauna at the back of the cottage.

"Edmund seems a bit curious," Porius stated while Leal washed in the warm flowing water that came from outside over the hot coals and then ran down under the cottage back to the river. An ingenious invention Porius developed by using the Roman bath plans from Bath and integrating some practical methods of coal-warming effects.

"As with Athena showing up in all her glory, curious indeed," said Thomas.

"Even if we were followed, I am sure Edmund would be unable to break through the forest and learn our location," Porius said.

Actually, while Porius made such a statement, Edmund and a band of ten men were searching the forest but in fact were so far off the track, leaving no concern behind.

"It must be here somewhere," Edmund said to his men just outside Hastings in the thick of the forest.

Franklin reported that in fact, Edmund and his ten men were miles from them and going in circles. Eventually, the search was called off as Edmund led his men back to Windsor.

Back at the cottage, Porius was still commenting on the previous night's special party at Dover. "Did you all taste the many cheeses au Fromage the French ambassador supplied from France?

"I did," Thomas boasted.

"Indeed, they were quite incredible," Simon said while wiping Leal's back with an elongated leaf-type material, making Leal's buttocks give a firm wiggle to the others. The questions started the intense conversation between them in admiration of the night's festive occasion—the meats, flowers, wardrobes. It was so lavish that Walters, Leal, Simon, and Thomas were hardly able to believe the treasures before them.

"I am contact," Thomas said.

"Right, it's getting hot in here," Porius said, standing and leaving the others to soak up the heat and steam from the burning embers' release. "Are you all staying for supper?"

"Well yes, but then we should be off. We have cattle, pig, and farm to attend," Walters said, following Porius to the outside dressing area where Parthenia stood with folded wardrobes for each. Once dressed, the men had a hearty meal. Walters, Simon, and Leal packed up and traveled to Essex where Walters's estate awaited them in green lush surroundings.

Thomas later that evening showed a blue stone to Porius in front of the fire.

"Girard made me a present of this blue stone," Thomas said, admiring its brilliance as it sat in the palm of his hand. "Girard would most likely enjoy a long furlough with Leal."

"Very perceptive of you, Thomas."

"No more two men could ever be more attracted to each other, which seemed apparent, and I am sure the separation must be devastating."

"True, it appears to be a sapphire, and a nice one I might add," Porius said, glancing at the stone.

"It seems to have an inner something deep within the blue," Thomas said.

"Let me see it," Porius said, grabbing the stone from Thomas and peering deep into its center.

"Reveal, oh jewel. Doth thy have presence?" Porius said to the stone.

Emitting from within seemed to be a shadow of movement.

"It's just the reflection of the fire, Thomas. You are very suspicious, but I find this to me a normal and beautiful sapphire."

"Are you sure, Porius?"

"Yes, it reveals no hidden message, but each stone has its memory, and though we may not view it, a history lies within all stones and jewels. They were formed from the earth and only the earth may know their histories."

"Interesting. I am glad of this stone, and I shall name it Pinox. Pinox the sapphire from Girard. And I will have a necklace made for it and wear it on many a festive occasion."

Thomas sat and placed the stone on the mantle place, the small floating band playing a soft romantic-style song in the background. Franklin was perched indoors on the top sill of speckled color glass behind him. As the chilling wind picked up outside, they eventually fell deep asleep.

CHAPTER 10

Walls of stone gargoyle and grotesque lined the walls and archways of the mighty Canterbury cathedral. Foalon the Mystical sat that very same night in the house of Fraun deep in the back streets of Paris. Men and woman walked by the outside of his two-story home. Pigs and horses were heard walking about in the Paris square. Rain lightly misted the walkways, and Foalon sat in black mixing mandrake and lizard skins to perform the changeling effect. Foalon drank the revolting substance and retched with pain, rolling about on the floor tearing his clothes from his body. With him were two apprentices frantic by the sight of their master rolling around in pain.

"Rapide ce qu'il a fait?" (Quick, what has he made?) one apprentice said, grabbing the paper from the table.

"The changeling," said the others, and they both grabbed a few items and exited Foalon's apartments as they ran, leaving the front door of the rue de Faun open. A goat wandering in and witnessing Foalon's body expanding and changing decided it may be safer to go back into the street. Foalon grew hair, whiskers, catlike eyes, and a long tail. Foalon walked with his new catlike body to the mirror after quickly slamming shut the front door to the rue.

"Ha, il fontione magnfiquement" (It works perfectly), Foalon said and put on a long cloak of dark brown skins, covered his head with an extremely large black pointy hat with a silver buckle attached in the front, covering his face from any interested party.

Foalon walked to Notre Dame and entered the grounds along the Ile de la Cite and entered unseen, walking up the staircase to the very top outer door and stepping out onto the roof where he disrobed and jumped from

---

161

the cathedral roof, expanding large feathered wings and spreading them in wide glides toward the earth. In full swing, many witnesses were in disbelief below, running and screaming in fear of this creature above them. Foalon laughed and flew over Paris, finally reaching home. He landed before his door, walked inside, and the bodily shape dissolved, the weight of it sending him to the ground. In walked the two apprentices who had recently fled, dragging his naked body to Foalon's bed and watching over him as he fell asleep. A word was heard by the apprentices in a whisper: "Success."

"Prosperite' Foalon," one apprentice said. It meant "We leave Foalon the Mystical to dream," dreaming of his ability to change nature.

"The nature of man has been brought to the test," Porius burst out in his sleep.

Thomas came in from outside Porius's chamber. "My lord, I heard you screaming," Thomas said, standing half naked before him.

"Foalon has achieved the changeling spell," Porius said, sweating with fear.

"The what, my lord?"

"It shall change him, and I told Foalon not to spend time on such an unpredictable spell." Porius ran to the center room and filled the pensive with water.

"Foalon, Foalon!" Porius shouted into the pensive.

"Porius, my good friend." Foalon was seen in the pensive smiling. "*Jou vous finite*, changeling."

"Yes, but how will control it?"

"Control, control, it is over, monsieur finite."

"No, it may return. Beware, Foalon. Drink plenty of wine, and try not to fall asleep for two days," Porius shouted as the image faded. "I hope he listens, Thomas."

Back in Paris, Foalon fell into a deep sleep; and while sleeping, his body changed from bird to dog, pigeon to rat, rat to fawn, fawn to bird, cat, pigeon, dog, endlessly rotating. His apprentices watched the spectacle until finally, hours went by and Foalon awakened, bruised and cut in several places, beckoning for wine.

"Vin seil vous plait, Vin," Foalon said, adhering to Porius's instructions.

Swans were aplenty in the rivers close by the cottage, swans of black, brown, blue, pearl, and white increasing in numbers, floating innocently above the two water goblins. Harold and Clarice slowly rose to take one swan into the deep of the river unnoticed. Clarice imagined that Porius may wish to have a tasty swan. She also slowed to the surface of the river and slowly took the swan into the deep. The neighboring swan looked a bit surprised, but went about its business most probably thinking that the once close swan that shared its pool of influence just went to another part of the river. Harold and Clarice took their prizes to their dwelling under the deep of the river and stored for an occasion closer to midnight when they would deliver the feast to Porius.

The next morning, Porius found two fresh geese, plump and ready for cooking.

"Parthenia," Porius shouted while his gaze was fixed on the pile of well-delivered fishlike fowl.

"Oh, my goodness, looks like we'll have feast on fowl this evening, Lord Porius," Parthenia said as she grabbed up and defeathered the once-gracious creatures to prepare for their next fate.

"Oh geese," Thomas said as he walked down to the river to bathe.

"Good morrow, Thomas," Porius said.

"Good morrow, Porius, Parthenia."

"A pleasant day for all," Porius said, lighting a pipe and walking around the garden. Franklin and his raven friends seemed to have gathered due to a plentiful supply of worms the bios had cast upon the garden. "Happy Ravens everyone, and Franklin circled in his usual pacing.

Searching over the forest, the cottage, small patches of snow still raining here and there, Thomas was seen by Franklin bathing naked quickly in the river, singing a very loud song.

Ye bountiful the mountain of the bountiful
Winds in the willows
Stalking fish in the breeze
This world is bountiful
Ye bountiful the mountain of the bountiful
Chalks and children walk the paths
White of day and black of night
The bountiful

Franklin shook his head at the spectacle, watching Porius proacting spells with his wand. First, he touched a lilac, which quickly grew before him from the cold wintery branch, seemingly lifeless, burst into lilacs flooding the odor throughout the garden and all the way down to the river. Thomas turned his soapy body toward the garden as he dried, smelling the whiff of Lilac.

"Reorganize, reorient, and repair," Porius said to the lilac bush, tapping the end of his wand.

A grin appeared on Porius's face as he giggled, watching the plant go back to its winter appearance.

"Oh dear, I almost forgot," Porius said as he grabbed a handful of flowers quickly before it returned to its natural state. Porius grabbed the flowers and went up to the kitchen window. Parthenia was pulling feathers from the fowl.

"Here you are, my dearest Parthenia." Porius handed the fully bloomed lilac Aquia to Parthenia.

"My lord, how wonderful." She grabbed them with a feathered fist smiling.

"Oh, I see the fowl is plucked," Porius said, grinning.

"Oh, my lord," Parthia said, blushing and placing the flowers in a water pot, arranging them at the center of the dinner table out in the main room of the cottage.

Franklin circled farther out and this time saw Simon walking with Byron toward the village, thinking, *Oh, it is most reasonably a date into town for supplies.* Then to the north he witnessed a small band of woodsmen hunting grouse but paid them no attention. To the south, the sea beyond the waves, a few ships were motionless in the distance, finishing the morning haul of cod, snapper, and whatever happened upon a hook. Circling to the west, dark clouds floated unnoticed over thick forests except by bird, deer, or other animal, which did not stand on two legs and was too slow to mortally witness the event. A lonely troll sitting next to another troll and a few elven participants fish, enjoying the isolation and safety of the forest from mortal men. The elf leaped in the air, spreading wings and circling Franklin.

"Morning." Franklin beaked in a square flat knot, but the happy elf got his meaning.

"Morning," the elf replied, putting his hand to his brow and quickly descending to the earth and plunging into the river.

Most joyous morning, Franklin thought to himself, knowing that this lonely elf was recently surrounded by many others before the church forced them into Elysium. The bios beneath the soil a mist with pleasure and living creatures in synchronized obedience to the earth. Worms, caterpillar, and winter.

Simon and Byron visited the tavern, and all were chatting insistently about the coming war with Saxony, the pope claiming parts of their lands and the lack of care for the old ways.

"My husband's been sent to fight in Saxony and has left us little," one woman shouted to a small crowd guzzling ale and wincing.

"My Molly been taken as slave to men in black cloaks," another woman said in desperation.

"Both my sons have been taken, or let me see, how did those rabbles say it? Oh yes, they were requisitioned. Well, I need them both unrequisitioned to help with the farming," exclaiming one and gulping a long-needed drink of ale. "Now how is our wheat getting planted and our corn seeds going down, I ask anyone able," he said, looking around.

"By god, count my two in," one man said, pointing at his two young sons in their teens drinking barley water."

"Yes, we will be glad to work," the committed to the crowd.

Simon told one man that Byron and he shall assist in the seeding. "Is tomorrow morning good for you?" Simon said.

The next morning, Simon and Byron met at the farmer's field and began the planting of rows and rows of corn and wheat, using ox and shovel, bag and plow.

Spring turned to summer and summer to autumn, winter and spring once more. Empires rose and fell, kings changed hands as time passed. Porius gained age and soon was mostly bound to the cottage and his memories. Thomas was still by his side; Walters, Leal, Simon, and Byron had aged but still stood in 1460. Athena and her guards were still beautiful and in the immortal realm. On March 4, 1461l, Porius lay on his bed surrounded by all.

"Edward, finally crowned at Westminster," Porius said in a weak voice. "Edward has assisted in hiding what is necessary. You, all of you, protect the cottage. Athena, come back from Elysium often and check on Thomas. Thomas will never grow old. I have given him the same as Franklin. To them, I leave the cottage and to them I leave the task to guard what is kept in the secret area below us and in Canterbury."

Walters, Leal, Simon, and Byron knelt beside Porius. He and his Thomas were dressed in white-and-golden grandeur, with Franklin perched on the windowsill. He died.

"Porius," Athena said, holding her hands over his body. "To Elysium."

Athena claimed Porius's body, and in the moment, both Athena and Porius disappeared before all to Elysium. They faded before them, her maidens following in a glow of light and in the smoke of dreams. Outside, the rain fell as a new king of England was crowned at Westminster. Thomas prepared for his new life without Porius and turned to everyone.

"We shall continue, and all that Porius has taught shall remain."

"It will not be easy, Thomas," Walters said.

Thomas turned toward the window. "We will miss you, Lord Porius."

And at that moment, while his mortal shell was left behind and Athena guided Porius to Elysium, Porius new unearthly body awakened, and he turned back toward earth and shouted. "Porius, Porius, Porius!" Porius shouted back toward earth below him. Thomas, Walters, Simon, Leal, and all other patrons of the old ways heard his voice and turned their faces toward the sky. "Feed my body to the river," Porius finished his last request.

"Replenishing the water and feeding the earth," Thomas said, tears streaming. "Porius always said that this is the way of the future."

"Yes indeed," said Walters. "At the time of death, the body shall return to the sea, river, or lake. That is the way to give back, Porius always said."

Thomas, Leal, Walters, and Simon carried Porius to the river; and the water goblins took him down. The body shall replenish the earth; the fish shall feed and populate.

"That which has been always taken shall be rewarded, and once the waters devour the body, a pathway shall be given to Elysium.

"In his writings, Porius mentioned the future world," Walters said while watching Porius's body disappear into the deep of the river. "Porius wrote that earth will become polluted and overrun with man and woman and the seas will suffer, the forest shall diminish."

"Yes, and the path to Elysium is by leaving your body to the sea," Leal said.

"I have read this spell as well," Simon said, wiping the tears from his eyes and waving to Porius as he descended.

"The coral reef shall replenish, the undersea grasses shall grow, the dolphin, shark, and butter hamlets will multiply and replenish the earth. This will be the new way forward, and every year on the eve of the equinox, all shall say, 'Porius, Porius, Porius.'"

At that moment, all around the world's peoples and their families who still followed the old ways repeated together, "Porius, Porius, Porius," heard from Egypt to Kenya. The new world tribes of Indians, the Asian peoples, all looked up toward the sky and whispered, "Porius, Porius, and Porius" once more.

Year after year, the ritual continued upon the eve of the winter equinox. "Porius, Porius, Porius" could be heard from all ancient civilizations and future groups who tried to cling to the old ways.

Mud rolled over the erosion of the earth as waves beat the endless rhythms around the earth. Animals converged, migrated, gave birth to their young, and multiplied. Simon wrote his chapter for the Malefactor, discussing the reasons for keeping the natural world apart from the destructions of man. Leal wrote his chapter in the great book and discussed the beauty of lovemaking and the importance of open-mindedness. Walters wrote his chapter for the Malefactor and described the importance of showing tolerance and sparing a life instead of taking one in battle. Walters described the importance of bringing close those who disagreed with you or had different faiths, which was a common theme among all their writings. The two soon faded over the years, and Walters gave his body to the sea eventually and was taken by Athena to Elysium. Simon and Leal followed this path in the years that followed. Thomas and Franklin eventually followed, but after descending under the currents, they remain to guard the cottage.

The earth revolved and split up its descendants, empires rose and fell, earthquakes and volcano shook the earth. Below the crust, the bios still continued and growing with each passing year, migrating and evolving. Men multiplied within all the earth's continents and built like an unstoppable mold unyielding. As Porius wrote, the earth did get polluted and became sour in places. The old ways faded into very small sects here and there, a few in Wales, some in England, smaller in far-off countries where religion had grabbed hold and shaken the common fold to their knees. Through battle and slavery, through family and unbelievers, the religions grew, taking almost all in its pathway. True, none who were not true of heart would never follow the path to Elysium. But still, some did follow, some who found the writings of Porius and heard the story, some who had followed other religions and at the end given themselves to the sea; they found redemption and resurrection by being escorted by Athena to Elysium.

Porius awakened after his travel with Athena, through the long winding roads of light, which all energy travels, until his destination Elysium.

CHAPTER 11

Elysium is basically another planet on the neighboring galaxy to earths and another green zone, which is to say another planet with its distance to the sun similar to earth's distance to the sun. Billions of worlds are green zones across the huge expanse of space. Energy with each soul or human form has this ability. Unfortunately, most will never know and may stay in the black of dark for eternities. But those who give their body back to the sea recapture the essence of light as the molecules regenerate into another easily described dimension. For Porius, he now appeared in his forties again, healthy, dressed in a long flowing white embroidered gown and living on a home atop a forest hill, which looked out of the Elysium seas. Within a tube of meniscus fluid rolling back and forth from finger to finger and hand to hand, from beings within Andromeda who lived among the chosen now housed on Elysium, Porius gained a new life to start new adventures within the many planets of the realm. Throughout the years, Porius had learned to communicate with Thomas on earth, and the cottage still held its never-ending dignity and hidden location. Wars and empires had come and gone among the races of the earth while science prevailed and from time to time doing good among the earthly warring factions.

Hidden deep underground lay the Malefactor with chapters by those who lived with Porius in his mortal time on earth. Thomas guarded the planet as occasional families, farmers, wizards, pagans, druids, water goblins, elves, and other creatures managed to live unseen. In 1650, Thomas had an adventure with a family from Dublin who moved there due to the insistence of Charles the First in 1625; the family was pagan and studied the old ways, their fathers and mothers giving their bodies to the seas when the time came and all said Porius three times. The Catholic pope always attempted to ravage their lands. Thomas gave them spells and amulets to protect the family from harm, making their harvests the best in Ireland and their minds the smartest in that part of the world. Charles was eventually executed in 1649, leaving Ireland and Scotland unprotected from Oliver Cromwell's army, defeating all and leaving a path of religious zealots in its wake, making it more difficult to survive for most magical and old-rule-abiding families. Most families gave in or eventually pretended to serve this new religion, but secretly met and set up sects that would live on for centuries; but here we see Thomas with Briar Wiltern, the leader of the magical families or spokesperson as he preferred to be referred. Thomas, still in somewhat human form, and though looking to the normal eye as a fifty-year-old healthy person, was able to reconnect and ride the Elysium highway when needed and return while Franklin still circled the cottage and its grounds daily. Parthenia's ghost in human form still cooked and cleans, Grendle still sorted and mended, the floating band ageless, still performing on rare occasions when they decided to visit from Elysium.

That night, Briar, meeting with Thomas, asked, "If we, Lord Thomas, all gather in Dunmow at the edge of Essex, we may be able to turn more heads in our direction."

"I would highly suggest an alternative. Cromwell is too heavy a foot."

"Oh, I understand, I mean, we don't want families to be jeopardized," Wiltern suggested. "How shall we communicate? Or still, how do we know the families are safe from Cromwell who are currently being tortured, who are imprisoned?"

"Hang on, Wiltern, just hang on," Thomas repeated. It was starting to rain most severely outdoors as the two men huddled around the table.

"I know of several in the tower now that could use saving," Wiltern said, wearing green cloth and beholding the emblem of a harp made of steel. "Jewels Cameron, the daughter of my second sister, and Frederick Genre are being taken to the tower."

"Yes, I have heard of them both and will call the chamber to discuss," Thomas said while opening the window and letting Franklin fly in.

"The famous Franklin, I see," Wiltern said, pointing to Franklin who came in and, shaking his feathers, perched himself on the inside sill.

"Yes," Thomas said with a hand extended. Franklin moaned with disconcert.

"A pleasure, and when shall I return to meet the council?"

"Mendicant or medicant order is forming in London as well. They will start begging along the streets and turning the money secretly to the farmers and old ways families."

"We will do this now," Thomas said and faced toward the window. He said in a calm voice, "Porius, Porius, Porius."

Within seconds, a face of Porius was seen out of doors through the window dripping in rain. "May I come in?"

"Oh my dear Porius, enter," Thomas said as Wiltern stood to greet the great Porius. Franklin was standing on his perch, unmoved by the event.

"My dear Thomas," Porius said as he walked in looking better than ever—younger in robes sparkling as he drifted by, bejeweled and smiling, long white hair, and braided beard.

"My Lord Porius," Wiltern said, bowing. "What an honor it is indeed to make your acquaintance."

"And, Sir Wiltern," Porius said, returning the bow, "you have need of some resistance I see, and a good thing you came to us. I will see to it, calling the others now." Porius held his arms out before him.

Walters, Leal, and Simon appeared, all wearing their usual leather outfits and black boots, swords at the side of each, and in the healthiest of figures greeted Wiltern and enjoyed a feast provided by Parthenia and Grendle, round the table discussing all the ins and outs of the tower and where each person who needed saving may be kept. Drawing maps and laughing, Leal was still beautiful though now able to change to his ghostlike figure and back into flesh at will. On one occasion, he turned into his ghostlike shape and flew back to Elysium while the act reached its highest high, but the memories of the one left behind would satisfy even the greediest of persons. Leal was able to fight for the causes, which he felt deserved his attention as to say freeing the two from the tower made just that distinction.

In the tower after easily passing the guards who slept that night in dreams, Walters, Leal, and Simon flew past; and while creeping along the lowest corridor, Leal was able to break the locks and release the two imprisoned and soon to put to the fire. Wiltern stayed far away in the cottage while this superb act of heroism was taking place. Walter struggled with the rusted lock then finally picked it with his knife.

"Follow us my friends," Simon said to the two innocent-looking captures now shivering and starving.

"Who are you?" one man said who seemed to be the thinner and mostly shaken participant.

"We are friends, now hurry," said Walters.

Jewel and Frederick look amazed at the three men greeting them with smiling faces. "But how—" Jewel began, but Leal put his muscular hand to her mouth.

"Silence," Leal said softly. "We still need to get you out of this forbidden place."

Leal led the way, and Walters went to the first guard who was awake and sipping mead at a small table. Walters floated past him to another part of the hallway and knocked over a stool, making a noise. The guard, dressed in red and black, quickly drew his sword and headed for the noise. Walters disappeared, and Leal guarded Jewel and Frederick to safety. Finally leaving the castle without a fight or being noticed, they all made it safely back to the hidden horses, Walters setting up Jewel behind him and Franklin circling overhead, squawking, "All clear."

They rode through forest and over river, past beggars, smoldering fires, and gypsies until finally they reached the forest near Hastings and the magical garden and cottage within its safe surroundings. Frederick and Jewel were greeted by the ghost of Porius, Athena, Walters, Parthenia with the usual handful of food and ale and Grendle. Still, there was shock of freedom on the faces and minds of Jewel and Frederick.

"Thank you, my friends, and the amazing, swift delivery is quite astounding," Frederick said to his heroes while Jewel bowed and entered the cottage dressed in pinkish gown dirtied by her previous captors.

"Come with me," Parthenia said and led them to the back rooms where they could bathe and remove their soiled clothes.

Leal appeared in at the naked backside of Frederick. "Not bad."

"Frederick is spoken for, Leal, behave yourself," Thomas said, laughing.

Porius lit the fire, and he was now in human form, his usual long white flowing wardrobe ornately patterned with elves and fairies pictured around the sleeves. "All is welcome here, and Frederick, Jewel, and others must begin a new journey, for they will be hunted."

"Hunt," Walter said, sipping his ale.

"Yes, they will be pursued by the knights who let them slip through their fingers," Simon said while removing his outer layers of mesh and steel and again fading into the invisible form as did Leal and Walters. "What's happening, Porius?" Leal said.

"Well, it appears we are back to Elysium,"

"But I wished to stay a while," Leal said while staring at his vanishing feet below him.

"Elysium only allows so long," Porius said as he vanished.

"Goodbye, my friends," Thomas said, holding his mug as he watched Leal, Walters, Simon, and Porius disappear and their goblets falling to the ground.

Grendle picked up the goblets and wiped clean the floor, and Thomas sat alone at the table while Frederick and Jewel washed in the back of the cottage. Parthenia carried their clothes to the river and, after beating them on the rocks at the edge, brought them back dripping wet. Thomas was still sitting at the table. Frederick and Jewel were wrapped in blankets and sitting beside the fire.

"I wish we could have spoken to Porius longer," Frederick stated while Jewel nodded in agreement.

"Where has doth Porius gone?" Jewel said as she reentered the main living area dripping in water and wiping her naked body with Frederick following behind.

"Your clothes shall be dried soon, but in the meantime, please dry yourselves in front of the fire. Porius and the others have gone," Thomas said, sitting with his feet up on the footstool. Franklin rested behind on his sill.

"Gone, Lord Thomas? Gone where?"

"Well, you must not expect Walters, Porius, and the others to hang around all evening. They are called elsewhere."

"Ah, Elysium, I imagine," said Jewel. "In the 700s, the puebloans made settlements in Mesa Verde and brought all the stones to England found in the digging, ancient stones which will no doubt come to heed our battles in the centuries to come, or is there no power within the stones?" Jewel said as she drifted off and everyone looked at her eyes fade to white, her hands to cream, her lips to red, and her soft skin floating as she meditated before them, a moment, a minute, a brief second of time as a soft memory was implant from an unexpected other world, penetrating deep within her skin, mind, ankles, and shivering buttock and thighs.

"Correct, my lady, but you shall both be safe here until we find out what to do with you both," Thomas said, witnessing the two drying themselves, unashamed of their nakedness, and soon they sat. Parthenia brought in some food, chicken, and wine and the feast to end all feasts.

"The tower was terrible in the extreme, and I do hope you thank Porius and Walters for us properly," Frederick said, sitting naked beside Thomas.

"Here, Frederick, speak into the pensive," Thomas said, holding a small round silver tray with water along the bottom. "Feel delight and take the mushroom of inner peace." She nibbled on a dried mysterious-looking mushroom. Caterpillars gathered on the verge outside the neatly leaded windows as frost formed, obscuring the view of the large yellow, red, and black caterpillars coiling and growing in the moonlight. Herds of deer danced within the surrounding forests and green rolling hills. Maple, acorn, willow, pine, and elm dotted the surrounding areas with double and occasionally triple stories that stood crooked building strewn here and there among elves, fawn, flowers, and delightful colors within the ever-changing images within the pensive as the storm brewed, blasting down rain, sending lightning and pocketing the woods surrounding them all.

"Porius," Thomas said into the pensive.

"Thomas, Frederick, and Jewel." Porius could be seen in the pensive with a garden behind him waving in the water of the pensive. "Listen to Thomas and protect the creatures below," Porius said as the vision faded back into the silver of the dish.

"Creatures below what?" Jewel said.

"Yes, in the morning, I have a splendid idea that will keep you both occupied for years to come," Thomas said mysteriously.

Men in horses covered the outside area just beyond the line of trees that protect the cottage. None find them, and soon they moved on and eventually headed back to the tower where the barracks of the king's men lived.

"They shall not find you here," Thomas said. Parthenia dressed Jewel and Frederick with dry clothes, and soon they had full bellies and warmth in their hearts that their futures were once again bright. Thomas showed them to the back room where a soft bed awaited them, and all slept until morning.

Rain beat down hard outside, and a storm filled the area. Wind blew the garden and forest trees, and even the animals stayed hidden in this miserable storm.

"Good morn, my friends," Thomas said while waking Jewel and Frederick.

"Good morrow, indeed, Thomas," Jewel said as she dressed, and they both walked into the main area, where there was a roaring fire and the rain was chucking down. Franklin even did not want to leave his cozy indoor sill until loud squawking was heard from the sky and, as the clouds part, the sun shone through and the flowers opened. Franklin flew up to meet his friends and circled the area of Kent.

"What a storm, Thomas, and I want to thank you for your hospitality." Frederick continued. "We seem to be bound to you."

"Think nothing of it," Thomas said. "Consider this your home and stay as long as you wish. Food is delivered daily by water goblins, just look outside."

Sure enough, outside the cottage was a pile of fish, vegetables, and fowl ready for the cooking. Frederick and Jewel could not have dared dream of the journey ahead of them. For after they had cleaned and dressed, Thomas stared into the pensive in communication with Porius. Porius's long gray beard image could be seen in the foreground with Leal dancing naked with Apollo in the background to some tribal dance tune that makes your foot tap. The two beautiful men were laughing and were soon out of sight.

"They are inseparable since Apollo and Leal met," Porius said, smiling. "Now, Thomas, I believe that Jewel and Frederick are the perfect two humans to journey to the underworld and study the inhabitants below."

"As you wish, Lord Porius," Thomas said.

"Come closer to the pensive," Porius shouted out at Jewel and Frederick as they dressed. "You need not dress for cool weather because the temperature is always perfect below the surface of the earth. Remember to study and list the beings which live below."

"Lord Porius, we would have never thought it truly existed," shouted back Jewel into the pensive.

"Yes, Jewel, now be kind to the creatures below and you will be safe among them," Porius said, and he started to fade away.

But then suddenly, Porius returned, face glowing, with Leal hugging Apollo behind him. "Oh mind you, beware of the dragon people. They can be rather strange. Give them candy or sweets if they attack you," Porius said as he faded.

"Attack?" Frederick said in a shaken voice. "Porius, is it dangerous?" Frederick shouted.

"He is gone, I am afraid, but you will know what to do I am sure of it," Thomas said as he laid down the pensive, and it disappeared before them.

Thomas went to the front door, and Franklin jumped into his usual circling of the cottage grounds. A few other ravens joined him, barking their unusual song, the clouds black as the rain had stopped momentarily and Jewel led Frederick out the front door.

Thomas was standing next to a spot to the south of the cottage. "Reveal," he said, waving a wand decorated with emeralds, rubies, and diamonds. "Take them and keep them safe."

As the earth trembled, the onlooking deer, squirrel, and small flock of bluebirds watched as a large hole appeared and within it a staircase that only led one way—down. Inward they stepped, one foot in front of the other, and hesitant with a thrilled skin and wisdom in their hearts. Minds full of wonder and excitement.

"What will we see?" Jewel said, stepping down step after step slower and slower as they lifted, fading to black.

"Incineration," Jewel said, holding out her palm as a light appeared and hovered upon it.

"Nice one," Frederick said and followed suit. "Flame appear," Frederick said, his light now hovering over his palm.

"The only trouble with this spell is that the flame goes out if you move too quickly," Jewel said as they descended step by step into another part of this world seldom seen by mortal humans.

Thomas stayed on the surface of the earth and waved to them as they descended and the hole became grass, weed, and hedge once more. Jewel held on to Frederick's arm.

"It is getting light," Jewel said softly as the walls started to shine the deeper. They descended, down further into the earth. The staircase winded, the walls appeared, and a glass between stone, granite, clay, and skulls and the occasional bones arranged in all different formations.

Below them further gleams a light at the end of a staff held by a man in white flowing gown and grey beard.

"Porius, I am glad to see you," Frederick said as they reach Porius.

"You didn't think I would leave you all on your own did you," Porius said pointing his lit staff toward the west tunnel.

"I want you both to follow that tunnel, you see it will get lighter as you venture on and soon you will witness peoples, cultures and fantastic beings like you have never dreamed."

"You shan't come with us?" Jewel whispers to Porius.

"I am needed elsewhere, and this is what you must both do," Porius said holding Frederick on the shoulder, "Study them and take notes with this and come back in a fortnight, remember to take notes and study."

Porius reached into his gown and pulls out a notebook bound in leather and hands it to Frederick. When you leave call my name and I will collect the book."

"Aye, we shall keep thy promise and venture on," Jewel whispered as they followed the tunnel further down the stairs, leaving Porius standing behind them until his features faded and he returned to Elysium. Jewel and Frederick turned back to glance one last time, but he had vanished, and the only light surrounding them were the crystals that lined the walls of the staircase upon which they descend. Winding, sometimes flat and then steep, the walls around them changed colors and occasionally gleamed and soon the efflorescence appeared of miraculous flowers and buds' vine and weed all aglow. Some aquamarine, some purple, violet, blue, and even gold and silver lined the walls with vast walls of quartz, amethyst brightly shinning. Small flying creatures spotted them and circled as in small herds. Several winged creatures about the size of your hand fluttered and circled and sounds could be heard of their flapping wings.

"Wait," Jewel said as they gazed around them taking in their elegant beauty. Startled by the sound of Jewel's voice, a few flying creatures stopped for a moment and then continued their fluttering and circling. Legs full of seeds and yellow-colored wings, bits of orange and starlight adorned their features, these amazing flying creatures. Some in purple and some in gray, some wearing wrappings of silken material and some with penetrating eyes, tiny but penetrating most assured.

"Porius said to take notes," Jewel said, reaching for the pad from Frederick.

"Let me see, SMALL FLYING," Jewel said, writing in the book as Frederick had two small manlike creatures with wings land on his shoulders.

"Greetings, my friends," Frederick said, touching one with his finger as the small creature flew off. "Thy creatures most assuredly are real."

"What's that noise?" Jewel said and they both stared into the glossing distance of circling lights and glowing, colorful plants that led to a widening of the area and a distance was seen before them.

"Look," Frederick said. Jewel, writing, said, "And the horizon lay wide and open and before us a noise, a buzzing."

"Put that book down and hold on to me," Frederick said as he started to panic and shake. The buzzing sound got louder, and just beyond an iridescently colored tree sat a few small house-like structures like miniature thatch-roofed cottages not unsimilar to the cottage. There was an infusion of smells like root vegetables and something sweet in the air. Soon they reached a normal-sized cottage, and in front a garden and beyond a black shimmering lake dotted with lights in the foreground. The backfin of a dolphin was attached to a creature who appeared to be sawing wood. The sawing stopped, and before them stood a five-foot-tall half-human-half-dolphin-type creature with arms and legs and a human head but some dolphin fin and gills along his neck.

"Greetings, you must be Jewel and Frederick," the creature said. "Porius informed me that ye will both seek a passage over the lake."

"Indeed, I am Jewel, and this is Frederick."

They both stood amazed, and Frederick held out his had to shake the hand or fin of their interlocutor. Setting down his saw made of amethyst and glowing wood, he walked toward them.

"My name be Worland of the Lake," he said, spitting water from his gills and grasping Frederick's hand with a slippery mucous-covered hand, which appeared half man and half dolphin-like.

"Our pleasure, Worland, our pleasure indeed," they both said.

"I am sure you have not seen a creature like me before and thus no one has for I may be the only one of my kind left on earth."

"Well, I am so glad to meet you," Jewel said.

"Many thousands of years ago, this area was strewn with thousands of my kind, but generation after generation, our forms changed and evolved and I was lucky to travel below earth and meet Horan. Horan is who you will both meet, and he is the king or, well, not really a king, but a leader for us below earth."

"Horan," Jewel said, taking note in her book and writing the name and making a quick sketch of Worland of the Lake.

"Just call me Worland." He noticed Jewel capturing his form on paper. "Make sure you get my best side," he said, turning to reveal a backside, which is humanlike except for the fin protruding out of his backside just above the buttocks and below normal human legs.

Several other creatures came out to greet Jewel and Frederick, one very curious with skin of shining gold and hanging lymph nodes like a squid colors changing as it ran the edge of the lake and swam out to the deep.

Frederick pointed and chased the creature to the edge of the water. "Look, ye can see thus creatures glow under the water."

Jewel rushed to the edge and, smiling, wrote down the event in her book.

"Oh yes, you will see hundreds of species within this realm and some I would not be so quick to chase," Worland said, now lighting a pipe and heading indoors. "Can I offer you refreshment?"

"Yes please, we are very thirsty," Jewel said as Frederick pushed his long black hair over his face.

"Come, I have apple brandy and several juices made from root and fern." Worland led them indoors. Inside was a one-room cottage lined with books, tweed-like walls, carved wood, and even a floating bandstand that appeared to be playing a sweet melody, its little creatures playing ancient instruments.

"Porius must have made them appear," Worland said as he stared at the floating band, handing two goblets of root juice and water to the two adventurers.

"A miracle surely," Frederick said, standing close and swaying to the music. Never before had he seen or even thought of such an oddity.

"Porius sends them to me occasionally," Worland said. The bandleader was waving his wand and turning to wink at them all.

"Well, sit please. Welcome and tell me of thy selves," Worland said, sitting around a table lined with benches.

"Thank ye, Worland of the Lake," Jewel said, writing in her book.

"Just Worland, please."

Frederick turned and joined them to rest his shaking limbs.

"Never would I have dreamed any of this was possible. Why for, here? Just to think only hours ago, Jewel and I were locked in the tower."

"The tower?" Worland stated, leaning forward to his interlocutor.

"Yes, Jewel and I were arrested by the king's men and set to die. You see, the pope came to our village and killed most of our people."

"Except the few that were lucky enough to escape or stay slaves to the pope's men," Jewel said, sipping her juice. "This juice is delicious, thank ye,"

"We come from the west country," Frederick continued. "Farmers we were and happy with nice crops, fresh fruit, kale, spinach, grape, and more. Hundreds of years, our families grew fields and fields of wheat, veg, and fruit and hunted. The pope was unhappy that we did not follow the new church and belong or pay homage to their will. First my family and then Jewel's."

"Too gruesome to mention, dear Worland," Jewel intercepted.

"My lord, I have heard of this new religion. Many will seek refuge under the earth. Or if lucky enough will see Elysium," Worland said, wiping the froth from his dripping lips.

"Welcome Jewel and Frederick, now to the lake."

Standing, his arms dripped. "I need to jump in the lake, please come."

CHAPTER 12

As Jewel and Frederick exited the cottage, a vast number of creatures greeted them. Standing room only around them while dozens of creatures, some manlike some beast, some fairy, some troll, oxen like heads with lizard or snake like body close to their bodies.

"I must write all this down," Jewel said to Frederick as they were separated. Many more creatures surrounded them. With arms outstretched, Jewel had several creatures sniffing, licking, eyeing, and alternating so many different creatures get the advantage place close to their skin.

One pair of water goblin–type creatures standing millimeters from Frederick and licking his face started to grab at his clothes. Others grabbed at the clothes of Jewel.

"Wait, stop that," Jewel was saying, somewhat miffed at why some of these creatures were so eager to disrobe them. Reaching for several bits of clothes at some point, it gets far too much for Frederick and Jewel.

"Jewel," Frederick shouted as she was now about ten feet away and dozens of multicolored creatures were between them, eyeing, pulling. "None of these creatures are wearing clothes!"

"I see," said Jewel.

"Let them have their way," Frederick shouted as the floating band came outdoors, some of the creatures dancing and singing in many types of songs. "I give in." Frederick smiled.

Many creatures finally removed their clothes, leaving nothing but their bare skin and jewelry. Frederick was naked except for his one ring, which was on his middle finger of the left hand, and Jewel wore a few necklaces and a wristband encrusted in jewels. Then from out beyond the crowd, two women-like creatures with brown hair appeared, holding silken cloth.

They draped the purple and golden cloths around Frederick's waist, and Jewel was covered across her boson with green silk and white silk across her waist.

"That is much nice. Thank you kindly," Jewel said to the two women.

"We need to have you in the clothes of the realm. Welcome," one woman said, wearing a long white silk gown, the other nothing but skin revealing a nude form as most of the other creatures. Some zebra-like canine sniffed their heels, circled, and went off.

"Some of these creatures don't look so friendly," Frederick shouted over the noisy crowd. Meanwhile as the crowd and party continued with even louder song, Worland splashed into the water before them. "Come, my friends," Worland said as they were both thrown into the lake by the noisy crowd, the floating band hovering over them as they swam beside Worland who led them out to the deep. Soon the crowd far behind them and the back of the lake swirled around them.

"I felt something brush against me," Frederick said.

"My book," Jewel said, realizing the book was left behind.

"The book is safe, Jewel, not to worry," Worland said. "Stay close to me."

The three went further and further out into the black lake, the darkest colors of water imaginable and only the occasional glowing of lights, which circled beneath them, and dots of light appeared and disappeared around and above. Jewel lined the ceiling, which got closer and closer to the tops of their heads.

"Where are we?" Frederick asked Worland.

"We travel west with the current, and sure enough, one shall come quickly so stay close." As he spoke, a current swiftly moved them along to the west and seemingly downward at a quicker pace.

Jewel was starting to panic. "I am getting tired," she said.

"Fear not, we are almost there," Worland bubbled.

A head popped up next to Frederick, scaring him out of his wits. There was one eye in the center of a long chicken-like neck, which blinked at Frederick and then disappeared under the water.

"I am really getting tired, Worland," Jewel said.

"Hop on my back," Frederick said.

"No, mine," Worland said and quickly circled around them both and holding Jewel as she rode, almost hitting her head on the ceiling. Soon the ceiling's height grew, and the color changed. Strange music was heard in the distance.

The floating band were far behind and silent. A new music appeared, and Worland landed them on a white shore. The sky sparkled with millions of lights, diamonds, amethysts spiraling in every direction. They all crawled up on the shore where there were more moss than sand, and they lay there sliding, backing into the lake.

Worland left them on the shore.

"Oh, you may need this," Worland said as he handed the book, which is dye as ever.

"Tell you are not leaving us here, Worland," Frederick said. Jewel grabbed the book and lay on her back on the mossy sand.

"You will be fine, my friends," Worland said as he splashed back toward the black lake and swam off.

Jewel rested on her elbows. Slipping in the mossy shore of warm water the inflorescence of many plants never before seen by Jewel surrounded them. Frederick's eyes closed, and his mind filled with the imagery of the spectacle that only moments before entering this large black lake with a half-dolphin creature, the crowds of alien-type beings thrusting them both into the lake. Jewel was beside him nearly naked except for the small piece of silk covering her breasts and waist, he wearing even less but a piece of silk wrapped around his waist and tied in a knot they roll into each other's arms.

"What dream is this, frederick?" Jewel asked as she regained her strength and stood holding the book and brushing the small spots of sand from her skin.

"You can attempt adjusting, but it's not much to adjust," Frederick said, giggling as he watched her try to cover her private parts with what little material she had been given.

"All those amazing creatures below and up above were called infidels," Jewel said.

"You are a beautiful sight, my Jewel," Frederick said, pulling her back down onto the sand, the book cast up further on shore.

"I do love you so, Frederick," Jewel said as they wrapped their arms around each other and pressed their bodies close, the skin and wet silk sliding in the moss.

Before they got too carried away, a large creature appeared, wearing what appeared to be a long red gown with gold trim, which was just lightly draped over the shoulder to reveal a human head and frog-like body. Large feet next to Frederick and Jewel, they jumped up to stand beside the creature.

"Your pardon, sir," Jewel began picking up the book.

"Your name, sire?" Frederick asked.

"Toby." The frog-like man draped in red cloth and holding a large stick poked Frederick lightly.

"My good sir, please refrain from poking me."

"A fine pair of humans you both are. Porius was right," Toby said.

"Ah, Toby," Jewel interceded. "Our extreme pleasure to meet you." She wrote in the book, "toad-like creature, Toby, we are in your hands."

"Porius again, any friend of Porius is a friend of thine," Frederick interjected.

"You will both find food, refreshment amenities, and a place to sleep. Follow me and welcome," Toby said as while circling around Jewel in wide-eyed appreciation of her beauty. The toad walked around them a few times, occasionally touching the silk bits of cloth and peering underneath.

"Please, Toby," Frederick said as he removed Toby's hand from Jewel's waist.

"Just such fine specimens," Toby continued and finally walked in front of the startled pair. "Please follow."

"We have not ever seen a, well, person like you, Toby," Jewel said.

"Oh, there are many of us down here, you know. Hermaphrodites we are, so not actually a sir," Toby explained. "We are a bit of both sexes that is why it always fascinates me to meet a strictly human form, truly amazing in its simplicity."

"Both sexes, aye, then how do you—" Frederick inquired.

"Well, let's just say we have many pleasurable ways and just leave it at that."

"Fine by me." Jewel walked and scribbled in her book of notes. "HERMAPHRODITE," she wrote, and Toby led them into a dark corridor.

"Now it shall be pitch black for a bit so hold on to my hand and each other and follow my lead," Toby said, reaching out to Frederick with one hand, and Frederick grabbed Jewel's hand. They walked in the black as what seems like a tunnel.

"The ground is very wet and slippery," Jewel said, grasping her book to her breast with her right arm and holding tight to Frederick with the left.

"Almost there, yes, it's just moss. Now look ahead of us."

Before them was a light-filled area with quartz ceiling and holes in the roof that shone patches of light. This 110-yard area was filled with plant life, small grass huts that held patches of mud and moss, and several small lakes with frog-like people as Toby in small groups. They all ran toward the new additions to the village.

"Welcome to Laffe," Toby said as the crowd of frog-like people stood before them, about twenty of them, some small, some short, some fat, and some thin. Harold and Cynthia, water goblins, were in the background splashing in one of the ponds until they disappeared under the water.

"My pleasure in meeting you," Frederick said as he bowed.

The crowd agreed to his bow, and all bowed back.

"Do you come from on top?" one frog-like creature asked.

"Indeed we have," Jewel said.

"Will you be meeting with Horan?" another shouted.

"Horan? Hmm, I have heard this name, but not sure as yet," Frederick said.

"Oh yes, they will be meeting with Horan," Toby shouted above the murmuring crowd of frog-like creatures with semihuman heads.

"We are here to study and record the underworld," Jewel said.

"Yes, yes, now all of you can go about your business," Toby interjected and waved them all off. Several came closer, but most went back to their previous places. Toby showed them into a small hut.

"May this dwelling comfort you both for a couple of days. Now please rest and refresh yourself," Toby said and pointed to a table holding fruit and some cooked meats.

"This food looks tempting, can you tell me of its nature?" Jewel asked while opening her book.

"Oh yes, indeed. Here this is passion fruit, and this is honey apple and this is . . ." Toby kept explaining the unusual meats and fruit juices and drinks while Frederick walked around the small hut, going back outside and walking around the pools while most of the strange creatures eyed his every move. Frederick walked into the bushes and studied some that were invasive and some plants that revealed hazardous thorns, one which pierced his thigh and almost broke the skin.

"Oh, my dear boy, allow me," one small forklike being grabbed the branches to clear his way.

The day went on and on, and after studying and drinking some moss-made mead, the two explores finally fell into a deep sleep, dreaming of the creatures and Porius. Finally Jewel had a frightening nightmare of her parents being taken away by men in black cloaks wearing large wooden crosses around their necks.

"Ma, Ma, Mama!" Jewel screamed as she awakened from the nightmare.

Frederick, awakened by the scream, held her and comforted her, hand on head and other arm holding her close.

"All in the past, my dearest one, all in the past," Fredrick said, holding her tight to his flesh.

"Gone, but never forgotten. Oh, my dear Frederick, soon we must return."

"Ah yes, but now." Thomas knelt on hands and knees and smiling. "Morning meal, do you smell it?"

"I do," Jewel said, and they both refreshed themselves in the areas obviously set up for such things, and then they ran naked to the back wall where others stood in waterfall and foam. They washed in the falling warm water shining metallically and wonderous. Then they ran back to their hut, replacing the small bits of silken clothing previously provided by the creatures where they met Worland; and after dressing and primping and kissing each other one last time, they exited the hut.

One short frog-like creature held rings of flowers that had been strung together with some strong ivy-type vine and attempted to place the rings of flowers upon their heads. Unreachable to the frog-like creature, Jewel and Frederick bowed toward the creature as the rings were placed on their heads. Jewel's flower ring was a type of blue pansy and yellow daisy, and Frederick's a greener-leafed gold mixture, and merrily they hear music playing and songs being sung by a few lined-up creatures.

Herald to ye from far away
They hath come down to bless our ways
Hail to those who come in peace
For here ye shall find peaceful days
For all our kingdom belongs to thee
For all our kingdom belongs to thee
A pleasant convocation we hath assembled

Several verses and other songs were sung by different groups of frog-like creatures, and with bellies full, hearts filled with joy, Toby appeared and walked through the dancing crowd that came close to the two. Toby was also wearing a new circle of flowers upon his/her head as he led them toward another wall of the village.

"Where are you leading us, Toby?" Frederick asked, still half dancing to the melodies, which were growing faint as they got close to the wall.

"But we have just started to enjoy and study you all," Jewel said.

"Ah, but I have strict instructions to see you on this morning."

"Wait, Toby," Jewel said as she ran all the way back to the hut and grabbed the book and writing instrument filled with graphite. While running back from the hut, one creature pulled at Jewel's cloth around her breasts, and it fell to the ground. Jewel picked up the silken cloth, adjusted it, and tied it a bit tighter.

"There, that should stay in place," she said and, kissing one frog-like creature on the forehead, reunited with Frederick and Toby at the wall on one side of the huge cavern.

"Here we are." Toby pointed to a solid wall of granite or what appears to be a solid wall of granite. For as they both looked closer at the wall, they noticed it was a tunnel and, inside the tunnel, white walls of diamond studded and crystal lined, gold, silver, bronze, and other colorful metals. Toby pushed them inside the tunnel impatiently.

Turning back once again, they saw a figure obscured by light as the distance grew between Frederick and Jewel as the soldier on toward the next incredible even. The sound of rushing water behind the walls, the smell of bat guano and mud under their feet, soon the mud became thick under their bare feet as their feet coverings have long gone since meeting Worland of the Lake. Dimmer still grew the walls swerving and turning and seemingly downward.

"I must say 'tis rather exciting, Jewel. Not many will ever see this part of the world," Frederick said, slipping and rubbing his legs along the walls of slime and mud but still occasionally encrusted in gold and crystal, emerald, and diamonds.

"I see a light ahead, hurry," Jewel said, picking up her pace.

The two eager young adventures came to another opening and even higher ceilings dotted with sparkles of light; long straight pouring waterfalls shower down in several places around them. Frederick put his hand in on and then stepped in to wash off the mud, and Jewel followed suit in another flowing waterfall. Duck-like creatures, large mushrooms, unrecognizable flora, vegetation and odd mouse-like animals scurried around the pair.

"Jewel and Frederick," shouted a voice from above them, and they looked up. Athena and her two maidens, dressed in usual Greek god theme with ankles wrapped in golden lace, ascended upon the.

"The great Athena," Jewel said, eyes wide and clenching her book.

"Well spotted, Jewel. Greetings and welcome to the underworld." Athena landed softly next to them, her jiggling flesh catching the eye of Frederick as Jewel nudged him.

"Welcome to the underworld. Porius told us that you were taking the journey," Athena said.

"Porius gets around," Frederick stated.

"Indeed he does and said great things of you two," Athena said while her two maidens Gloria and Alexandria also bathe in the waterfalls and landed beside them.

"This is Gloria and this is Alexandria." Athena presented her two soldiers as they relaxed and bowed.

"Oh, my dear ladies, I have heard of your tales and a pleasure to meet your acquaintances," Jewel said, giving a soft tap on Frederick's shoulder to bow. They all bowed graciously toward each other, and Gloria came closer still.

"For your feet," Gloria said, dropping the two pairs of golden sandals at their feet. Quickly, they put their sandals on their drying feet.

"Thank ye, Gloriana," Frederick said, gazing into her beautiful brown eyes and watching her golden hair dry in the air.

"And for drink." Alexandria also handed them a leather satchel filled with water, and they drank.

"We want to make sure you are still in one piece because in this section of the underworld, there are on occasion several types of man-eating creatures, so we will stay with you until you are safe. Mind you it is rare that anyone gets actually eaten," Athena said to the bewildered couple.

"Eaten," Jewel said grasping her book to her breast and holding Frederick tighter.

"Well, look over there." Alexandria got between a snakelike creature with many legs and a snout showing large teeth. "We call these snappers."

"Ah yes, very scary," Jewel said as the slithering creature was shooed away by Alexandria.

"Oh, and these." Gloria pointed at a large spider the size of a cat or dog.

"Wow, well, I am bound to agree. I am glad you are here just at present, Athena. Thank ye," said Frederick.

"I smell smoke," Jewel said.

Before them, through a clearing of golden dried herbs and hedges, was a small hut with smoke coming out of the top, birch burning under a few fish roasting.

"Horan," Athena said, and they all stood quiet. "Horan."

Out from the hut smoking a long pipe was an elderly man wearing typical Grecian robes, gold sandals, long white clothes with a mixture of red, blue, green, and white stones around·his neck on a golden chain, every finger covered in rings, swirling tips on his sandals, obviously sewn on after the fact.

"Ah, Athena, a pleasure. And you must be Jewel, lovely indeed, such beautiful skin and nice lips," Horan said, walking around her and touching her here and there.

"My extreme pleasure to meet you, Lord Horan," Jewel said.

"OH MY DEAR, please, just Horan," he replied, now gazing at Frederick standing beside with a bewildered look on his face. Frederick was still only wearing a silk piece of tied material around his waist and another small cloth over his shoulder. The true image of the ancient Romans.

"Frederick, Porius said you both were easy on the eyes."

"Porius once again seems to have preceded us," Frederick said, pulling his short piece of silk in an attempt to cover his behind while Horan took a closer look.

"Welcome and come in to eat. You both must be tired, confused, mystified, and worn out after all this excitement," Horan said while leading them toward the hut. Then all at once from above them, first light, then form, then flesh entered Walters, Simon, and Leal, ascending from the sky one by one.

Leal dropped down in front of Jewel, Horan, Frederick, Athena, Gloria, and Alexandria.

"Welcome, Leal, Walters, Simon, my old friends," Horan said, hugging them all in succession as their bodies of light turned to flesh before the startled.

"Aye, may I inquire for is thine as Athena, Porius Gloria, and Alexandria?" a nervous and startled Frederick asked while Leal grabbed him, hugged him and held Frederick close.

"Porius said you were both visiting Horan," Walters said, "This is Simon,"

"A pleasure to meet you both." Simon bowed.

"Yes, we are as Athena, Frederick, and our pleasure to meet you," Leal said as his form turned to flesh and his form changed from old to young, weak to muscled. The usual black leather pants, leather straps, and sword. Simon was wearing a blue short skirt over tights and Walters his usual battle leathers, Simon a thin strip of blue silklike material, which just covered his waist while Athena, Gloria, Alexandria, and even Porius finally arrived in his whitest robes lined with golden drawings adorning each sleeve and along the bottom.

"You both must wonder why this has all been happening to you," Porius said as the light that he rode to arrive from Elysium faded, standing before the two travelers.

"Indeed, Lord Porius, and all of you. It is our greatest honor to be amongst you all," Frederick stated.

"My deepest thanks for fleeing us from the Tower and what beastly despair awaited us," Jewel said, bowing.

"We are as one, together within you," Porius said, stretching his hand out to Jewel. "Please to give me back my book."

"My lord, I have only written twenty-odd pages," Jewel replied, handing him the book.

"Blessed are thee, and this is all I need," Porius said as he quickly turned the pages and viewed them while all the others looked on.

Horan lighted a fire outside and hung some meat of what looked like very large caterpillar-type creatures, unmoving and obviously poached for the day's feast. Jewel and Frederick stood before them, and Porius led them to the lake.

"The lake before us lies earth's first single-cell creatures. Allow me to present the prokaryotes."

While he spoke, many large moths flew up from their nesting place on top of the lake. Large white and gray Boarmiini moths circled and dived around them, one landing on Jewel's shoulder. Jewel and Frederick noticed that though the moths landed and dodged Horan, Jewel, and Frederick, they were able to fly right through the others. Leal had moths flying toward his neck and seemingly fly right through, Jewel realized.

"Right through you all, it is because you are the Elysium Elite, those who have come," she paused.

"From Elysium," Frederick finished.

"Good to see you are both in sync, that's good," Porius said, walking behind them and leading them to the food and drinks. Athena had brought food and drinks from Gloria and Alexandria. Leal and the others grabbed fresh meat on plates of silver, with Horan pouring wine.

"But, Athena," Jewel said, "how doth thou drink?" Jewel stood watching the beautiful princess hold the goblet and drink from it. The liquid just disappeared.

"We have ways, my dearest Jewel. The ways of the Elite will someday be known to ye both," Athena said as she sat close to Walters and hugged him, their bodies now flesh, yet sometimes only form.

"We enjoy the flesh and are able to travel as form," Leal said handsomely while drinking down some wine.

"The journey so far has been surprising," Frederick said to Porius. All listened to his reply.

"Well, Frederick my young lad, you are going to go through the hall of stone, past the black water, and discover the way home. This is something you must do to see beyond the normal. You will both be able to understand what others are thinking. Now, music," Porius said, snapping his wand in the air, and the miniature floating band once again appeared. This time, the band members all wore white bits of cloth to cover them only in part, looking like ancient Roman or Greek gods sweeping, swiping, plucking, and blowing instruments to make a magic melody; and Simon grabbed Gloria, Porius got ahold of Alexandria, Jewel and Frederick stood and waltzed. After Leal looked around at some bizarre half human, half what seemed to be a doglike creature, he looked at Horan.

"Horan," Leal said as he reached out to Horan. "May I have this dance?"

Horan blushed and took ahold of his hand. Swirling in circles, laughing, and singing, the party ensued.

"Music, good companions, food, and drink," Porius said while spinning Alexandria and they began to float about three feet from the ground. Walters with Athena at his hand also began to float and circle.

Jewel and Frederick stopped dancing and giggling, looking to see the other couples floating in midair while dancing. Even Leal and Horan now levitated. Three feet, four feet, five, the dancing circled around them until finally they all landed, Leal and Horan splashing down into the lake.

"I thought I could hold him," Leal said, sitting in a foot or so of water. Porius stood with a hand on Frederick's shoulder, Leal and Horan still laughing and walking back to Horan's hut and going inside. The others crowded around Jewel and Frederick.

"Now, my two beautiful darlings, your journey home begins. Once you arrive, you will stay with Thomas at the cottage. You will learn to speak with water goblins, occasionally visit this kingdom below, and hold the sacred flame alive for our kind. Generations of men will call upon thee."

"My Lord Porius, can't we stay longer and visit?"

"We all must ride the light shortly as it appears there," Porius said, pointing to a circle in the high amethyst-covered ceiling as a beam of light appeared.

"Porius," Frederick said as Porius and the others walked slowly to the gradually growing beam. "Where are we now?"

"Oh, I see, actually somewhere underneath the village of Rye," Porius answered quickly. "Now listen to Horan, he will tell you what to do."

The group walked to the light, and one by one disappeared back to Elysium. Jewel, Frederick, Horan, and several other grunting creatures gazed up at the vanishing Elite's head back to Elysium.

"Beautiful, aren't they?" Jewel said as she was filled with the inner joy of being in the presence of such magnificent beings.

"Beautiful, indeed," Horan said, turning back to Jewel and Frederick, their eyes shining with the light as the sun moved its position and the beam of light disappeared, the light leaving the travelers' eyes and the focus on Horan.

"Now, come with me," Horan said, leading them to a dark tunnel beyond the lake. He pushed open a stone door. Inside attached was a raft made of wood, bound by leather and upon its sides a small brass plaque that reads, MOBILE RAFT.

"This my dears will glide you home, but be cautious because it may get rough in there. Listen," Horan said, holding his ear out toward the tunnel. Within the obsequies' blackness could be heard crashing waves and rolling rivers.

"Frederick," Jewel said.

"Yes, my dear," Frederick replied.

"Help me onboard." Jewel sat on the raft, and Frederick helped her legs up. Horan gave them a cloth to sit upon.

"Watch out for splinters," Horan said, laying his hand on Frederick's upper thigh. "Don't want ye to get stuck." They adjusted themselves, and he pushed them toward the black.

Pools of black watery waves bubbled under the raft, knocking as it went against the black stone walls that lined the tunnel. Quicker and quicker they flowed, the right side hitting the wall.

"Oh, Frederick," Jewel said, clinging to the raft as the river widened.

"Hang tight," Frederick shouted. The raft flowed quicker and quicker, swirling through pools of black.

"I cannot see anything," Jewel shouted while tightly clinging to the leather straps, which appeared to be shaking loose.

"This raft isn't the strongest, is it?" Frederick stated as they whirled back and forth, round and round.

A large black creature with lit-up white eyes rose beside them and quickly returned to the black water surroundings.

"Augh, my goodness," Jewel shouted at the startling creature, which Frederick had missed.

"What is it?"

"Before thine eyes look." Jewel grabbed Frederick's thighs and turned him to see the once again visible black creature.

"Dear me, hang on," Frederick said as the raft began to fall apart.

"The leather, it's breaking," Jewel shouted to Frederick as the raft slowly pulled apart.

"Hang on, jump on my back."

"I can swim," Jewel said as the rafts leathers ripped apart, leaving the two floating in each other's arm within the black waves.

"We shall be carried with the river, hang on to my hand," Frederick shouted and tried to grasp Jewel's hand they loosened and parted. Waves crashed over them; they rolled and went under the water and out again, swirling and swirling on an on downriver with the current.

"Jewel," Frederick cried out while several slimy river creatures slipped beneath him and slithered along his flesh.

"Here, Frederick." Jewel could be heard ahead of him farther ahead in the current.

"I am headed toward thee," he shouted, still rolling in the waves.

"Do you feel them?" Jewel shouted back to him.

"I do indeed, I do."

"Let's hope they don't bite," Jewel shouted.

"I think I felt one nibbling," he replied.

"Look ahead, LIGHT."

Soon the quickly flowing river's tunnel ended though they quickened in speed then passed a shore.

"Look." Jewel pointed at many creatures sitting on chairs, watching them as they passed and waving.

"Hurrah!" the crowd shouted as they sat in much amusement watching the two tumble and roll passing them. One creature was turtle-like, another cat-like, several naked mortals lying along the shore waving to them as they passed.

Green lights and purple hues aligned the paths with foliage upon foliage of many remembered styles of glowing plant life surrounding them and the river ending at a sandy yet rocky shore. Clothes long lost, they lay upon the shore naked as the day they were brought into the world.

"Those plants look familiar," gasping, Frederick said as he crawled on his hands and knees until he lay on his stomach just breathing.

"I think we are back," Jewel said, lying beside him. She stood up.

"I have sand in everywhere," she said, "and I need to wear something." Jewel grabbed a vine thick with ivy and wrapped her waist and upper body with a few vines, and Frederick followed suit.

They walked and walked along the river until they reached a stone wall.

"Jewel, aye say," Thomas could be heard shouting down from above.

"Are we glad to see you!" Frederick shouted back.

"Stand thee clear," Thomas said and threw down a handmade ladder. They climbed out and stood with Thomas wrapped in ivy.

"Nice clothes, did you have a nice trip?" Thomas said as Parthenia and Grendle came up to meet them.

"Food awaits you," Parthenia said, ushering them back to the warmth of the cottage.

"Welcome home," Thomas said. "Welcome home."

The next morning when Jewel and Frederick awoke from their chamber at the back of the house, breakfast was ready and books out by the dozen. Thomas greeted them with a big smile, and even though he was half clear and half human, eventually he came to flesh.

"Good morrow, my splendid young students." He handed them both books made of thick leather and ancient writing on each page.

"What's this, Thomas?" Frederick asked while scratching his head and eating fresh bacon from his platter set before him by Parthenia.

"Book of spells and potions," Thomas said promptly.

"How wonderful," said Jewel, wrapping her hair behind her neck and tying the long golden locks with a ribbon made of blue silk.

Frederick opened his book, and within it on the first page reads,

"Oh yes," Thomas said. "Now that ye have both been through the underworld, Porius has informed me that ye shall both have the spark to do magic."

"War Water Spell," Frederick said, reading from the book. "First, write name of adversary on strip of brown paper."

Thomas stopped him. "No, let's not get ahead of ourselves. In fact, this spell was given to Henry the Fifth at Agincourt, which proved to be very successful."

"I have often wondered about that day and if our world assisted," Jewel said through the side of her mouth, ignoring her breakfast and skimming through the book.

"Maybe we should all eat first and the lesson will begin shortly. You both need your strength, and I need you both clean. So off to the river to wash and scrub."

"But the water is freezing," Jewel said.

"Well, I have just the spell to make you not feel the cold," Thomas said while turning to a page of water spells.

"Let me see, yes indeed, this will do it," Thomas said, pulling out his wand and hovering over Frederick first. "Lemon squeals and donkey heals, give thy the warmth to heal."

Then over Jewel he read, waving his wand, "Girls of cold and ready or bold, make thee not feel the cold."

"Seriously, my good Thomas, you think that will—" Frederick started to say and then looked at his hands.

"My gracious, look I am glowing! Quick, Jewel, to the river," Frederick said, grabbing her hand, and they both ran to the edge of the river, remove their clothes, and jumped in, splashing, laughing, swimming, and washing. Then they came back to the cottage, Thomas greeting them at the front garden. The mushrooms were sprouting all around them and in many colors, flowers opening, deer playing, squirrels rushing to and fro, the bios of insects beneath in their early morning routines all together.

"It worked, Thomas, it worked!" Frederick said, standing naked before Thomas and looking at his body dry very quickly. Then Jewel and Frederick dressed in their nicest clothes to begin the lessons.

Franklin circled overhead with a watchful eye.

CHAPTER 13

Frederick came out first dressed in roman a short skirt revealing his muscular thighs and feet bound in golden sandals. Jewel came out in a short skirt that matches the gold-trimmed lace of Athena, Gloria, or Alexandria, her upper body gently laced with golden depictions of tulips and daisies strewn together by some gentle hand.

"These clothes are beautiful, Thomas, thank you," Jewel said as she gazed into the pensive to see her reflection.

"Thank Parthenia and Grendle for it was their steady hands that darned the trim, and the fit is perfect, such talent."

"Thank ye, Parthenia and Grendle," Jewel and Frederick both said as they ran into the kitchen excited to be wearing such beautiful clothes.

"Oh, my dears," Grendle said while Parthenia scrubbed the morning dishes. "I just would not wear them into town, they may be a bit revealing for common folk. In the wardrobe, you will find better-suited clothes for the village."

"I say those as well, and they also look splendid," Jewel said as Frederick hugged Parthenia from behind and then Grendle and Jewel gave them both a squeeze as well.

"My word, you both did turn out well," Parthenia said, drying her hands and smiling.

"The beauty of youth and the happiness of the young," Grendle said.

"We are so glad to have you and just let us know what you need and call our names and we shall appear," Parthenia said as she untied her apron, sets it on the counter and then snapping her fingers, they both vanished before them, leaving the kitchen sparkling clean. They both run back out to Thomas.

"We love this place, Thomas," Frederick said excitedly.

"We just saw Parthenia and Grendle appear or disappear right before us," Jewel said, rubbing her hands and holding her book.

"Goodness in the extreme," Thomas said. "I think a little morning music." He waved his wand, and the floating band appeared, playing a flute alone on the stage a happy little tune. Franklin came and sat on a branch chewing a large worm.

"Psephomancy is the art of divining with pebbles. Mark these pebbles to make your pebbles to indicate your choices," Thomas said, handing them both a bunch of different-colored pebbles and a writing quill and ink blotter. "Then take the bag and shake the pebbles inside the bag, then we will pour them out onto the floor and begin the art of psephomancy."

They both wrote on the pebbles and did as instructions required; then after a few shakes in the bag, they released the drawstrings and poured the pebbles on the outdoor wooden table while a very curious deer leaned over Thomas's shoulder to watch the rolling stones. Thomas pushed the deer back and so the deer walked behind Jewel and leaned over her shoulder gazing at the pebbles.

"Well, good morrow to thee, you are a cute one," Jewel said, petting the deer's head, and it blinked its large brown eyes at her and rubbed her neck against Jewel then backed away.

"I believe the doe likes thee," Thomas said.

"Indeed, and a sweet doe you are as well," Frederick said as a larger buck with horns bowed his head over Frederick. "Well hello, you're a big one," Frederick said, looking at the buck somewhat startled.

"The animals have no fear from humans in the garden of the cottage, my friends. In fact, some of these spells will ask for assistance from several animals, and in time you will get to know them all personally."

Franklin jumped into the air and started circling again with a few of his other friendly ravens circling to keep an eye on the grounds.

"Next we will learn the Dirt Anti-Stalker spell, which is done by grinding graveyard dirt or dirt where someone has been buried below. This spell will come in handy when you go out to the village of farther," Thomas said opening the book to page 2.

"This sounds quite practical," Jewel said while Frederick followed along.

For the next few days, Jewel and Frederick practiced with oils, feathers, even powwow protective spells with honeysuckle. They planted herbs, flowers, tended to the animals, and learned a whole new way of farming, living, loving, and soon they even learned some Latin.

In a few days during Frederick's and Jewel's bath in the warm waters of the river and as the water goblins circled below them looking up to watch their bodies against the sun rays, Thomas came running down to the water's edge. "Come out, come quickly, we have visitors."

Jewel and Frederick swam to shore and threw on their Roman or Greek-style clothes trimmed in gold and stared upward to a colored light ball. Porius appeared, glowing in multicolors and landing on the grassy bit by the front door of the cottage. Jewel and Frederick ran toward him, and Thomas was filled with glee.

"My friends, my heart goes out to thee. Come for I have brough thee gifts," Porius said and handed them their first wands. "These wands have been made in Elysium and once used by Athena during the revolt in Roma for you, Jewel." Porius handed the wand to Jewel and turned to Frederick.

"Thank ye, Porius, many thanks indeed," Jewel said, holding the wand firmly.

"Here my boy," Porius said, handing over the second wand to Frederick. "Use it well and listen to it when it speaks."

"Wands speak?" Frederick said, shocked.

"Most assuredly they speak. You will hear them without sound, and you will hear them with sound," Porius said while Thomas poured them all peach nectar in goblets.

"Tasty," Porius said, now sitting and sipping from his goblet. "It is so good to be home."

"Will thy be staying a while?" Thomas asked excitedly.

"Yes, in fact, maybe a month or so," Porius said.

"Your room is prepared as always."

"Parthenia and Grendle," Porius asked. "Still around, are they?"

Parthenia appeared, and Grendle was tying her apron behind her. "Here and present, Lord Porius," Parthenia said.

"So good, my dearest Parthenia and Grendle, I am most pleased beyond measure."

"How many for dinner, my lord?" Parthenia asked.

While she asked, a splash could be heard from the river, and up popped the two water goblins with arms of fish, running toward the cottage.

"Harold and Clarice," Porius said. "My two favorite water goblins."

Harold and Clarice bowed to Porius, dropped their load of fish by the front door, and quickly ran back to the river and hid below the depths.

"You have to love their style," Porius said.

"This is the first time I have seen them though Thomas has informed us of their presence," Jewel stated.

"Yes, they are quite shy," Thomas said, taking the fish indoors.

"Well, it looks like fish is on the menu. Now let's see you both hold your wands out," Porius said as they began practicing the flick and wave, stammer and blast. Hours passed and spell after spell was rehearsed, learned, and memorized. Days passed, weeks passed, and with the heat of summer upon them, it finally came time for Porius to depart. Before he departed, back to Elysium, he gave them their first mission. Porius stood before them and raised his hands in a loud clap. He shouted, "The underworld."

Jewel, Frederick, Thomas, and Porius fell from their chairs, and one by one they fell to the shaking earth. The ground swallowed them up, and then they all stood naked upon the underworld, lying next to a pond of pure blue sparkling. Porius shouted even louder as the earth rattled around them. Pieces of wall fell to the ground. One large piece of amethyst was close to hitting Frederick as he put his hand back into the water.

"Swim all of you, and search for a light under the water. If you see it, grab it and bring it back here to me."

They all jumped into the water, and the clear blue surrounded them. With eyes open, they watched odd fish and creatures mostly curious as to what these humans sought.

"Light of Elysium!" Porius shouted and raised his wand. A bright white and golden light filled the chamber, lighting the lake's blue waters to a white azure.

Thomas saw the underwater light, which appeared to be held by a small nude youth, possibly male but feminine in the extreme with large black eyes and pale white skin. Thomas pointed to the figure and waved at Frederick to retrieve the light. Frederick quickly went up to the surface for air and once again descended. Swimming with all his might, he came face-to-face with the youth of pale white skin and put out his hand toward the glowing object.

"Tell Porius this is his gift from us," the youth said as water bubbles came from his mouth and he handed the stone over to Frederick. Frederick clasped it and began to swim back to shore. Jewel and Thomas lay on the shore watching the water bubble above the spot Frederick was last seen, but alas, no Frederick could be seen.

Porius lowered his wand, and the light dimmed as the three stared out toward the quiet lake.

"Where art thou, Frederick, where art thou?" Jewel yelled and began to cry.

"Worry not, my child, he will come," Porius said, eagerly awaiting. But below the lake's surface, Frederick was enraptured in flesh to flesh with the youth as the underwater being held him tight and tried to take Frederick further below. Surprised, Frederick by this time was almost out of breath and put his head up for a moment out of the lake, gasped a breath, and was quickly pulled back under the sea, the youth wrapping his milky white arms around the waist and gripping tightly to Frederick.

"Come with me, come with me," the bubbling words came from the youth as he began kissing every inch of Frederick's backside in quick succession.

"Come with me, come down to the bottom with thyself." The youth grabbed tighter, but Frederick pulled away and the youth released. Frederick looked down at his captor and aggressor, but the look on the youth's face as he looked up toward Frederick seemed sad and sullen. Frederick slowly went to the top, and the youth fell deeper and deeper into the abyss. Frederick, feeling a sort of loss, gasped a breath of air and put his head back under the water to view the youth, his long black hair waving around his falling skin in a sensual display. Frederick, in a state of arousal, watched the youth fade. In pity and some type of unusual feeling, Frederick waved goodbye and swam back to shore. In his hand was a stone no longer shining, and he handed it to Porius.

"Thank you, Frederick. Now wasn't that amusing?" Porius said while putting the stone back into his pocket. "Now let's return."

Porius raised his arms and shouted, "The surface!" All were magically strewn through the earth as it opened up around each of them and seemingly spit them out onto the surface of the earth among the bios. Slugs, beetles, and ladybugs crawled away from each of the traveling participants. Porius wiped his robes. "I must say it's a lot more dirt than I remember."

"You could have warned us, Porius," Frederick said, lying naked beside Jewel and Thomas.

"Porius, why do your clothes stay on and ours are ripped from our bodies?" Jewel said while redressing into her white and gold skirt.

"There is a lily and fig spell that we will teach you. It will make you able to do the same," Porius said. "But we did not have time to teach you that spell, plus it is very difficult to handle."

"Why did you need me to get the stone?" Frederick said.

"You can't expect me to get my robes wet before I travel back to Elysium."

"Well, possibly not," Frederick said, smiling, and Jewel laughed with them all.

"I also thought it nice that you had a short adventure. Did you see some wonderful creatures under the waters of the lake?" Porius asked.

"Yes, many," Jewel answered.

"I met a beautiful youth, male I believe, but female in a peculiar sexuality," Frederick explained.

"Marco," Porius said. "Marco is a most beautiful creature who seeks, well, who seeks the company of another, but it is difficult for him at present."

"He seemed sad," Frederick said.

"I am afraid that Marco was taken to the tower, tortured, and was one of the Lyons of Cambridgeshire, many years ago and the King through him to the water grave as example to ward off others from doing spells."

Porius said, shaking his head, "Very sad indeed, he was a beautiful youth."

The sun dipped into the black of night, and after they had feasted, laughed, and drank, Porius said his goodbye, and on a wave of light, he returned to Elysium. Figures passed and shadows grew, and Porius was surrounded by light and time. He had sickness in the pit of his stomach and was nauseous until finally arriving safely in Elysium and greeted by a nude Leal, they walked back to Porius's newest home in the Shadow Hills. Shadow Hills was a deep dark forest strewn with fairies, elves, the occasional dragon, unicorns, and water goblins, animals, hundreds of types of bird, and fowl-type creatures that may only be found on Elysium. The walls of this palace were grand, and Athena bathed among her maidens while Walters gazed upon her and Simon gazed upon the maidens and Porius gazed at them all among the lime green-and-cream-colored walls some thirty feet tall with long elegant windows of stained glass, silk, and satin green-and-purple draperies tied by golden thread. Several other creatures walked among them all, and music could be heard being played by an even larger floating bandstand of musicians than the floating bandstand back at the cottage. Here lay the unusual, the different beings of night among the beings of day, creatures of many worlds and many green-zone planets that visited Elysium from far-flung worlds and galaxies.

Thomas prepared tomorrow's course of Turkish divinations and was preparing wax from the beehive kept from a neighboring farmer slash beekeeper and a molded figure of a man sitting on the outdoor table. A cloth and a dish of water were waiting as Jewel, Frederick, and Parthenia stepped outdoors.

"Today, we will study divination and will explore psychic vision in all its glory," Thomas said for all three sitting around the table.

"I want to sit on this class, if you don't mind," Parthenia said.

"Why not? The more the merrier, and if it is something that interests you, by all means."

"Thank ye, Thomas." Parthenia sat, her large arms lying upon the table and her face beaming with interest.

"Now first we make a figure of a person we believe to be the person of interest, and note that this method goes back thousands of years to the Egyptians and pre-Egyptian where they once hailed Anubis using this method. What you don't want to do is bring Anubis forth because that could be dangerous so make sure that you wax image looks like the person you are willing to manipulate. Then take the wand and touch it to your forehead and close your eyes, then think of the person made of wax, hold the water bowl over the statue, then bring the water to you, and cover your head with the cloth while peering into the water bowl," Thomas said while acting this out.

"Interesting indeed," said Jewel. "But the figure is of you, Thomas."

"Yes, and the likeness is very good," Frederick said, Parthenia trying to keep up.

"Correct, correct, because you will all see me in your bowl and will be able to tell what I am doing.

On the day Richard came home early and on the night a man claimed to be Eros, Jewel said to herself while glancing into her water bowl.

On the day Richard came home early and on the night a man claimed to be Eros, Frederick thought to himself while quietly tucked under his towel and peering int the water.

"Until a man named Richard doth what?" Parthenia said, scratching her head.

Then they all removed their cloths and looked at Thomas with a puzzled expression.

"Well . . ." Jewel, Frederick, and Parthenia now listened carefully and spoke slowly the words they heard in the water. Thomas eagerly awaited their words.

Parthenia remained silent, but Jewel and Frederick began together, "On the day Richard came home early and on the night a man claimed to be Eros." Then they both exhaled greatly.

"We did it," said Jewel, smiling at Thomas.

"You see, it wasn't that difficult," Thomas said, full of glee.

"I knew it was something about Richard, but I bound my mind could pick it up," Parthenia said as she stood and headed back toward the kitchen. "I shall prepare a nice evening meal. You both are quicker than I which I do so admire. Keep up the good work," Parthenia said, scratching her hip and waddling back into the cottage.

Deer, rabbit, fawn, and toad all played in the garden of the cottage. Flowers wet with rain dripped, and the sky opened to reveal light, and the peaceful wind steadily blew through the grounds, a true testament to the animal kingdom since they were so unconcerned with religions and ideas, which put each class of individuals above others in the mazelike goings-on of organized groupings of people, from Roma to Paris to Londinium and soon beyond. At least until all the playful natural animals still existed, there will always be freedom of mind and thought. For the future may cage, farm, and feast on animals, they will never be able to take over their minds.

"You see, this could easily come in handy," Thomas said.

"Well yes, they have good countenance upon thee, Thomas," Frederick said as they kept practicing the spell and the evening came closer. More time was spent gardening and planting then drawing, then practicing mathematics and Latin.

"Building your minds every day, you two shalt rule the area," Thomas said at dinner, Franklin perched out on the window ledge under thatch.

The black raven had long befriended the inhabitants of the cottage, his black eye and keen hearing alerted to the bushes in the moonlight. Franklin fluffed his wings and squawked louder and louder, but whatever was rustling the bushes stepped out and the noise of Franklin's alarm could clearly be heard from the indoor participants. First, Thomas came out, and now flesh held his comet of burning embers toward the shadowy figure.

"To whom do I have the pleasure?" a startled Thomas inquired.

———

Jewel and Frederick stepped out, and Frederick shouted, "Who is it, Thomas?" But only a growl from the large black figure could be heard.

The bushes again rattled, and the figure headed back into the branches and bramble of thick forest.

"Come, Frederick, let us follow this creature," Thomas shouted back to Frederick. "Jewel, you stay behind."

"I am unsure of this, Thomas," Frederick said, cowering. "It seemed quite large and formidable, shouldn't we wait until morning?"

"No, we must follow it. Come and come quickly," Thomas said, waving Frederick to his side.

"I am getting armed just in case," Frederick said as he picked up a wooden rake that was lying about from his earlier meanderings in the garden while planting tulip bulbs earlier.

"Thomas, don't forget, I am still mortal and can be injured."

"Oh, don't he such a child. Plus, if this creature was able to enter the grounds, it must be magical. Now stay close."

"Be careful, my loves," Jewel said as she wrapped herself and stayed by the front door.

No sound was heard, and at the moment Thomas and Frederick reached the edge of the forest, a scream was heard.

"Thomas, it is here," Jewel said as the large creature in black grabbed Jewel and took her back inside the cottage, slammed the door, leaving Thomas and Frederick outside. Inside, the creature was merely a man covered in black robes and speaking an odd language.

"It'll be fine, lady, it'll be fine." The man let loose of her. Thomas, Frederick, and Franklin all came in. Franklin flew at the large man and then perched himself on the windowsill staring at the now-seated figure.

"I mean ya's nay harm," the man said.

"Who art though? Out with ye!" Thomas said.

The man threw off his hood and robe and was dressed in the finest purples and green, a family crest of a knight and raven on his chest, and his features seemingly changing continuously before them from young to old and back again.

"I am captive of the forest, and my ageless body is rapidly changing as you can see. I was sent here by Porius who said you can assist me," the man said.

"Well, well, well, well, this does pose a problem, but I am Thomas, this is Frederick—"

Thomas was interrupted by the man. "An' thee must be Jewel. Porius said you can help me." The man had bright-green eyes, long black stringy hair, dry mouth, and was sweaty.

"Here, have some water," Jewel said, giving him refreshment.

"Thank ye," he replied, gulping the liquid, his face ever changing from young to old and old to young.

"Is it painful?" Frederick asked.

"Nay, I feel nothing only when I look at a reflection, I see the ever-changing ages. I was practicing the spell of youth, and this was what happened."

"Where is thou from, the speech is different to ours?" Jewel asked.

"Sounds like he is from the Americas to me," Thomas said inquiringly.

"That I is, from Virginia to be precise. My family settled there when I was none and I was practicing the spell with my brother in Virginia and he was injured, and all had thought I had killed him. I escaped and took a ship toward England. Porius visited my onboard ship with another man, name of Leal."

"Oh Leal, yes, a good acquaintance of ours," Frederick replied.

"You are very kind, all of you, but Leal and Porius sent me here with these instructions." The man drank more water.

"I be Martin, Martin Allensworth."

"Well, welcome Martin," said Thomas. "I must admit I've not seen such a curse go wrong, and I must say your face is amazing."

"My body as well," Martin said, opening his shirt and showing the wriggling skin go from wrinkles to flat youthful skin then back again in a perpetual uncertainty.

"We knew of some Allensworths," Jewel stated.

"The Allensworth and the Peeks live side by side in Dunmo by the ford in Essex by Suffolk. Maybe they are relatives of thee," Frederick said.

"Might be, but surely I cannot be seen like this. This state of revolving ages is quite tiresome."

"Porius told you to come and see us," Thomas said, pacing back and forth. "The only reason that Porius could not treat you onboard the ship is that something must be here which will cure you."

"I do hope so," Matins said. Now standing beside Thomas as Thomas thumbed through book after book.

"I have it," Jewel said. "The stone that Porius had Frederick fetch from the underworld, where is it?"

"I believe Porius took it with him," Thomas said.

"Nay, he did not taketh the stone in fact, look," Jewel said, pointing to a small box on the mantle. Written on the boss, it said "FOR THE CHANGING OF TIME."

"Perfect," Frederick said as he grabbed the box and opened it, holding the stone of bronze in color yet rough like sandstone or granite.

"Try holding the stone," Thomas said and motioned Frederick to hand the stone to Martin. He did so, and Martin's hands clasped tightly around the stone. He began to shake and quiver, falling to the floor, and began some convulsions and screaming.

"Leave him," Thomas said. "Look, it's working."

Martin rolled to and fro. "Ay, ay," said Martin, very placably. "You all do me the greatest honor. You know, Jewel, I think I love the."

Jewel gazed down upon him, her hair hanging over his retching body, squirming back and forth. "You don't know me," she whispered above him.

"He hath not passed through the complete phase," Thomas said, watching the spectacle of the squirming Martin. Now ageless, protruding lings from changing hair color systematically changing from white to black and back again.

"My dear Thomas, when will this poor fool stop? He appears to be in agony," Frederick said.

"His agony may endure for some time to come," Thomas said while the now-naked body of Martin lay squirming on the stone floor.

"We may as well just leave him and keep an eye on him," Jewel said, standing back now just a step closer the fire.

"This poor being," Frederick said.

Martin rolled around for at least another twenty-five minutes until finally he stopped and was silent, motionless, and rather handsome. Long pitch-black hair, high cheekbones, bare of hair covering his muscular breast, he awakened.

"Jewel," he said, looking up at Jewel again looking down upon his naked body.

Frederick, Thomas, and now Parthenia and Grendle looked out from around the corner of the kitchen door.

"Handsome," Parthenia said, bringing him some ale.

"Lovely," said Grendle as she gazed down at Martin.

Age about forty, rugged, muscle on every crevasse of his features, black hair, green eyes, he stood at least six foot eight inches tall. So tall in fact that he bent down to enter any of the doorways. Where he was once knotted, he was now of perfect figure and obviously very well endowed in every meaning of the word. Even Frederick blushed and quickly threw a robe over Martin.

"There then, you take it quite easy now. How doth thou feel?" asked Frederick.

"Much better, thankee, Frederick I believe," Martin said, standing over a foot taller than Frederick and at least two feet over Thomas and the others.

"Thank all of ee, I have not been myself for several months, and it feels grand I am bound to say."

"I would like to welcome you officially to the cottage, Martin," Thomas said as he began setting the table for a feast.

"Well, finally I can do what I need to do in England, and that be no small matter, I can tell ye," Martin said as he stood and walked out of the cottage and back toward the woods.

Outside, Jewel shouted after him, "Where is thou going?"

"I will be right back," he shouted back at them. Thomas, Frederick, and Jewel stared at them by the front porch, and his robe came off as he walked bare naked into the forest. Trembling with emotion, Jewel was nervous that she would never behold this beauty again even though Frederick was green with envy and becoming extremely jealous of this beautiful shape, face, and demeanor that surrounds this visitor in mystery.

"Ah, it is as I thought, a perfect fit," Martin said as he stepped out from the forest completely dressed in black leathers and cap, red vest and blank-and-white pantaloons, black buckle, silver-colored buckles of course, and even a bracelet and necklace that now adorn Martin.

"Please to excuse my previous appearance and accept my deepest apologies for my behavior."

"Appearance was all right by me," Parthenia said, giggling to Grendle as they cackled, peeled onions, plucked a chicken, and shredded some carrots.

Jewel sighed gently as she held out the pastry toward Martin, his white perfectly aligned teeth and smiling green eyes melting her soul as she looked over toward Frederick. Her eyes said to Frederick without speaking, *Adorable, isn't he?* The secret thought was transferred to Frederick's mind, and Frederick himself looked on Martin who gave the same sexy smile in Frederick's direction. A gaze was met by Frederick to Martin, Martin to Frederick, Jewel to both, and Frederick to both; they all smiled during dinner.

The next morning, the sky was filled with a downpour not unusual by inclement and most conducive for spending a day indoors and chatting over past experiences. Martin was saddened to hear the tale of Jewel and Frederick's past, the escape from the tower, and loss of their parents. He piqued a particular interest in the underworld.

"If it was not raining, I would like to go through the underworld myself," Martin said, and at that moment, the earth trembled, the cottage shook, and Parthenia and Grendle came rushing into the main room.

"We will be going now, but back tomorrow," Grendle said as the aprons lay on the floor after being dropped by the disappearing pair of house maidens.

"Tomorrow?" Thomas exclaimed. "What about supper?"

The house kept shaking, and the ground opened up beneath Martin.

"He mentioned the underworld, I guess he will see it," Jewel said, standing back as the floor opened and swallowed Martin before their eyes.

"I suppose he will visit the underworld," Frederick said, holding on to Jewel.

The ground became solid, and the shaking stopped, leaving Thomas, Jewel, and Frederick staring at an empty space where Martin stood only moments ago.

"He really should not have mentioned the underworld," Thomas said as he nonchalantly sat to sip ale with Frederick and Jewel. "But I am quite sure he will have an excellent journey."

"He'll be fine," Jewel said, shrugging her shoulders and squeezing Thomas's hand with her right, and Frederick with her left. All gazed upon the heap of clothes that once adorned Martin. "He will get these when he returns."

CHAPTER 14

Below and magically cast through the earth's crust in the throat of mother earth, Martin flowed between spaces and experienced a loneliness that few men ever know. Landing on the ground among unfamiliar surrounds of fluorescent plants, many types of creatures, Horan stood beside his nude and muscular appearance.

"Welcome," Horan said.

Porius, Leal, Walters, and Simon appeared, surrounding naked Martin and Horan.

"This is Martin Allensworth, I told you," Porius said, pointing down on the naked Martin lying on the floor in confusion.

"I must be dreaming," Martin said as he lay flat on the mossy ground, insects scattering around him.

The caterpillars were large, the butterflies huge, the fireflies many, and Porius lingered over Martin.

"Martin, come to, come to, awaken."

"Porius, I thought I was dreaming," Martin said, confused looking up at the miraculous plant life, animals, creatures, Horan, Porius in his usual white robe and bejeweled staff, Leal, Walters, Simon wearing battle leathers. Martin stood and covered his private parts, which Leal had already taken notice of its size.

"I seem to have left my clothes behind," Martin said, blushing.

"Horan, if you please," Walters said, waving his arm toward Martin.

"Oh yes, of course, of course. Let the fairies dress him," Horan said, clapping his hands, and three small flying fairies together holding a blue piece of silk, which they cover his waist with and which he tied in a knot.

"You spoke of the underworld, and your wish has been granted," Leal said and let out a full load of laughter as the others joined in.

"It is commonly known that companionship is made in dark places. We just came to see you off," Walters said.

"Good luck, Martin," Leal said, patting him on the shoulder as he stood tying the blue silk around his waist nice and tight though the piece of blue did not cover everything but was comforting just the same.

"Good luck," said Simon.

"Yes, you will follow the tunnels and meet the creatures. Take ye this pad and writing tool and write what you see and then return once you have reached the other side."

Martin's journey began, and alone he traveled the same path as Jewel and Frederick. Once more a traveler takes the path and once more the beautiful youth of the lake falls in love; and this time, it worked.

The next morning out in the garden of the cottage, Thomas read, allowing Frederick and Jewel, the deer, and other animals to graze, meander, and play in the garden.

Forest below the ground, forests above the ground, all that we see.
Chains of other worlds unchain thee
Folds of time and space, light, purple and green
Chains of spiritualism set thy free
Bones of long departed and tombs run wild
As departed souls join infinity

"Here we have the writings of Alibastor Fraun, to whom I had the most delighted pleasure of meeting while in the company of Porius."

"He was from France, I believe," said Jewel.

"Indeed he was. Oh, a great wizard he was as well," Thomas said. "I've heard he was by the side of Leonardo de Vinci at the Chapel of Saint Hubert in 1519 and transported his form, not flesh, to Elysium, where I am sure he rests today, as many great artists currently reside."

"It does beg to wonder and hope that once we die and our bodies cast into the waves, we will also meet at Elysium." Frederick exhaled.

"We will now make a hole about three feet deep and contain within it a few hair follicles, nail clippings, and possibly some urging of the mind. We shall put our essence into the earth and wait for the sun to go down, then we will practice the—oh, and walnuts because after all, it is the walnut security and protection well-wishing spell," Thomas said, digging a small hole just beside a fresh-growing bushel of thyme.

"Here are some walnuts," Jewel said, tossing two walnuts into the pit.

"What happens at dusk?" Frederick asked.

"We will wish Martin well and a safe return," Thomas replied.

"Excellent," Jewel said.

As for Martin, once he met Worland of the Lake and ascended below to retrieve another bright start under the surface of the lake, the beauty of the feminine youth within the lake was too difficult a magnet for his manhood to resist. After they had copulated and swum in the waters of the underworld, Martin was finally able to depart, and once again his nude body was sent up to the surface within the garden. All rejoiced at his presence; and once he had dressed, eaten, and laughed with Jewel, Thomas, Frederick, Parthenia, and all the animals of the garden, they rested and dreamed of far-off shores, Porius, and Elysium. Owls made their noises among the other finely hidden birds of the night, rain slowed, and the water goblins delivered their nightly load.

Tales of the underworld were remembered as the new band of friends discussed the coming day's journey for Martin as he departed one sunny day. Bag of food over his shoulder, he waved them farewell, tears in his eyes as he lived his wondrous friends as he headed for home. Once he reached Portsmouth, he boarded a ship that took him far across the Atlantic Ocean to Virginia where his trials and tribulations were only just starting. Martin never wondered east of Essex to visit the Allensworth family and bound for home.

Jewel, Thomas, Frederick, and occasionally Porius learned, read, studied, and examined the potions, spells, herb lessons, alchemy, and nature.

Knowledge lies waiting for us as it sleeps, just waiting for an awakening and most probably cures, which will mend thousands of ailments, light which may be traveled, storms to fight, and battles to win awaiting us all.

Edward the Fourth allied with Burgundy and all seemed well with the world, excepting the rebel forces here and there who occasionally popped up fighting small battles over lands, religion, or the usual fight over title. Frederick and Jewel became better and better and herbal remedies to assist the ill, magical spells too invoke inner spirits, gardening, farming and even embroidery and music. Their skills occasionally lead them to visit Hastings as on this occasion. Franklin came squawking with a few fellow ravens one winter morning.

"Wake up, Wake ups, help is need in the village, help is needed," Franklin shouted waking the sleepy occupants inside the cottage, Thomas prepares a quick breakfast while Jewel and Frederick dress in their warmest clothes. Outside the sky black with rain clouds but holding back an impending downpour.

"William Hastings from the house of York is ill," Thomas said.

"Influenza?" Jewel asked.

"Indeed, something most unpleasant I grant thee," Thomas replied, still packing his bags.

"Do we have the rye seed and candles?" Frederick asked.

"Yes, and good memory, Frederick," Thomas said, rushing them out the door and on to two white horses. They rode out of the safety of the cottage grounds and beyond the protective safety of the area. They finally reached the edge of Hastings, and small cottages lined the coast, a large ship is anchored with men working to refurnish bread sellers and fishmongers setting up their morning stalls. Jewel dismounted at the first large home, and the guards allowed her in while Frederick tend to the horses then followed, carrying bags.

"Lord Hastings, my baron, we have come to tend to thee," Jewel said.

"I am Frederick, and this is Jewel," Frederick said, laying his bags beside the seemingly dying courtier of Henry the Fourth.

"My lordships—" Jewel began.

"Oh, I am not bothered by all that royal clap trap, young woman. Can you save me?" Hastings blustered and shouted while he rolled away from them and vomited a bit then rolled back. "As you can see, I am very ill and I shall reward thee handsomely."

"Yes, we can help you. First, we need some hot water to wipe you down," Frederick said.

Hastings shouted at his servant, an elderly woman rushing with a hot pale of water, and they cleaned him while another servant wearing blue silks raised the heat in the fire by adding more logs.

Smoke billowed from the fire, making Hastings round figure cough. "Don't use green wood, you will smoke up the place, you fool."

"Now you must relax," Jewel said as she mixed rye and oils in the mortar and pestle, reaching out to Frederick who handed her a lit candle.

"Don't let my wife see you doing this. She doesn't go for the witchy stuff and won't allow the name of Porius in the house," Hastings said.

"We understand, now quickly drink this down. All of it," Frederick said as he watched out for her ladyship.

Hastings gags sips, winces, and said, "Oh, that was awful."

"Now, close your eyes," Frederick said, holding the candle over William Hastings's head.

"What is going on in here?" Lady Mary shouted as she entered the room, Frederick pouring hot melted wax on Williams' forehead.

"Witchcraft, oh no, not in here!" Mary said, rushing toward them.

"Hold thy tongue, woman!" William shouted. Mary knocked Jewel aside.

"Thee shalt not perform such—" Mary started to say when a soldier of Henry the Fourth grabbed her and carried her away.

"Good, take the bitch to the far end of the house and lock her there," William shouted with eyes still closed and the hot wax dripping down his cheeks, Frederick wiping his eyelids so the wax does not penetrate the eyes.

"My face feels hard as stone," William said.

"It is just the wax, my lord. Soon we will peel it off and you will be on the road to recovery," Frederick said, finishing his duty.

Jewel mixed another batch of rye, honey, and a few other herbs. "I shall leave this potion with thee and to take every four hours until gone, one spoonful. I shall even leave the spoon."

"Thank ye both and here, take this as payment and blessed are thee both. You come highly recommended by the way."

"Porius?" Frederick asked.

"Indeed, I believe his spirit occasionally visits the royals with guidance," William Hastings said while he rolled over to vomit a bit more into a wooden bucket, which was quickly removed by the elderly servant and taken away as another servant brought a fresh pail.

"Now, lots of bed rest for the next few days and you will make a full recovery," Jewel said, grabbing the large blue jewel given to her by Hastings. "Thank thee."

"You're both most attractive. I expected wort-covered, long-nosed hunchbacks or something revolting," Hasting said in amusement. "Thank you both and I shall recommend thee to the king."

"No need for that," said a voice who just entered from the front.

"Your Highness." Jewel bowed to King Henry as he entered and rushed to William's side, patting Frederick and Jewel on their heads.

"So you must be Jewel and thy Frederick," Henry said, giving them each gold coins. "I was hoping to meet you both, and hath thy helped my friend William?"

"Indeed, we have, Your Highness. He will make a full recovery," Jewel said, Frederick amazed at his good fortune in meeting the king of England.

"It is a great honor, Your Highness," Frederick said, bowing.

"My dearest boy, we need more like thee," Henry said as William began to snore. "He is off."

"We must peel the wax, Your Highness," Jewel said as they bothered peeling the wax from Hastings's head and threw it into the fire.

"Thy wax, take thee sickness and never return," Jewel said as she cast the sparkling wax into the raging fire.

"Truly amazing," King Henry said.

"I hope you will both do me the honor of dining with me at Dover in a fortnight," King Henry asked.

"It would be an honor," Frederick replied.

Back at the cottage, Jewel and Frederick told the amazing tale to Thomas and gave him the jewel and gold coins.

"Thomas, these finances will feed many families for years," Jewel said, holding her large jewel in her hand glistening in the glow of the fire.

"Indeed, it shall," Thomas said. "I am so proud of you both and an invitation to dinner. Most overwhelming. I will embroider you both the most beautiful clothes for the occasion. Black with gold trim and a serpent to match King Henry's, it will be the time of your lives."

That night, Jewel and Frederick dreamed of dancing, feasting, and mixing with court as a guest of the king; and the excitement lasted for days. Two other villagers got sick, and Franklin alerted them. Out they went to treat the farmers and foresters one by one, mixing the rye potion and peeling the wax, one by one, family to family. The following weeks, Jewel and Frederick were known throughout the country as the best healers in the area and became most sought after and requested.

Two weeks went by, and they arrived at Dover Castle greeted by the page, led into the fancy chamber and the great hall, where a party of spectacular colors and lights awaited. Piles of food and ornate dresses adorned the guest. William Hastings greeted them, looking fit as a fiddle. The Duke of Burgundy was present; King Henry, even Mary, William

Hastings' wife, greeted them with charm—courtier after courtier, lady after lady, poet, musicians, world-renowned artists, some Italian, some English, French and Danish, all great for Jewel and Frederick. Frederick turned at one point and came face-to-face with Leal, looking as perfect as ever and wearing his usual black leathers; Walters; Simon; Porius; and Athena. Athena greeted them as they all stood in a circle toward the back of the great hall.

"What brings all of you to this amazing palace?" Jewel asked as Frederick smiled and greeted each of them.

"Leal, I have never seen you wearing so many clothes," Jewel said, blushing.

"Well, when in Rome," Leal said, grinning, showing his perfect white teeth and rounded high cheekbones. Apollo stood behind him in golden hair and a white Grecian dress.

"My friends from Elysium, thank you all for coming and saving the lives of so many with your potions and good nature," King Henry said.

Henry silenced the room and spoke. "Hear ye, hear ye, among us tonight are those from legend and myth, chaos and confusion." He pointed to the group of magical fellows.

The crowd hushed in amazement, quietly only whispering to each other while stepping closer to the magical legends who stood before them.

"For one night only, I demand that no religions be discussed and make this a peaceful evening," Henry continued. "Our peoples have ruined many lives through religion, and beside me are Jewel and Frederick," Henry said, pulling Jewel and Frederick by his side then place their glasses on tables and joined him, facing the large crowd of famous and royal humans.

"We are delighted to be here and amongst you," Frederick said aloud. Jewel bowed to the crowd.

"Is that Porius?" a woman was heard whispering in the back showing concern or disbelief.

"These two beautiful young souls saved William Hastings from death by using their learned skills of medicine as taught by the house of Porius," Henry said as all bowed and stood staring in amazement.

"They actually all exist," a man was heard whispering.

"Jewel and Frederick, I wish to extend from all of us a deep apology," King Henry continued to his castle full of followers. "For you see, Jewel's and Frederick's families were tortured or killed, made to serve or taken by the pope." The crowd was silent and in remorse. "We owe all now in debt to thee, please may you from now on live among us in peace." Henry gulped his mead.

"Hail thee to Frederick and Jewel," Filippo Lippi a well-known artist shouted.

"All hail to our new friends!" Henry raised his glass.

The entire population of this merry castle raised their glasses and shout, "HAIL."

The party continued for hours, laughing, dancing, singing, and even one song, which was put together during the party.

Together forever, freedom for everyone
Jewel of our Hearts and Frederick's behind

Laughing, joking, and the occasional performing artists including a small dog act where three poodles danced while wearing small red hats and tiny booties, jugglers with balls and pipes, poets, dancers of sexual exploitation who make all but the king blush, an alligator, pink-colored horse, and other peculiar oddities.

"Frederick, this is the best time ever," Jewel said, hugging him close during a dance in the main ballroom. Leal and Apollo were kissing in the back while Filippo Lippi eyed them in arrestment. No mortal beauty could seem less natural was thought by some, but others seemed rather keen on the idea—men with men, women with women, it was a possibility. Rarity though it may be, it has been going on since the beginning of all species throughout the galaxies. Back on Elysium, the quiet waters of time melted with ray and light; scientific experiments continued from earth to beyond Elysium. The bios grew and shrank with their usual progressions in constant flight and struggle. Caterpillars morphed to moth and butterfly and then to dust, their aging and seemingly dead cells changing and turning into the next phase.

Our bodies and energy collide with time and space within the understanding of all things metal, seed, fire, water, air, and star. Churning ever churning throughout the ever-expanding universe. Morphing, billowing, gushing forth in expression and delight, seeds ever growing until retuning to the earth or whatever planet may the progression serve.

The next morning, Jewel and Frederick awakened in a small room with a small window overlooking the crashing waves upon the shore. Only the sound of the waves, gulls, and the occasional clink and clank from somewhere else in the castle could be heard. Thomas appeared before them.

"Thy presence is requested. Grab thy coats," Thomas said and they held his hand with hands on coats. Thomas grasped them, waving his wand as they dissipated from this place, leaving no remnants of their having been visitors in such a lavish place.

Thomas used the traveling spell from the ancient Egyptian wizard Khufu. Khufu lived many years prior and had developed the transporting spell done simply by mind and wand. This spell had taken years to master, and Thomas was one of the only beings, living or dead, with the ability.

"My hope is that I will teach thy this spell," Thomas said to Jewel and Frederick as they floated above the earth in some misty haze, unable to see but mists of white and electric light.

Frederick tried to open his eyes during the transportation, and Jewel did the same; instead, all they saw was white and felt the wind and Thomas's hand, cooling and warming while the sensation went on for several bewildering minutes.

"Transport complete," Thomas said.

Chapter 15

Amazed upon reflection, Thomas dissipated, leaving the two helpless souls to figure out on their own where they were and what he needed to do and by all means something quickly because before them were houses in fire and men in black cloaks taking children from their screaming parents, two large men in black holding the parents. While attempting to shackle and bind them, Jewel and Frederick stood and began to run toward the scene with wands held high.

"We have seen this before," Frederick shouted as he ran up the first man in black wearing a large wooden cross around his neck.

"Qui Sunt!" the man shouted in Latin.

"I think he is asking who we are," Jewel said.

"Why has thou come?" the other asked, holding two children by their necks.

"To avenge thy parents, Parelizio," Frederick shouted, pointing his wand at the man holding the children. The man fell back. The children got free and ran away screaming.

"Back, you demons," Frederick shouted. "Jewel, my blade." Jewel tossed him a small blade.

Frederick plunged the blade through one man's heart. Blood squirted a bit, then he fell as Jewel thrust a long thin blade she found on the ground beside this large black figure.

"You shalt not hurt others," Jewel said as she landed a blow to the side of his head, and he died before her. Parents ran to the men and kicked their dying bodies as they quivered on the ground, a mass of black clothes, skin, and blood.

"To the devil with thee," one father said as his children clung to his waist in fear.

The men died, and Jewel wiped and replaced her blade. Frederick did the same, and they walked to a nearby tavern and drank with the locals.

"What er the doin' 'ere," said the man serving behind the bar. "T'ain seen nothin' like 'em b'for."

"Not from round 'ere," an old woman said while sipping ale with a few other villagers who also drank in the tavern called the Cat and Crow.

"Welcome to the Cat and Crow, sir and miss. What shall ye 'ave?" the man behind the bar asked while wiping off goblets with a dirty rag.

"Best bitter, please," Frederick said.

"Mead shall suit me fine," said Jewel.

"Thank ye both for showin' up and getting rid of that church scum," said the father of whom Frederick had saved from the beastly man in black.

"Sent from the pope, I 've no doubt," Jewel stated.

"Nice ale," Frederick said, gulping back. "Where are we anyway?"

"Where are thy, 'ere in Oxford or Oxenforda, mostly Saxon round 'ere," the bartender stated. "Glad you like our ale."

"Thank ee most welcome," Frederick said. "May we find a room here at this tavern?"

"Oh aye, you can stay upstairs and there be a bath at the back of the garden."

"Will this do thy?" Jewel handed a coin to the man, and his eyes lit up with joy.

"Aye, shalt do thee nicely, my good friends, but all drinks on house for thee and room as well. No savior of the common folk pays 'ere." He handed Jewel back the coin.

Sipping more ale and mead, Frederick turned to Jewel. "Doth is seem like time has flown byeth?"

"I wondered about that as well. Its seems moments ago we awoke in Dover in early morn, then Thomas, then here, so quick and smart."

"That journey with Thomas was no quick journey, though it seems like moments, hours more the truth of the matter," Frederick replied.

"The cottage lies far now past Suffolk, Essex, and then Kent," Jewel said.

"We have no horse, no cart. Do we walk?" Frederick, wondering, asked.

"Fine to have thee amongst us, where art thou from then?" asked a cobbler. The material of his trade mattered about his person.

"Kent, and we were just wondering how to return," Jewel said.

"Oh, that is no bother, my brethren Francis travels to Kent every week to do the pig trade or whatever else he can carry in trade," he said.

"Francis sounds perfect, where is thou?" Frederick asked.

"Oh e'l be in round suppertime, mark my word," he said.

"These are the two that saved my children from the Catholics," the father said, bringing a small group of people over to meet Jewel and Frederick. One man carried some fresh carrots and peas, one woman carried some grain and stock, another with clothes obviously newly made from her own hands.

"It was nothing truly, be assured," Jewel said to the small crowd. "Nothin', nothin'."

"They have my children now," one woman said, putting her carrots on Jewel and Frederick's table.

"They've my children workin' in some far-off land," another said.

"Both me sons were taken, and God only knows what has become of them, most likely slaves, but nothin' ye said. Where hath thou come frometh?" the father said. He was happy he had his saved children at his side.

"Kent," Frederick said, and his wand was revealed from under his cloak.

"Aye," said the father, noticing his wand. "Good to have ye both in our village."

"Food on the house," the barman said and the cooking began. Jewel and Frederick talked to each person individually, hearing their familiar stories and wondering or thinking up plans to retrieve their families from the clutches of the church's grasp.

"They called me a witch, a witch!" one woman shouted, laughing. "If'n I were a witch, I would have given them a spell to send them back to their own hell."

"Well, Frederick, maybe we don't head back to Kent just yet," Jewel said to Frederick when they finally had a moment to their own while the crowd rambled on and on, and cooks poured more mead and ale and gets louder as the evening goes on. Then finally even Francis the cobblers brother shows up asking.

"Doth thee need a person to take ye back ta Kent?" Francis asked.

"Well, my good man, not just yet, I believe we have a few missions to set in place with these good folks."

"Listen up all," the father shouted, silencing the tavern. "These two fine travelers from Kent have agreed to assist us in getting our young ones back."

"Hurrah!" the entire crowd yelled as they began singing and shouting praises at Jewel and Frederick.

"What have we gotten ourselves into, my love?" Jewel said.

"I think Thomas knew exactly where he was taking us and why we are needed in this place," Frederick said in her ear due to the noise rising from the eager crowd, ready for revenge against the Catholics thieving their brethren, sons and daughters, wives and cousins.

Jewel met with each person who had suffered a loss as did Frederick. Finally, the list was complete and they had twelve names, three under the age of six and nine over the age of thirteen. Most were suspected to still be within the area. They started searching within the county, checking all the churches, monasteries, and anywhere the priest in black may have appropriated and hidden the twelve missing youths. They searched the east, west, north, and south.

Finally, they found the three youngest baking bread in one monastery, ankles changed to table legs, thin and hungry. Frederick unlocked the chains by prying open the weakest link and setting the three youths free. Quietly, they absconded the youths and walked back to the road where a local farmer hid them in a pile of hay and took them back to their parents' loving arms. Rumor was told that the other nine missing youths were taken to Benedictine Canterbury to assist in building the houses behind the cathedral so Jewel and Frederick set forth to Canterbury, knowing it was on the way home to the cottage and Thomas and all they desired.

The days passed as Francis and his team of horses with loaded cart set finally reached Canterbury. Francis informed them of the fullers, ironmongers, spurriers of which the youths once lived and worked within the peaceful villages before priests in black stole them from their beds or ripped them from their screaming parents' hands, who were given the lash as they protested the taking.

"Do not defy the word of God," one priest repeated as he shouted, giving justification to his stealing of the youths.

Once in Canterbury, Francis waited at the side road while Jewel and Frederick walked slowly and unnoticed toward the slave barracks, which after Frederick's cool hand at breaking the locks, they crept inside. Just as they were opening the large wooden door plastered with large bolted hinges up and down the sides, they crept in. The smell was disgusting, and Jewel tied a cloth around her nose and mouth. Sure enough, as the rumor was told, there lay nine youths shivering under hay while shackled to their cots, which were bound by large metal spikes into solid stone.

"How will we remove thy shackles?" Frederick whispered to Jewel as she shook her head in disbelief at the poor health of these starving youths.

"Not to worry," a voice said from behind them, slamming the door and locking them inside. Behind them stood a large man in black waving a stick and dangling a wooden cross around his neck.

"Frederick, no!" Jewel shouted as the man came toward them in fury.

"Absolutum Molefander, Porius, Porius, Porius!" Frederick shouted while holding his wand to the charging black demon.

The figure heard the words Porius repeated three times and stopped, looking around. "Porius, long dead Porius, he won't come to help you, what are thee?" the figure in black stated and once again charging.

"Thy are our brethren and disciples," shouted Porius who appeared in a flash dressed in his white flowing gowns, and then in a flash of colored light came Leal, Walters, and Simon who blocked the path of the charging villain in black.

"Release the youths!" Porius shouted. Pointing his wand at the shackles, all nine thick chains became snakes, slithering out of the barracks, as the man in black stood in amazement. Leal grabbed two of the snakes, and with his mighty arms thrust the snakes upon the villain in black. The snakes bit and wrapped themselves around the priest.

"Adder's bite is harsh, as thee shalt feel the bite," Walters said.

Simon and the others took the youths outside the odorous barracks and one by one rushed them back to the cart where Leal was with his unforbidden swagger or muscle and good looks then loaded the youths onto the cart, lifeless and waking, weak from lack of nourishment. Five girls ranging from thirteen to seventeen wore hardly the clothes to keep you warm on a cool winter night, and four males lay lifeless.

"Take them quickly to the tavern and knock on the door. Have the innkeeper feed and clothe them, no quickly," Leal said, smacking the ponies on their backsides and sending them less than a mile up the road. Once reaching the tavern, the youths were nourished, washed, and given clothes from several villagers eager to assist in the youth's escape.

Though run by the church or "underfoot of the church," as Porius liked to describe the ruthless rule of Christianity, back at the barracks, all that was left were the few workers who were originally taken and now remained bound to the church.

"You poor sods, good day to thee," Porius said, ushering Jessica and Frederick outdoors.

"Here, take these branches and put them between your legs. Say the words, 'Lift thee, take thee by Porius's lead.'"

"Lift the, take thee by Porius's lead," Jewel said as the branch lifted her about ten feet above the ground and she tried to hang on." Frederick did the same but had more difficulty.

"Oh, I have forgotten," Porius said to them. "Take thee thy shape." The branch opened under Porius, making a kind of seat to carry his weight. Frederick and Jewel said the same.

"Take thee thy shape," together they said while the branch unfolded to a wider shape and they sat more easily. Flying above the ground, the three flew toward the wilderness and over the trees, passing a flock of squawking geese heading south from this wretched cold weather. Soon in the distance was a small flapping bit of black. Joy was brought to Jewel's and Frederick's eyes as above them flew Franklin. Being filled up with grief from the long journey and moaning every now and then, Jewel and Frederick finally landed on the garden grounds, the wood falling beside them, and once again becoming just branches.

"I shall well remember that spell," said Frederick to Porius and Jessica, Franklin landing on top of the cottage, resting upon thatch.

"Welcome home, my friends," Thomas said, arms outstretched to hug the weary travelers. Parthenia and Grendle also came out aproned as usual and smiling of the fish left behind by the water goblins' nightly vigil.

Jewel turned to the cottage with gladness in her eyes, dirty from the long travels and pleased to be home.

"My Lord Thomas, Parthenia, Grendle, and Franklin," Jewel said while there were the deer, quail, squirrels, and even a pair of barn owls. The deep dread of their journey was at an end.

Butterflies hummed among the earth surrounding the joyous reunion as the bios below perpetuated its multicreature world below.

"Well, I think a few days' rest and pleasure will do. Where are the boys?" Porius said, looking back for Walters, Leal, and Simon.

"I believe they went back to Elysium, Porius," Frederick said.

"Oh my, possibly true, in fact most likely," Porius said.

"I would have loved to have seen them longer. Did you see Leal through the adders on the terrifying priest?" Jewel said, removing her clothes and walking to the back room to refresh herself in the running warm waters of the cottage.

"Terrifying in the extreme," Frederick said.

"Come, you must tell me all about it, and I'll have the clothes washed and hung." Thomas removed Frederick's outfit and took his and Jewel's outfits, handing the huge piles to Grendle.

"I'll see to it, Thomas," Grendle said, whipping the clothes from Thomas and taking them to the river. "Don't tell the tale until I return, I shan't miss a word."

But as soon as Jewel and Frederick dressed, ate, talked of their journey and discussed tales of Elysium with Porius. Another cry was heard from Franklin as he landed on the open windowsill.

"You are needed," Franklin screeched.

CHAPTER 16

The alarm sounded, and Jewel and Frederick felt they needed a more important matter. They thought they were well fed but not yet as rested as to be considered. Jewel sat back.

"By the elves, what now?" Jewel said, just resting back in the armchair opposite Frederick, warming his naked backside by the fire.

"But we've just arrived, Porius," Frederick said as he loaded a dried black leather short over his shoulders.

"Plus, this weather is being so harsh," Jewel said, now standing to dress.

"Hand me the pensive and stop your complaining. This is our call, and we must fight on," Porius said, hands outstretched toward Thomas who handed him the pensive, which was set on the table.

"I always say music makes this work just a little bit better." Flicking his wand, the tiny floating band appeared in some sort of odd South American wardrobe—the tiny conductor in grass skirt, the woman wearing coconuts in the back playing some odd-stringed ancient instruments.

"Ah, much better. Reveal," Porius said, gazing into the pensive as the others looked on over his shoulder.

The scene within the pensive was the same sad story of men in long black cloaks yielding big sticks and grabbing all the youth of Hastings.

"It appears to be six or seven this time," Frederick stated as he buckled his boots and adjusted his long black leather trousers.

"Yes, it will take all our cunning," Porius said.

"Quick then, no time to lose," Thomas said, handing Jewel and Frederick their cloaks, and Jewel eying the large dead branches, which once transported them as she opened the front door.

"You know the spell," Porius said as they flew off toward Hastings, over forest as the sun disappeared in the sky and the moon rose, wind growing to a bluster until finally below the two flying witches' houses on fire, people screaming, a scene as they had witnessed before.

"I shall take the tall one there," Frederick said as he headed toward a tall bony figure in black who carried two small children, kicking and screaming.

"Halt, non prohibere!" Frederick shouted as his wooden traveling machine landed in front of the charging black-hooded demon.

Frederick took his sword from his waist and plunged it deep into the heart of the charging villain.

"Destry dues eorum." The priest dropped the children and died as his blood splattered until he lay lifeless. The children ran for home.

"Mama, Papa!" the children ran screaming toward the parents who battled the house fire, several villagers grabbing buckets of water to douse the flames.

"Felix namque et," one large priest over three hundred pounds of a stone began to shout as Jewel plunged her dagger.

"Two down," Jewel shouted.

"Let them go!" Frederick shouted at another struggling with some farmer's wife and ripping the top of her dress, exposing her full bosom as she grappled with the beast.

"Let her be!" Frederick shouted again and plunged his still bloody sword into the heart of another. The woman gestured to Frederick her thanks.

"A most particular three," Frederick said, jumping over the third now lifeless priest.

"Ego Dominus." The next smaller figure in black cloak faced the charging Frederick.

"Ye shall what?" Frederick said as he stopped to face blade to blade.

"Morietur!" the priest yelled, plunging his sword full strength at Frederick.

"Frederick, no!" Jewel yelled toward Frederick as she battled the fifth demon.

But Frederick was quicker than this angry villain and moving swiftly to his left. The charging priest's sword missed Frederick by an inch. Frederick's blade entered the belly of the priest with tremendous force as

Frederick rolled his hand and the belly was slit clean as the insides spilled out along the grass and stone.

"Morietur!" shouted the gurgling priest as he died.

Frederick fell to one knee to catch his breath. The woman he recently saved handed him a goblet of water. "Thank you," Frederick said as he drank and stood toward the last priest.

"You win, you are the victor," the priest said, throwing down his sword and releasing his catch.

"Help them put these fires out," Frederick said, and the last priest obeyed and assisted in carrying water buckets as did Jewels resigning offender.

"Well done, Frederick," Jewel said as the same woman brought Jewel a goblet of water to quench her thirst and they both sat on the grass for a moment.

"We had better see these fires out," Frederick said as they also assisted until the injured homes only have smoke in places, damage control under way. After which Frederick and Jewel met up with two priests who had relinquished their selves in shame.

"Simul Autem apologize," the priest said.

"Well, we are familiar with your kind, and I hope you will leave these people in peace," Frederick said.

"You should be ashamed of thyselves," Jewel stated.

"We are commanded," the priest said in broken English.

"We cannot promise you that others will come in our place. The order is strong, ruthless and cunning," the second priest said.

"Hand me your crosses," Frederick said, grabbing the crosses from around their necks.

"Ego te condemnabo," one priest said.

"Aye, you may condemn us, but thee shall one day fall," Jewel said as the priest looked to Jewel in amazement of her understanding Latin.

"What inducement shall I say to thee other than take me home, Frederick," Jewel said, holding him tight to her body.

"Let's go," Frederick said.

Grabbing the branches, they said, "Take thee thy shape," as the branches once again expanded and carried our friends toward the cottage silhouetted by moonlight, chilled to their bones. The forest below was active with nightlife as the owls flew from tree to tree, poor running victim to tree once more. Frederick pointed down at the river, and they saw splashing. They followed his finger to a lower elevation, and three goblins were playing in the water and some fairies hovering above the splashing water goblins, giving a wave toward Frederick. Jewel waved as she passed. "Visiting fairies, or are they to start a family?"

"Porius said that some magical creatures will return in small numbers," Frederick exclaimed.

"My dear friend, let's just hope they stay hidden, for you know what mortals can be."

"Indeed, watch the branch," Frederick said as they once again gained altitude up into the moonlight, which slowly got covered by some black clouds.

"Time to head for home," Jewel said, pointing at the soon-to-burst thunderhead, lightning spurting within. The rage of the sky burst around them as rain pelted the grounds of the cottage. Jewel and Frederick landed and went inside, somber, burned out, fueled by Thomas's pigeon pudding. Sleepy and staggering, they both fell asleep.

Morning came, and the rain still poured over the elated world while the bluebirds chirped. Franklin and his two raven pals circled in the rain for a bit, then tired of the water, landed under the ledge of thatch that fell over the top window. Jewel lay by the fire inside still resting and healing the few bruises and scratches from the previous days.

"Come on sun, shine, bring us a sunny day," Frederick said, holding his wand out toward the heavens, but no change occurred.

"You know, Porius said you cannot change the weather. Why doth thou try?" Jewel said, standing almost naked inside the doorway, her long golden hair draping over her pouting breast and watching Frederick getting soaked in the downpour.

"It is rather chucking down, make no mistake," Frederick said, looking back and gazing at Jewel standing there as beautiful as Athena or any other goddess known to man.

"Come inside, take meal and rest," Jewel said, waving him indoors.

"Building up a new home, sounds like the plan for the day," Frederick said and took her to the warmth beside the fire, stripped her naked, and followed suit. Flesh to flesh and breath to breath, they enjoyed an early morning sensual feast.

Afterward and hearing the rain stop, the sun broke through the clouds, and light fell among the plants, trees, and animals now circling the cottage. Thomas came from the outer back of the cottage and made his usual swap in the air as the floating band appeared, playing something uplifting, and the afternoon began.

"Training time, Jewel, Frederick," Thomas said as he walked outside holding a large book of spells.

"On our way," Jewel stated while tying her hair back. After splashing with water, Frederick and Jewel followed Thomas to the benches and oak table with the carvings of animals on every spot of weed, chairs, or bench-type chairs and the one spell after another the practice.

"Wrapping a wound, cleaning a wound, holding the pensive correctly, and palm reading," Thomas said. "I truly feel that you both have mastered these methods and spells. Now we need to learn connecting spells."

"Connecting spells, you mean like mind reading?" Frederick said.

"Not exactly, for you cannot learn to mind read, nor would ye wish to. But ye can learn to visually examine a person and watch eyes—up to left, mostly lying, downward, most probably sadness. No, no, the connecting spell is important because you will be able to connect with other magical or rare creatures. Most definitely something you both need to learn," Thomas said, turning pages through the Malefactor while sitting on a bench with squirrels carved upon its sides.

"Page 40, Connecting Spell One."

"Put to stand legs wide and arms outstretched," Thomas said, waving toward Frederick and Jewel to perform his instruction by the fountain, birds chirping all around them.

"One, two three," Thomas said and flicked his wand toward them.

Eyes wide, legs apart, and facing each other, Jewel and Frederick tried it with their wands.

"ONE TWO THREE," they both said and then held their arms out wide. Before them stood a man with long white beard about four feet high and looking at least one hundred if he's a day.

"And ye are," Frederick said, looking at the old man who had magically materialized before them.

"I am Horan. You met me under the earth, but here I show my real age due to the atmosphere being so heavy."

"Horan, it is thee," Jewel said, delighted.

"And look amongst ye," Horan said.

As he spoke, several other creatures appeared around them, and two fairies flew by as the deer chased them and scampered. Five elves walked by and waved, and several trolls walked by bowing.

"What, all these beings here?" Frederick stated.

"Always around you but getting fewer. I actually called them all here today because I knew you were going to practice this spell," Thomas said as they all disappeared.

"Where hath thou all gone, Thomas?" Jewel said.

"Home, I imagine. They can't stay around all day, now relax," Thomas replied and eventually the rain came back, and they retired to a meal prepared by Grendle and Parthenia.

Franklin and his raven brothers circled and squawked. "Come out, come out."

Frederick and Jewel awakened to the uproar and quickly primped and dressed, drinking a spot of juice and ran outdoors looking up at the screaming ravens.

"What is it, Franklin?" Jewel shouted.

"A shipwreck of the coast," Franklins squawked back while Jewel and Frederick mounted their wood and spread the seat while a mild rain tingled their faces they fly out beyond the forest and over the sea. Below them, thousands of fish could be seen, some jumping in and out of the water, large cod, schools of haddock, halibut, bass, and other multicolored species.

"See all the fish?" Frederick shouted to Jewel, who nodded in agreement.

Frederick and Jewel had not flown over the sea to see such a spectacle of the ocean life below, and beyond was a ship at half-mast and sinking. Two men stood at the bow, and many in the water screamed, one fighting off a shark attack, but alas, that sailor went down below the waves as a blast ripped apart the midsection and fire and flame burst forth. Frederick, feeling the heat of the blast, hovered over the sinking ship now engulfed in feverish flames.

"Stay back, Jewel. Another blast may come," he said

"Save them." Jewel pointed at the two men nearly touching the water at the top of the bow, which was still holding its safety away from the swirling fish life and bubbling water, the fire ship still blasting below the waves.

Frederick and Jewel circled the two men, thin as they were in the extreme condition with white silver pantaloons, black silver buttoned cloak, and long straggly hair and beard of black and gray.

"Qui defenda nos," the larger of the shouted toward the flying Frederick, their eyes in amazement not only at the sight of a man flying before them on a piece of wood, but the water rushing toward their feet and the ship disappearing beneath them.

Jewel swooped toward one and grabbed his hand, but he was too heavy and fell into the sea, a multitude of fish surrounding him as he sank beneath the waves.

"I have thee," Frederick said, grasping the final survivor of the wreckage and holding him with one arm as he dangled inches from the surface of the ocean, carrying him back to shore then quickly dropping him on the beachhead over Dover.

"I tried to save the other," Jewel said as she landed shivering from the cold. "He was too heavy."

"It is fine. We saved one, and look at the sight of him," Frederick said as he looked down upon the sailor wearing his best sailor uniform, not French not Spanish.

"What are thee?" Jewel asked.

"No intelligo," the man said as he stood wavering a bit once on his feet, most likely due to having solid ground beneath his feet for the first time in a long time.

"He does not understand," Jewel said as she spoke just enough Latin to get what his meaning was.

"Qui es?" Jewel said.

"I Fernando, Capitan Fernando."

"A pleasure to make your acquaintance," Frederick said.

"Quod tu es?" the stranger asked, wondering how two seemingly mortal beings can fly upon a piece of wood.

"We shall take him to William Hastings," Jewel said.

"Agreed," Frederick said. "Ye are safe, follow us." Frederick tried to repeat in Latin.

"Mali Tempus."

"Oh, ego intelligus, intelligus," he said. "Gratius tibi, gratias tibi."

"Te gratissimum," Jewel said. "You are so very welcome."

Walking the long road to Hastings, they finally stopped at the Ole Crow tavern and drank a quick flagon of ale, Jewel sipping slow, while Frederick and Fernando drank theirs down in two quick gulps.

"Gratis," Fernando said as an older man stood staring at them like they were from a far-off planet and not allowed in a place such as this.

"Where ye from then?" the old gentleman asked Frederick.

"He is from out of the area, and we rescued him from a ship," Frederick said eagerly as Jewel jumped in.

"This gentleman swam to shore, and we were lucky enough to find him," Jewel interjected.

"Interesting," the man said as he gazed back into his goblet.

Once Ferdinand had been delivered to Hastings and far removed from the prying eyes of the village, they found a quiet spot in the woods.

"I shall try the connecting spell. One, two, three," Frederick said, arms and legs wide. Yet looking around him, there was nothing. No fairies, elves, water goblins. The sadness or disappointment annoyed them both, so they flew toward home.

CHAPTER 17

The tale of Jessica and Frederick continued, year after year of living at the cottage; and occasionally, Thomas, Porius, and the others visited or set them up with a new spell or charm until they grew old and following the lead of those before parish among the species and gardens of the cottage, their bodies taken to the sea and released into Elysium until once again, Thomas, Franklin, Parthenia, and Grendle watched over and cared for the grounds. Time passed, and nature continued its never-ending circles season to season and king to king.

On January 1, 1605, our raven watcher Franklin signaled for Thomas to come out of the cottage and into the garden. Horan from the underworld also came up top to see what all the commotion was about due to the immense sound of hooves and men somewhere outside the boundaries of the garden. Charging, stomping, shouting, and slushing through the first-of-the-year cold morning.

"Why can it be?" Thomas said as he came out no form and flesh, to peer behind the edge of the forest and saw men sitting across the river.

"Rebels," Franklin squawked.

"Quiet, you foolish fowl, do you want them to know we are here?"

"James is not a right king," was heard from one man who was starting a fire to obviously cook something that still squirmed on the ground before him.

"But thou is the king, and ye must not interfere," another said, kicking and cleaning with his knife the poor creature bound to sticks and set to dangle in the fire's edge.

"Be thou not ready anyhow, my lord?" he stated.

"Tell the other men that we head for Dover tonight. Let us rest here for one day and catch our weight in this fine river. I see it full of fish ready for takin'."

Thomas noticed the water goblins hiding below the water, just their heads occasionally popping up and quickly down so as not to be noticed.

"Di ye ere a splashing?" the obvious leader of the two said.

"'Tis the wind, the wind."

"Aye, ye must agree. 'Tis a wicked chilled night." The man wrapped himself in a thick black bearskin fold.

"Come, Franklin, let's go in. Thy shalt not find us," Thomas said and turned to go back from the edge of the woods, and an elf was before them standing on a frozen bit of wood.

"Thomas, I am Joray the elf. A man is here from Roma, Senior Talis, coordinator, extractor, and keeper of the elven commission here on earth. Be kind and take us to your side to escape the cold, we beseech thee, Lord Thomas."

Thomas was rather startled by the elven creature with skin of green, eyes of black, and wearing a bit of cloth just large enough to cover his genitals and wrap his tiny feet.

"By all means, do come and stay for dinner. Where is this Senior Talis?" Thomas said, walking quickly toward the center of the garden.

"Sono qui," a booming voice came from behind the eastern side of the hedges at the foot of the forest. Out stood Senior Talis, who stood five feet tall, with black long hair and wearing a silver pantaloon outfit with thick black belt, black boots with silver ornate buckle, feathers that were soaked from the rain, which has just started to pour, and wand in hand.

"English, *si*, I do speak English, Lord a Thomas, my pleased to of course meet thee," Talis said.

"Aye, the same, come in and warm yourself by our fire and eat, drink, and tell us of your tales," Thomas said as he ushered Talis into the cottage.

"I have several bottles of wine from Roma and Florenza to offer thee," Talis continued. He was quite loquacious and also carried a pipe and flute-type instrument.

"I wish thy Porius was here. He would like thee and can speak Latin fluently."

"It is okay. Oh, greetings," Talis said as Parthenia carried a large cooked chicken and placed it on the table. She curtsies with a slight blush, Grendle peering around the corner with her usual giggle.

Senior Talis carried on telling Thomas of his journeys and his hiding from priests in his pursuit of the old ways.

"You see, my friends, Christianity is not everywhere in Roma or Florenza but has taken a toll on us all. Few *familias* remain, and many big houses have long since fallen.

"Indeed for we are acquainted with Athena who has fought against the Christians in Roma," Thomas said, sloshing back some ale and enjoying the good humor and companionship of this odd stranger and his elf, Joray, who sipped ale and warmed his half-naked body by the fire.

"Warmth, nice thank yee, thank yee," Joray said.

"Pleased you have come, but how has thou found us?" Thomas asked as he set down his goblet and stared at Talis who seemed to get better looking by the glance.

"I have come from Athena's direction."

"What an amazing coincidence! I was just going to mention Athena."

"Ye know of Athena?" Talis asked, Joray peering on with interest.

"Well, well, we are very old friends, and I also know Gloria and Alexandria, her—" but before Thomas continued, Talis rushed his usual excited conversation.

"Athena, you are acquainted with my queen?"

"Indeed."

"My heart leaps for Gloria," Talis said and was so excited. "I shall perform magic for thee." He threw his large coat off and his top shirt and pantaloons out—boots, socks, and everything else except a small blue cloth to cover his waist.

"Unda greantiado!" Talis shouted, standing before Thomas. A bit of smoke came out of his wand, and a little band appeared; in fact, the same band, which Thomas and Porius occasionally hailed.

"Voila, music," Talis said, still standing and waving his wand.

"Geometric," Talis said as Franklin squawked and, not needing this excitement, flew out the front door to perch on the roof. Thomas giggled at the performance as another puff of smoke came out of Talis's wand, making them both cough a bit but giggling nonetheless.

"A signpost," Talis said and another bit of smoke followed by Porius, Athena, Walters, Simon, Leal, Jewel, and Frederick.

"Greetings, everyone, greetings," Thomas said as Leal smacked Talis on the bum, Walters and Athena dressed in nothing but flowers and wrapped in vines.

"Talis, ye must be playing magic tricks," Porius said, looking bewildered at what he is doing.

"Paenitet, so sorry all of you," Talis said as he laughed and looked at his wand. "I did not think a you all a would a coma." Talis fell back into Leal who sat at the table.

"While we're here, we may as well have a bit of that wine," Leal said, holding Talis and laughing on his lap.

"Parthenia to the rescue." Parthenia came in carrying several goblets, one for everyone, Jewel, and Frederick wrapped in some kind of silk blue cloth and looking as if they had been out gardening.

"From our garden to here so quickly," Jewel said, taking the goblet full of wine to her lips.

"Nice to meet you, Talis," Frederick said.

"Well, now that we are all here," Porius interjected, "what of these two men across the river?"

"Well, my lord, it appears they are planning on reaching the king," Thomas said, looking out the window. Athena and Walters, Simon and Leal toasted to Talis.

"Nice spell, Talis," Athena said, and they all raised their goblets and cheered.

"Keep an eye on them, Thomas," Leal said. "Oh, and just use Talis's spell to bring us again."

"A bit of warning would not go amiss,". Simon said, still wet due to have been bathing with Gloriana on Elysium. "I must return. Gloria will be quite taken a back." Simon turned to light then vanished back to Elysium.

"Oh, and I for we were in the middle of, well, just say something special," Walters said as he grabbed Athena, and they both disappeared, Athena waving to all of them as she evaporated before them.

Jewel and Frederick also made their notice of leaving, and off they went back to the garden from their garden from which they were so suddenly taken.

Leal was still sitting in front of Thomas and holding the squirming and laughing Talis on his lap. "I'll stay for a bit longer if you don't mind," he said, standing and tossing Talis on the rug by the fire while they both grinned.

"Aye, and what of these gentlemen by the river?" Thomas asked.

"Thee shalt not be required to leave in this weather. Dress me later, and Talis and I will follow thy roving men to see what scandal they are up to," Leal said, picking up Talis and taking him to the back of the house. "Give us an hour."

Two hours later, Leal and Talis came out of the back rooms, washed, and clothed in black leather fittings, black silver buckled boots, tying their sworded belts.

"Now let's go see of these inquiring travelers," Leal said.

"Paratus," Talis said, stepping out and looking ready for apparent battle.

"You both look fit and most ready. Shall I show you the way?" Thomas said, opening the front door, rain getting denser outside. But Leal ran to the edge of the forest and noticed that the tent was pitched and the men seemed resting.

"There be no reason at this time," Leal said.

The next morning, the men's tent gone, Leal and Talis quickly got on the trail as the two curious travelers and, relying on Franklin's directions, headed toward the village along the dirt road. They see the horse tracks and follow with eager anticipation of meeting these rascals.

"Pleased that the rain has stopped for the walk ahead," Leal said. "My intuition informs me that we shall find these two men of interest at the Golden Lyon tavern."

"Me Like to visit ee Eglander Tavern, laetus," Talis said, walking behind the muscular and ever gorgeous Leal and catching up on his right side.

"Laetus?" Leal said as he stopped to look at Talis, deer running past him and squirrels running along a branch, which extended from one side of the road to the other. Overhead, they scramble one after the other.

"'Tis meaning Happy," Telis said, not knowing the word for *delighted* in English.

"Most Laetus," Leal said, regaining his gait toward the village.

Finally, they come around a corner and hear, smell, and see the village folk running about, laborers building some constructive building of stone and mud, thatchers adding the branches to a cottage a few layers of building up, but seen between the narrow path. The baker shouted at his wife for committing some form of fidelity and other productions fitting the growing village.

Waving in the wind stood the Golden Lyon and Robert Catesby standing under the sign talking to two other Jesuit priests. They noticed Leal and Talis walk into the tavern and order a drink. Catesby, rebellious

Catholic and unwanted in these parts, seemed to be planning some sort of plot no doubt.

"He shall not start any trouble here," Leal said, drinking down his goblet of ale back to the bar. Two young women were blushing and making eyes at Leal, Talis fully aware.

"They seem interested," Talis said, eyeing the girls.

"We've no time for that," Leal said, putting a coin on the bar. "For these two lovely princesses."

The two women curtseyed., "Thank ye, Sir Leal." "Nice to see you in the village."

"Nice to see you both and stay clear of the three men outside," Leal said.

"We can a' take um," Talis said, touching his sword.

"Now don't be hasty, young Italian pup," Leal said as he put his arm out to steady Talis.

"They are a-comin'," Talis said.

"As soon as they cross that threshold, keep calm," Leal said, watching the three men dressed in black enter and walk to a table. Leal and Talis were still standing at the back of the bar to the three unwelcomed Jesuit priests.

Foolish talking and chattering in a circle and not paying attention to the villagers, Robert Catesby chattered and sipped his wine, not ale.

"Robert Catesby is not one to be trusted," Leal said.

"Catholics, after what they did to my countrymen, why, I—" Talis said when Leal quickly put his hand on his arm, pulling him slightly.

"Charm, my friend, now just stay your charming personage," Leal whispered, the girls eyeing them. An old man walked by Leal, speaking very to as he passed.

"Nice to see you, Sir Leal, notice the priests?"

"Indeed I do, but not to worry," Leal reassured the man eyeing Talis.

"This man is with me," Leal said.

"Good, greetings." The man bowed slightly to Leal and Talis.

"If a fight breaks out, please to keep bystanders away. My family is feeding horses outside," the man said to Leal.

"We are just watching and won't start anything here, but here sits Robert Catesby in the village, now what is he doing here?" Leal asked in soft voice.

"Plotting no doubt, plotting as usual," the man said knocking back a quick ale.

Robert Catesby and the two priests wearing of course the color black, and also the two which took and evenings rest along the river by the cottage.

"They are a-leavin'," Talis said.

"Let them go, we will follow shortly, for I know these paths and woods like the back of my hand, they shall not go far," Leal stated as he turned back to the bar. "Thy shalt not go far."

Leal watched the men leave, Robert Catesby boarded a coach that was prepared by villagers and sets off in the path of London, leaving the two men on horseback.

"Quickly, bartender, where may I find horses?" Leal said, but as he did, the man they were speaking with earlier came out.

"I have two ready," the man said, smiling and hay sticking out of his teeth, smiling.

"Very well, thankee." Leal patted Talis on the back, and they ran out behind the tavern and mount two large black horses.

"Tender and Pegasus"—the man told them the names of these nicely fitted horses—"bring 'em back here when you are finished."

"Tender is an interesting name," Leal said as he handed Tender to Talis and he mounted and adjusted his weight.

"Pegasus, can you fly?" Leal said, steadying himself on Pegasus.

"Thank ye, and I shall bring them back unharmed," Leal said, tossing a small coin to the man who so nicely supplied the men with fresh horses.

"No need, please." The man attempted to run alongside Leal, but Leal and Talis had ridden off.

"Leal, always the perfect gentleman," the man said, watching Leal on Pegasus and Talis on Tender ride off a far distance behind the two priests.

They followed far behind for several hours, and soon the two priests noticed them and quickened the pace, soon a canter, then a full out run. Leal and Talis on much more solid animals and they headed them off and raised their swords.

"So ye want to fight," one priest said and jumped from his horse to the ground and pulled out a long blade from his cloak.

"This blade shall greet thee," the first priest said, turning to Leal as Leal jumped from his horse.

"Thy sword may be long, but mine is quick," Leal said, and they started a fight.

Talis and the other priest followed and dismounted as the four men clinked, clattered, sliced, and diced, waving and shackling their swords.

"Take the sword to thy heart," the priest fighting Leal shouted as he plunged his sword to Leal, but Leal was far too quick; and as he stepped aside letting the attacker's sword miss him, he plunged his shorter blade into the priest's neck and pulled down on his pommel and the guard met the priest's chin, slicing his neck open. The priest fell to the dust. Talis, not doing as well and backed against a large stone as the other priest, lunged toward him; but Talis also was too quick and rolled from the stone, landing on the ground and swiping at the priest's leg; he fell. Blood squirted from the priest's leg all over Talis's face, and the priest grabbed his leg.

"My leg, my leg!" But as the priest yelled out, Talis finished him off with another blow to his back and through his heart.

"Ye shall not suffer," Talis said, standing and meeting Leal.

"Nice work," Leal said. "Quick, let's remove these villains from the road." Leal dragged the men into the verge. Then he grabbed the other two horses and stripping them of saddle, only leaving the reins in Leal's palm and handing one to Talis as he mounted Tender and Leal mounted Pegasus.

"The prize not bad for a day's work. We most likely foiled a plot against the king and was handsomely rewarded with two horses," Leal said as they ride back to the Golden Lyon tavern, where once they reached was full of villagers and the occasion traveler from Hastings or Dover.

"Thank ye for the horse, and here are too from our trouble," Leal said, handing Tender and Pegasus and patting them kindly on their mane and neck. "Nice pair, indeed, they served us well."

"No, I could not take these other horses because they were recently stolen from Birchwood farm," the man said, walking up and leaving the horses to be dealt with by a younger boy who leads them round back of the Golden Lyon.

"Well, return them with my heartfelt feeling that justice has been served," Leal said, Talis smiling as the man bought them two large goblets of ale.

"When you say dealt with, Sir Leal, do you mean . . .," the horse provider said.

"Dead. Both I am afraid," Leal said.

"You made quick work of it, Sir Leal."

"One must not take horses," Leal said, raising his goblet. "Thank ye."

"His sword is fast," Talis said to the man and onlookers as they also hear the tale of Leal taking out two Jesuit priests and cheering them on.

"Wish I could have seen him in action," the man said, and the uproar could be heard far out in the village. With music playing, the occasional singing some folklore song, lutes playing, women dancing and more. The tavern has not had such an outrageous party in a while.

One woman walked up to Leal, hair piled up high, and large breasts almost fully popping out of her corset. "Leal, those two men here earlier, ye took them out?"

"Aye," Leal said confidently.

"Sue Lynn, Sue Lynn, come quickly," she said, ushering a beautiful girl of no older that thirteen. "Leal took out your priest."

As she said this, the young girl walked up to Leal and kissed him on the cheek and hugged him then walked back into the crowd.

"She was recently raped by one of those evil men. Thank ye, Leal," she said, also pecking him on the cheek and curtsying to Talis.

"You, a hero," Talis said, gulping his ale.

"Correction, we are heroes," Leal said, repeating his gulping of this most wonderful ale.

Soon, a large pile of cooked pheasant, game pie, greens, and more ale were set before them and they feasted. Even Thomas walked in later wearing brown pantaloons, golden tied vest, and looking quite the ticket. They stayed till late in the evening and then all three walked back toward the cottage.

"It has been a pleasure meeting you, Talis, and fighting alongside you, but I am sure Porius shall soon come and take me back to Elysium," Leal said as the cottage garden came into view as the walk through the thickest part of the woods which hides the cottage grounds and farm.

"Ye are leaving," Talis said with a look of extreme disappointment and sadness on his face.

"'Tis not the light in which we travel that is easy to grasp. I cannot travel alone and look up," Leal said, pointing up as a large multicolored ray of light came down to earth, Porius standing in all-white embroidered gold mesh and bejeweled in the most extravagant fashion.

"Leal, your mission is complete, come," Porius said as Leal waved goodbye and the light disappeared, carrying Porius and Leal back to

Elysium, fueled by ambition and looking forward to relaxation on Elysium the closure of another day.

Between this world and the next, fire from the aftermath of legends and mystery and fazed-on beams of golden rays sourced other worlds of magic. Insects in their bios congealed and directed each in syncopation a collective whole and meandering and perpetual in existence. Throes of endless life coil, spiral, touching, growing toward the sun or toward some other distant light. Performing the ritual of cell multiplication, integration and perplexed amongst all time and space. Fortunes of kings coming and going like their families. Battles ran in scattered views of domination and manipulation, country to country and world to world creating the endless shouts of anguish by the meek losing to less-kind beings. This unbalanced world and others where goodness does not always win over sorrow within its propagation of hurt. Generals stayed far behind their regiments in anticipation of victories and not for the will of people or sane thinking but for some unobtainable honor. Honor that filled men and women's minds, which compete continuously until no one is able to actually win, unless you take the small victories, conquests, corralling, pinching, thieving, whoring, feasting, engulfing the essence within man's reach. Until all control is a final goal missing the reasons for regret, conscience, and science.

"I don't know," Thomas said, looking at Leal after the others had gone—Talis, long back to Italia; Porius and the others on some distant journey between Elysium and millions of other worlds, civilizations, cultures, and creeds. Beings whose physical makeup may be three of four heads, parts which may be heads but unrecognizable as heads due to the chemical makeup of a certain atmosphere.

Thomas looked at Leal, standing together in the cottage warming themselves by the fire, the floating band playing on and on until the next journey takes them, holds them in a later time.

Porius and Mercurius

"Mercurius," Porius began, looking down at the almost-naked Mercurius, "riches unbound and all these centuries, you still amaze me."

"My Lord Porius, you must join us," Mercurius said, standing to greet Porius in his usual white robes of satin and golden sandals.

"If it is thy wish, what awaits our challenge?"

"Two beasts larger than a Roman castle have surrounded a village on the third green planet," Mercurius said now standing before him on the green fields of Elysium. Monuments and small thatched-roof huts arranged in disordered fashion lined the hills surrounding them. Between the houses were paths of sand, scatterings of flowers, millions of butterflies, bees, grasshoppers, and other vibrant insects, animals, reptiles, and humans.

"If it must be done, then I shall pledge thy hand," Porius said reluctantly.

"Thank ye, Porius, and come, I shall give you all I know," Mercurius said, leading Porius into one of the small huts.

Inside the hut were a few small nymphs running around playing some sort of game, Athena lying on a swinging cloth-made bed, which was held up by a lean-to-type mechanism, Simon also was present.

"Ah, Athena, Simon, I had no idea you—"

"Yes, Mercurius also took our pledge for this journey," Simon said as he leered at Porius, in the full knowledge that the noble Porius would leave nothing to chance when another civilization faced ruin.

"I call upon the light sail," Porius said, raising his wand toward the heavens and a ray of multicolored light extended before them. Far in the distance, a ship of gold and metal, laced with dark wood and a figure of Apollo at its head, rushed toward them, all eyes widened as the massive ship got closer.

"You see, my dears, the light sails are powered by the sun, controlled by Giuseppe on the other end. Now we all must board, have thy sword, armor in place because we will arrive within the blinking of an eye," Porius was saying as they all load the ship of golden metallic sails.

CHAPTER 18

Wind beginning to grow, rain began falling as dark clouds cover the grounds and only the ray of multicolored light protruded from the clouds. The ship had large golden metal masks held up by a black metallic wood-like substance, which seemed unearthly. One by one they climbed a stair made of thick rope and wrapped in brass circular hoops. Floating, the large structure had a large bubble-type clear barrier, which covered the ship on the sails of gold piercing through the bubble ceiling. Bound for another planet, another world, and even another galaxy, Athena, Porius, and Simon sat and strapped themselves in to golden chairs.

On the farthest end of the ray of light, Giuseppe, a large elderly man standing with white beard and ragged robes, shouted, "All aboard!"

"We are ready," Porius said after looking around at Mercurius staying behind with others now surrounding and waving to Porius, Athena, and Simon.

"I failed to mention this ship only can carry three, so here we go," Porius said as an elven man in metal armor and black boots stood behind a large wheel like that aboard ships of the fifteenth century.

"Beautiful sails," Athena said, gazing up at the large golden sails now glowing in the rays of some distant sun, and then there was a blur and the light faded. As if yawning mental feelings that seemed like sleep for the shortest of moments, they all opened their eyes. Hundreds of feet below was a world of green hills, rolling fields, running rivers, and a small village that resembled some ancient French village of the fifteenth century. People were running and scattering. Cartloads of hap, food, produce, and meats headed for the outer areas. Smoke filled parts of the air from burning huts, stables, and stores. In the background and up on the highest hill stood a great castle, close in style to Dover, with a drawbridge, moat, and sea on the other side, winged animals flying about as the ship hovered over the castle grounds descending until it landed.

"Porius, Athena, and Simon, so very good of you to come and lend a hand," Giuseppe said, greeting them out front of the castle and up on a hill, the village in turmoil below and the noise of shouting heard far in the distance.

"Our most sincere pleasure," Porius said while Athena and Simon bowed to Giuseppe, and then both turned to watch the view of chaos in the lower elevation.

"You see," Giuseppe said, pointing from one side of the valley to the next. "Terror I tell you, terror. They will destroy the village." Giuseppe told Porius of the past night and the huge monster with several heads slithering down one from the west and one from the east bearing down on the village, its inhabitants scrambling to grab what they could and get out of the village.

"Not if we have anything to say," Porius said, looking at Simon and Leal.

"The three branches," Athena said to Giuseppe.

"Yes, here, all prepared as requested." Giuseppe clapped his hands, and there came two dark-skinned men wearing loincloths made of some purple material and fitted with sword hands Simon, Athena and Porius each a large wooden branch.

The all whisper something to the branch and answering to the whispers the branches widen and ready for carrying.

"Let's mount," Simon said. Eagerly the three mounted their branches and flew, Athena toward the eastern monster; Simon the western, an even larger beast; and Porius circling the village and flying over the burning huts one by one, shouting an d pointing his wand.

"Accumulati oprenda," Porius shouted, pointing his wand as the fire weakened and froze with some snow-like covering. The amazed villagers once running stood still, looking back at the miracle, realizing of course that Porius was good and on their side, their eyes filling with hope.

"Hooray, Porius," many shouted victories and returned to assist in putting out the fires.

"Now you will taste my blade," Athena said, circling the large beast with several heads and snakelike limbs. She dove, plunging her sword toward one in which the eye floated of its head. Swiping, the severed eye fell far to the ground below. Both creatures stood about twenty feet high and swirling snakelike limbs toward Simon and Athena.

Simon tried the same method and severed an eye. But as both creatures' eyes fell, two more grew back in their faces; and fueled by hurt and pain, the monster roared and screeched a mighty roar, which almost toppled Simon. Athena's creature turned toward her and roared as Athena angered the creature. She lured him away from the village, and to follow her up the will, Simon did the same.

"Take this," Athena said, plunging as she dove toward the creature's heart. Hitting her mark and retrieving her blade, she regained her altitude and Simon followed suit.

"Careful, Simon, these beasts are tricky," Athena said to herself, hovering ten feet over her creature, her eyes on Simon as he plunges. "Steady, Simon, steady."

Simon hit his mark and, pulling his sword out quickly, also regained altitude and hovered over the beast.

Simon's eyes were on Athena to watch her next move, and she did another go for the heart of the beast, hit her mark, and Simon followed suit. Both regained altitude and watched as the creatures weakened and eventually die in a pile of slithering limbs and blood.

Unlike the insects and bios of earth, the third green planet where Giuseppe ruled was full of multicolored flying, crawling, slithering, and swimming species. Athena paid homage to Giuseppe later that evening during a lavish table of fruits, stuffed pork, pheasant-type creatures, and quail.

"Many of your species are not unsimilar to our home planet," Athena stated while sipping a goblet of wine. The goblet was silver and surrounded with multicolored gems of many shapes and sizes.

Porius was at one end of the table in his most splendid white robes, the crowds of villagers in masses outside the castle singing praises to Porius, Athena, and Simon, preparing legends of the day when the monsters were slain by our victors.

"Yes, my dear, I have visited your world, and although you are seven times our size, we are similar in many ways," Giuseppe said before filling his oral cavity with some delicious fowl.

"Oh look, a praying mantis–type creature," Porius said as a large reddish-colored insect flew in the window over the table and back out again. This made Simon jump a bit because unlike our praying mantis, this species was ten times the size.

"Actually, Lord Giuseppe, I rather feel our insects are far less intrusive," Simon said as he eyed the room for other miscreants and ate most cautiously indeed.

"Yes, wonderful place you have here, and I noticed nothing but wood and this occasional metal, but your home world is not unlike ours in 1605," Porius said then sipped his wine daintily.

"Thank ye, yes, our scientist have learned to work with our natural products, and birth control is of most importance here, for we must never again grow in population to minimize the risk of overfishing our own small planet. It works quite well. But the creatures do occasionally land and attack," Giuseppe said in sympathy for the large beasts recently slain on the hills surrounding the village.

"This is a wise and noble approach to maintaining a healthy world," Simon replied.

Athena, Porius, Giuseppe, and several of the waiters stood around the table ready to pour more wine, fill plates, or offer water. All nodded heads in a congenial agreement and murmured some foreign tongue.

"Unfortunately, I don't see the discipline in our world. I am sure it will be years from today, but I feel our home planet will not control nature properly. I see battles, overpopulation, the poisoning of sea and air," Porius began.

"Why, Lord Porius, do you suppose of this of man?" Giuseppe asked.

"Well, Lord Giuseppe, the nature of man is possessive, combative, religious, overly ambitious, and very competitive in the extreme, more this, more that," Porius said, shaking his head in disapproval of his own statement and looking at the agreement in Athena's and Simon's eyes.

"I see, sounds very primitive. Well, at least your world is so large it can withstand the populace," Giuseppe said.

"No, it will get smaller and smaller in time with less open spaces for animals, distinction for many are under way as we sit here speaking," Athena said wisely.

Once men get the taste of turtles they will wipe them out,
Once they get the funds from selling metals they will dig them all out
Once they get the knowledge of flight and combustion engines and eventually split the atom

"It will exponentiate the population of the earth. Empires will fight for land and rights, pillaging and plundering as they go.

"Religions collide with daily dislikes and pointing fingers and the competition of who has the bigger and most assuredly better god will rule. Unfortunately, the myths which they call gods are nothing but evil wrapped in stories to weaken the mind and create endless wars," Porius said.

"And we will be there to fight them," Simon said as he eyed a large bee, which has flown in the window and landed on the top of an unlit candle. Athena was being eyed by one of the strong young men standing behind her and to the left.

"And what is your name," Athena said to the muscular blond-haired, tanned by the two suns that circled the third green planet.

"I am Richard," Richard said as he bowed to Athena. "Your every wish is my extreme pleasure to fulfill."

"He will do that, Athena, that I can promise you," Giuseppe said, smiling.

They all laughed while Athena blushed as her present state of living flesh provided the blood to do the trick.

"I hope we will be staying the night," Athena said while undressing this muscular blond beauty from head to toe.

"My guest for the night, and we will have dancing and a few magicians who would like to put on a show for thee," Giuseppe said eagerly.

"Oh yes, then we must stay," Porius said happily as the doors to the outside opened outward.

Men dressed and undressed with balancing balls and skipping rope, women wearing only blue ribbons wrapped around ankles danced before them, and the large hall outside was filled with villagers, shopkeepers, musicians, cobblers, and knightly participants who also looked to be of royal blood, slaves, and footmen surrounding these richly clothed participants. The night turned into a splendid affair, joyous in every respect, the swirling music, flowing wine and smoke, feasting and amazing shows performed by poets, musicians, dancers, and erotic acts many of which Athena, Porius, and Simon had never witnessed before.

Much later in the wee hours of the morn, Athena ascended the stairs to her awaiting chamber with Richard in tow. Simon retired with two beautiful maidens; Porius was given a large room with a large tube of bubbles fueled by wind and was disrobed and caressed by several male and female professionals for this type of occasion. All was well, and when the morn came on the third green planet, another ship awaited the three; and upon a ray of light, they descended until they all returned peacefully to the cottage, Thomas pouring tea, the floating band playing a tuneful happy song, the deer, squirrels, pigeons, and Franklin going about their daily routines among the garden and forest. Meanwhile, rumors of another surge lay waiting at the village.

"Lord Porius, Lord Porius," a voice was heard shouting outside the cottage. "Thomas, Lord Porius, are you present, are you present?" shouted frantically this old peasant-looking gray-haired rather strangely looking individual.

"Why, if it isn't Renour Pletogini!" Porius said, sticking outside his wet head due to a morning cleaning in the back steam room, which Porius used daily to primp, design, and adjust his morning look. "Come in through the front door, we are all up." The bluebirds swirled around, the leaves falling in the slightest of breezes, and Renour came into the cottage.

"Renour, what brings you this fine morning?" Thomas said as he handed a warm cup of mead to Renour. "Welcome, my friend."

Porius came out from behind the wall dressed in his finest white and golden-trimmed robes of the finest white silk made by elven families who still hid in the forest. "What has excited you to such a most exceedingly apparent mood?" Porius asked.

"My lord, and sir Thomas, please come to the village for beyond the old hay farm are vicious men who have taken my two daughters and my teenage son. They plan on turning them into slaves and use at the monastery. They are full of their gods' spiteful words and attacking everyone who is different or unchristian. You must come quickly."

"Pious, aren't they?" Porius asked, looking toward Thomas. "Contact the pixies."

"My lord, what a splendid notion," Thomas said while running across the room for the pensive and some water.

"I think a touch of milk, more the ticket," Porius said while Renour stood sipping mead and watching the magical event unfold.

"I call upon thee, Norman, Randall, Felicia!" Porius shouted into the pensive, and three small pixies floated in the air above the pensive, obviously just waking up.

"My Lord Porius, what a pleasant surprise," Felicia said. Norman, Randal, and Felicia were all green-skinned wearing small clothes and rings of green above their bushy brows and circling the blackest hair, tiny green robes draping over their three-foot-high bodies. Randall and Norman were to the sides of Felicia.

"My need is great, and we ask for your pledge of loyalty to defend the village against some rotten intruders," Porius shouted.

"They will enjoy this invitation, to be sure," Thomas said, whispering to Renour while Porius grinned, watching the three pixies in hologram form only discussing among themselves until finally Felicia, who is usually the spokesperson of the three, spoke.

"We pixies would be delighted," Felicia said in her almost unheard voice.

"But, my lord Porius," Renour stutteringly said, "surely it will take more than pixies." As Renour spoke, Porius put his hand up and said softly, "Silence."

"We will be honored to foul the beasts, what is their appearance and local?" Felicia said as the other two disappeared for a few moments them and came back holding wands and tiny branches.

"The usual black dress, most assuredly large wooden crosses hanging from their necks." Porius turned to Renour to see if he agreed with his description.

"That is about it, but not to the far east side of the village, there is a very pleasant monk called Christopher, who is always thoughtful and kind like Christians are supposed to be."

"No, we know Christopher and shall not harm him," Felicia interluded.

"By the hay farm," Renour said.

"The hay farm it shall be," Felicia said as a loud rattle on the windows occurred throughout the cottage. Porius pointed his wand toward the pensive and shouted, "Fly!"

The three pixies in a mist of sparks and flew toward the village.

"That's most fascinating!" one woman shouted while running away from the villains who laid siege on the farm, dressed in black. Four large hooded figures were holding swords and dragging a large cage on wheels covered in think wooden planks, creaking and full of screaming children.

"Those two, beyond them mill, get them!" the leader of the pious men in black shouted while pointing to two teenage youths who ran for the river beyond the mill. They escaped by jumping naked into the icy river to flow downstream where if they didn't freeze to death would be able to crawl out to safety.

"Damn, they got away," one figure in black said with a Welsh accent.

"You fool," the leader said as he whipped the other.

The pixies circled overhead, dove down from the sky as sparks dispersed from their tiny wings. The unknowing four men in black robes still scrambled to grab more children and shove them into the cage.

"Take this morsel and feel the bite," Norman the pixie said and dropped a large spider on top of the hooded fiends.

"Ontayo bees," Randal the pixie said and waved his tiny wand by a tree that was home to a fairly large swarm of bees, the bees attacking on Randal the pixie's command.

"Take ye, thy snake," Felicia said while waving her wand near a hole in the ground and out popped three adders. "I've done this hundreds of times, and I can teach ye in several minutes," Felicia said to Norman and Randal as they seemed quite fond of Felicia's snake spell.

"Wind of high and wind of low, bring these men to their knees," Porius said back in the cottage as he and Thomas witnessed the events through the pensive through Franklin's keen eyes as he circled the event even higher than the pixie flight path.

"Muddle thy minds with tick and spike," Randal said and acting proud that he knew such a spell, but as he spoke, the bios of creatures came up from the ground, all filled with irritational beings to infest the underneath of these black robes.

"Very lovely spell," Felicia said to Randal in congratulations, and the three pixies circled and waited. Then finally altogether, the four beasts in black began shouting.

"What on earth is biting me?" one said.

"My ear, oh, my scrota, something is biting me," another shouted while shaking his robes. Soon all four men in black were now persecuted by bee, snake, insects, and other creatures who joined into the fray. Rolling, stomping, screaming, and shouting the men battled the insides of their own robes. Two men took the robes off completely as the children in the cage on wheels started laughing and pointing at their nudity. The two men jumped nude headfirst into the freezing river and floated downstream. Finally, the leader, while ripping off his robe, all three pixies flew down upon their discarded robes, grabbing their crosses left behind and tossing them one by one into the river. Norman and Randal landed on the cage and opened the lock to free the children.

"Look, pixies," one child with long red hair stated.

"Herald the pixies," another said as he ran free and went to ground.

"Stop, ye devil children, I command thee!" shouted the leader while rolling on the ground as an adder wrapped around his neck and bit his cheek. Bees swarmed and attacked the two rolling men in black robes blistering their faces as tick, spider, snake, and mole bit, irritated, and smothered the priest. The leader finally realized that the fighting was useless and jumped into the river. Downstream, they rolled and shouted as the children were freed. Felicia, Norman, and Randal flew away; and Franklin headed for home.

"Most assuredly brilliant, Lord Porius," Thomas said as he placed the pensive back on the shelf.

"Oh they will feel those bites for a while," Porius said.

Renour stood in amazement of the past half hour's events and went to his knees.

"Porius, my lord, we owe you greatly," Renour said, kneeling.

"My good friend Renour, ye shall have no need to thank. Thy would have done the same for me."

"But how and what did—" Renour began with his interlocutor but could not find the words to describe.

"Well, I should have said that if you knew the spells. Well then, I am sure you would have done the same for me," Porius said in delight that he was able to assist in preventing another desperate and cruel act committed by the church.

"Thomas will always be here if you need him, but this is something that is happening everywhere, unfortunate for most that we are not there to prevent it; but in this small island, we will do our best to protect all the families who believe in the old ways."

"Your kindness is a blessing on all of us," Renour said as he left for home.

"Quickly now, go home and let me know if the men come back in even a worse temper," Porius said, standing at the front door of the cottage watching Renour fade into the forest on his way back to the village.

"Time will tell," Thomas said to Porius.

"My fear is that these priests will now be more angered and shall return, but let's let them lick their wounds and let Franklin come home and rest." While Porius said this line, Franklin landed safely on the roof.

"You see, right on time," Porius said as he turned to see Franklin resting. "Good job, my lovely raven, very good job indeed."

"My lord," Franklin squawked.

"Now, Thomas, we need to plan something nice for our three pixie heroes, I say a party," Porius said as he gathered his pensive once more to congratulate the pixies.

CHAPTER 19

Later that evening, Porius, Athena, a few elves, and of course, the floating musicians treated the pixies to some of Parthenia and Grendle's home cooking. Even Leal, Apollo, Jewel, Frederick, Simon and Walters appeared for a short time from Elysium in form not—flesh but at least for them to make an appearance to toe victors, congratulating the pixies on a job well done.

Far below the earth's green crust, an unforeseen event began of such eventful grandeur that Horan, his local creatures, the serpents, elves, trolls, worms, snakes, and other creatures crawled from their caverns and climbed to safety. Some without protection of the sunburn and disintegrated while others sought refuge in the forests, rivers, and oceans, which circled the globe. Horan gasped for air and knocked feverishly upon the cottage door. "Porius, Thomas come quickly."

Thomas opened the door to see Horan standing drenched in water and wearing only a small waistband of a blue cloth.

"The earth is collapsing on the underworld." Horan explained, "We were all sleeping and heard the cracks, the sky began to call, the earth shook, the people and creatures ran for safety and now the underworld is collapsing."

"Quick smart, Athena, Walters, Simon, Leal!" Porius shouted into the pensive, and they all peered into the milky liquid and viewed the falling ceilings of the underworld.

"I will be back," Porius said, grabbing his staff and wearing his white. "Take me to the underworld," Porius said, and his body began spinning before them until he disappeared and they all gasped.

"He is gone," Thomas said to the others.

"I shall assist Porius," Athena said. "Take thee to the underworld."

Porius appeared in the underworld, and the ceiling was falling on the houses, huts, getting smashed one by one by large falling rocks. "Murum ascendere!" Porius shouted, and the blast of his voice echoed amid the crashing walls and failing ceilings of the underworld.

"Athena here by your side, Porius," Athena said as Porius saw Athena glistening beside him.

"Murum ascendere!" Athena shouted, holding her wand. The earth cracked all around them.

"Murum ascendere!" Porius shouted, and a large piece of moss-covered earth fell beside him only missing by an inch.

"That was close," Athena said as the rocking stopped and what was left of the ceiling remained.

"Quick, the other chambers," Porius said, running toward the next tunnel.

"Murum ascendere!" they both shouted as they went. Running creatures, splashing serpents, sea creatures, toads, frogs, lizards, snakes, all were in turmoil. One by one, Porius and Athena visited each cavern, shouted the spell, and the collapsing caverns eventually stopped. Dust and the sound of wounded creatures filled the air. Porius and Athena attended to the wounded.

Horan, after making his way back down, greeted them, and all the other creatures follow.

"We must rebuild the underworld, Porius," Horan said, hugging Porius and Athena. "You have salvaged our world, and we must find the cause of these events.

"It was thee shaking spell of Egypt, for I saw within the pensive," Porius said while touching the tip of his staff and grabbing on to Athena.

"Take thy to our host," Porius said as Athena and Porius disappeared, leaving Horan bewildered but unshaken.

"Thee shall find and deal with the fiend who tried collapsing our underworld," Horan said as he began rebuilding while elves, trolls, serpents, and other creatures came back home to the underworld, apprehensive to the extreme, most keeping a watchful eye on the ceiling, which only moments ago was falling piece by piece and bit by bit.

Porius and Athena landed in Roma at the foot of the pope's three elders. The three hooded men wearing black were surrounding an altar, and upon it a stone, the stone of purity glowing on the altar. Porius and Athena were suddenly joined by Alibastor Fraun, the Wizard of Paris.

"Alibastor, I thought you were long dead?" Porius said, startled by Alibastor's arrival as was Athena.

"Oh, Porius, I read your tale and also went into the sea when I died and have also been resting on Elysium. But I heard of the destructive attempt on the underworld and followed the same trail as thee," Alibastor Fraun said.

The three men of the pope turned to see Porius, Athena, and Alibastor behind them and raised swords to attack.

Porius raised his staff. "Be still!" Porius shouted, and the three froze in place only their eyes wide and following Porius as he circled them. Athena grabbed the stone.

"Now how doth thee have taken charge of thy stone of purity?" Athena said, placing the stone safely in her pocket.

"Jewels of my forefathers," Alabaster said. "How dare thee!"

"Well, these fools cannot move now, though they can follow us with their eyes. Take the stone back to Canterbury," Porius said to Athena and Alibastor. "Oh, and a pleasure to see you again, Alibastor of Fraun."

"As always, my Lord Porius, we shall travel back to Canterbury." They dissolved.

"Well now," Porius said with focused attention to the three frozen men in black hoods and wooden crosses. "First, I shall take thee symbols of torture from thy necks." Porius took the crosses and threw them all three into the fire, which burned bright in a large hearth along the west wall of the Roman cathedral.

"You three will be frozen for a good twenty-four hours to remain a spectacle for ye parishioners, which come to visit or your flock as it were," Porius said, circling the three still frozen only their eyes following Porius and, of course, hearing his every word as he spoke in Latin.

Eyeing the men, Porius searched their robe, and finding nothing but cloths and a few coins, he removed their hoods.

"Ahh, the map of Canterbury," Porius said, retrieving a small map with the steps of Canterbury cathedral, which showed the hiding place of the stones where Walters and others had hidden the stones.

"Oh, map and all who have gazed upon thee, forget what thee hath seen and distort the minds of those witness to the hiding place," Porius said, waving his wand over the map and then tossing it into the fire to burn.

"The look in the eyes of confusion and they forget all, the journey, the destination, and beyond walks in the pope. Pope Leo XI or known to many as Pope Alessandro de Medici.

"Alessandro, take thee a fever and may thy reign be short," Porius said to a bewildered pope and, spinning, disappeared before them, leaving the pope to sweat and fall to the ground. The others remained frozen for a day then once thawed also came down with fever and eventually died. Alessandro lived until April and then died of fever.

Athena, back on Elysium, glanced into the large mirrors that lined her walls of golden painted wood, plush purple-and-green satin overstuffed pillows, and deep blue silk and satin bed coverings surrounded by green and gold cushions. Walters stood above Athena's beautiful figure, her full lips of pink and ivory skin, feminine yet muscular, smiling yet yearning for Walters. Walters's hair-covered chest, muscular stomach, muscles of deep indentations, which she rolled her finger down as he knelt down to her and embrace. Far for time is the distance of love, yet close together they embraced. Athena rolled in coquettish giggles, long blond and golden strands of hair, which when released thundered down her back. When the emotion of Athena's sensuality reached a peak, the sky outside thundered, rained, and winds appeared. As Walters reached his final burst of excitement, lightning penetrates the earth from beyond the clouds made by Athena on Elysium.

1700 England

"The earth and time treat thee kindly," Porius exclaimed, peering into his pensive while sipping wine among the creatures of Elysium, no one paying any attention to Porius most days.

Years have passed, and Thomas was still at the cottage in form not flesh as it had become of often lately. Someday, Thomas would join Porius in Elysium, but not until the earth was safe once again for all the magical creatures who were sent from the earth so as to not live side by side with the Christians who now rule the earth. Thomas, the cottage, and several small patches of witches, druids, freethinkers, and other mystical beings must remain in isolation for many years until the hatred went from religion. As the centuries passed, long had earth been visited by Porius as they used or abused the power of turning from form to flesh and traveling back to earth from the safe surroundings of Elysium.

William of Orange ruling England was known as William III, sovereign Prince of Orange still enjoying his victory of Battle of the Boyne ten years hence. This monarch believed that authority derived directly from God. The Dutch territory made William stadtholder of Drenthe; Jacobites then plotted to assassinate him in an attempt to restore James to the English throne. Then William and Louis XIV prepared the Treaty of London, Charles of Spain lay dying in bed, and other countries were in turmoil—boundaries, borders, religions fighting of gods, territories, farms, inheritances. The church was scourging across Italy, Spain, France, and England. Porius, Leal, Walters, and Athena, even though in Elysium, heard the news of the day and watched through their home pensive the events, battles, hangings, massacres, which had become a daily event on earth.

"Thomas, Thomas, anyone there?" Porius's voice was heard shouting out of the pensive, which rested in isolation upon the main room table within the cottage. Thomas came rushing in from out in the garden.

"Porius, my Lord Porius, how art thou?"

"Keeping rather well, my good friend."

"Nice to see you, my friend," Thomas said, looking down at Porius's reflection in the pensive.

"What are those creatures beside you?" Thomas asked.

"These are lemur-type creatures from some other galaxy. I really don't know, but they are quite pleasant creatures."

"I see, my lord, what makes you call?"

"I want to make you aware of an ordeal happening not far from the cottage in Dover. Stay out of Dover, in fact, don't travel at all for a while. Stay home."

"Yes, my lord, I have heard of the battles here, jacobian, you know."

"Indeed, most unfortunate."

"Wait a moment, I have someone for you to meet, his name is Bryan," Thomas said, and he ran to the door and introduced his new student to Porius.

"Greetings, Bryan," Porius said.

"My lord Porius, it is quite an honor, I have heard of you."

"Yes, I am sure Thomas has kept you well informed and a pleasure to meet you. Study hard," Porius said as they chatted, briefing on spells of new and old, asking where in his training Thomas had spent on the boy.

"My Lord Porius, will I get a change to by thee?"

"Yes, Bryan, I shall be there within the year. Stay close to Thomas and learn the spells of protection, we need you. Make sure he tells you about the ancestors and dreams. Bye for now," Porius said and disappeared.

"Aye, dreams, ancestors?" Bryan asked.

"Indeed, you see, Porius believes that all our dreams are just memories that were transferred to us from earlier ancestors who share our bloodlines. So in theory, all ancestors know what the future generations are up to, and current peoples can know what their ancestors went through."

"Interesting."

"My Lord Porius has mastered the art of following those dreams and pinpointing who, what, where, and on and on. His interpretation of dreams gives proof that our mortal shell withers and dies, but our energies, or aura as Porius likes to call it, goes on for eternity. To bring back form is the difficult part and only a few who have blood from alien lives who transcend molecular ratability," Thomas stated, winded.

"Sounds most confusing," Bryan said, wearing short britches and leather straps and holding a white owl who took off from his hands and soaring up to the treetops then landing and scanning for its next scrumptious meal. The owl in question was called Oliver. Franklin was not a huge fan of this obtrusive white owl, but they got along.

"Bryan, tomorrow is your twenty-third birthday, and I want to make it special," Thomas said as they moved to the garden benches and table made from ancient white oak and beech.

"How doth thy know my day of birth is tomorrow?" Bryan said, sitting with books of spells displayed on the table and writing quills, paper, and a few half bottles of mixed potions.

"Oh dear boy, Porius was most precise when he gave me your background information," Thomas said, sitting behind him. "Our lessons today will include using pastel-colored candles to make a home more agreeable to others, taking small leafy branches and string to keep the home happy to passersby and a few protection spells."

"Both spells you mention do sound rather useful." Bryan was in agreement of his daily lessons.

"Then you and I will visit the village, buy a few items from the market, and stop to see how Mrs. Brenville's knee is doing, possibly change the bandage."

"I believe Mr. Brenville owes a piece of gold for attentions to his wife performed already," Bryan said, rubbing his chin.

"Well, I will leave you on charge of Mr. Brenville," Thomas said, opening his large book and sitting in front of Bryan. "Begin, wand to the ready."

Later that night on the way back from the village, Bryan's owl Oliver and Franklin the raven swooped down, almost hitting Bryan and Thomas.

"Silly fowl," Thomas said as Franklin swooped by playfully, the moonlight piercing through the treetops as the sounds of the forest consumed them, rabbits, deer, wolves, and pigeons aplenty mixed in with the hundreds of other creatures of the forest.

"Life is grand," Bryan said, patting Thomas on the back, but his hand swept through his form.

"Thomas, you are fading," Bryan expatiated as Thomas's form glowed, softly moving as if walking but leaving no prints behind.

"Yes, saving energy, saving energy." Thomas waved his wand at a large thick patch of trees alongside the river and the trees moved aside and let them pass. Bryan's bare muscular thigh was getting slightly grazed by the conifer branches as they wisped back once the two gently enter the garden of the cottage. Bats and other owls swirled and played, Franklin and Oliver at rest on the thatch.

"Get in here, you men," Grendle and Parthenia said at the front door carved with deer and rabbit, which was open, revealing a large plate of fresh food.

"My good women, this is feast," Bryan said as they stepped inside and beheld a pile of cooked pheasant, greens, cakes, and wine.

"My Lord Bryan, this feast is for thy birthday, you prince of men," Parthenia said as she gave Bryan a peck on his round blushing cheek.

"Thank ye, my dear friends," Bryan said as Thomas regained full form and tucked in.

"Did you tell Bryan of tomorrow?" Grendle asked in anticipation.

"No, not as yet," Thomas said while chomping down on a big piece of fowl and washing it back with wine.

"What is it, Thomas, you must say?" Bryan said, sipping his wine and putting his hand out to Thomas.

"Tomorrow you will visit the underworld," Thomas said, standing and opening his arms toward Bryan.

Bryan stood and hugged Thomas. "I have made it. Oh, I am so pleased."

"Your lessons have been achieved, your deeds of goodness received. Thy place awaits you in the underworld," Thomas said lyrically as the small floating band appeared and played a late-sixteenth-century volta. "Our friends are arriving."

The light of the outdoors glowed from the garden, and the garden was filled with magical lights, golden chariots, horses with wings, as the rays shone through the windows.

"What is going on?" Bryan ran to the cottage front door, and in burst Porius in the flesh.

"Well done, Bryan, well done and congratulations. Well done indeed," Porius said as he entered dressed in the finest long-flowing white silk robes laced with gold, his head covered in a wreath of vines, holding berries, flowers, and wines in his hands.

"Porius," Bryan said, hugging him.

Following Porius was Leal wearing only a small thin blue cloth tied to one side, the rest of him bare as well as his feet.

"Leal, I have heard so much," Bryan said as he stared at Leal, possibly the most beautiful male specimen he had ever seen and stood unable to speak.

CHAPTER 20

Leal hugged him. "Congratulations on passing all the course, my dearest Bryan, a pleasure to meet you and welcome to the group." Leal bowed to Porius, Thomas, and the door through which entering was Athena and her two golden guards waiting for her outside and standing, one on each side of the door, swords at the ready.

"Athena." Bryan stared at Athena's most alluring and beautiful golden threads that circled her naked body, breast covered slightly in white silk, and a small waistband of silk, golden threaded shoes, which laced up to just below her knees.

"Pleasure to meet you, Bryan. Well done and welcome," Athena said, putting out her hand toward Bryan who kissed it lightly, and tears of joy filled Bryan's eyes.

"Short of Walters and Simon, Jewel and Frederick," Porius said to Bryan as the others grabbed the delicious food and tucked in.

"This is my most absolute dream, to meet all of you." Bryan stood still in amazement of his good fortune, growing up in Kent with all the stories of past adventures, sea serpents, other worlds, the underworld.

"And you are going to the underworld?" Leal said, sitting on the back area by the window, wine in one hand and a large piece of pheasant in the other. "I look forward to seeing you off."

"Yes, my lords and ladies, my heart beats with excitement. Not sure how I will sleep tonight," Bryan said.

"Oh, you must sleep later. You will be thankful of rest once you have spent your first night in the underworld," Thomas said with everyone in agreement. Porius and Athena were in a small type of dance.

"Room of thee expand and we shall dance within," Porius said, waving his wand in one hand and holding on to Athena's waist with the other. The cottage main room expanded larger and larger, the cracking and creaking of the expanding walls, Leal laughing and falling to the floor, the tables rattling and shaking, and Oliver and Franklin squawking and hooting in complete annoyance of the expanding room. They hovered for a moment and circled the garden once then found a new place to rest on the new large roof.

"Dance, dance. Gloria and Alexandria, come in, come in, dance with us," Thomas shouted, and the two guardians of Athena entered. Alexandria picked the nearly naked Leal up from the floor as Gloria danced with Bryan.

"I am Gloria, and she is Alexandria," Gloria said as the start to swirl to the waltz now being played by the floating band, who by the way was dresses in the finest silks.

"I am Bryan," he said, almost stuttering as her breast presses against his and their eyes smile at each other.

"Yes, we have heard that you visit the underworld tomorrow. We came to see you off," Gloria said as they all danced. Thomas exchanged partners with each in turn, Bryan with Alexandria, Athena, and Bryan, even spending some time with Leal and Porius. The party ensued, the night came late as a slight rain fell outside until later, they all rested. Thomas was back in his bedchamber with Alexandria, Leal asleep on the rug beside the fire, Bryan in his chair, Athena and Porius vacating completely, and in the morning only Bryan, Leal, and Thomas remaining. Bryan woke up and saw Leal, naked and snoring in front of the fire. Thomas was heard among the running water in the back of the cottage and came out toweling himself.

"Don't mind Leal, he will wake up soon. Your turn," Thomas said, pointing Bryan to the running water area to refresh himself before the long journey.

"Wake up, Sir Leal," Thomas said, leaning over the beautiful Leal who rolled over onto his back, eyes shining blue, thick pitch-black hair, and pearl-white skin.

"Is it time to send the boy to the underworld?" Leal said, standing and tightening his thin cloth of blue silk tight around his thirty-inch waist.

"At last his time has come, for once he reached Horan and journeys through the underworld, Bryan will be more useful to us in the future than one hundred men," Thomas said.

"One hundred, oh, that many?" Bryan stepped out from the running water and toweled his body then reached for his clothes.

"You won't need those," Leal said.

"What, dear Leal, my clothes?"

"Well, it is mostly true," Thomas explained.

"All my clothes?"

"Well yes, you see—" Thomas began, but Leal interrupted.

"Thing is, young sir, you will not be able to hold them through the journey," Leal continued. "Clothes don't travel to the underworld and the only way to enter is as you entered this world, naked."

"Oh, I see, well then, I am ready."

They all walked outside and stood by the fountain.

Birds circled and played, the images of Porius, Athena, Alexandria, and Gloria all surrounded them. Bryan was standing close to a rock by the river.

"Open thee and take thy whole person," Porius said, waving his wand, and Bryan spun and turned into the ground, lower and lower until he can be seen no longer.

Tumbling, bouncing, turning, and swirling was the pathway to the underworld. Bryan's mind filled with images of dragons, mushrooms, elves, and legends as he fell. Deeper into the earth he rolled, wiggled, shook, and was filled with new sensations that made his silky white skin electrified with stimulus never before felt. Exhausted, enthralled, emotionally charged, and slightly aroused, Bryan finally landed on the green mossy ground of the underworld.

Bells far off were heard ringing, light far-off melodies of song, a sky filled with jewels, darts of light, creeping vines covered the walls as Bryan stood and ran to a bush of vines, tearing them and wrapping them around his waist, leaves hiding the pink bits.

"The underworld," Bryan said to himself as creatures came closer.

Elven peoples, lizards and turtles, snakes, and other crawling species surrounded him as he began his journey step by step, fairies circling him, tugging at his leaves.

"Amazing," Bryan said, eyes wide and watchful of his surroundings.

Large turtle-like creatures with human heads and two three-headed lizards waddled below his feet, making him jump a bit.

"Intense," Bryan ejaculates to the large manlike creature in front of him, covered in hair from head to toe, the creature eyed him up and down and then scampered back into the thick foliage. "What type of creature art thou?"

No comprehensible reply from the turtle-like creature, and two-foot male and three female fairies fluttered around Bryan as he slipped on the mossy floor while slimed by the mossy floor beneath him, rolling naked on the moss as the fairies dressed him in wrappings of leather and gold. Laced golden sandals fitted to his feet, one fairy placed a mesh belt around his waist while two flying fairies fit Bryan with a mesh-laced pair of trousers, which smiling Bryan accepted with gratitude.

Bryan took a path toward a small hut made of vines, leaves, straw, and amethyst that sparkled gleamed, and glowed from every angle and beyond a black sea, the same sea as others used to venture as they journeyed through the entirety of the underworld. Rats, mice, lizards, owls, and other animals raced around him, dashed about him, hundreds in the distance and scattered between many other unfamiliar beings as the door of the hut opened and out came Worland.

"You must be Worland," Brian said, pleased to see someone normal looking human wearing baggy trousers, black vest, and a French-looking hat.

"Indeed and ye must be Bryan?"

"Pleasure to meet you, Worland. I hear you are to show me how to proceed and get through the lake."

"It won't be difficult, and I see the fairies have dressed you nicely."

"They have made me quite comfortable, thank ye."

"Welcome, Bryan, student of Thomas, house of Porius."

Worland offered Bryan a plate of cooked eggs, bread, cheese, and some greens with a bottle of mead. Inside the hut were three pictures of other dwarf-type images cut into wood.

"It this your family?"

"Yes, yes, my wife and two daughters," Worland said, smiling, offering more mead to Bryan.

"You must try these mushrooms as well. It will make your journey all the better," Worland said, handing two small mushrooms, and Bryan chewed them both and swallowed them back with a big gulp of mead.

"You ate both mushrooms?"

"Was I not supposed to do so? My deepest apologies."

"Oh, not to worry, just remember whatever you feel, it will soon pass."

"What kind of mushrooms are these?" Bryan asked.

"Special I grant you, and thy will be glad of its effect."

"Now, Clarice and Harold, the water goblins, have agreed to swim alongside you because there is no current boat. Don't worry about what swims or splashes close to you in the lake. They are for the most part not vicious. Scary looking, but not vicious."

"Doth thou not have a raft or floating device for me to use?"

"Unfortunate to say, no," Worland said with hesitation. "The last raft fell apart due to the bumpy ride through the third tunnel. You will love it, my boy. Now come to the lake." Worland led Bryan to the lake, and he walked in up to his waist.

"The waters are most warm," Bryan said hesitantly.

"Now look up, see the pink in the sky?"

"Indeed I see it," Bryan said, edging out to the depths, the colorful fish circling, popping, weaving. Up a few feet ahead were Harold and Clarice.

"Keep going, my boy. Safe journey," Worland shouted as Bryan disappeared in the black.

Bryan saw the black oily water on the horizon while curious fish, eel, turtle, and the two water goblins kept an eye out for anything too unfamiliar.

"My heavens and greatly world around thy, what awaits me further beyond. This cold-looking underworld, which surrounds me," Bryan said, whispering to himself and only Clarise and Harold listening.

Harold ran his leg against Bryan's and popped up inches from his face. Startled, Bryan explained, "Oh, Harold, I have never seen thy so close." He spoke about Harold disappearing and swimming to a safer distance, tiring and continuing, swimming with a current now and watching the pink sparkling spot in the sky. Black covered the area with only occasional glimpses of lights from diamonds, jewels, and other geologic species.

"Thy shall be safe now, and we shall leave thee. Keep swimming toward the pink in the sky," Clarise gargled in her water goblin voice, and they departed quickly under the lake.

"But wait, don't leave me, wait!" Bryan pleaded, but they vanished before him.

"The loneliness is abounding in the place. Porius's ghost, what are they slithering under my legs?" Bryan said as a large serpent maneuvered between his legs,

"Oh, that is big," Bryan said as the large serpent below him not coming above surface, moved and brushed its scaly soft skin between his thighs and then disappeared.

"I feel the effects of Worland's mushrooms," Bryan said, now giggling, "Swim toward the pink. That pink seems to get farther and farther away."

A school of carp-type fish splashed around Bryan, one hopping out of the water and getting caught for the briefest of moments in Bryan's hair as he dipped below the surface and releases.

"I never knew you could be so close to fish. I feel as I am one of the fish of the lake," Bryan said as the pink shiny ceiling now stood above him.

"Ah, land ho," Bryan said, his toes now feeling soft sand beneath him until finally his ankle and foot walked toward the beach.

CHAPTER 21

Black-and-gray sands beneath him, Bryan sat on the shore to catch his breath looking far in the distance, and all he saw was black with tiny far-off sparkles as he peered out at the journey he had traveled. This beach was seemingly void of creature or fowl until a group of a small duck family with feathers glowing in purples and iridescence waddled by squawking.

"Greetings, Bryan," one duck said, passing by.

"Ducks that speak? Well, greetings to thee," Bryan said, rolling onto his stomach, resting on the shore, his feet still touching the warm soft waves.

"I had better make a move," Bryan said, standing.

But as he stood and returned to the lake to rinse the sand from his body, two women appeared before him, dressed in leather skirts and battle garb and rushing up to Bryan.

"Ye must be Bryan, house of Porius," asked one woman of black hair, black eyes, and the whitest of white skin like looking into a cloud's white softness.

"And you are?" Bryan asked.

"We are Jessica and Amy." They bowed.

"Pleasure. Bryan." He bowed.

"Brave Bryan, and quite the muscular figure indeed," Jessica said as she rubbed her hand down his chest to his waist, rolling fingers over the deep-cut stomach muscles.

"Doth thy have a wife?" Amy asked.

"Not as yet, my training forbids such an undertaking at this particular juncture," Bryan said.

"Juncture, what is this juncture?" Jessica said inquisitively.

"Never mind. Well, are you two assisting me in my journey?

"Nay, we have just come to see what the other creatures were eager to confirm and thy have not disappointed me, hath thou, Amy?"

"He is perfect," Amy said. The two women plunged toward him, rolling him to the ground; and the lovemaking ensues, the three of them rolling, kissing, feeling, and cackling. The orgy began. For several minutes, the women licked him, squeezed him, kissed him, and he returned the compliments.

After about an hour of, shall we say, some very particular delights of the flesh, the three parted ways, Jessica running to get some fruit, which she had stashed up on the edge of the forest.

"For thy journey," Jessica said, handing the grapes and other unusual-type fruits to Bryan.

"We love ye, Bryan," the women say, laughing as they disappeared into the edge of the woods.

Bryan began walking toward the rapids and submerging into the lake once more, taking the cave to the next cathedral-high cavern that awaited him, floating and swirling over slime-covered rocks and tunnels of deepest pitch black. Bryan saw nothing, and only the waves and an occasional eel, fish, or tortoise grazed his flesh until he was on the rough part of the river, rolling him and tearing him back and forth. The small bit of mesh-laced silks managed to stay on, but his sandals he had lost until finally when he reached the end of the tunnel, he saw the sandals resting in front of him on the next shore. Tying the sandals in place, he noticed this large ceiling covered in glowing rocks, the brightness of this cavern so bright it almost blinded Bryan.

"Such a brightness," Bryan said, walking to the middle of the cavern. Large bat-like fowl circled above and gave piercing screams, the sound of someone screaming in the distance.

"Get away, get away!" a voice cried out from behind the walls of jungle and foliage, which appeared teeming with life, rats, worms, snakes, caterpillars, and monkey-type creatures crying and running in all directions.

"Get back, move away from me!" the voice said now, getting closer.

Bryan turned around another bend and saw two large men in black robes. "How hath thee penetrated the underworld?" Bryan said, jumping out and screaming as he ascended on the figures in black. One figure held a large blade.

"I shall have thy blade," Bryan said to the startled figures.

The figures were obviously pillaging the youth as their captor. Bryan arrived just in time to free this youth from these fiends with crosses dangling around their necks holding large wooden crosses.

Bryan lunged low at one and hit him below his knees. The figure in black robes fell into the lake, flinging the blade into the air. Bryan rose to the challenge and grabbed the blade by its handle in midair and then plunged it into the belly of the other figure, blood pouring out of the gut, and he also fell into the lake, to his water grave. Bryan pulled the long blade out of the hole he had made. Then he swung at the head of the other figure who came back at Bryan in anger form the lake. Bryan swung and decapitated the fiend, blood gushing in every direction and covering the bound youth who had been tied facedown over a large fallen tree, naked and buttocks raised toward the sky. Bryan cut him free, and he fell into the lake, washing the blood from his body.

"I hate blood, and I don't think much of these Christian-types either," the youth said.

"Seems I came just in time, but how did they penetrate the walls of the underworld?" Bryan asked as he bowed to the now freed youth.

"I am Bryan, house of Porius."

"And I am most glad to see you Bryan, house of Porius." The youth walked up from the water. The youth appeared to have wings, pearl-white skin, and long brown hair, which hung to his waist.

"You are," Bryan asked as they both walked to the shore out from the lake or more of a pond actually.

"Steed Flanders," the youth said, bowing. "Oh, house of Worland."

"You are the son of Worland, whom I had the fortune of meeting earlier today."

"Yes, he raised me in the underworld, but I first came with my parents but before we could make the entrance to the underworld, my parents were both taken by captors of the church in Paris. I have not an idea of what fate came to them because they were adamant about not following the Christian way."

"My parents did the same. They were slaughtered in Oxford, and Porius brought me to the cottage."

"Ah Thomas, you know Thomas?" Steed said.

"My tutor and a brilliant tutor as it happens."

"Lucky you, I have had to learn from goblins who are not the best tutors, but luckily, I have learned a few things."

"Well, you have not learned the protection spells for you were in quite the precarious position when I arrived."

"Indeed, priests do like to make their advances. Though I am close to my eighteenth birthday and priests usually attack the younger boys."

"How did they get down here?" Bryan asked.

"That's the question of the day," Steed said.

"Come with me on my journey and keep me company," Bryan said.

"It is not allowed, you must face the journey alone," Steed said. "Oh look."

Behind them in the water, several water goblins, serpents, and other creatures tore at the two priests' carcasses and devoured them. Even the robes got ripped into pieces as one serpent was shaking its head ferociously as bits of material scattered around the lake.

Bryan and Steed watched the splashing and saw the blood fill that part of the pond until the blood and particles floated downstream, the fish and serpents, goblins and multicolored birds who circled picking off bits the others may have missed in the feast.

Bryan was walking with Steed along the seemingly endless white sands and jungles, ceilings of fire and studded with every imaginable jewel. Pearls lined the ponds as oysters, crabs, mussels, and crawfish populated the pools.

"You would never run out of food here," Bryan said, opening an oyster and swallowing it down.

"Would you like to visit some aliens while you are here? Oh, and these caves all lead to other caverns," Steed said, pointing at the walls surrounding the huge cavern. Monstrous in size a league and filled with jungles, lakes underwater, and rows and rows of quail marched by the boys as they feasted on oysters.

"Those quail look similar to the quail on top, but the lights, amazing."

"Yes, these quail have a tiny lantern on the beak when on top they have feathers. Below the earth is its own world, just beneath the top."

"Aliens?" Bryan said. "I would do anything to see aliens."

"Thy will is thy command or savior of the underworld, Bryan," Steed said and he led Bryan into the thick of the jungle.

Several hours passed, and they journeyed through many water pools, lily ponds with fluorescent-colored creatures and some lily flowers, which were over ten feet long, caterpillars the size of your hand, trolls, fairies, elves, and a rather odd-looking man with one leg with several blond men and women sitting around a campfire waving as Bryan and Steed passed. They passed fields of rice then wheat and then another jungle and beyond the large multijeweled wall of this massive cavern.

"The walls are so tall I cannot see the top."

"Oddly enough, clouds do form here and sometimes the top of the caverns may shed rain upon us. You should see the spectacle of rainbows that happen on this occasion. It also brings out the unicorn which hides among the jungles of this cavern."

"Not hath I ever seen or dreamed of such a place," Bryan said, peering into the large black with sparkling occasional glistens of light among the jewels embedded in the walls, ceilings, and floors of this tunnel.

"We call this tunnel the Parway,"

"The Parway," Bryan said, following Steed into the tunnel. Steed was about five feet tall, stocky, with large shoulders and strong back muscles, round pearl-white buttocks, and long muscular legs. Bryan asked, "Don't you feel vulnerable not wearing clothes?"

"The body does offend thee?"

"Nay, not in the least, just for your own safety," Bryan said nervously.

"Vulnerable form ye?"

"Nay, just the—" Bryan began when Steed turned back to him, stood close, and pecked him on the cheek and then winked into his eye.

"Thy lord Bryan would bed thee and fill hours with beauty?"

"My thoughts have rather passed in that most delicious persuasion," Bryan agreed.

"Then it's a date, now get ready, look." Steed pointed ahead, and a green moving pack of lights rolled back and forth the next cavern, and after a few twists and turns, the tunnel ended. Before them were several buildings made of emerald green, odd-looking mechanical machines that hovered and gleamed. Many ropes tied the floating machines as one would do a horse to the wooden fences. Two elongated green beings came toward Bryan and circled him. Both aliens stood at least eight feet tall. Long legs, knobby knees, greenish skin, bulging eyes, and long stringy hair, white but stained with dirt and filth cloth robes draped over their shoulders.

"Aliens, aliens, a pleasure to meet thee," Bryan said as the two large beings circled him and touched him, a grab here, a pinch there, studying every crevasse of his body.

"What do they want?" Bryan said to Steed who stood back watching the observing alien beings circling Bryan.

"He will do, he will do nicely," the first alien said to his partner, ignoring the speaking and motioning Bryan.

"It's like they don't know we are here."

"You are like a test subject to them."

"They are most peculiar," Bryan exclaimed.

The two aliens went back and discussed in private a matter that they seemed interested in. Bryan looked and them in perplexed annoyance.

"What are they discussing?"

"Not quite sure Bryan, house of Porius."

Then a large light came from behind one of the large machines that were tied and hovering.

"Porius, what brings you here?" Steed said, running up to greet Porius.

"Steed, my good fellow, how art thou? Looking good," Porius said, walking up to Bryan and Steed.

"What are the two of you doing in this tunnel?" Porius said, someone bothered.

"Porius, I have seen aliens," Bryan said in excitement.

"Yes, dearest Bryan, but there is a price to pay when you meet them."

"A price," Bryan said, standing in dumb stupefaction.

"I forgot to mention, you may have to do them a favor."

"Favor?" Bryan asked.

"I have a funny feeling that Steed here was tired of doing favors for the aliens and brought you here to take his place for at least one favor. We shall see."

"What kind of favor, Porius?" Bryan asked, a bit frightened.

"A journey, an exchange, anything. These fellows are crafty and strong. Leave it to me for I doubt highly that they will want to exchange conversation with one as young as you," Porius said, walking up to the aliens still discussing the likes of Bryan.

"My good friends, good morrow to thee, and may I assist you in your concern?"

"Hail higha dn hail low, Porius. Nice to see you," the first said as the other was still whispering items of interest about Bryan.

"Nice to see you both, now can—" Porius tried to continue, but they ignored him and continued with their closed session, one putting his hand out toward Porius.

"One minute, Porius. Okay, we have decided," the obvious leader finally said, standing before Porius, Porius positioning himself down breeze to avoid the stench of these creatures.

"He will not do, after all, Porius. You may take him." The alien bowed to Porius.

"Why, thank ye, thank ye, my good fellows and peace be with you," Porius said and then rushed back to Bryan and Steed, grasping them forcefully by the arms.

"Let's get out of here before they change their minds," Porius said while innocent Bryan lingered a bit and then the aliens turned.

"Wait, wait, wait, wait," the aliens said and they ran back to grab Bryan while Porius raised his wand.

"Now, Porius, your wand holds no power over us."

"I know, but this is one of my best students. We have plans, we need him."

"Oh, we will only borrow him for a short while," they said, walking back to one of the floating ships covered in metal mesh, ropes, and bits of electronic metal wires, which appeared to be filled with moving currents. One of the large aliens picked up Bryan by the waist and set him into the ship.

The other untied the ship and smacked on the obvious rear of the ship, and it shot off into the distance up and out of the cavern through a large hole now closing and gone from sight. Only the voice of Bryan could be heard screaming, "Porius!"

"Well, Steed, I hope you haven't killed him," Porius said, the other two aliens laughing and walking back to their odd green buildings.

"Well, there is nothing we can do but wait. I shall go with you to Worland's and sleep there for the night."

Panning to his left, Bryan saw lights quickly passing and making him a bit nauseous from the start. He looked to the left, and it revealed the same. Pressure building in his head and feeling sick, he slept the deep black pressure-filled sleep. Memories flooded his mind, his father egging him on to meet the girls in the village, yet Bryan's mind would rather be filled with magic. Yes, the thought of kissing and rolling in the hay with the breadmaker's daughter filled him with delight, but his studies came first.

"Dad, the old ways are leaving, and I must dedicate myself." His father hugged him and with a smile closed the bedroom door, candles flickering from the rush of wind provided by his father's nightly wave from the closing door, leaving Bryan in his room with his studies. Then the images of the ravers, priests, and angry mobs that the church ignited under his family, taking his parents and leaving Bryan. "Mother, Father!" Bryan called out in his sleep on his way to the stars as his memory and dreams were next filled with the struggling with men in black cloaks wearing the large wooden crosses of Christianity. In one struggle, Bryan managed to rip a cross and throw it into a fire-smoldering ember from what was left of his neighbors after several struggles to escape. Bryan ran for days and knew of the cottage. Once Franklin spotted Bryan circling the hidden forest, Bryan finally was guided to the right garden and permitted to enter.

Bryan slept over. He was ship docked in a green-filled land of other alien creatures that looked a lot like the two that first sent him or whisked him away on this particular journey. The ship landed, and Bryan, with blurred vision and head spinning, puked over the side of the ship.

"To be expected. Wait here," a large alien said, holding one hand on Bryan's head, his large green alien hand easily palming Bryan's head.

"This one is quite spectacular, my lord," the alien shouted back to some other ominous figure who apparently was in charge of this mission.

"Does he have wings?" the voice from behind his captor shouted back.

"No, my lord, it is another and even more beautiful."

"Bring him to me," the voice commanded.

Picking up Bryan by his waist and placing him in front, pushing him toward a large alien with thick black hair wearing red and blue silk robes, a four-feathered hat, boots on finest leather, and big silver buckles upon well-polished boots.

"Bring him closer and turn him," the large king-like figure said, motioning for the guard to spin Bryan so he could view his body.

"Spin," the alien guard commanded.

Bryan turned slowly.

"A very skimpy thing you have chosen to wear," the king stated.

"My lord, I was visiting the under—" Bryan said when interrupted.

"Yes, yes, we watched your arrival and Porius trying to stop them from sending—" the guard said.

"Silence!"

"Why, my lord?"

"It is all right to let the boy speak. Are you friends of Steed?" the king asked.

"Not particularly friends," Bryan replied.

———

275

"But how did he convince you to take his place on this journey?"

"Actually, I do not see the opportunity for choice in the matter. It all happened so quickly," Bryan said, standing in nothing but the waist covering provided by fairies when they added his mesh skirt, which only barely covered is genitals and buttocks with gold chains around the sides holding it up.

"Yes, well, let your fight begin," the king said and sat on a throne made of gold and bejeweled and set on wheels.

"Come, come," the king said and waved to two other apparently female aliens, their large green breasts which hung naked over a skirt of white silken and woven with butterflies and toad images. The two women stood behind the king and punched his throne on wheels toward a path that led to a large stadium filled with people.

The crowd roared as the king entered.

"Our champion!" the king shouted to the crowd.

Bryan pushed into the center of a large stadium grounds of at least a forty-feet-long field where he stood, the crowd cheering and whistling, some yelling out comic quotations and ridicule.

"Oh, he's a pretty one, bring on the killer! He won't last a second, but I'll take him after, hooray, champion!"

"Now this one is from earth so please, manners, manners don't forget your hospitality to our guests," the king shouted through a large microphone, which reverberated around the screaming and excited crowd.

Bryan noticed a branch of tree at the edge of the stadium.

"Portillo ambana, come the replicant wand," Bryan whispered and reached toward the branch, which stood thirty feet away.

"What's this?" the king said, eyeing Bryan's gesture.

"Portilli ambana, make thee thy replicant wand," Bryan said again, remembering a spell Thomas had taught him last season. The branch broke and magically flew safely to Bryan's hand.

"Not fair, you brought me a wizard!" the king shouted into the microphone. The crowd went quiet, and a large ferocious beast with five heads was released. Large gates pulled back, and Bryan was standing with his wand pointing at the charging creature, all heads roaring with a scratching yell.

"Tatalum fretato," Bryan said. Pointing his wand at one of the five heads, the head shrank from fifteen feet long to about two inches, the other four heads turning to look at its fifth shrinking head.

"Tatalum fretato." He pointed his wand to another, and the second head shrank. But it was still charging now with three heads and only a few feet from Bryan. Large octopus-type limbs reached out toward Bryan, wrapping his tentacles that suction cups stuck around Bryan, leaving his one hand with the wand free.

"Poricocoman!" Bryan shouted, pointing at the chest of the beast. A large blast came from the wand and hit the creature dead on. The creature fell back, its tentacles releasing from Bryan's body. Popping was heard while the tentacles released his skin, leaving perfect red circular hoops all around his body.

The crowd roared to an incredible volume, cheering the victor and chanting, "Bryan, Bryan, Bryan."

"Yes, yes, by all the rules provided by our directions, Bryan is the victor," the king said, standing, smiling, and even joining the crowd in clapping.

"Earthlings never stop to amaze me," the guard said to Bryan as they left the center of the stadium through the gates were once the large beast once stepped in to kill Bryan.

"Disgusting," Bryan said, noticing the crowd come down from the stadium and start tearing apart the beast who had lost his honor and title to Bryan.

"What are they going to do to the poor creature?"

"That will be dinner. For many in the villages, a beast with five heads is a delicacy, found mostly in the island of Turin behind the coastal mountain," the guard said, wearing what on earth would be called battle fatigues made of brown leather and silver buttons.

"Makr yhey sheath," Bryan used his makeshift wand create a sheath that appeared on his waist, and he placed the branch inside the sheath.

"Hmm, okay," the guard said, leading Bryan into a long chamber full of cells along the side with all types of creatures moaning and howling inside the cages. "Let us out, mercy! Stranger with magic, let us out," they all yelled toward the guard and Bryan passing.

"What fate becomes these creatures?" Bryan asked the guard.

"The same as the creature you defeated, I am afraid," the guard said. "Now don't dawdle, quickly the king must not be left waiting."

"One moment," Bryan said. He turned to the line of cages and whispered, "Free thee." He flicked his wand toward the line of cages. Creaking and opening locks could be heard, and all the beasts broke free. Bryan ran toward the end of the hall, the guard running behind Bryan.

Bryan reached the end before the large awkward-walking alien who was once his captor. Shutting the gate before the alien had time to exit, Bryan said, "There, now you have your captors." Bryan turned and heard the screaming captor behind obviously being taken by the now-freed creatures awaiting their fates.

"What has thou gone and done to my slaves?" the king said, standing before a large crowd behind him laughing.

"I knew he would be useful," another well-dressed alien said behind the king.

"I could not resist," Bryan said.

"Never mind, Bryan," the king said in joyous fervor. "Come and meet our committee, friends and royal family. Eat, drink, and be merry."

Bryan looked at the party, which has erupted into quite a ball. Hundreds of people crammed into a ballroom of not as large a size needed for the occasion.

"It is so rare that any champion beats a five-headed monster. I am sure Thomas will be proud of his star pupil," the king said, walking Bryan to meet lines and lines of people, aliens, figures of many shapes, weights, and sizes with all types of wardrobe, some in golden threads, some in seventeenth-century exotic garb from earth, some in futuristic battle outfits that looked like something another far-off futuristic planet would wear. A large orchestra played loud pumping danceable music with several girls in cages wearing bikini-style outfits and dancing with sexual contagious rhythms. A large table held several cakes, and muscular earth men paraded in the party wearing only golden slippers and bowties. One came up to Bryan and offered him a goblet of champagne. Bryan accepted, and the muscular waiter went on through the crowd, occasionally getting fondled by the passersby.

"What an amazing place, and I see very multicultural as well," Bryan said as he was led to several lizard-type people, rabbit-type people, and one with a mule body only below the waist.

"Centaurs?" Bryan asked, pointing to the large beast leaving the party by hoof.

"Indeed, Bryan, centaurs are extremely useful at moving large bits of furniture, and we needed to get this center table in for your party."

"Now everyone, lords, ladies, friends," the king said to the crowd as he stepped up on a small platform and motioned for the orchestra to stop playing.

"Silence for a moment. Allow me to introduce you to Bryan," he said, pointing to Bryan the circles of red finally disappearing from his skin made by the once nearly fatal creature.

"Greetings to you all," Bryan said.

The crowd yelled, shouted, screamed, whistled in congratulations of Bryan beating a five-headed monster. This was such a rare occasion on this far-off alien world.

"We Altarians give you freedom to stay or leave as you choose, we name the Lord Bryan."

"Why, thank you, my Lord," Bryan said, bowing to his most generous king and thinking Altarians.

"Altar has found a champion, and when you need of us, we shall be there for thee," the king said. The crowd cheered; the music began again; the dances, performers, jugglers, and sexy intervals continuing throughout the night until midnight when a piano player came out and played a most beautiful piano piece, which made everyone cry, even Bryan.

"What a wonderful evening this has been," Bryan said to the tired king of Altar.

"Yes, would you like to sleep alone or visit the orgy or—" the king said, interrupted by Bryan.

"Orgy?"

Morning came too quickly, and Bryan freshened up in the river beside the large green castle among the forest of Altar. Many people, aliens, animals, and working folk were outdoors also bathing and doing morning chores each day's normal activities ensued. Bryan eventually was set back into his traveling ship, and after he had traveled through the proper tunnels of light, he ascended once more to the underworld and a smiling Porius. Porius took him from the creatures.

"Now, Bryan, please stay on the path and try not to take too many more detours. Oh, and by almost any means, do not listen or believe what Steed may say."

"Morning, Bryan, morning, Porius," Steed said as he fluttered by them about fifty yards toward the edge of the forest and disappeared into the trees.

"Right you are, Porius, but it was quite an adventure, and the orgy at the end, well . . ."

"I can well imagine," Porius said, setting Bryan back on the path toward the rest of his journey through the underworld.

———

The rest of the journey went as usual, and after a few days, Bryan returned to the cottage, greeted by Athena, Walters, Leal, Simon, Jewel, Frederick, Porius, Thomas, Grendle and Parthenia, and of course, Alexandria and Gloria who guarded the outer garden of the cottage. Tales spun between them, and the floating band played on and on in the cottage. Athena, who followed Alexander the Great since 330 BCE assisted with the Antigonid Kingdom, Hellenized Kingdom, and the Seleucid Empire. Athena would have never guessed that in 476, Italy would succumb to an advance led by Odoacer, who was an intern supplanted by Ostrogoths under Theodoric the Great in 493. The Roman province of Britain, which had broken away from the empire in 411, suffered complete political collapse as Angles and Saxons mounted invasions across the North Sea. Athena had assisted in rescuing thousands of Old World families from Greece, Rome, Wales, France, and now though residing as immortal among others in Elysium. Leal, claiming his honor in Bourges, France; Cognac; and Troyens as he battled and Porius as he saved thousands during the 1523–1544 reformation in Sweden. King Gustavus Vasa sought to establish his national church, still in communion with the papacy. Catholic church property was finally seized in 1544, and Sweden was declared a Protestant nation. And here they were once more together at the cottage, refueling, singing, playing, and bathing in the waters of Kent, England, home of magical creatures and transportation contact and location to Elysium and all other far-off planets and civilization whose distance was too far across the universes to travel by practical and known science. Porius and his bloodlines went back through many millennia long before the 3000 BCE life of King Narmer of Upper and Lower Egypt.

Deer played and scampered about with fawns. Large quails walked by in straight lines. Pigeons, doves, swans, hawks, Franklin and his friends, rabbits, turtles, squirrels, possums, and all the animals of the forest were in their normal realm. And below the bios, the insect kingdom, building, pushing shoving, creating new pathways, enriching new kings and queens in the ant and butterfly kingdoms. Ants, bees, ancient spiders, worms, flies, and every insect of the bios construct and reconstruct their worlds upon this one until all were in harmony together. From other worlds to ours to the bios and the undersea, underworld, and every molecular combination of being generates their own tales within and among the garden of the cottage.

CHAPTER 22

Turning, spinning, and forever weaving the casual processes of life flowing amid the energies, which lay endlessly around the immortals of the cottage where Thomas and Bryan remained. On the eleventh day of November 1727, George Frideric Handel finished the version of the soon-to-be-commissioned piece *Zadok the Priest* in preparation for the day in which King George the Second was to be crowned at Westminster Abbey. George was rather Germanic for the taste of Porius and close to the church. Thomas and Brian awaited the next chance to defend those in need of medical attention, food, relationship issues, mental illnesses, loneliness, and other annoyances to the human soul. Bryan was much older, but Thomas since long has been able to change shape become form and not flesh or just flesh. Bryan would need to wait until his body grew elderly, withering before submerging into water and becoming reborn with a new immortal image and acquiring a pathway to Elysium and the immortals. But many adventures awaited Bryan and Thomas with the coronation of George II.

Franklin circled in the November midnight moon over the cottage and smelling its smoldering embers beneath the chimney. Thomas was asleep with a coronation celebration hat in his armchair, Bryan sprawled out like Leal would usually do when visiting in front of the fire. Franklin widened his circle and over the conifer treetops where owls stared at his circling before he plunged down upon his next victim, which happened to be an innocent unknowing rat. Caught in his talons and brought back to his steady branch toward the tip of the pine, Franklin saw the fireworks across the villages celebrating their new king. George Augustus, Parliament ruling in its own way as not concerned as much with this monarch having spent so much time in Germany. As Handel's four pieces played over and over around the castle, the king, highly dressed, painted, and stuffed with the most delicious food in all the world, sat back in his bedchamber that evening and peered out his window at a raven that circled the sky. George walked to the window and stared for a few minutes, and the raven, which soon widened his circle and then returned to his more favorite haunts.

"Odd seeing a raven this late at night," George said and walked back to his bed and went to sleep, soon to dream of ravens, angry mobs, spiteful politicians, spurned women, and others who may have a cause against the king. A large black cat ran under his bed while he dreamed, spilling his bedside water and sending a glass picture to the floor smashing into thousands of pieces and waking the household.

"What is it, Your Highness?" A thin man broke into the door of the bedchamber, rushing to George.

"It was nothing. Nothing, just a bad dream and the pitcher fell," George said, calmly waking from his bizarre dream, which may have been caused by too much drink after the coronation.

The black cat ran out the door, and both men watched it quickly move by.

"Ah, you see, the cat," George said, lying back down.

"Yes, Your Highness, the cat," he said, closing the door behind him.

Deer, fox, otter, owl, and rat feasted in the garden as the low-lying mist floated around the foliage and shadows appeared beneath the treetops. Since Franklin was usually afraid of large unwanted shadows, he squawked, fluttered, and went to warn Thomas. The sound of marching hooves and men out somewhere in the forest could be heard.

"Where are they hiding? They must be here somewhere," a gruffy old soldier said who was the scout for the campaign.

"Porius's cottage, surely legend," another said, now dismounting by the river next to a clearing. Water goblins poked their heads just slightly above the water. Back in Wales, another phenomenon was occurring.

Melisende, Queen of Magical Realms, was in her castle. Piers Galveston and all the other ghosts hid among the ruins or fallen temples, castles, sacred grounds, pagan temples, and rings of rock, stone, or other identifiers not known to the Christian segments of the earth. Egyptian, Asian, Indian, pagan, druid, warlock, witch as Melisende's ghost in white and red flew, half form half essence of a new flesh. It had been hundreds of years since the begging for Melisende as she awakened from her crypt and floated, hovered, and spied over Wales, Cornwall, Devon, and Suffolk, traveling.

"My body, my form, fy dial, fy dial, my revenge." Melisende held her hand out for the wand. "Acio wand." The wand landed in her hand, her form seemingly in her thirties, yet hundreds of years since original birth. Melisende floated higher; the clouds darkened; the rain fell over Wales; flowers withered and faded; trees turned to autumn; generations of animal, fish, plant, and insect evolved and withered one by one; species by species as Melisende hovered and patrolled the realm once more.

"Fi dial," Melisende claimed revenge over the ancestors of those who betrayed Wales, Scotland, and England for to her mind, the generations of lost rituals, civilizations, and ways had been taken over, bound and gagged in the form of Christianity; and she would have none of it. Piers Galveston was also released from a long dream from since he was strung up and tortured.

"Ich bin zuruck" (I am back), Galveston said in his Saxon tongue and rising from the earth half form half flesh and as he was once in his thirties. With brown and red beard, muscular form wearing his French battle gear and wardrobe, he floated and looked up at Melisende, waving him on.

"Come, we shall journey together," Melisende said, looking down at his rising body, half ghost half flesh.

"Are we shadow, my lady?"

"We are flesh and shadow," she replied.

"My lord Porius is not with us."

"No, but he will be called and ready."

"Where shall we journey, my lady?"

"The cottage, Galveston."

They journeyed over field, village, river and stream, forest and farm; and the occasional farmer looked up to see the two flying ghostlike beings and ran for shelter.

"Devils, we have devils!" one woman said, tossing her clean linens in midair and, screaming, ran into the shelter of her thatch.

"Fear, you see fear in their eyes," Melisende said as she swooped down close to the screaming woman. Galveston, laughing, followed her and also took pleasure in flying past a couple of farms. One scratched his head, and the other ran in fear.

Once they arrived at Exeter, they entered and dressed in hauntingly old-styled clothes and entered the tavern "the Old Cock," which was full of many drinking and laughing and a few singing songs around a harpsicord that stood against the west wall, Galveston catching the eye of a few prostitutes and youths and all eyes watching these two unusual beings coming into their village pub.

"What do we have here?" a man asked behind the bar wearing working clothes and cap. "Welcome."

"Greetings, my good man," Galveston said to him with a large smile. "Two large goblets of ale if you please"

"Your accent is French, I detect. Welcome, traveler," the barman said, pouring two large goblets. "And your woman," he inquired. "Also French?"

"Welsh, actually," Galveston said, sipping his beer and handing the other to Melisende.

"Thank ye and good day to thee, sir," Melisende said, sipping and curtseying to the barman.

"That will be—" the barman started to say but was interrupted.

"No need, good sir. These are on me," Porius said, now standing beside them and offering a few gold coins to the barman.

"Thank ye, Lord Porius, I did not see you come in," the startled barman said.

"I travel lightly," Porius said, waving for a goblet for himself. The barman's eyes were full of glee seeing such beautiful gold coins like he had never seen.

"Melisende and Galveston, it's been years," Porius said, out of breath.

"Lord Porius, my greatest pleasure to see you once more," Galveston said while Melisende hugged Porius and grabbed a table from a couple of prostitutes or ladies who came into the pub for a bit of cash and maybe a good time to be had by all.

"Porius, I don't know what happened. First, I was holding a stone, the next minute I was asleep and as I can see why the dress around us for many years."

"Finally, the good year 1750," Porius said. "George the Second, Duke of Brunswick, is in charge and here you are."

They talked for hours while Porius caught them up on all that had occurred and what work was being done to preserve the old ways, telling them of the stones hidden in Canterbury, Thomas and the cottage, and students like Jewel and Frederick, George and others who trained at the cottage and fought for the old ways against the ever-growing religions that to their minds plagued the world. Porius stood beside the table and lowered gently into his seat, the long white rune-stone-covered robes getting stepped on by many a passerby who led up toward the bar past the table where the three now sat. The loudness of the pub mostly was filled with discussions of these three unusual travelers—Porius in white gold and tapestried trimmings, Galveston, and Melisende in red-and-white gowns like she just stepped out of a medieval castle moments ago from hundreds of years back in time, not bothered by the reactions of onlookers. A woman was pointing. "Maybe there be a fancy dress at court," she said.

"They do look fine and most assuredly royalty," another said, glancing out of the corner of her eye.

"The rich are occasionally eccentric," an old man said, leaning to the woman from another table.

"My friends," Porius said, standing and facing the crowd, "drinks on me, help yourself to the bar."

A soon as Porius gave another gold coin to the barman, the crowd cheered into a louder roar, and everyone piled up to the bar.

"Now now, wait for your turn."

"Thank ye," one said, passing Porius toward the bar.

"Thankee," said another. Soon all were laughing, filling the goblets, glasses, copper mugs, and wooden cups. Standing room only except for those seated at their well-guarded tables, the night lingered on toward midnight.

"Where has Porius gone off to?" Thomas said back at the cottage. "One minute here, then off." Frustrated, Thomas, Bryan, and Leal sat around the table.

"Porius is on his own, it appears," Leal said.

"The soldiers out in the forest. What of them?" Bryan said to Leal.

"My good Bryan, there is nothing to worry about at all," Leal said. "I have handled soldiers before, and it's not like King George is amongst them anyway. He rests at Dover this evening, and the soldiers are most likely looking for the cottage, which thee shalt not find." Leal walked outdoors in the midnight moon, Bryan following.

"I am going to bed, good night," Thomas said, leaving the two to go spying on the soldiers who rested beyond the forest.

"Porius is meeting up with other friends, no doubt," Thomas said and was right. Because while Thomas suggested that Porius is with others, Porius, Melisende, and Galveston climbed upon fallen branches and rode toward the cottage over hill, river, stream, forest and farms, villages, and around London until they finally reach Kent and the outskirts of the cottage forest. Below, Porius spotted Leal and Bryan below. Leal looked up at Porius flying above him and waved, pointing toward the patrolling soldiers.

"Oh, look," Porius said as Melisende and Galveston followed closely behind. They all nodded in agreement at seeing the soldiers by the river and two drowsy guardsmen watching over the three tents.

Porius and Galveston landed by the front door, and Melisende landed but tumbled and they assisted in getting her up.

"Now there, dear, come in and relax," Porius said, ushering them all into the cottage, Leal and Bryan not far behind.

"We have visitors I see," Porius said to all.

"Shh, Lord Porius, Thomas is asleep," Leal said quietly.

"Yes, well, we'll not wake him and I'm sure we can all do with some sleep. Leal and Bryan, allow me to introduce you to Melisende and Galveston."

"Pleasure," Leal said.

"Lord Porius has informed me of your exploits, Leal," Melisende said, shaking his hand quietly.

"Leal," Porius said.

"You are beautiful, and I must say that is an understatement," Galveston said, blushing as he looked into Leal's beautiful muscular body and deep-blue eyes.

"And, Bryan, who traveled through the underworld," Melisende said, greeting Bryan.

"You will have to tell me about the underworld," Galveston said. "I have not the courage to visit."

"Oh, ye must visit the underworld," Bryan said.

After the usual pleasantries, they all find a place of rest and settled until the pots and pans, the smells of breakfast wake them as Parthenia and Grendle delivered a hearty breakfast of kedgeree, mead, eggs, bacon, and apple juice. Water goblins peered through the leaded windows and disappeared just as quickly.

"Leal," Porius shouted. "Hath ye the ambition of a new journey with Galveston and Melisende to France?"

"Aye, it will be my honor to protect these rare individuals. I have heard so much of the great Melisende and would be glorified to protect her. My honor and sword are at thy disposal."

"Such a beautiful being you are, Leal," Melisende said, running her finger between his muscular protruding breast only partially covered by leather and down the alleyway between two luscious sets of budging stomach muscles. Then she turned to Porius. "What is the quest?"

"I see Galveston has an attraction for Leal as well," Porius said while Galveston stood deep in arousal but only slightly flushing and pushing his hands toward his groin. "It's not uncommon, and Leal is so beautiful it actually comes in handy because most mortals are afraid to stab or lance someone of such perfection.

"Done," Galveston said.

"The journey is going to be argued to say the least," Porius said, sitting out front at the garden table, and all followed with plates of food.

"The Mesopotamians in oh, I would say 2,650 years before our current numeration system. For the ancient city of Ur has several members of the final old ways families, and they need protection and an escape to the teleportation devices which will arrive in two weeks. The ghost of Nubia shall light your way." Porius rested, and an image of Nubia glowed before them inside the pensive, her naked body only slightly covered in gold mesh around the upper hips.

"I shall direct the warrior lord Porius," the ghost of Nubia said, and her beautiful form of flesh disappeared once more into her abyss.

"Nubia," Thomas said, coming outside and wiping his hands on an apron.

"Yes, Thomas," Porius said, everyone still both shocked and bothered that Walters, Athena, and her two beauties guarding her appeared as if made of lights and then faded. Soon only Porius, Bryan, Galveston, and Leal sat beside Melisende while bluebirds circled and played, rabbits jumped, and swiftly running by squirrel and dove.

"My Lord Porius, what of these soldiers outside the edge of the forest?" Melisende asked.

"They are friends of George the Second who I am sure is wanting to learn the whereabouts of this particular cottage," Porius said.

"They shall not find it," Leal said.

"Well, they do have a sort of wizard who claims to know divination and transference of mind with them who is most assuredly reading our mental activity, but I have blocked her vision through the forest. They will walk in perpetual circles for a few days, and surely the water goblins will play simple tricks on them and annoy them enough until they finally depart," Porius said. "You will most likely see them running about naked because I believe the water goblins stole their clothes and armor last night.

"How do you know that?" Bryan asked, getting ready for them to be off.

"Look, that pile of clothes is, I believe, theirs," Porius said, smiling and pointing to a pile of clothes, pipes, and a few pots and pans.

"Oh, Porius," Leal said, laughing.

"That will make them leave quickly," Melisende said. "But how has thy relic from Ur made it to Paris?"

"From Abydos in Egypt to Elba, then Greece with the assistance of Athena because it stayed with a family in Roma for over two hundred years, and once the priests set loose the prisoners who destroyed most of the old-way families of Italy, a small elven courier took the parcel to France and hid it in Bordeaux for several years and yesterday was given to an artist in Paris, whom I am most familiar—Jean Bardin, who awaits you tomorrow, so best to be quick."

"Right, let's be off then," Melisende said, mounting a large branch. Leal and Galveston on their branches and whispering the branches to life, they departed for Paris. "Many years ago, I lost Geoffrey and James to the fires of Paris. I shall not see this terror continue in the future."

Over Dover and over the channel to Calais, they rested and join others in a tavern. Two women were singing competing operatic songs outside the tavern, hat sellers, merchants, prostitutes, beggars, sophisticates, men dressed like women and some women dressed as men. A pool of water, lilies, and croaking frogs were spotted along the coast just beyond the reach of channel waves.

"Le Pole Tachetee," Leal said. "The Spotted Hen pub sounds good to me."

"We shall find an ancestor of Fraun here this evening, let's have a bite to eat," Melisende said as Bryan. "Jean Bardin should be here shortly."

"'Coq au vin' is written on the board," Leal said happily.

"Make that deux," Bryan said, standing beside Leal and ordering a few goblets of wine served in brass cups; a large loaf of bread is given to Leal and Bryan carried to the bench where Melisende sat pruning her out-of-date wardrobe as others looked on and of obvious curiosity ogled the three strangers. Then all at once, the front door opened and two rather tall well-dressed men appeared.

"Melisende," a black-haired man with a straight, long, wide black moustache said as he removed his hat and the other followed.

"Yes, I am she."

"I took that to be the case. Porius mentioned that you may have a certain look to you, excuse my English for it is not of the best quality," Jean Bardin said.

"It is fine," said Leal as he shook his hands and ushered Jean and his companion to sit with them.

"Oh, I see you are eating. We shall also," Jean said, sending his partner to the bar.

"His name is Phillip, but he speaks not a word of English," Jean said, sitting down to chat with the three travelers. Upon Phillip's return, his arms were full of food and drinks, and he placed it among them.

"Merci," said Bryan to Phillip who was dressed in the finest purple and golden silks with black shoes buckled with silver and some mild paint to the face, his perfect pitch-black hair tied in a ponytail with red ribbon.

"*Mon plaisir*, Bryan, Leal, Melisende. I am Phillip."

"We have brought you something from Paris," Jean said, handing a small wrapped object.

"Yours, I believe," Phillip said as Melisende unwrapped what appeared to be a small rock of no major beauty but sandstone, very plain. "When they died at the stake in Paris years ago, both men were robbed of all their belongings and were not even left with a handkerchief for weeping."

Melisende looked anxious and rubbed the stone between her palms harder and harder, sweat forming on her brow with the thoughts of ancient times, masses of freethinking individuals killed, lost, separated from their families, or cast out of society.

Birds of night chirped in the distance, and the pub noise receded into a blur of obscure senseless noises, and a rat scuttled across the floor while grabbing a half-eaten piece of bread, carrying it off while chewing.

"Indeed, it is, and I am so pleased to see it," Melisende said as she held the sandstone in her hand. The table shook, the publicans alerted at the rocking room.

"Earthquake," one man said, running out the front doors and others following. The crowd was in chaos, the room shaking, and pans falling in the kitchen, beer glasses rolling around the floor, and smashing periodically. Bardin, Phillip, and the others stood and fell, fell and stood, leaning against the walls, and a few women moaning crawled out the front door. A large crack went from ceiling to ground, and bits of plaster fell to the floor. Inside, the walls fell bits of bottles, cotton, petrified dung and other ancient objects which were placed inside a century ago when the tavern was built, which was actually a stable turned into a home then a pub. Two youngish teenage boys vomited just outside the pub while the shaking continued for several minutes.

"Need not worry," Melisende said as the once plane rock now turned to a beautiful diamond before them all and jean stares on eyes wide.

"My lady, it is thy stone."

Melisende stood and held the stone above her, and a wind came through the tavern all those huddling still at their tables or quivering in fear behind the bar stare and the scene of Melisende holding the stone above her head.

"I had no idea," Jean said.

"Inscrutable," Phillip said as he stood with Melisende and the others stood as the wind knocked over goblets, pictures on the walls, and a cat ran quickly from the kitchens out the front door. Melisende held the stone above her and shouted, "Tecca Elysium aluminatum!"

Melisende vanished before them, and in amazed confusion, the people in the bar reacted in different ways, could not believe their luck on being witness to such an event.

"She's gone," Leal said, holding Bryan by the waist and looking at Phillip who ducked down below the table and Jean sits eyes wide open in shock.

"Qui, she is gone," said Jean, looking around for a sign of her and then seeing her bag, "Regardez."

The bag vanished to follow.

"That was brief, what shall we do now?" Leal said, Bryan still gulping a bit of ale and dumbfounded on what they should do next.

"Is that it?" Bryan said.

"Surely Lord Porius would not have had us come all this way," Leal said to Jean and his companion.

"No, I say no. Come, let's drink and then off to Paris. Phillip and I will take you and show you the families who need you. You see, we feel a revolution is coming in France, and war is not a place for Old World families. The national assembly is close to abolishing feudalism, the Catholic church at Saint-Eustache opening its doors in 1632 the beauty of the building has a power over peasants and working class alike. Gens or people easily get swayed once they are awestruck by the buildings, and that helps spread the church which disagrees with most of our new scientific discoveries which unfortunately will be bought and sold by the church."

Jean, sitting back in his chair, shook his head with hands pressed on his temples.

"Well, we found people once they start believing in Christianity, they don't always need science," Leal said, finishing his copper goblet of ale.

"Science isn't needed because their plan and directions in their writings take the will of the reader away, makes them less dependent on science and evolution."

"Yes, science and knowledge is on the run," Bryan said as they all stood and walked toward the exit then to two horses. Phillip carried Leal on a large red horse named Jiff, and Jean helped Bryan up to lead as Jean got on the backside of another even larger black horse named Showtra.

"This is Showtra, horse of my best breeding stock," Jean Bardin said pleased with the beauty of this magnificent creature.

"Very nice," Bryan said as they all rode off toward Paris, which they reached about midnight and not far from Notre Dame once opened in 1345. Looming over the river and just across was a black-railed townhouse where they tied up the horses and leave with a small man covered in suet and grumbling due to his obvious annoyance of being woken at such a late time. Leal, Bryan, Jean, and Phillip dismounted. Three male drunken men walked by wearing silks and sipping wine from a large glass bottle.

"Bounje l'homme veut une fete?" one drunken youthful man with long black hair said and smiling as he eyed Leal as the passed by, pausing and looking at Leal from his beautiful eyes down to his muscular calves, arms, and exposed rippled stomach muscles. "Tu serais un regal."

"Tu n'es pas mauvais toi-meme," Leal replied as Jean remarked at his French skills. Jean quickened to break up the distraction of these apparent interested men in some sort of party with Leal.

"Peut-etre une autre fois," Jean said, tipping his hat, and they went about their way, whistling and giggling. The cackling was heard as they went further down the street, the four men entering Jean's house.

"I speak a little French, Leal, was that man asking?" said Bryan.

"Yes, and I politely said another time," Jean said, ushering them into his beautifully designed home with gilded curtains of green silk, purple ground cover overstuffed pillows, and gold painted ornately decorated wood carvings, nude statues of the Roman style, ceramic figurines, and a boy of about twenty finely dressed in finest butler clothes entered and handed them all a drink.

"This is Fenaur, our houseboy and very good at his employ," Jean said as Fenaur bowed and left them in the main living room, beautiful Italian blown glass chandelier above them, and a high ceiling painted with cherubs and angels and muscular men mixed with fair-skinned ladies nude as angels with wings.

"I like your place, Jean," Leal said, looking around.

"Very nice," Bryan said, removing his cloak and giving it to Fenaur, Leal taking off his leather vest, still wrapped in leather strappings across his shoulders and waist.

"Please make yourselves at home, you can bother sleeping in the blue room just left at the top of the stairs. You will enjoy the view of Notre Dame.

"Thank you," Leal and Bryan, both pleased, and they all went up to look at the blue room at the top of the stairs.

"Magnificent room," Bryan said.

Jean opened the wardrobe and saw two robes of blue silk hanging. "Help yourselves to these robes and come down for a nightcap if you like."

Leal undressed and alongside the room was a built-in water closet and shower with running water.

"There is not much pressure, but feel free to wash up, and here is some scotch whiskey which you may find most delicious," Phillip said as he eyed Leal's nudity, every muscle magically in tune with his every move.

A few moments later, Leal and Bryan came down in their blue robes, and they all had a new drink made with coffee, cream, and whiskey.

"This is called a hot toddy," Jean said, looking at Leal with his white upper lip filled with cream.

"Delicious," Bryan said.

The night soon became morning, and a nymph dressed in green silks with long blond curls leaned over Bryan's sleeping ear. "Come to Caledon, Bryan. Come below the lake to Calidon," the nymphs said as Bryan awakened and sought Leal beyond walking toward the waking Bryan.

"Good morrow, Sir Bryan," Leal said, dripping with water from his morning swim and putting on his leathers and singing the tune from the previous night in French. "Dole role o, bonjour, mon cherie."

Bryan looked at Leal and interrupted his song, "What is Caledon?"

"Why, that's the mystical city below the lake," Leal said, pointing his large muscular arm and finger pointed toward the lake.

"It came to me in a vision," Bryan said as he removed his clothes and walked to the lake, jumped in and swam, cleaned, and dove down with eyes open. Under the surface of the lake were long stings of underwater grass duckweed, watermeal, hydrilla, and curly leaf pond weed. He went up for air then swam deeper toward the middle of the lake. There were some large catfish, perch, trout, northern pike, bullfish, but no city to be seen.

Leal stood on the shore waving Bryan back from the depths, worried that his excitement may tire him before today's expected efforts, and Bryan came back to shore. Dripping wet and naked, he walked back to Jean's home. Stacks of books, dust, paintings, and wooden models filled up most of the main living area. Bicycles hung from the east wall, leaded windows, and every room was filled with sleeping, snoring, or waking visitors, men in silks. One elf ran out and quickly turned, looked him up and down, smiled, snapped his finger, and vanishes before him.

"Interesting pestilential elf," Leal said as he dried off his muscular physique and not the slightest bit bothered by the fact that others were watching him, eying his every curvature.

"WELL, WELL," Jean said as he placed several crescents of fresh bread, cheese, and a few cooped tomatoes before Leal. Leal popped a few tomatoes and took a bite of bread.

"Delicious, Jean."

"Merci, Sir Leal. Now get dressed because the Markus family awaits us. Today, the pope has ordered for several protests to remove them from their lands and we need to stop them," Jean said, handing Leal his leathers, and they dressed and left jean's home. Bryan was straggling behind until he finally caught up and they passed Notre Dame as workers on scaffolding worked on placement of objects, washing windows, and other odd jobs. Bryan, Leal, and Jean rode out to the county about four miles from the safety of Jean's Paris home. First, two women walked by, one selling flowers another kindling bulks and the further they got toward the forest fish sellers, wheat sellers, vegetable sellers, and onion sellers set up stalls and shout their usual sales pitches to the three eager men. Several horses with carts passed them, steered by local farmers who seemed very polite and tipping hats or shouting "Bonjour."

Finally, they got to the woods, and just beyond the first set of trees lay beyond the splendor and grandeur of this vineyard, orchard, and fields of vegetables. Two teenage boys and three women wearing apron and cap greet the men proudly bow.

"Bonjour, monsieurs," said the tallest and eldest of the Markus boys, hugging Jean and introducing Leal and Bryan to the rest of his family.

"Beau garcon," one girl said, blushing toward Leal as they all noticed his overexaggerated beauty and form.

"Bonjour," Leal said while Bryan rolled his eyes and pushed Leal toward the farm, which was quite nice indeed.

"Wait," Bryan said, holding back Leal. "Look." There were large black horses riding toward the barn far off in the distance; the family ran from water as the large black figures carried fire to light the stacks and barn.

"They are burning the barn," one girl said, crying and running to the barn with the others. Leal, Bryan, and Jean dismounted near the barn as the figures in black threw lit torches into the hay.

"Think not," Jean said, dismounting and reaching into his pocked, his wand out, and he pointed to the sun.

"Tall and dark clouds come forth, take this life and make it rain," Jean said, pointing his wand toward himself, and Leal dismounted and ran to Jean.

"No," Leal said, but before he reached Jean, Jean's body evaporated and the sky became black, the sun became black. Even the riders with torched looked up to the sky, and within the blinking of an eye, rain poured down upon all, the torches extinguished.

"Heresy!" one priest said as his torch became wet with water impaling every dry spot on his being, downward it rained. The family rejoiced as they threw stones at the departing three black demons, which foiled at their plight of ruin for the Markus family.

"Heresy," said again the figure in black, riding off.

"I'll show you heresy, my black demon," Leal said as he mounted and rode toward the three figures in black, crosses dangling. Leal reached them and rode alongside, swiping his blade at his shin and down he fell, the blood spilling over the rain-soaked black as he fell to the ground, mud spurting in his face and his horse circling and stamping him in a rage.

"No, what has become of thee?" the priest yelled as the stomping horse landed firmly on his head, spilling blood, brains, and teeth around the hoof and mud, the other two priests in horror looking back to see the withering flesh become mud in the storm.

"Never return!" Leal shouted to the departing two, and the dead priest's horse got alongside Leal's and bowed then rode calmly alongside Leal to the farmer's house where the others gathered together in thankfulness that Leal, Jean, and Bryan came in the nick of time.

"But how di thee know that we were in such danger?" Mr. Markus said as he poured wine for Leal and Bryan.

"Still raining I see," Bryan said as they hung their cloaks over the hearth to dry amid the burning fire. The home had a high ceiling and elegant for a farmer, and plucked chicken were being prepared by Mrs. Markus and the girls as they watched Leal through the doorway as he draped his clothes to dry. Mrs. Markus was a bit over two hundred pounds and dressed in typical red and white apron, dress, and pink bows. Mr. Markus had quite the thin build of a hardworking farmer, and horse brasses lined the rooms.

"Thank ye," Mr. Markus said. "This could have been the end to all our dreams and we have worked so hard all our lives. My father's father built this home, and our wine is some of the finest in Paris and at a good price as well."

"I can attest to that," Leal said, drinking back a large gulp.

"But what of Jean, did he really use magic to make a storm?" Mr. Markus said inquisitively.

"Indeed, but he shall return," Leal said proudly.

"You see," said Bryan, interrupting, "the only way to get a storm that quickly is to evaporate and become the storm. I am sure he will join us soon."

"My word and on our farm, we will tell this story for generations to come, that is, if we have more time here. They will be back and with more fire."

"No, they won't be back ever. I have placed a stone from Porius, and the spell will be completed at midnight. May this farm stay free from religion and always remain in your family," Leal said, grinning.

Jean walked in from outside and naked as the day he was born.

"Jennifer, get thee some clothes for Jean," Mr. Markus bellowed to the oldest girl, and she quickly tossed a white and blue robe to Jean.

"Welcome back," Leal said.

"Nice storm," said Bryan.

"Yes, it did work out rather nicely, but I have to confess, I believe Porius assisted my magic, for I said his name while in the midst of evaporation. You see I've never done that particular and most elaborate spell before."

"Well, thank you, for tryin' 'cause it worked like a charm," Mr. Markus said, bowing, and the family came out and bowed together to Jean then applauded, and the party began. Bryan and Leal prepared a few fireworks out in the field and several townsfolk, neighbors, and passersby enjoyed the sparkling blasts of colored light and popping sounds, which could be heard for miles around. The celebration wind down, and Leal left Bryan on his own to return to the cottage, Franklin circling overhead once Bryan returned to the safe English forest that surrounded the cottage.

Porius and Thomas were sleeping, snoring as Bryan made his way to fall asleep on the main room's overstuffed couch.

Leal, upon return to Elysium, was greeted by Apollo, naked except for his winged golden sandals and wreath crown of feathers and golden braided threads that rested on Apollo's brow. Leal undressed the moment he saw Apollo and the two men retire inside the small turret atop the midsized castle, which Apollo and Leal called home. Several servants holding silver trays out to the men as they passed to their chamber, some trays holding fruits and body oils, towels, and lotions, wine goblets of gold and crystal. Naked, they walked arm in arm and ended up in a large pool of warm waters, which was lighted by candled sconces.

Porius woke up at the sound of Bryan's return, walked in to check on his well-being. Nothing seemingly out of the ordinary, Porius returned to sleep, where he dreamed of his youth and the beings that held and raised Porius in earth amongst the wizards and druids of old, Ely near Cambridge was his home. His earth mother was Priscilla who cared for several children during that period. The secrets of Ely cathedral built in 1109 is surrounded in mystery, which played a big part in the life of Porius, for deep within the dungeon bricks was placed the stones and writing, which depicted the unearthly or alien ancestors and bloodlines of his past. The ability granted to Porius, which gave him the sight and eternal life once form and flesh and giving the ability to assist the passing of humans once their mortal life ended and they donated their bodies to the sea or rivers to replenish the earth. Molecular change processes all that was living to another beginning of those lucky few, pure of heart, and resourceful minds.

During the war o5 the Jenkins 'Ear, a British colonial raid on Cartagena in 1740, which resulted in the death of quite a majority of the raiding army.

Hence ten had passed for two escapees brought spells from Jamaica and were given to Apollo to hold until he next visited the cottage. Once inside the safety of the cottage grounds. Apollo would work with Porius and Leal to make sure the spell was credible and will then submit to the Malefactor by the molecular transformation of unearthly pages that held the letters of each page of the Malefactor. In 1745, the French fortress on Louisburg fell to Americans during King George's war. Porius studied the notes sent to him through the pensive, and the reflection of American Indian chief and pagan Markus waved back across the miles to Porius, smiling, waving through the water waves of the pensive.

"Safety be with thee," Porius said, and waved his elegant hand over the water in the silver pensive, Thomas looking on.

"America?" Thomas said.

"Indeed, such turmoil and tremors," Markus and his Indian friends called out occasionally for assistance, "and the elves had been sent to America as relief, for we must not leave them with no magical armor."

"My thoughts exactly," Thomas said, leaning over Porius to see America through the pensive. Porius accidentally dripping his long white beard into the pensive's waves.

"Be careful, Thomas, pensive water can stain my beard," Porius said, alerted to his flowing white beard dipping into the water.

"Quick, pull it out," Thomas said apologetically.

"Too late I fear," Porius said as he stood up quickly and looked down at his multicolored beard of yellow, light green, pink, and purple.

"Actually, it doesn't look awful, Porius, maybe fashionable," Thomas said, laughing at Porius standing to notice his beard's lower half was full of rainbow colors.

"Oh dear, it will grow out in some time. In the meantime," Porius grabbed a pair of copper scissor-type machine and trimmed his beard, sending the colored beard adrift to the floor. Porius called for Parthenia.

"Parthenia, I have something for your attention," he said, pointing down at the pile of colored mass of hair.

"Oh, dear Lord Porius, quite a lot of colored beard. The pensive, I imagine," Parthenia said sweeping up the hair and taking it out doors.

"I wonder what type of life will come of it."

"What do you mean?" Thomas asked as he and Porius followed Parthenia out into the garden. Deer, faun, squirrel, and fox scampered about, and a few birds tweeted here and there.

"To the wind may you fly," Parthenia said as she tossed the discarded, colorful hair to the sky.

Porius took his wand and pointed to the flying tossed hair and said, "Yes, fly, hair fly." As he said the words and with a quick short wave of his wand, the colored hair came together as one mass of color and light, forming, rotating, and then finally a beautiful hummingbird appeared made from the beard of Porius.

"Such a little creature for all that hair," Parthenia said, laughing as the hummingbird immediately adapted to its surroundings and flew over to white flower and sucks its essence of sweet energy.

"Yes, I anticipated something much larger, but alas," Porius said as walks out into the garden.

"It's quite lovely out today, would you like your tea here in the garden?" Parthenia asked.

"Yes, that would be most pleasing," Porius said as he patted a young deer on its head and fed the large-eyed creature some raisins from his pocket.

Thomas sets the table and Parthenia brings out a large plate with cut tomatoes, cheese, game pie and a few goblets of ale.

Bluebirds circled and chased each other while Franklin watched, thinking, "Pestering showoffs," as he witnessed the quick-flying, turning, and souring bluebirds.

"Thomas Newcomen's steam engine has given me a wonderful idea on how we can use steam to heat our water. I worked on it last week, and as soon as the ironmonger came back with the pieces I ordered, we will have hot steam bath and steam room. First, we need to make sure that once we build this contraption it will work," Porius said.

"Lookin' forward to it, Porius, and even though Isaac Newton is getting all the glory currently, William Whiston to whom visited the cottage and sorry that he missed you. William let you some interesting articles and boxes, was that a part of the contraption?" Thomas asked.

"Indeed, keen eyed you are, and yes, nothing more pleasing than talking about mathematic equations and debating theology with Whiston. Sorry I missed him and yes, it would be a pleasure to meet him again, try sending Franklin with a note," Porius said, watching Franklin whose disagreeable expression for a raven is not the slightest bit interested in flying all the way to Cambridge with a note strapped to his foot.

"Franklin, do fancy a bit of a journey," Thomas shouted out at Franklin jokingly and seeing the expression on his face as he nestled in deeper into the roof thatch. "Maybe not."

"No, Franklin is a bit too old for such a journey," Porius said to Thomas, knowing that Franklin does not being considered old at any time by anyone.

Franklin flew off the roof, circling the gardens and edge of the forest, proving he is fit and forever young. While milling about in the garden, the ironmonger came up the path shouting for signs of the cottage.

"Reveal thee," Porius said and the trees parted as the ironmonger stumbled into the gardens as the deer scurried and Franklin landed once again upon the thatch.

"Good morrow, Porius," Timothy the ironmonger said, placing a few large wrapped packages.

"I say good morrow to thee, Timothy, we were just wondering when you would deliver our odds and sods," Porius said while Thomas greeted Timothy, wearing a dusty brown workclothes and apron.

"Lord Porius, such an honor to meet you again, and thank ye for such generosity to not only me, but all the others in the village who profit buy your extreme generosity," Timothy said, laying the last item at rest in the cottage.

"It is no more than all of you wonderful people deserve. Why, look at the this craftsmanship, superb," Porius said, taking out the pieces of metal and quickly matching them up to eventually become his steam room boiler. "I am so excited to see it working."

"As I make certain. May will build this device together now?"

"Why yes, come, bring all the packages to the back room," Thomas said and the three went into the back room.

"Most well crafted, Timothy," Porius said, putting on pieces together with pipes that extend from the outdoors. The pipes hung from the ceiling where Timothy's eyes were fixed.

"Yes, the pipes hold water that is kept in a tank up in the attic," Porius said. "I stole the idea from plumbing I witness being built for a place in Italy."

Porius paused, setting down the parcel and looking momentarily distraught. "That poor family who once lived in lavish surroundings now live in ruin. Italy has been through so much and that family in particular was one of the first removed by the pope. It was 1202 and though now that palace is long over run by. It was the middle of the Fourth Crusade, and the pope who called himself the Innocent, but his real name was Lotario de Conti and not a very pleasant man. Just ask the families he removed from beautiful estates and palaces all across Italy, makes me sad just to think of it."

"I would so much like to hear more of your adventures, Porius," Timothy said, wiping the sweat from his brow and taking the last piece from Porius.

Porius looked up. "Here I digress, and you both have finished the project, yes fine fittings fine indeed," Porius circled the large steam kettle and metal barrel. "Turn on the water, Tomas, bring some kindling and let's warm up this water closet, and we will have our own personal steam room and hot running water," Porius said, pleased with himself, and they all went in to a nice meal prepared by Parthenia and Grendle.

"Pleasure to see you, Timothy," Grendle said, pouring him some warm fish soup and fish cakes.

"Fish cakes, most agreeable," said Timothy as he dug in to the feast before him, Parthenia pouring mead into their goblets.

"Nice to see you round 'ere," Parthenia said, knocking Timothy's head with her elbow in a playful manner.

"A pleasure to see you Parthenia," Timothy said, eyeing her every move. "One question always passes my mind. My grandfather and grandmother both have long passed, and they had mentioned all of you in tales from over a century ago. Why do none of you look any older?"

"Well, you see, Timothy, all of us are long past the mortal time which you are bound to because we have already passed through the portal or the other side or whatever comparison to death you can state. We have all been through it. Here, watch my hand," Porius said, holding out his hand to Timothy, and his hand became transparent then flesh once more.

"Oh my," Timothy said, a bit in shock and his mouth open with bread held close to his lips.

"Nothing to worry about, but when you get to our age and your heart remains true, you will also give your body to the creatures of the water and replenish the earth and even coral reefs," Porius said and the others held their hand hot as Timothy watched it move from transparent to flesh.

"My word." Timothy gulped down a large glass of wine. "I am so fortunate to know thee, Porius, will I?"

As Timothy spoke, the front door crashed open and in walked Bryan, Leal, Apollo, and Athena while Gloria and Alexandria waited outside facing the forest and watching the deer play before them.

"Yes, it all comes from 1147, the outpost of Edessa," Porius said, turning to the door.

"Welcome all, Leal, Apollo, Athena, well what brings your to our humble abode?"

"I see you have company," Leal said, bowing to them all as he burst into the cottage wearing his usual black leather battle clothes, Apollo in Grecian skirt and golden sandals, Athena her usual see-through silk and gold with golden sandals.

Timothy quickly jumped to his feet. "Athena, Apollo, Leal, and . . ."

"Bryan, just human and as normal as you, my friend," Bryan said.

"Oh yes, I have seen thee in the village."

"Ironmonger, aren't you?" Leal said.

"Yes indeed, I was here to help Porius install his water feature."

"Water feature?" Athena inquired.

"Well yes," Porius interluded. "I will show you all later, now come inside and enjoy some nice fish soup. call Gloria and Alexandria in please," Porius said loud enough to fall within the beautiful guards' earshot, and they entered for a nice glass of wine.

"I was just explaining the fall of the outpost to Edessa," Porius said.

"Ah, boring our young friend with history lessons," Athena said, reaching over Timothy, and he smelled her beautiful sweet lily of the valley perfume.

"Is that lily of the valley?" Timothy said. His words slurring and his eyes gazing upon Athena's beautiful face, lips, long golden hair, curvy hips, ample bosom, which can be seen clearly through the silk, he was dumbfounded by her extreme perfection as she turned and walked. He could not take his eyes from her back side and long elegant muscular legs.

"Are you all right?" Leal said, snapping his fingers in front of Timothy's eyes. "Athena has that effect on everyone, it's the perfume that will get you."

They all laughed, and Porius waved his wand. The miniature band appeared, floating over the mantel, Timothy watching in amazement. They exchanged stories with Timothy, and Bryan explained some of his training while letting him know that he was only mortal as Timothy and hoped to one day when his life ran out to be thrown into the waters and reborn with a pathway to Elysium.

"In the early fifth century, Germanic invaders breached the Rhine frontier of the Roman empire. Dalius Crimp was the noted wizard, who most wanted to make armor that befitted an unbeatable knight. Laced with lead, iron, and sandstone-filled lace, the suit would be perfect. No one would be able to spike the wearer an injury," Porius said to Timothy.

"Indeed," Timothy said, not sure what to say.

"You see, my boy, I have the armor and you fit the bill. Care to do some adventuring?"

"It would be an honor, Lord Porius. Command thee and I shall conquer," Timothy said, bending down on one knee before Porius. The gentle glow and rays of colored light came through the windows. Deer and rabbit, fox, squirrel, and lizard played out in the garden. Blackbirds faced each other in playful flight. The band playing music, harmony filled the air.

"Now which adventure best suits you, Timothy my boy?"

"Whatever your lordship choses, I imagine." Timothy undressed and laid his clothes on the small sideboard opposite the fireplace.

"Yes, you have been following Leal's exercise routine," Porius said as he noticed the curvatures of Timothy's arms, bulging muscular chest, wide shoulders, very small waist, and deep-cut lines between the stomach muscles that rolled like rolling hills.

CHAPTER 23

"Jewels beneath the tropic of cancer, Jupiter, Uranus, and Mars," Porius said, holding his wand over the naked Timothy. Before them floating in midair swung the gold, silver, and bejeweled mesh and armor from the fifth century. "For thee I give thy task," Porius coughed. "Oh, and Mr. Crimp, thee who first made this suit, may his powers oblige thee." Porius put down his wand, and the suit hung over Timothy and slowly covered him, molding into his body and becoming one.

Sheathed with two majestic swords good for thrusting and fighting. Timothy looked himself in the mirror, his glowing jewels and metal mesh, thin tight silver and gold ribbons pressed against his form, making him a formidable victor.

"Now, in Canterbury cathedral," Porius began to tell him where and how to get the stone, which will take him to France, where there he will fulfill his mission.

"Told, received, and memorized," Timothy said as he opened the door and began his journey.

"Remember, family name is Fraun," Porius said as he left and Thomas entered the room.

"Do you think the dear boy will fulfill his deed?" Thomas said, walking out to wish Timothy a safe journey.

"The Fraun family depends on it. There is trouble in Paris, and he must get to the bottom of it. Tomorrow the family will be assaulted by Louis XV men, and they are brutal. He must succeed, lives depend on it."

"But alone," Parthenia said, coming out of the kitchen. "I for one can't think of that beautiful Timothy in Paris and dressed like that." Parthenia walked back into the kitchen.

Porius flicked stones into the pensive and held his wand, waving in a circular motion over the watery substance floating within.

"This one is for Timothy," Porius said as the water became an image. Porius occasionally glanced in the pensive to make sure that Timothy was doing well.

"House of Fraun, Paris Black cat club, Delius Crimp suit," Timothy said to himself after reaching Canterbury and taking the stone of purity to transport him to his predestined portal.

"All that is waiting for thee," Timothy said and the stone transported him into a vicious tunnel of light, revolving round and round until just before he vomited he awakened, standing in his most luxurious armor in the middle of a crowded street so fast moving around him no one really noticed his royal armor and the busy street just buzzed, rather exciting him.

"Pardon," Timothy said to a noble-looking gentleman passing to ask where the Black Cat club was. "De club de cat noir?"

"Oh yeah, you will enjoy it," the man said, smirking as he looked Timothy up and down and pinched something between his fingers and sniffs it down hard."

"What vill you give me if I tell you where it is," the man said in gentle smirking.

"Well, I-I . . ." Timothy was stumped and knowing not what to say.

"Neverr mi-ind young may, I was only kidding," he said. "Just around the corner, twenty feet, you were close, if you want company come to number seven just down the road,"

"Thank you, kind sir," said a blushing Timothy, and he walked the Black Cat tavern or Bear and Wine bar as it was becoming the correct conversational description. Along the Rue de la Roquette was a hanging sight with a painted black cat sitting and wearing a red collar. Inside the smoke-filled black wood walls, thick wooden way with barstools, brass fittings, mirrors with images of cats. Several small groups of three or four individuals, laughing and smoking, some of the smoke giving off an odor or skunk which Timothy has never smelled, and he saw one man taking a long drag from a large pipe and coughing his head off while others laughed, as Timothy walked up to the bar.

"Que est se quille," the man behind the bar started, but Timothy interrupted him.

"Vin de blanco," Timothy said, hoping that the man understood a goblet of white wine.

"Oh, ye Englase, Vite vine?"

"Oui, merci," Timothy said.

"Ve don't get many in full armor," the man said, giving him is glass of white wine in a tumbler.

"I am looking for the Faun family," Timothy said, gulping his wine.

"Oh, uui, pour sure." The man walked around to the front of the bar and quickly led Timothy behind a curtain and quickly closed the curtain, leaving Timothy on the other side then continued to serve other patrons of the fine, yet someone questionable tavern.

Timothy on the other side of the curtain faced a large hallway full of rooms. He opened one door, wine in one hand and the other slowly opening the door that revealed candles burning and a youngish muscular man wearing only a belt around his waist and bejeweled vest and the rest of him naked except for lilies of the valley in full bloom around his angelic face and neck kneeling on a table and rubbing oil around his chest while a couple of people egged the boy on in some sexual advancing and not showing much concern for the opening door, which a shocked yet excited Timothy viewed with wide eyes all and then Timothy quickly closed that door and moved to the next.

"Oh dear, well, let's try this room," Timothy said, opening the next door. Two women wearing some sort of silk see-through garments and garter belts faced a small group of onlookers.

"Entrez," one woman said to Timothy as he quickly closed the door and the sound of laughing was heard behind.

The next door that Timothy opened had a table with a crystal ball in the center, candle sconces dripping wax over the floor, and two older men talking in English.

"Now the plans 'ere, take these plans, and oh hello," one older man said, eyeing Timothy.

"Ye must be Timothy," the other wearing green long silken clothes and a large black sad hat smiled with white teeth toward Timothy and startled though Timothy heard his name. He entered, closing the door behind him.

"My lords, yes I have come to see Fraun," Timothy said nervously.

"And how is old Porius?" the first man said, standing and walking to greet Timothy wearing another dark green outfit that looked a bit outdated but practical for woodland living.

"Porius is well, and I am here to report to Fraun," Timothy said, looking at the ball.

"Welcome and I hope you will enjoy some leisure time while you are here. You will be most popular, make no mistake."

Smiling with pleasure, "Allow me to introduce myself, for I an Fraun, wizard of Paris and longtime owner of the black cat, my ancestors go way back with Porius, of course I have only met him once. It must be wonderful to know such a great wizard."

"What is this an actual crystal ball?" Timothy said, never seeing the like and pulling is tight material away from his trouser which may be a bit too tight for complete comfort.

"Indeed, 'tis one from the mines of Africa," Fraun said, "and this is Simon."

"Yes, I am Simon and I am also long-time friends with Porius, Leal, Walters, Athena."

"Yes, you I have heard of, a pleasure," Timothy said in his surprise and meeting Simon, a legend in his own right.

"Ye hath traveled to Elysium?" Timothy asked Simon.

"I have, dear boy, I have indeed, but I have come to assist you with this current mess outside Paris. Together we will make sure that the family of Jon Luis Olden lives on. For tomorrow the priest from Our Lady of Frantevod, or something of that nature. They planned on removing the eldest son from the farm and replace the kin with monks. We must ride and defeat them. Are you up for the challenge?" Simon said, standing and placing his hand on Timothy's shoulder.

"My skills are quite good, and no one will touch me in this armor," Timothy said proudly.

"That's the ticket, young Timothy," Fraun said, and he laid out the map. "We are here, and you need to get all the way over the Seine, past here and land there." She pointed to a spot of green and some writing Orle family.

"Let's ride," Simon said and they finished their wine and walked out back down a long hallway with noises of all sorts and smells of coconut, wine, and other odd sensational odors follow them out of doors.

"Soon the priest of Our Lady of Fantevod will show themselves," Simon said to Timothy, balancing his steed.

"Lord Simon," Timothy said, sipping from his flags since five miles past the edge of Paris. "Thy closest wood looks thick and dangerous."

"Nay, just beyond lay the farm, and if I know priests they will have men waiting in the woods, probably some lowlife scum that they brainwashed and then trained to do their bidding," Simon said, slowing his steed.

"I have witnesses such priests and beings," Timothy said, arm close to his blade for readiness.

"The saddest of all was that these frail beings who gave themselves to God all do it from fear of what will happen on the other side," Simon said, slowing to almost still at the edge of the forest.

"Near half mile through this along the path. Stay ready for here we go," Simon said, both holding the reins with calm and ready for battle.

"Nay, thy shall not know we're near but thy are close I smell them through my left nostril, so watch out to the left. Plus the priests are beyond these fighters and quite close to the family now."

Trees of acorn, pine, elm, ripper, and white buckeye lined the tightness of the bushes in this forest of overgrown and difficult to travel part of France.

"We are not alone seeing to the left up high," Simon said, pointing to a black spot in the sky that quickly approached to reveal a large hawk of grey and white feathers.

"Jeremy, my hawk," Simon said as the visiting Jeremy flew close to their heads and swiftly flew through the forest.

"I see them," Simon said as he closed his eyes, and seeing through the hawkish eyes of Jeremy, he investigated.

"To your left and about three trees up," Simons said to Timothy in their slow pace.

"My honor for freedom," Timothy said and swiftly drew his silver blade that shimmered in the sunlight.

A man in black appeared with sword held high and flailing his sword toward Timothy as if to dismount Timothy from his steed while another came after Simon. But Timothy caught the light from the sun on his blade, blinding the aggressor who covered his eyes. Dribbling saliva and greasy hair, smelling of uncleanliness, he rushed close to Timothy. Timothy quickened his horse's step twofold and plunged his sword into the onrusher and Timothy's sword plunged through the priest's slave as Timothy quickly pulled out his blade and the man dead where he stood, as Timothy wiped his blade on the man's thick black cloak, which hung across his shoulders. Blood squirted out like a fountain then stopped suddenly, making a perfect pool of blood. Timothy returned his blade; Jeremy the hawk circled overhead and flew off. A quick gnashing of swords, which Simon handled with ease and pleasure; they ran through his black dresses and smelly attacker, plunges him through the heart and meets Timothy back on the path as the barn homestead of solid French gray and bluish stone, well designed and fountains sorted with lovely hedges, rows and rows of flowers, tarragon, spices, and all other herbs are growing in straight lines to perfections surrounded by forest and a large lake beyond.

"Most a welcome stock hath thee planted, enough for an army," Simon said with Timothy in agreement.

"Listen and look, the carriage of the priest and three horses. Mind you, three," Simon said, drawing his sword and listening as he dismounted and Timothy followed suit.

"Come, the horses," Timothy said to Simon in a whisper as he rushed to the horses and removed all the leather straps, bridle, saddles, and left the horses standing there as the day they were born.

"Take thy freedom, my friends, run for Porius hath set thee free," Timothy said as he waved his wand over the horse's head and the horse bowed then spoke.

"Thy help is welcomed these riders were not of our liking," the big black horse said.

"We shall ride to the other side of the forest pastures green," the larger red horse said and the horses ran off, leaving the priest and his three men with no return transportation.

"Come, listen to that squealing," Simons said as he burst into this beautiful stone home of more than one hundred feet long with four bedrooms and a cloak room where Simon and Timothy made their crashing entrance.

"Who art thou?" the priest said, turning, looking like one of those ex-con priests that were released from prison for sentences that were quite appalling yet the pope and many posed before him, setting them free. Free to do the bidding of the pope to come to be enriched we bred pagan homes and kill and destroy until they take every bit of land and leave the homeless to fend for themselves or enslave the young and mostly the pretty ones.

"Ye are not welcome here!" the priest spurted, smelling of wine and bad odor, halitosis breath, and standing six and two feet high. Standing on the stairway was a weeping woman naked and bleeding with hands bound and feet bound while two other men in black carried her down the stairs.

"Is this thy home?" Simon asked the priest.

"It is now," the priest said, drawing his sword and shouting toward his men. "Drop her and come fight!" he screamed.

"You may try, but we shall kill thee," Timothy said. All three froze, Simon poised to defend as the priest stopped in wait for his men who drummed the poor woman on the stairs, making Timothy wince.

"She shall be all right," Simon said, yet also wincing.

"Rebound thy lady," Timothy said, pointing his wand at the falling woman. She froze in midair. "Clothe thee," Timothy said, and clothes flew down from the top of the stairs and landed in place on her body, including shoes and a nice golden necklace with beads.

"Magic, kill them," the priest said, now plunging toward Simon with full force.

"Fierce, I see," Simon said as he parried and knocked the priest off balance and he stumbled where he quickly rebounded and stood, mildly wounded, against the far wall, checking himself for a wound, which may have come from his swift behavior.

"Enlightened with a sword, he shall burn in hell for eternity," the priest said, sneering and holding his blade ten feet back and circling the blade. "I've heard of your sort, pagan or Israel or something."

"England," Simon said.

"Come and meet your destiny," Timothy said, and he swiped his sword in a downward motion toward the charging miscreant.

"Your world has gone long ago. I have heard of thee, but look how few you are now in number," the priest said. "Leave this place."

"Ye shall leave this place, but not alive," Simon said as a scream was heard, and they both looked over toward Timothy, his sword coming down close to the right side of the charging monk's head and Timothy removing an ear. Then up and then down again and another ear, the man fell screaming as the next charged and another came from upstairs, pulling up his trousers drawing a blade and noticing the woman who was slowly floating to safety, the earless man screaming in pain as Timothy swiped sideways and removed his head, rolling out of the open door left by Simon.

The other charged at Timothy, and Simon fought with the priest. Round and round they went, Timothy fighting the large man from upstairs, who was apparently also good with a blade, back up the stairs down the hallway, into one bedroom, over three people tied up in a bedchamber, one an eighteen-year-old boy tied naked to a counter and two young girls strapped to each other and rubbed with makeup in a hideous way like someone took vengeance with makeup, which was actually quite startling and grotesque.

"Sauvez, nous S'il vous plait," the child said, weeping and with tears running down her and all the others' faces. Trembling, Timothy got pinned down against one wall then thrown against the cabinets; he dropped his sword.

"Hail thee, young prince of such fine clothes and armor! What has thee got under thy armor, hath thee drunk his last wine and shall I kill thee?" the heavily breathing man said. At that moment, there was a crash in the window, and Jeremy burst into the room through the leaded panes, glass flying in every direction and two other hawks flying in with Jeremy and rushing the large intruder, one to his eyes and one clawing his hands.

Simon finally ran the priest through downstairs and dragged the priest's body and the headless body outdoors as the freed horses came back and dragged them away, leaving a trail of blood.

Timothy rushed the man as the hawks invaded his nature and ripped his skin. Rushing, Timothy plunged his shoulder into his groin, quickly grabbed his sword, and pulled it through his palm. The man screamed, "No, curse the pagan villain!" The man looked at his hand sliced by his own blade and then looked directly into Timothy's beautiful blue eyes, knowing what was to come. Timothy turned his head slightly, still staring the man straight in the eyes. Timothy grinned. "Goodbye, villain, hope thee enjoys thy hell."

Timothy ran him through with his own blade, slowly and with great force, watching the hawks circle the room. The bound family watched in surprise, and all averted their eyes from the large bloody man lying dead before them. Timothy untied them all and took the man with Simon's assistance. They all thanked him, hugging him and running to dress, straighten, and check on each other's well-being. Two older daughters were in their early twenties with the hardworking elegance that a large farm demands. Buckets of ale and food was brought into a large dining room fit for a king.

"I bet they have fine ale here," Simon said, smirking.

"I need to remove this armor and take a bath. The lake looks promising. Yes, the horse will throw these men into the lake as well—no better fish food," Timothy replied. The two men walked outdoors and enjoyed the grounds as the family returned themselves to their rightful estate.

"We, I fear, are in a rather somber abyss, my lord Simon and Timothy," said the eldest son as the others went to rest.

"We shall take thee our leave, and Timothy shall be ever near to you if anything else occurs. Take heed of this pledge. Repeat after me," Simon said, staring into the boy's eyes.

"Draw Timothy to thee, and think on thy face," Simon said, pointing to Timothy his innocent and caring face before him.

"Draw Timothy to thee," the boy repeated.

"Good lad," Simon said, patting him on the head as he turned to rejoin his family and Timothy took Simon out into the night. Eventually they parted ways, back to Elysium for Simon and back to the cottage for Timothy.

Horses later came back for the final intruder, dragging his body into the lake and keeping watch over the farm and grand house until the family was restored, the house secured, and all was well.

Two days passed, and Timothy finally returned to the cottage. Porius lifted the forest veil to allow him entrance and walk through the thick of wood, thistle, adder, squirrel, chipmunk, deer, fox, and feathered creatures. Porius stood with open arms.

"Welcome to thy victor, Timothy, and well deserved," Porius said, handing him a wand of his own. Parthenia, Grendle, and Thomas clapped with glee knowing of his adventure and clearing the French farm from its assailants who perished due to their cause.

"Thank ye, Porius," Timothy said as he removed his armor, held his wand, and looked deeply at its wooden shaft and thick handle.

"May she serve thee well," Porius said. "Now some ale and I'll take that armor." Timothy undressed and laid all the bits of beautifully crafted armor upon the ground before Porius and his wand on the outside table and ran naked to the river to bathe while Porius disposed of and allowed the armor to be returned to hiding.

"Sanguine asis newmall," Porius said. "Armous Autem Absondum." The armor began to float and levitate with all its shining metals in the sunlight then floated into the cottage, past Grendle, Thomas, and Parthenia until it miniaturized and returned to a small cabinet in the hallway.

"Watch out for that flying metal, Grendle. It will get you every time," Parthenia said, smirking as she ducked down while the floating armor passed over her head, the cupboard doors opened, and shut with the sound of crashing metal inside the cupboard.

"The Honeywells in Adena 200 BC also left a parcel buried deep in the mines of Creek Mound burial, place of the Adena people. There the wizard Fraun was born with mixed blood as mine, otherworldly coming at us," Porius threw a rack at the naked Timothy who came running back from his bath in the river.

"I am hungry as an ox with two bellies," Timothy said, wrapping himself in a loincloth to barely cover his manliness.

"My dear young fellow, I am pleased to say that you will be of some use indeed to our cause. Here are the maps of current battalions, fighting, skirmishes, and trials." Porius laid out a large map, which covered the entire table so much that Porius decided to wave his wand, enlarge the size. And holding his wand above the map, the floating band stopped to play and peer with the others at Porius, the glowing map below him open, but as if alive.

"Secrets revelera tuum," Porius said softly, and his wand, glowing, emitted a soft mist from its tip. A slight moaning could be heard for only a moment. The map opened wide, stretching itself over the heavily carved table, which for centuries had held its position in service to Porius and the others. The map burned with smoke in certain areas.

"Italy," Porius said, pointing. "Athena holds these two areas and these families."

"Paris." Fraun, Simon, and others held and kept watch on the four remaining pagan families with large vineyards, orchards and livestock.

"London," Porius said while several fires burned and went out and continued around several areas. "Yes, you see London?" Porius closed in on the map. "The east side, several religious gatherings have caused many beatings and prejudice." Porius wept as he looked over London.

"London, my favorite town, home of arts, literature, and all things beautiful, and religion is tearing it apart, feeding its pious folk, changing them from honest freethinking individuals to one god-praising piece of a collected force."

"I had no idea," Timothy said.

"Yes, always skirmishes, beatings, and the taking of farms," Thomas said while lightly kicking a fox who was running out of the place, a small mouse on its tail.

"Enough, yes, there is plenty of activity, and we need fighters and messengers and bringers of goodwill. Timothy, we need you," Porius said.

"And I shall serve. Did you say Athena needs assistance in Italy?" Timothy said, leaning over the map.

"I think a few lessons with the sword before the evening," Porius said, playfully smacking Timothy's bottom, and quickly stood.

"What?" Timothy said, rubbing his behind and smiling.

"I watched you in France, and one of them nearly got you," Porius continued after a sip of wine. "Practice after we eat. You must win all your battles, Timothy, and it will not be easy. But thy fortune will multiply. I mean, look, you are all set in France from your deed," Porius said, munching down on a large piece of game pie.

"And the oldest daughter is quite a looker, I felt it in my loins," Timothy said, blushing.

"That may be true, but ye shall find women in every mission. Stay alert," Porius said as he waved to the band to continue playing and closed the map with a wave of his wand.

"Now don't misunderstand, you did exceptionally well in France," Porius said.

"Exceptionally well," Thomas said as he had Timothy a gown to drape over him for the evening. They laughed and chatted, dance, and sing, talked about mathematics, science, nature, and all the things, which make the cottage home.

Deep below in the bios, ants crawled industriously and followed by step or lead by design, their antennae's transparent waves communicating with the leader. The leader communicated with the queen, the erroneous multileveled brain of the ant so workable in every order. Caterpillars burrowed and migrated them, molding to become changed, one species intertwined with others. Flowers amongst flowers, and to the occasion, Timothy also brought Porius's seeds fresh from France. Packages tightly wrapped of seeds including roses, lilies les, pomme deterre, carrots, onions, and asparagus, pansies, and even wheat. Porius looked at the lot and planted instantly.

"You can never have too many varieties. Thank you, Timothy," Porius said as he grabbed a shovel and seeds, planting them in rows on the east side of the garden, Timothy helping and keeping the rows straight and mounds for seedlings, deeper row for water.

"Perfect when all is said and done," Porius said that evening after, planning and teaching Thomas and Timothy some slick tricks with the blade.

"I am also quite fond of the new cards. Card games are well and good. But to boggle someone's mind from use of a deck of cards is quite amusing," Porius said.

"Show us some card magic, Porius," Thomas said, Timothy in agreement rushing back inside and sitting at the table where once a map revealed the many areas of earth under war or conflict.

"Here both of you, take a care," Porius said.

"Hold on there, Porius. I want a card," Parthenia and Grendle came rushing out of the kitchen to grab a card, wiping their hands on aprons.

. "Oh all right, everyone pick a card," Porius said, extending his arm, deck spread like a peacock, handwritten cards of beautiful design. Dragons were around the 3s and snakes around the 7s; 8s were witches, 10 warlocks.

"Right, everyone, remember thy card and place back into the deck." Shuffling the cards, Porius gave them each three cards, peering at the three cards. Each of them noticed their originally picked card among the three.

"Are you all ready?" Porius said. "Lay all your cards facedown and in a line in front of you, and I will tell you which card is yours."

"Parlor games, perfect," Timothy said, adding his card to the center and placing them in front of himself.

"Timothy, your card is not the middle one but indeed on your left," Porius said.

Timothy knowing full well that his middle card was actually his choice, he turned it. "Ah-ha." Timothy looked at his turned card in complete confusion. "But I—"

Porius interrupted. "You did, but I actually changed it while you were not looking."

"Not looking, Porius, surely I would have seen you. What's the trick?" Timothy said, laughing.

"Grendle, yours is on your left." Grendle was smiling and nodding in agreement when she saw her card.

"Parthenia, center."

Parthenia turned her card. "Oh, lord Porius, you are good! Once more please," Parthenia said though quickly sniffing the air and rushing to the kitchen. "My bread!" she said and rushed back to the kitchen.

"Thomas, you're right." Thomas turned the card, and Porius again was correct.

"Quite humorous, Porius," Timothy said as he looked up to see Franklin squawking his normal cry when visitors were arriving from the forest.

"Ah visitors," Porius said, pointing his wand toward the forest beyond the fruit trees, and the procession began. Three large horses were pulling a golden carriage in full regalia, and out stepped the prince surrounded by three peacocks in white and gray, a tame zebra with reins made of bejeweled leather straps, two guards in finest armor who turned and stood facing the forest wall and back to the garden, which thickened after they arrived, closing the outside world from the garden.

"Good morrow, Prince George, son to Frederick," Porius said, delighted at the visitation of the prince and his bizarre, yet delightful entourage, yet knowing that something is afoot.

"Porius, my good man, a pleasure to see you and thank you for granting me passage to this garden. As you can imagine, I seek your assistance in a very odd matter," George said, taking his robes off and placing them back into the golden carriage with Timothy and Thomas circling with great exploration and wonder at the amazing carvings, beautiful velvet and finest woods and craftsmanship that went into the building of such a fine carriage.

"Come in, have some ale and tell me of your need of assistance," Porius said, leading him into the cottage, where Parthenia and Grendle bowed and curtseyed as they left goblets of ale.

"Oh dear me, let me change that cup to fit a prince," Porius said, waving his wand at the goblet set out for George as rubies, emeralds, and large diamonds pop out magically from the sides of the silver goblet amazingly turned into a bejeweled chalice filled with ale.

"You are the right wizard for the job, make no mistake," George said, eyes wide and grabbing on to the now transformed chalice and sipping the ale.

"Simple parlor tricks that I seldom get to use," Porius said, smiling. "And music." Porius waved his wand, and the miniature floating band appeared, playing a stately chorus of royal marching and dressed in the finest royal silk to match the prince in color and style.

"Most impressive, Porius, most impressive. You know my predecessors would have called you a heretic or worse," George said.

"I fully know of your predecessors, but they also all knew when to use my skills and they all secretly leave me alone."

"My good Porius, let me assure you that while we are taught strict religion, there is always the secret books taught to each royal of the old ways, which include stories and adventures of the great Porius. Oh, and you must be Thomas."

George laid eyes at Thomas who sat on the other side of the table.

"Yes, my prince, Thomas, my deepest pleasure."

"Leal?" George said, looking at the young Timothy.

"No, my lord, Timothy," Timothy replied and bowed as he stood back from the table in respect for the prince.

"I have always a royalist wizard, my prince," Porius said, sipping ale.

"Timothy, what a delightful name. I know a Timothy in Hanover," George said. "And I miss him too."

"Leal is much older now and seldom visits us, but still of our company," Porius explained then inquired about this abrupt arrival. "Now, what brings a prince to the cottage?"

"My lord Porius, the pope is close to visiting Dover castle and holds with him a box taken from Etruscans found in Tarquinia, Italy. The gems were depicted in the frescoes painted and pots of ceramic images, which showed the story of an ancient stone," George said, becoming quickly out of breath.

"I know of this stone, but how did they find it?" Porius said with deep concern.

"I bet they are excavating Greece," Thomas said inquisitively.

"Indeed, they must be," Porius.

"My lord Porius, the pope is to perform a ceremony at midnight tonight," George said. "We seek your guidance."

"Thomas, Timothy, call for Athena by way of the pensive. Tell her to meet us at Dover," Porius said, standing and grabbing his wand, which fit among the leather and beaded belt, which wrapped his white silken robes holding the details of fine sewing.

"What shall we do?" George.

"You were right to come and now do not go back to Dover but keep riding to St. James," Porius said, heading for the door after finishing his ale. George, Timothy, and Thomas followed suit and headed outdoors.

The sky was beginning to cloud, a cool breeze blowing by while Franklin circled, the trees giving up their branches to Porius and Thomas to use as their flying transport.

"Timothy, stay with George and see him safely back to St. James," Porius said, noticing Timothy's despair as he would rather go on the journey.

The pensive was left behind floating in the air and Parthenia told Athena, "Dover, my lady, Dover at midnight."

Porius flew over the forest with Thomas flying close behind. Timothy was riding in the coach with George and gazing at the zebra that walked alongside the carriage playfully. Two monkeys were playing on top of the coach, one swinging in and landing on George's lap.

"Oh, Filo, watch your hanging items, they like to play," George said to Timothy as the monkey jumped over to Timothy and pulled out his sword slightly.

"No, you don't, Filo," Timothy said to the monkey, shooing him off, and the monkey swung back up to the coach roof.

"I hope Porius can stop them. All we need is for the pope to have even more power," George said, offering a bag of wine to Timothy who obliged.

"Porius and Thomas will deal with this pope," Timothy said and they set forth for St. James. They passed through village after village, each catching the fond eye of passersby who bowed to the prince, waving to come up and offer food. One young man dressed in fine linens offered to buy them lunch, but George was headed straight to St. James.

"You never know who may want a lift to take advantage."

"I shall protect thee," Timothy said, hand to sword as they traveled further to their elegant destination.

As Porius and Tomas got closer to Dover, the clouds were becoming heavier.

"Oh good, these clouds will disguise our arrival, but for now just our watchful eye," Porius said.

Thomas was circling the castle high and heading out to sea; they both flew past the castle and over the sea further out until they saw the ship.

"Ship ahoy, Porius!" Thomas shouted, pointing down to the large ship that will most likely be letting go its anchor and sending a smaller ship to shore within the hour. They circled back to the castle.

"We have plenty of time to get ready, follow me," Porius said as they disappeared from sight among ever-growing darker clouds. The three-mast ship dropped anchor with several small boats holding five men each including the pope Pius VI, Giovanni Braschi, with a few Jesuits from his school days in one boat and one woman, the woman dressed in black and who seemed mysterious. The pope was holding the box, which hid the ancient stone.

"Let's land there," Porius said, pointing to a spot along the edge of trees toward the side of the castle.

"Lord Porius!" yelled a man of great form running toward Thomas and Porius as they landed.

"Take thee the wood," Porius said to a tree as he handed his branch and pointed to touch the tree. The tree took it as its own and also took Thomas's branch, and before a moment, the tree became home to the branches once which not a moment before transported our heroes to Dover.

"Leal my good friend," Porius said. "Nice to see you."

"Hello, Leal," said Thomas, "Come for the fun?"

"Indeed I have. Athena is busy so she sent me and said something about a stone, but I did not hear the whole story," Leal said in his tight-fitting battle leathers, short leather pantaloons, sword dangling at his side and shield with a lion molded to its front.

"Yes, we seem to have about fifteen coming our way, and the rain will be in our favor."

"What rain?" Thomas said.

Porius pointed to the air, and bucket loads started chuffing down around them. "This rain," Porius said, and the three entered the back of the castle, climbed the back steps, and two soldiers let them enter and bow as instructed earlier by George.

"Let them come," Leal said as he was offered a drink of water by a blushing lady-in-waiting.

There was lightning followed by thunder, and water crashed around the pope. They walked from their boats up the path to the castle, swords drawn and the pope holding the large wooden box covered in leather and lacings.

"Aperto nel nome di dio!" the pope shouted, walking up to the guards. "Open in zi name of God."

Porius stood at the entrance with Leal and Thomas behind.

"La peitra non deva entrare nel castello!" Porius shouted, catching the pope off guard.

"What do you mean and how dare you! Who are you?" the pope said angrily, and the men behind ran up to Porius, swords drawn. Thomas and Leal came from behind and entered into the fray. Leal ran a few of the pope's men, easing his blade once a lady was noticed.

"One is a woman, Porius," Leal said, and they all stopped fighting.

"What has thee brought within thy box?" Porius asked as the pope now knelt in the mud and drenched with rain. The pope shouted back, "Thy land is unpure and this opening shall bring thee peace."

"We have peace in these fields, we have peace in the villages, marshes and counties, what peace doth thy mention?" Porius asked as the others stopped fighting.

"Porius, the last wizard. Is it thee?" the pope asked, and Porius pointed his wand at the box.

"It is, and the stone is mine," Porius said, waving his wand toward the box. It opened, even with the pope fighting its opening. The stone floated in the air while the pope jumped after it, but his long black-and-red robes were drenched with the weight of the water that he fell once more to the mud.

Porius grabbed the stone and small medallion from midair and tucked them safely into his pocket.

"I will see war with thee, Porius, and the English king shall know of this interruption. You will all die, and we will take over these lands," the pope screamed. "Now let us in, we need food and refreshment."

"Enter as friends and come take shelter from the rain," Porius said, waving his hand toward Leal. "Let them pass."

And as they passed, Porius waved his wand toward the box, and it shook and rattled and mystified its holder the pope.

"Bury the dead," the pope said to the largest of his priests dressed in black with long black hair.

"Yes, Your Grace," he said, bending down with the help of others including Leal. "I will see what thee hath done to thy box and stone."

"Not you," the man said to Leal, and Leal backed off and headed into the castle with Thomas, the pope holding his shaking box. Just inside the entranceway, the pope dropped the box as it shook.

"I believe there is much more in thy box than a stone," Porius said, smiling as the box shook harder and the lid popped open. The sky murmured, and soft winds blew unusually with short bursts from every direction first from the west, then the north, east and south. Small cracks of lightning descended in piercing cracks. Groups of birds were flying but in swooping swirls—sparrow, crow, robin and even a few toads croaked as they leaped past one way then another, confusion among the natural creatures.

Inside, the guards stood along the sides watching the pope and his men's every move, the woman walking but not speaking next to the pope covered in black and red silks. The pope cast off his coat drenched with rainwater, rushing toward the box as its lid opened.

"The stone is mine!" the pope shouted, dragging his sopping wet cape of black and making a large puddle as the others took off their outer garments and gave to the men in waiting who swiftly took the robes and went to dry them while watching the spectacle before them.

"Ah, Lithorien, elf of Essex and Mingor, elf of Kent," Porius said as two fully grown elves dressed in the finest silks and jewels appeared.

"Thank yee, Porius, for releasing us from the box," one elf said who went by Lithorien.

"Lithorien, what brings you and Mingor to be in this box and traveling with such a foe?" Porius said.

"We were called by the stone to protect thee," Mingor chimed in.

"Well, just in time too," Porius said, pointing to the pope. "This man wishes to own the stone."

They all laughed. Thomas and Leal went out burying the dead.

"Well, the elves are sure to handle it, let's see to the dead," Leal said after removing his leathers, drying them, and replacing them strapped to his every curve, the pope mesmerized at his misfortune.

"Porius, you may not have that stone," the pope said, rushing past the two elves.

"Morian and Litigrell, whatever your names are, where is my stone?" the pope said, looking into the empty box and only seeing the elves. "Which one of you are hiding the stone?"

"We have no stone amongst us and therefore the stone can only be seen by the worthy," Lithorien said, pointing to the box. "I can see it plain as day," Lithorien said as all the others saw the stone sitting alone in the box.

"I cannot see it. What magic hath thee performed to hide the stone?" the pope said as he desperately searched for the stone, even rummaging through the pockets of the two elves.

"Isn't the basilica Giovanni missing you, Clement?" Porius said, avoiding the question. "You may see when you are worthy."

"You mean this?" Lithorien said, holding the stone at the level of his eyes and waving goodbye. "Arrivederci, Mr. Pope." Lithorien grabbed ahold of Mingor's hand, and they vanished before them, stone in hand.

"No!" The pope fell to the ground, crying, slamming his fists one after the other like a two-year-old who has had his favorite toy removed.

"It never really belonged to you or the church," Porius said, Thomas and Leal looking on laughing.

"And what of my dead men?" the pope asked.

"You should know of what happens when death occurs, or so you preach," Porius said. Two guards came out with dry overcoats, and the pope in red and black removed his overcoat and scurried away angrily, mumbling, "No stone, dead men, this trip is a disaster."

After they had rested, feasted, toasted with fine wine, and mingled with some very unpopular or lower-down-the-lines royalties, Porius, Thomas, and Leal rested for the night in a room offered by His Excellency, the pope charging to his chamber, never to be seen since they arrived.

"I thought he would've come down and breached the argument," Porius said. "But alas."

"Coward if you ask me, hiding behind men, trying to use a magical stone. The man is an idiot," Leal said, walking to refill his goblet with dark red wine as a couple of dancers came out to perform, one male and wearing only a fig leaf, the other a female and painted with gold on her breast and waist but otherwise naked as the day she was born, a man with two drums, and a few other musicians played a danceable tune and performed their historical dance.

"I believe this dance reflected the ancient mystics. How kind of His Royal Highness to offer us such splendid entertainment. They all applauded as they finished, the male performer coming up to Leal.

"Lord Leal, it is an honor," he said, bowing and then turning toward Porius and Thomas as they reclined and bowed back to the dancer. Then the painted woman bowed and performed a few steps more for them before retreating.

"The rain hath stopped," the pope said in broken English. "I am going out to say words over the dead. You there, Thomas? Come and show me where they lie."

Thomas led the pope out into the night to perform his ritual.

"Not very loquacious, is he, Porius?" Leal said, still eyeing the male dancer with such fine round buttocks. Then he stood and, seeing the dance, turned back to Leal and waited for him at the edge of the corridor.

"I will see you in the morning, Porius."

"Very well, good night and thanks for the protection, appreciated as always," Porius said, looking at the two dancers waiting for Leal. "Don't stay up too late." He smirked and sent waves to Leal as he walked toward the dancers and the three disappeared down the corridor to a room somewhere in the east of the castle.

"Tenacious Leal," Porius said, whispering and sitting alone in the large room of Dover castle, only on guard standing along the hall. Porius remembered past times here at Dover. James the Second, Charles the First,

Edward the Third for Porius surviving these many years on earth. Half human and half something else, something he had always wanted to know.

"Mysteries, mysteries, where will I end up?" Porius was thinking to himself and all the past rushing through his mind. Looking down to his empty goblet and a footman came in with his dried cape of white silk.

"My lord Porius, it is a great honor to meet thee," the man said.

"And you are?"

"My father was descendant of Salazar," he said.

"Ah, Suffolk, many a good folk in Suffolk."

"Thank ye, and thank ye for the drying of my clothes. Is there any more wine about?"

"Yes, here, my lord," he said as he filled a goblet.

"My name is Pierce, and I always wanted to study the old ways. My heart is beating quickly as I stand so close to such a noble wizard," Pierce said.

"Pierce, my good man, it is an honor to meet a fellow pagan. What family?"

"Jacques. Pierce Jacques," he said.

"Not a name I am familiar with in Suffolk."

"My great-grandfather was taken to France as a young boy and came back years later with a new name and no knowledge of his past name, but he feels it is Lovell."

"Lovell, now that's a name I have heard of, a small farm outside of Dunmow," Porius said with delight as Thomas and the pope reentered from the once again rainy night.

"Talking with the help," the pope said in a nasty way. "Go about your business." The pope smacked Pierce on the backside and moved him on.

"Now, now, now, Clement, it never hurts to be nice," Porius said and stood and rushed to Pierce, grabbing him and stopping him and turning him around. "It was my sincere pleasure to have made your acquaintance, Pierce." Porius reached out his hand to shake Pierce's.

"And you, Lord Porius," Pierce said, shaking his hand, smiling and then turning his head toward the pope quickly then away.

"Pierce," Thomas said, nodding toward him.

"Lord Thomas," Pierce said, bowed, and went about his business.

Porius turned to the pope. "Are you not supposed to be representing a man who would do the same?" Porius asked, a bit miffed at the pope's character and snobbery.

"How dare you speak to me of Jesus!"

"I have absolutely no wish to discuss religion, politics, or the hierarchy of humankind. I shall go to bed and leave back for Rome in the morning, all this way and no stone."

"O, that is too bad, I was prepared to spend a good hour discussing just those particular items. I would also like to discuss how far the Catholic church plans on going before they are done."

"We will never stop, Porius. My leagues of followers are set in motion to cover the world, the Orient, India, Africa,"

"You will devour the earth," Porius interrupted.

"It is our destiny and the one true god," the pope said.

"But will you please leave the old ways families alone, at least those who have royal ties to the ancient ones?" Thomas pleaded.

"It is all foreseen. Thy shalt be washed, and the world will be cleaned," the pope said as he turned and sat at the table, most likely deciding that this conversation may be worth having. "And you cannot kill me because another shall come behind me."

"We do not kill. We protect and try to slow the machine your church has used to take the freethinking minds of families, turning them against each other, showing them sin and giving them forgiveness."

"And how better to rule their simple minds?" the popes said, sipping some wine.

"People's minds are not so simple, and mark my words, not now and far in the future will men start to use their minds again. They will not need the belief that you offer," Porius said.

A few bats flew into the castle from the time Thomas and the pope came back into the cottage circling.

"Bats, I hate bats," the pope said, waving them away as they circled over his head.

"They will not hit you, and I will show you how to get them out," Porius said, slowly running to the far end of the room. "Now you there, open the front door," Porius said to one of the guards who obliged the request.

"Open," Porius said and ran at a mild pace toward the front door then out. All the bats completed their circling and followed Porius until they were all out save for one.

"You see," Porius said to the pope, "bats are just a part of nature, a part of us all."

"Well, thank ye, Porius, but they are not a part of me, Bats, really," the pope continued. "How can you say we are part of everything?"

"I think someday science will find that to be true. Fish in rivers will have the same building blocks as the trees and bushes that surround the river, birds will share atoms of all they fly over, and man will be a part of everything," Porius said though he knew that this is something the pope may not quite be able to digest.

They discussed the living, the dead, and all in between and Porius agreeing with some items. The pope spoke of the good of mankind, and the pope listened to many ideas and thoughts of Porius and also agreed on may points. By the end of the evening or actually early morning, both men stood in respect for the other on some points, but Porius was not satisfied with many others. They parted, and in the morning, Porius, Thomas, and Leal headed back home, the pope returning to Italy.

CHAPTER 24

Deer scampered and played, doves willow and cooed, foxes picked off the occasional chicken that roamed endlessly among the gardens of the cottage. Wheat safely planted; tomatoes ripened on the branches held up by strings; rows of carrots, cabbage, corn, and herbs lined in rows here and there between flowers, fruit trees; and one cupboard grew a complex assortment of mushrooms that Porius, Thomas, and all the other occasional students that passed through the cottage. Timothy was still with George and most likely being knighted as a guardian of the palace built by Henry VIII in 1536 where Timothy walked the halls and was given a room and allowed to mingle with the staff, women in waiting, and lesser relatives of the crown. Leal was back with Apollo in Elysium, Athena and her maidens stayed in a castle in Italy, which was still hidden from the church among the northern provinces, which became a refuge for those who fell outside of the church's grip. Walters was also given the extended life by turning his body into the waters and made to travel between Elysium and his farms and land in Kent, now being run by his relatives. When Walters visited earth and his lands, the family told the tales of the ghost of Walters who haunted the grounds and may occasionally become form, exposing himself to ancestors and some believe while others called nonsense. Simon wandered between Athena where he spent many a night in ecstasy with Athena's maidens. Many others who had stayed, learned, and possibly traveled to the underworld under Porius's guidance now traveled from planet to planet, helping all who sought preservation.

Porius, Thomas, Grendle, and Parthenia were happy among the magic grounds of the cottage, allowing only those worthy or in need to enter the secret gardens hidden in Kent. Hops growers traded good ale with fish, wheat, and the occasional visit from Thomas, Porius, or Parthenia when sick or in need of medicine. The villagers still knew how to reach Porius, and even though many had turned to the new church, they had respect and need of the old ways. Porius occasionally was sought out by individuals who had heard the tales and had the desire to seek him and learn the ancient ways. Though ancient remedies and medicines, many would be even more relevant in the future because one of the standard teachings from Porius is the teaching that even though Porius did not have the technology or machines to measure all sicknesses, he feels that someday the human race will have the medical knowledge to possibly cure all diseases but not the will of the mind.

"Good morning, Thomas," Porius said as Thomas walked out front to go and bathe in the river. Porius was out in his white robes, bluebirds circling and playfully swooping down at Franklin who sat on the thatch, annoyed with the pestering bluebirds.

"They only wish to play, Franklin," Thomas said, watching the event, and both Porius and Thomas giggled at Franklin's stern face of feathers until Franklin flew off with the bluebirds after succumbing to their annoyance and finally beginning to play.

"It appears the Americans are hunting the pumas, I'm afraid. I have sent a note by pensive to Leal and Apollo, requesting that they transport to America and salvage a few pumas. I think there are a few safety circles around the areas that contain these lovely beasts, the Apache, Navajo, and a few other natives are killing pumas it's very sad."

"Will Leal and Apollo go?" Thomas asked while drying himself and slipping on his purple pantaloons. "To America, I mean."

"Well yes, not sure. I haven't heard back but seem to have lost touch with some of the other tribes and not sure what havoc the colonialists are posing, but I am sure they will require their independence. George has other worries now between France and Spain. Leave America to the Americans because it will end up their own at some point anyway," Porius said as a couple of butterflies land on his shoulders and fly off.

"Feudal, I imagine, Porius," Thomas said inquisitively.

"Yes, that is what everyone is saying. Let them have it," Porius said as he pulled out a pipe from his robes and set it alight with his wand.

"Ale, Porius?" Thomas asked, heading for the front door, almost tripping over a festive faun who was playing with a squirrel who ran directly under Thomas's legs, the tail slapping the purple pantaloons.

"Purple is very becoming, Thomas," Porius said in jest.

"Thank you, Porius, I picked them up in Paris," he said proudly.

"I can well imagine you did. Very Parisian of you, Thomas, very Parisian."

"Afternoon tea at the tavern I feel for this day. Doth thy wish to accompany?" Thomas said as Parthenia handed him a yellow and purple and green top made of the finest silk.

"Yes, and will you be wearing this new purple, green, and white Paris garb?" Porius asked, squinting his eyes at the spectacle of Thomas's Paris collection.

"Wait, look at these shoes," Thomas said as Porius tried to keep from laughing.

"These are very nice, Thomas. Sit down and let me slip them on you," Parthenia said as she set Thomas down on the outside table bench, wood carved of many animals. "Sit tight and there we go, a nice fit indeed." Parthenia smiles then rushed back into the kitchen to finish kneading the bread already once risen.

Thomas stood, his silver shoes with heels, white silkiness up to his puffy purple pantaloons.

"I would not miss seeing Thomas in public dresses in his finest Paris clothes if my life depended on it," Porius whispered to a large deer who was poised with vacant expression, wide eyes on Thomas's purple extremities. The deer looked at Porius, rolled her eyes, and continued to gaze with one eye on the fawn who still ran playfully with two young squirrels.

Later that evening, Porius and Thomas walked into the Fox and Hound, newly named from the latest owner, June and April, two sisters who inherited the tavern from their father, a stately man who was caught giving papers to the French, which the king thought were secrets, but actually the papers passed were nothing more than a recipe for coq au vin, one of the latest crazes in London, chicken with wine stewed in pearl onions and mushrooms.

"Hello, Porius and Thomas," June said, standing behind the bar and passing out drinks as fast as possible, two large goblets of ale were given to Thomas and Porius.

"Nice clothes, Thomas," the farmer said behind them, waiting to order a drink.

"Going to the ball?" another shouted.

"Very fancy, Thomas," a woman said, winking as he passed.

"Well, I like it, Thomas," June said. "A real fancy gentleman you are." She rinsed and wiped a glass with her apron.

"I knew you would be the toast of the town," Porius said, smirking in his usual way.

"Thank ye, June, and your ale is splendid," Thomas said while Porius held back laughter, found an empty table, sat, and gulped. Several young men walked by Porius and tipped their heads in greeting. Three small kids shouted as the mother shook each one, telling them to be quiet or go out. The three kids ran outside and left her to enjoy the tavern folk, and a fiddler stood outside the door in case they open it for scraps or change as played beautiful music, which filled the air, creating a peaceful yet elegant perfume of sound. Porius, Thomas, and the farmer spoke of crops' care. A young physician, Morley, came and chatted with them about the latest medical discoveries.

"One is where we can take the blood from one and give to another," Morley said.

"Wonderful idea, and the life can be saved from loss of blood," Porius said, amazed.

"Yes, Porius, I have performed the operation twice with success on both occasions," Morley said, sipping some wine as he was not a fan of ale.

Three fancy-dressed men entered, obviously on their way back to London. One spotted Thomas and quickly came up and sat on the chair next to him as he shouted. "Get me an ale and join us here," the man said, wearing white silks and red pantaloons.

"Very nice to meet you," Thomas began as Porius looked at the sight of them, both wearing the latest Paris fashion.

"William, and my friends are Colin and Steven. Your wardrobe's from Paris. I was just there and bought from Madame Droussier."

"Ah," Thomas said, looking at Porius for a way out of the conversation. "Well, I am no fashion expert, but I did like the purple and thought this may be the future." The others came up, bringing their large ales and gulping them down. The table turned into a loud and rapid conversation of "Where did you last visit in Paris?" "My suit came from another place," the usual midtwenties gentlemen who were mostly confirmed bachelors who obviously had close relationships with each other and the talk and gossip and drank more ale as the night went up to just past ten. Porius made his good night to many of the villagers, fancy men, June the bartender, and some others with Thomas in tow for the walk outside and which has started to rain.

"Perfect," Thomas said. "I am not sure how well this outfit will react with rain."

Colin ad Steven hovered around some of the prettier girls from the village, vaguely paying attention to Thomas, Morley, and Thomas eventually landing among the company of interested women, goblets clinking, some smoking the latest tobacco or herbs from other parts of Kent. Two young gentlemen were in silver threads with silken stockings and black shiny silver buckled shoes.

"My good woman, we would like two pints of your finest Kent ale," one man said at the bar as she curtseyed to the splendor of such immaculately dressed fancy gentlemen.

"On the way to London?" she asked, serving them but they ignored her and dropped some coins on the bar. She curtseyed again, used to being ignored by the gentry.

"Very fine ale," the other man said, his face painted white with black painted dots above his eyes and upon his cheek.

"You see, Porius, more fashionable men," Thomas said to Porius as they witnessed the two fancy men tipping their heads forward as they passed and find a separate table at the far end of the tavern.

"Just a drizzle, I am sure of it," Porius said, looking up as the rain slowed a bit and they walked along the road back to the forest.

"Porius," a voice was heard from behind.

"Ah, Morley," Porius said, stopping to greet the such an eager messenger.

"Porius, Lord Thomas, I fear that I forget to invite you to the new rooms I have let and turned into a medical office and operating room to support Kent."

"My good man, we would be delighted to visit your medical facility with pleasure," Porius said with Thomas in agreement.

"I have written the address here for you just outside Dover, not far from Hastings patch and close to shore. I thought it wise in case someone comes from ship seeking medical attention."

"Very wise," Thomas said.

"How about tomorrow?" Morley pleaded.

"Yes, tomorrow will be fine," Porius said.

"Perfect, let's see at noon and I shall provide lunch," Morley said, wearing a gray outfit made for any basic townsmen, the usual gray and leather, tuck and buckle outfit. The hardworking folk consider this outfit most practical and pleasing.

The next morning after breakfast, they rode upon two horses, Jill and Jacopo or J&J as Porius liked to call them as they usually came on loan from one of the local estate owners who owed Porius one or two favors for medical treatment. For this particular owner who raised horses, Porius once saved his youngest son from the rack due to being labeled a heretic even though the boy was just caught naked with several others splashing about in a pool of water. The priest's men found them and made them all walk four miles naked to the magistrates and after calling them heretics telling the magistrate that they were found performing satanic rituals. Well, nothing could be further from the truth; in fact, just the opposite. They were doing, well, let's say some sort of sexual experimentation that may have gone a tad too far.

"Morley sure seemed pleased to show us the place," Thomas said back to Porius who followed on Jill riding and watching the forest life off to the east and west of them.

"He may be on to something and also a good ear for our cause," Porius said.

"You noticed it too? I think Morley comes from a very old family," Thomas said.

"I knew them. His father was a blacksmith and ironmonger for several years out of the village."

"I thought I recognized Morley. I remember him as a child," Thomas continued to his interlocutor. "That child who brought us the new hinges."

"Correct, the time we had to fix the front door due to one of Cadmus Upton's great-grandson son."

"Yes, that's right," they wondered whatever happened to the Upton family since.

"We sure have seen and done a lot together, Porius."

"My dear boy, there is much more to come. Much, much more to come."

The dark clouds covered and let loose a bit of rain but stopped after a while as they finally reached Dr. Morley's new three-story monstrosity, a large towering building built of crossed wood, thatch, brick and stone, crooked lines, a smaller base with upper floors that leaned over the front porch. Ivy was growing up around the front, and thick vines circled the posts and a sign out front that said DOCTOR MORLEY.

"Welcome, Porius, welcome, Thomas," Morley said, wearing his tight-fitting black suit and white gloves. He took them through the parlor then through the kitchens and up to the second floor. He opened room after room, quickly checking inside to make sure nothing was taking place. Finally, Morley came to a door on the west side of the building.

"The study," Morley said as they walked in like people admiring a home for sale, all in smiles and agreement with the fine woodwork, shutters, wardrobe.

"Now, Porius, do you mind staying here for a little while?" Morley said while Porius gazed out the window, Thomas by his side. Porius noticed a small group of people walking beyond the treelined edge of wood. "Just sit tight," Morley said and slammed the door as he left Porius and Thomas in the room and a click was heard.

"He's locking the door," Thomas said, panicking and rushing to the door.

"Morley, what is this all about?" Porius shouted, not liking the thought of being locked in Morley's surgery library. "Morley, come back here, man."

"Porius, it is only for a little while, and then I will return," Morley said as he ran down the staircase and rushed out into the street to join the others dressed in black and walking into the forest.

"What is beyond that wood, Thomas?" Porius asked, rushing back to the window.

"It appears they want you out of the way, Porius," Thomas said. "He did not inquire after our state of being."

"The Cat House, yes, the Cat House lies just beyond the woods," Porius said, looking around for a way out of this wooden cage.

"Do you mean the Cat House, opium den, wild people, naked dancers, and rooms for, well, this and that?" Thomas inquired.

"The very same. We must get out of here, for I know what is going on in Morley's mind. I was wondering how he could afford this place, not by his doctor skills, of that I'm sure."

Porius took his wand and pointed it at the door. "Roman tick and tock come forward and release this lock," Porius said, still pointing.

"Ah, here they come," Porius said as two fairly large spiders walked out of the cupboard with broken hinges and from behind the wall they both crawled toward the lock, one spider digging into the lock and manages to disappear within.

"Spiders are so helpful," Thomas stated, watching with care.

"And so easy to command," Porius said, smiling.

Meanwhile, Porius was most accurate in his thought of the Cat House, which was usually filled with the gentry buying favors and enjoying illicit pleasures, renting girls who eagerly line up for the riches among them. And men who handled the other persuasions with delicacy and force when the occasions called for such force. Inside the large two-bedroom stone building stood several large smoke-filled rooms, clean kitchens holding maybe five workers, a chef, waiters, and a few topless girls who served drinks and offered other favors.

"Yes, that's it," Porius said as the locks opened, spiders running quickly back to their home behind the broken cupboard.

"Let's go, Porius," Thomas said as they rushed outdoors far behind Morley who was most probably meeting the henchmen from the pope, who even more likely paid Morley to lock up Porius before attempting to raid the Cat House.

"I believe a diversion is necessary," Porius said, waving his wand upward. "Clouds holding back, release and slow these black hearts." The clouds burst with lightning bolts one after the other, cracking, pouring, chucking down rain by the bucket load.

Morley and his mates were only one hundred feet from the Cat House; the water poured on them, soaking their black robes, slowing their pace.

"Ah rain. I augmented you shall have your reward, and the place is most busy," Morley said to the largest men in black.

The man in black turned to Morley and did not say a word but shook Morley cold to the bone. For Morley was not really a bad man, just when the pope offered one hundred gold pieces for locking Porius up and showing his men the way to capture one of the hidden dens of iniquity. Morley slowed his pace and, wiping the water from his face, followed them more quietly. Then about ten feet from the Cat House, one of the men put his hand out toward Morley and stopped him. "You will not be needed," the man said, and the three large figures drenched in rainwater pulled large blades out from underneath their black wet robes. They burst in.

To their wonder and excitement, the three men stood eyes wide and face-to-face with three tables surrounded by peoples of all kinds, girls in leather, men in small straps around their waists. Several card tables and several dropping off food and elegantly dressed tables, pheasant, champagne, smokes from large water pipes. A woman walked up to the three. "May I take your coats and dry them?" she said innocently, her wide black eyes circled in black makeup, pitch-black long hair that ran down her naked back all the way below her buttocks. "Are the swords necessary, sirs?" she said, moving back from these men who didn't seem or feel to her like the usual customer.

"You may leave," said the largest man in black, motioning for the girl to run outside, and she did quickly. Plush curtained lodgings or not, she knew when danger was present, and out she went, leaving. She bumped into Porius.

"Stay out here, you fool," Thomas said to Morley as he and Porius rushed in to save the helpless victims or soon to be victims of this raid.

"Stand down!" Porius shouted at the men, all eyes in place on Porius and the three men.

"Scatter, hide, run!" was shouted and heard from many of the patrons as many grabbed their winnings from the gambling tables, rushing to and fro. Some men and women just remained still and looked at the three large ominous men in black holding large cutlasses, and it began. The largest of the men in black plunged his cutlass into a man who wore tights and carried round balls painted of many colors.

"Leave these innocent people alone," Porius shouted. Thomas pointed his wand at one of the men and whispered, "Snake bit tonight." He pointed at the bottom of his coat, and a large black adder came from the wand, entering under his robes and bit hard.

"Jacob, a snake!" the man winces in pain, and Porius went for the largest of the three and parried with his wand instead of a sword.

"I need not a blade to destroy you," Porius said and waved his wand at all three. "Freeze thee villains and petrify in thy midst."

The three men moved slower and slower until their bodies stopped moving, only their eyes seeing the crowns, and one man's fist gripped with the hair of a woman who, screaming, released her hair, ripping much that stayed in his frozen fist but the man still watching the crowd.

"Pulled from the hairs and all for a wooden cross," Porius said, holding the angry mob back.

"They are frozen stiff," one man said who slowed his charge due to Porius giving instructions.

"We shall show mercy to these men," Porius said, circling them and removing their robes with the assistance of others. "Take all their clothes and burn them once they dry."

"Porius, may I ask what you are planning?" Thomas said, watching four men and two women disrobe the three men in back.

"I wish to see what is present on their skin," Porius replied.

All three men had expressions of questioning upon their faces. Two women took the robes back to the kitchens and left the three men standing naked bearing marks of previous torture, tattoos, and worse, the indentations of cruelty.

"You men have had rough times, I hope moving forward you will forget the church and rejoice in thy new skin," Porius said as he waved his wand over their wounds and slowly the three men now defeated succumbed to the earth and lay crying. "Forgive us, forgive us," they pleaded, but the crown does not wholly forgive.

"Thy fate is thy own, what you make of it now," Porius said.

The card tables started playing again, music from the far-off chamber was heard, the rustling of change was heard among the whispers, which turned eventually into sounds of joy. The Cat House saved Porius and Thomas. Heading out into the street and walking back through the forest they went back to Morley's new facility. They burst in and found Morley crying in the downstairs smoking room, his wife standing over him.

"Forgive him, Porius," she said.

"Oh, I do indeed. Everyone wants to make a bit of money," Porius said earnestly.

"Thank ye, Porius. I did not know, but the money paid for all this," Morley said apologetically.

"We understand," Thomas said.

"Now show us the rest of this magnificent hospice," Porius said and they enjoyed the rest of the evening.

"And remember, Morley, lack of discretion will be fought with unforeseen consequences," Thomas said as the apologetic Morley showed the rest of the surgery, kitchens, and lab, which Porius found most interesting.

"This lab can be used for many purposes within the next few years, especially since new inventions, discoveries, and remedies are happening daily," Porius said while he greeted his wife Sarah, who was pulling a baked pie out of the oven.

"Porius, a pleasure to meet you and sorry I wasn't here to greet you, but baking takes quite the attention. Oh, and Lord Thomas," Sarah said as she placed a fresh game pie out of the oven, placing it on the wood block counter.

"Smells most scrumptious," Porius said, rubbing his hands together.

"Oh here ye two, have a slice while it's hot. The pheasant has much better qualities when hot," Morley said, opening the wine while Sarah sliced the pie.

The next morning, Porius walked out into the garden and noticed Franklin already up and circling high over the town side of the forest, usually meaning that someone was approaching from that direction, whether the traveler was worthy or lucky enough to be granted access to the cottage and its grounds.

"Franklin, what hath thou seen?" Porius said softly while Thomas came from within the cottage walking past Porius to his usually morning bath in the river.

"Mumbling to yourself this morning, Porius?" Thomas said.

"Oh no, it just seems Franklin is in some holding patter," Porius said, pointing to the black dot high and off to the west.

"Visitors?" Thomas said, leaving his robe on the garden and running in to clean in the waters, stepping over the soft mossy grass at the river's edge.

Soon the sound of a carriage and then about twenty minutes passed as the well-known and familiar carriage drove up, a young driver sitting on top with red and white silks. Timothy jumped out of the carriage in royal garb. George and Caroline stepped out in grand dress and bejeweled.

"Prince and Princess from Hanover," Porius said proudly as Thomas quickly dressed, Parthenia and Grendle coming out in good cheer carrying a tablecloth covered in many lace made animals by some delicate hand at needlepoint.

"My dear Porius," George said as Grendle took Caroline by the hand and whisked her off to a private chamber at the back of the cottage, which was seldom used and prepared for mortal royal visits. The room has pink and gold trim with veined marble flooring, running water, perfumes from France, and some Swedish soaps, which Caroline most admired. Grendle left Caroline to freshen up and returned to the kitchen and rushed together some broth, turkey pies, canapés as Parthenia came back to the kitchen in great enthusiasm and excitement.

George handed Porius a box, which held two bottles of red wine, which Porius gladly took and after opening one poured them all in goblets and

George removed his large cover, placing it over a stump outside while they sit around the outdoors table, deer, fox, squirrel, and hound watch from the edge of the forest with ears perked up. Until once the conversation grew into a comfortable flow, the animals went about their playful day as usual. Timothy and George were telling the tale of their adventures with George of the past few days and his good fortune of being given such splendid clothes. Porius complimented George of the excellent wine as Caroline came out.

"My Lord Porius, an honor to meet thee," Caroline said.

"My good princess, is that a Swedish accent I detect?"

"Indeed, Lord Porius and Thomas, I presume," she said.

"My lady, the pleasure is all mine," Thomas said, bowing. His eyes were cast upon her dainty ankles bound in golden threads and handmade white shoes with pearl-beaded linings, her dress purple lined up to a waist of nineteen inches wrapped in white silken bonding, whale-bone structure and pink, purple and blue bows lined up her sleeves and neck. This outfit pretty much matches George as they were the most becoming of beings, elegant in the extreme.

"We would like to learn a bit of magic, Porius," George said in earnest.

"You would, wouldn't you? Well, that is a new one on me," Porius said. "A prince soon to be king wants to learn magic?"

"Yes, Lord Porius, France is becoming a problem and just in case," George said, "something special."

"I will be right back," Porius said, walking into the cottage and then back out before they had time to sip their drinks, deer coming closer.

"Porius, I will be king, you know," George said.

"Yes, and you may not want to wear so much powder on thy wigs and head," Porius said inquisitively.

"Nonsense, Porius, it's all the rage and I must look divine," replied George.

"I would not wear the powder, but your fate is your own," Porius said as he quickly placed a small stone in to George's side pocket.

"Do no put your hand into the pocket until after you remove thy clothes," Porius said, patting the pocket with his hand. George glanced down into the waist pocket.

"Why, it's only a pebble, Porius," George said, worried expression and smirking.

"A pebble, yes," Porius said. "But magic"

"Oh, how pleasing." George patted his pocket with a secure smile and knowledge that came from safety, and all were filled with glee.

George discussed his last adventure to Hanover and his need of the many outweighing the few in court and government, his hesitations as the role of king awaiting him was filled with dangers, and the usual fears of France and Spain. Parthenia and Grendle laid out a meal, which would please anyone as they gorge themselves, laugh, and eventually dance to the small floating band, which Porius made appear and gave a splendid performance while George, Caroline, and even their trusted coachmen went up to the band within inches and watched the tiny musicians play such miraculous-sounding music.

"You say the bandleader is called Jack Tanner?" George asked Porius while eyeing the happy conductor, who occasionally picked up an instrument himself aside from conducting.

"Yes, Jack the Lad is his nickname, and he is rather shy," Porius said, warning George from getting too close and putting his hand on his shoulder, pulling him back a bit.

"You see, he is temperamental," Thomas said, laughing as Jack the Lad and his magical floating band disappeared in an instant.

"Oh dear, what have I done?" George asked, watching the band disappear before them.

"Not to worry, Jack is temperamental, but they will be back," Porius said, leading them outdoors and round the garden pointing out certain vegetables, fruits, and rare plants and herbs. Caroline was taking a special interest and commenting on the superb wine that George had brought for their enjoyment. In fact, after two bottles of wine and a gallon of mead later that evening, everyone rested and finally dozed into the wee hours of the morning. There were talks of America, the battles ahead, and the cages on the minds of so many, now bound to new religions, politics, theater, and anything else worthy of captivation.

"What is worse?" George asked. "Being in hospital ill and no one knowing you are there or caring? Or someone you love being in hospital and not telling you?"

"My dear prince, both are equally bad and will add to loneliness of the heart and self-loathing, not particularly refreshing any way you look at it. Why?" Thomas replied.

George patted Timothy softly on his behind as he jumped into the carriage following Caroline.

"I shall miss our conversations, Porius," George said, hugging Porius. Outside the carriage, a slight rain began to fall, and the coach wandered off through the woods that opened like a large orifice and closing thick behind the carriage. One hit the road beginning its long path back to London. Spectators watched the coach and waved as it passed the villages of Kent. Past fields, waters, houses of thatch and stone, wood, and ivy. Children came out to the carriage occasionally in the rain to wave to the prince and princess as they wheeled by, horses erect and stately, as Caroline cast occasional rose petals at the people who walked up close to the carriage. These mortals were happy in their stride, and word traveled from tavern to tavern and home to home: "en las casas serendipity, all hail the future king George."

George took Timothy back to London with Caroline in tow while Thomas and Porius went fishing the following day, and all seemed right with the world. Until about six the following evening and a flock of crows went screeching overhead and boar, deer, and other woodland creatures went running through the gardens at a fierce rate, as well as sheep, cow, hawk, and badgers went through one by one.

"What is happening, Porius?" Thomas asked as they ate a plum pudding for after.

"Intuitive of you, Thomas," Caroline said as she sipped some brandy made of the berries in the garden.

"Something is coming, and I sense rage," Porius said as he quickly whipped his wand into action and the pensive appeared, floating before them.

"Reveal the nearest dangers," Porius said as the pensive liquid revealed three men on foot with oxen and cart, wheels turning in rickety wobbles with brown ox towing as a low hum of muffled notes moaned out of the obvious monks, one bleeding down his leg from his previous night's cilices and red where the small of the three's tonsure razer closed. The large moaning mouth was wearing a long wooden cross, sword, shield, and blades about his person, leather pants, black muddy cloaks misted in the rain as they marched down the road pacing farther with cart in tow to London, one giggling under his breath as he sipped from one of the dangling bags of whatever liquid substance hung upon them.

Porius closed the pensive, and walking out into the garden, he looked up at the sky as it began to rain, popping slightly among petals, leaves, veins of ivy, water, and earth. Droplets fell, penetrating everything in its path, which replenishes the world. Ants and beetle were under fire as one dropped blasting next to their being, knocking the beetle and changing his direction slightly. Ants under fire ran for cover or to the hold that led them safely to the bios, grasshopper clinging to the branch that bobbed up and down with each pellet of rain. Deer, woodpecker, badger, mole, rabbit, squirrel, and fox wandered back to there, burrowed, rested, or whatever home they have made while birds flurry, catching the inquisitive worms uncovered by the rain.

CHAPTER 25

Deep below the raging waves amid a storm at sea, two large blue whales bellowed and swerved among hundreds of species within their realm of blurry water, seaweed, octopus, and eel. These huge magnificent whales rose to the top, and beside them a comet-type hot ash descended from the heavens, punching a hole in the ocean the smoldering hotness of this molten rock that caught the eyes for both blue whales swirling downward, following the embers as they cooled in the deep of the ocean, then finally to rest among the underwater seaweeds, thick kelp gardens housing red algae, seagrass, and underwater animals, and creatures of all kind. The whales in turn swept over the still-smoldering stone and its size of twenty feet wide, thick and long. But even the whales noticed its peculiar shape as not being round but rectangular, and as it cooled, the outer crust fell away, leaving something unusual. The whales surfaced and thought hard about Porius. Using their large elaborate brains, they transmit the idea through thought, emotion to Porius.

Porius awakened with the blue whales' vision as witness to the falling debris to rest upon the surface.

"Stay, my friends, and we shall be there," Porius transmitted his thought to the large beasts of the sea.

"Come, Porius, a visitor has landed," the whales transmitted back. "We shall mark thy spot."

"Thomas, awaken, come quickly!" Porius shouted.

"What is it Porius?" Thomas said, wiping the rightness from his face.

"We must get to Portsmouth by tonight, board the HMS *Princess Amelia*, and ride out to sea," Porius said, grabbing his best and warmest robes, wand, and sword. After they had freshened up and packed a few dried fish, bread, and wine satchels, they were off. Taking the branch from two trees who gave gladly, they rode their wooden transporting branches and made it to Portsmouth by night fall and boarded the HMS *Princess Amelia* unnoticed and in secret. They sneaked into a small covered rowboat that they eventually lowered into the sea the next morning when the *Amelia* reached the area where Porius's mental stimulation was strongest, lowering the boat slowly. Two sailors hearing the noise came to check on the distraction, but Thomas placed a spell that made the person less aware.

"Take no notice of this boat," Thomas whispered, pointing his wand toward the sailors as he whispered.

"Well done, now help me lower and keep it even," Porius said as they finally reached the waves, the ship leaving them off in the middle of the sea.

"Hear me, whales, hear me, see me," Porius said while Thomas put the ores inside the dingy.

Beside them, large as mountains, the massive whales rose, one winking to Porius and the amazing sounding noise of their voices echoed a defining sound under the sea, which the men heard loud and clear.

Athena, Walters, Simon, and Leal appeared in their transmolecular form they like to call form not flesh, which made them appear in ghostlike form, giving the ability to transport from place to place and planet to planet when the beam of light permitted.

"We heard your call," Walters said as they all hovered over the seas, coming to rest in the dingy, save Leal who rested on the blue whale, resting on the surface of the sea and adding ample dry space for a team of Leal's.

"I never thought I would get to ride a blue whale," Leal said, waving down at the others in the boat until the whale began to submerge and Leal joined the others in the dinging.

"Barely enough room for the six of us, Porius," Athena said, wearing her usual golden threads, white silken skirt, golden hair, and smiling.

"We thought this may concern us all, Porius," Athena said as all looked down.

"Indeed, somewhere down there are trapped living creatures, where from I do not know. But we must save them," Porius said. "The whales shall guide us."

Thomas was puzzled. "I am not as such a fine swimmer who may reach the bottom of the sea."

"You will stay and watch the boat. Whales guide us to their resting place," Porius said as he plunged into the sea after pointing his wand to the top of his head and then to his feet, a bubble appeared and Porius stepped inside.

"Man in bubble," Leal said, laughing. "Very good, Porius." Leal jumped into the sea, Athena, Walters, and Simon following.

"I will follow your lead, Porius," Simon said as he created a bubble following Porius's lead. Athena, Walters, and Leal, as they were form and not flesh, had the ability to dive to the bottom, and there among the seaweed and red algae sat the large boxlike metal ship—basic, rectangular, silver reflecting the greens and blues of the sea. The large whales faded away in the distance and shouting back "good" by the sound waves, moving the five of them. Thomas sat alone in the middle of the sea peering down into the dark blue, not a sign of life. But below the waves and in the dark blue, Porius led them to surround this large crate. Porius looked in and knocked, Athena bending down to feel the sides; then she nodded to them, and Simon, Walters, and Porius stood at a corner each and lifted, raising it to waist level then all handling a corner, Athena on one, Porius, Walters, Simon, and Leal pushing underneath the others. They swam toward the surface slowly; swimming while holding was not an easy feat. Porius called a large squid, octopus, and several turtles to join in on pressing the underneath. One squid let off a little ink, which made the sea black and finally at the top.

"Squid ink? Really, Porius," Athena said, black with ink as she washed off on the surface.

"I thought since we are form and not flesh," Porius said, frantically swimming and holding the box or craft.

"Why is the sea so black?" Thomas asked as they rose up to the surface.

"Porius found it necessary to call on some squid and octopus to assist."

"Yes, and they are still holding it up. Bombardier," Porius said, pointing his wand at the crate, and it burst open. Within was a small green-skinned creature wearing a silken white outfit with silver linings, and a bug-eyed little creature it was, unconscious and sleeping.

"Porius, is it alive?" Walters asked, picking up the being and placing it into the dingy. Porius took out two pieces of wood, which he hid in the dingy and prepared for flight.

"Come, Thomas, we need to get this creature home," Porius said and then thanked Athena, Walters, Simon, and Leal, waving goodbye and grabbing on to rays of light. Each was on a beam of their own, and they disappeared within the twinkling of an eye. Porius held the creature or little green man in his arms. They mount their pieces of tree and ascended toward home, over Portsmouth and following the coast all the way back to Dover and several hours later over the forest and finally home.

"Why would this poor being be sent here in such a small craft?" Porius asked Thomas.

"Why, indeed, maybe he or she escaped some war," Thomas replied.

"It's waking up," Porius said, laying the small green being dressed in a leather-type wrapping not unsimilar to Leal's battle leathers.

"Greetings, my friend, you are safe," Thomas said, offering a plate of food to show their harmlessness. The creature smiled. It had large eyes, a green head, and small hands with four fingers on each hand, four toes, and wearing no shorts. Otherwise, it was mostly looking like a human structure in a four-foot-high alien green-skinned being.

"Porius, are you the great Porius?"

"Yes, I am he," Porius said, leaning over the creature as Porius placed him on the sofa in the main room by the fireplace.

"My time is short, but I am to give you this map," the creature said in a high-pitched screeching voice. "My time is short."

"I am Porius, and you are?"

"My name is not important. This map is important. Follow the stars on the north ray and head for green planet five. The planet is planning an attack against your planet, and this means war."

"Well, as you know, this planet is far from being able to defend itself against an advanced civilized world, who obviously have discovered the path to space travel by reusable light."

"Yes."

"You will tell me what to do, please?" Porius said, wide eyes watching the creature sit up and hold its head, shaking.

"You must reason with them and stop them. It is the only way," the creature said, breathing rapidly.

"To whom am I to discuss this very important item?"

"Harris Valmont, the king of druid peoples of Valmont, the fifth green planet."

"I shall find Harris."

"Your planet is heading in the wrong direction, Porius. Warring amongst themselves and not focusing on science but other theological paths, which will slow your race here. Others are watching," the creature said.

"This is true," Porius said.

"Yes," Thomas agreed and handed a goblet of wine to the creature, not knowing if wine is to its liking, but oddly it satisfied it greatly.

"I do fear the early stages of the internal combustion engine coming," Porius said.

"It is the wrong path. The internal combustion engine will pollute, betray, and lead science into the wrong direction," the creature said.

"My dear friend, tell me how—" Porius stopped midsentence as the creature began to fade, the goblet falling empty to the floor.

"I said my time was short. Find Harris, discuss, save your world," the creature said as he waved at Thomas and faded. "Thank you for the wine, it was lovely." It vanished, leaving only a small map and his leather wrappings.

"Gone," Thomas said, staring at his once-occupied space.

"This calls for all the peoples of our world to show solidarity. We must convince Harris Valmont not to send his Druid armies to threaten the people of earth."

"I see," said Thomas.

"Quick, the pensive," said Porius, turning toward the main living room and finding the pensive already floating above the table and within the reflections of Athena, Walters, Leal, and Simon.

"Porius, the whales informed us of the fifth planet," Athena said.

"What shall we do?" Walters asked.

"Gather the two elves who escaped from the church in Italy—Remis and, oh, what was the other's name?" Porius said, not remembering.

"Gena. I know how to find them," she said from within the water pensive.

"Yes, perfect, we need to make a case for Harris Valmont to believe that the people of earth are worth keeping. He thinks we are all brutal murderers and warlords not worthy of having our world or deserving it."

"Serious indeed," said Leal who stood, wearing a loincloth with no back, Apollo showing up behind him.

"He may have a point," Simon said. "Look at the atrocities the church alone has committed."

"Agreed, there will be many instances pointed out by Harris, I am sure. We must gather the most loving, caring, and emotional beings to present for our discussion."

"Porius," Thomas said as he fiddled through maps and books. "By my calculations, if we take this map and the time of year, in one week, a beam of light will be available from the cottage to the fifth green planet."

"And we shall show pageantry and care with our demonstration, remember all. Earth depends on it being a grand show."

And a grand show it was for at ten o'clock in the morning on the following week, a clear sky awaited the splendor regaled by the great Porius. A large golden carriage engraved with cherubs, angels, animals, and vegetation in every inch. Red velvet cushions lined with white piping and set between beings of all kinds of amazing creatures. Two elves, two dwarves, several fairies. Athena, Walters, Leal, Simon, and Porius held flowers, wine, grapes, and other offerings for Harris the druid king on the fifth green planet. All dressed in their finest jewels, foods, and royal garb, excepting Leal who wore his light black leathers, a vest and shorts, and black boots. Athena's two beautiful guardswomen Gloria and Alexandria floated close in golden threads, holding swords and shields and hovering beside the large carriage.

As Porius entered the carriage, another carriage came up alongside them and stepped out George and Timothy.

"We have come to wish you well and to thank you for taking on this important mission," George said in his best robes and golden bracelets, necklace, and rings of emerald.

"My dear George," Porius said, "We shall do our best."

"Timothy filled me in on this ordeal, many thanks and the hopes of all the world go with you."

Porius waved away as the sun hit the carriage. "Sun of light, sun of day, take us through time and point our way," Porius said as the carriage slowly faded and blurring obscured by space and light. Colors of light moved beside the carriage and the occupants within. Dizzy, sleepy, and all frozen in motion, the hundreds of millions of miles unknown to each. Porius only standing and seeing a blurred world closes his eyes and then opened, revealing a new world and distant world and what a world.

Colored hills of green, deciduous, and conifer forests surrounded them and a large castle in front of the carriage. One would most likely compare the fifth green planet or druid planet not unlike our fourteenth-century architectures with gabled and turreted tops, stone, and wood carvings upon every inch of material used. Hundreds of people were dressed in a mix of silks and leathers, crowds cheered as the carriage appeared before them, and Harris Valmont stood before them with open arms.

"Welcome, Porius, welcome," Harris said as he was surrounded by others in silver dressed gowns and see-through garments. Two teenage boys wearing only a thin strap around their waists held large pitchers of wine, and as all the passengers including Porius exited the carriage, the boys gave them each a goblet and filled with wine. The crowd began a chorus of some otherworldly chant. Gloria and Alexandria stopped hovering and stood beside the carriage guarding Athena as she stepped out.

"Ye shalt no need for thy weapons here," Harris said to Athena, and she waved to the two guards as they placed their swords, shields, hidden knives into the carriage and walked with the others toward the castle. Harris was leading with his entourage filled with colored feathers, dresses, skirts, many people not dressed at all only for the minimalist covering of some parts. Leal, Simon, and Walters eying all the feminine females waving and throwing bits of golden flakes, which sparkled in the sky, which has two moons. Thomas handed the large bouquet of flowers to Harris and his wife, and they were accepted gladly. Porius was holding his large dress staff as he called it.

"My good Harris, a pleasure to meet you and what a beautiful place this is to behold," Porius said, his eyes contacting Harris's eyes. Porius studied his eyes for within the eyes of Harris Porius saw plans, plans within plans, knowing not to take him lightly for in Porius's mind, he knew that this may be the only chance to convince this great king of the earth's purity and to prove that all men are not evil.

The large doors of the castle opened and within were jugglers, dancers, horse-like creatures paraded past in splendor as they pranced, not ridden but seemingly human. Hundreds of white doves flew above them all from within the castle and soaring outside into the open sky as our troop watched with glee.

"Amazing," Porius said, watching the hundreds of doves fly out and swooping over their heads, the elves and fairies watching and amazed.

"I thought you would like the doves," Harris said, smiling.

"Impressive in the extreme," Porius said.

"Yes, for here all peoples are trained to speak with our animals, doves, fish, lion, bear and fox, all have their own language, but our minds can reach them. As I know some of you have the same within you," Harris finished.

"Yes, the blue whales I assume filled you in," Porius said, smiling.

"Indeed they did," Harris answered politely. While butterflies by the thousand poured from within the castle out in the open air, above the cheering crowds and between the silken flags adorn the outer vehicles roaming the green planets. Light turned to silk turned to energy.

"You see, Porius, my two billion worms weave silk enough to clothe our world. The silk is also used for traveling energy screens you see in dotted colors in every direction," Harris said, pointing away from the castle as Porius, sun in eyes looking out over the crowds, buildings, fields dotted with colored flags, which made by silk assume all the light from the sun, hold it and use in in hundreds of ways.

"You have mastered the light indeed, you have."

Porius said, "Light travel is the only clean way."

"You make sure your planet doesn't fiddle with internal combustion engines. It will make a mess of the place," Harris said.

"Humans are unpredictable, but I shall try," Porius said, knowing full well that he will be powerless against humans using, exploiting, and destroying earth with internal combustion machines once the industrial age began back on earth.

"Soon we will have your challenge, and all of those you brought shall be challenged," Harris said as together they walked among the crowds of cheering people, dancing animals, and beings of all sorts.

"We have visitors here to greet you from other parts of our planet," Harris said, pointing to one green-skinned man wearing sixteenth-century silks, buttons, garters, pointed black shoes, white wig and painted face bowing to them as they passed. Porius was in his delicious garb and returning his bow.

"My fondest greetings," Porius said, bowing as two men passed wearing loin and leather; a few frog-like and slimy creatures passed and bowed to Porius.

"From Elysium," Harris pointed out.

"Yes, we've met before," Porius said, bowing as he flicked his wand and there appeared his floating band.

Harris became wide eyed and, surprised, said, "Oh, you brought them?" Harris said, grinning.

The band started playing and mixing with all the other music in the far corners of the room. Small pipe bands, horn bands, string and symphony bands, each to their own part of the castle. Rooms with large bath facilities, rooms with detailed laced artwork, cushions, wood carvings and more. Rooms filled with people having parties which seem almost secondary but soon blend toward the main ballrooms. Hundreds of people, beings, and several unusual birdlike creatures of many colors flew overhead, swooping out of the long corridor exits.

"Quite a splendid gathering," Porius said to Harris, looking around confused. "But I have seemed to have, well, misplaced my companions."

"Yes, come with me, Porius, we need to talk," Harris said, swiftly tucking Porius into a room off the hall corridor and locking the door firmly behind Porius.

"Alone at last. Be at ease, good Porius."

"Thank ye." Being alone with Harris was not to his liking, but Porius was feeling calm.

"You know, we have the pensive here as well," Harris said, waving his wand and the pensive floated over a wooden table shining like black.

"So you have been watching us," Porius said.

"Not often but many times, yes. And splendid work you have done, all the way back to Cadmus Upton."

"That was hundreds of years hence," Porius said, startled.

"My lifeline is as yours, slowed to the common man."

"'Tis true, Cadmus tortured, maimed, and killed for his god. He enslaved hundreds, changed villages from old ways to the new religion. Destroyed magical creatures," Porius said, deflated.

"Him and many more like him, but not all bad. Actually, all the religious folk are not that bad," Harris replied.

"Some find goodness and spread it, 'tis true," Porius pleaded.

"These magical creatures you brought to us, how can they plead their case to save the earth? Man has all but made fairies, elves, druids, pagans, and witches extinct."

A quiet came over them as Porius thought hard for the reply. A long pause and silence as Harris walked to a cabinet and poured two large goblets of ale.

"I will give you until the year 2050 to prove that man can live alongside each other, get along, care for each other, and have no combating religions. No Muslims hating Christians, no Christians hating Jews, no Buddha hating Hindus, and so on and so forth."

"That seems far. Three hundred years," Porius said and they clicked glasses.

"Three hundred years, I will give you the change," Harris said, grinning. "But I still want to see what your people has prepared and plead their case. I still must be satisfied."

"Well, let the show begin," Porius said, sipping and walking out into the immense party going on inside the castle. King Harris walked through the crowds and climbed a circular star that brought him to the center of the large ballroom. "Come forth and plead your cases."

The murmuring crowd moves back as Porius, the elves, fairies, and others plead their cases one by one. First the fairies talked about the wonderful world and how it was over a thousand years ago, the peace, the working together to create a brilliant world. Elves had a similar story. Leal looking as beautiful as ever told the story of love for Apollo and others, and earth's riches in humanity, Socrates science, foods, wines, beautiful women, and music. All gave their tales and all rejoiced, the crowd cheering after every expressive and exceptional tale. Athena performed splendidly not only telling of the battles but of the joy the human race has hidden within and finally Porius.

"Lord Porius, give us your tale," said King Harris, pointing down at Porius.

"I give ye this," Porius said. Pointing his wand at himself, he levitated higher and higher up to the level of Harris's eyes.

"You give me, thus," Harris said and he became drowsy, eyes rolling into the back of his head. Unknowledgeable of his surroundings in an instant, Harris fell asleep.

The crowd goes quite with awe, trepidation, and a worried sigh murmurs across the great hallway.

"Awaken," Porius said as Harris glowed and floated down from the pulpit in midair to touch the ground as Porius floated beside him; they touched down together, and the crowd went wild.

"What, where, Porius, how did I get down here?" Harris said, shaking his head in amazement.

"You see, my friend, I do have magic that you do not possess," Porius said, smiling and sipping his ale from the silver goblet.

"Lord Porius, thee hath proved thy case."

Of this and any world, fair or not, cruel or kind, all worlds must have the power of kindness and delight. Ants among the great bios on earth or any other green planet connected, infused, mingled, and compassionate with no thought of greed, with no thought of hurt, and with no thought of creating pain to others all these worlds must remain.

Later that evening and cast among the many rooms of chambers to the castle was lovemaking, private or otherwise. Farmers outside prepared the early morning chores while the mayhem slowed, and to sleep, all within the castle went, one by one and two by two until sleep presented itself to these amazing travelers. Porius dreamed of all the items he wished to see outside. Athena, Walters, and the others enjoyed their dreaming until they all awakened and within the great castle they bathed among cherubs, exotic washers dressed or hardly dressed but soaking them, bathing them, powdering them. Two girls were bathing Leal in a large pool, rubbing soap over his muscular physique and smiling with coquettish delights.

"Are they all as beautiful as you are on earth?" one beautiful girl said. Leal flicked soap at her and juggled, her rather large bosom giggling and jiggling.

"No one is." They laughed and Leal stood, the silky white water dripping over his perfectly round buttocks, dripping on the floor.

Athena was naked until dressed by flying fairies. "So beautiful, may I?"

"Please, Your Highness," the smallest of the fairies said as Athena placed a beautiful diamond-studded silver crown upon her head, Harris walking down admiring Athena's figure that many had carved in stone. Even Harris had a stone version of Athena on his balcony off the west side of the castle that looked out over the river Time.

"We shall take a boat down the river Time today and I shall you show you our amazing silk factor," Harris said, leading them all onto a boat made of wood, silk-colored flags adorned with splendid artistic figures of naked bodies, animals, and other alluring decorations.

Farther down the river they go until landing upon a greasy empty shore behind a large tentlike structure that stood hundreds of feet long, wide and tall.

"Immense structure," Porius said, stepping out onto the grass from the boat followed by Walters, Leal, Athena, and Simon; all the others had gone back to earth on the early sun rays light travelers.

"Looks like our fourteenth-century architecture bank in England," Porius stated.

"I must come and visit," Harris said, patting Porius and moving the others to the entrance of the large structure.

"My worms," Harris said as they walked into the large chamber.

"Very colorful in here," Athena said, arm around Leal as Simon and Walters ran to look over the railings at a watery substance and billions of cocoons floating in the water to be boiled and stringed. Harris took them around, pointing out the massive colored flags set up on the roof catching the rays of light, which generate the power in a system that fueled the power on all this druid planet's energy needs.

Worms and their cocoons made the silk of life, which gave the most beautiful of colored wardrobes for Harris and all his people. Leal noticed all the areas they explored and traveled and searched within the village different parts of the city, one with artists, musicians, dancers, and slaves, slaves by choice for no one on the fifth green planet does anything under pressure and is true to themselves within their families.

They came upon another port, this time all lit up as the evening sun went down. The banner said Light Traveler Port 1. A large muscular blond-haired and tanned man wearing a French short-sleeved dark blue and white striped shirt, white shorts, and sailor hat said, "Welcome. Star to star and planet to planet, the universes are all connected for this light connects all. Beware of nothing and travel to the extreme of your imagination and travel to what star you like."

Leal eyed him and licked his lips. Walters and Simon turned Leal away, letting Harris explain the fundamental ideas around this extraordinary invention.

"Are you always thinking about sex?" Simon asked Leal, laughing.

"Most of the time to be sure, yes," Leal replied.

Later that evening at the library of Harris's castle, they went through the works of many English writers including Shakespeare with Chaucer, which was Harris's personal favorite. Porius and Harris discussed the future.

"So you are giving me three-hundred-and-twenty-odd years to have all the peoples of earth get along? That may be a difficult task," Porius said, shuffling a few playing cards as Harris tossed him one after the other, playing a few hands of piquet while philosophizing together like two elderly wizards in an attempt to save mankind.

"I am sure your great race will welcome the task," Harris said, grinning. "What of the Minoans of Crete? The Thera volcanic explosion? Myceneans' invasion from Grece?"

"Yes, I see your point that we have been fighting for a very long time, but don't most civilizations enter into such times, rivals who is more influential and on and on?" Porius said calmly.

"Yes, it is indeed and we have trouble to this day of approaching civilizations who may be discovering how to travel by light. But we cannot allow anger, fighting, and warmongering civilizations to obtain this knowledge. Because that is all it is, not magic, knowledge."

"Children of the sun find their own ways on earth, Harris. My amount of communication with all people is exceedingly rare and nearly impossible. Politicians, preachers, teachers, and professors have a better chance of relaying messages of peace, but it is difficult," Porius said, in despair for the human race in the knowing that his putting all peoples of the world to live and respect each other seemed impossible.

"Why?" Harris said, "Why do you despair?"

"The children of earth grow little by little, dreaming and building themselves into what becomes them, but all the while being bombarded by ill influences from every direction. If they are Jewish, then the ancestors, parents, synagogues teach and manipulate to their way as a way of life. Christians the same, Muslims and so one, each making the importance of staying together in their own factory of acquaintances. Bewildering to imagine, but few break away from their parents' teachings and only the strong became freethinkers while most would not spend the time or energy changing to a nonreligious way of life. They honestly believe and follow the ancient teachings to the ruin of all," Porius said, walking to the drink's cabinet. "Now how about some white wine?"

After three hours of discussing science, ancient civilizations, other worlds' chemistry, and medieval quantum mechanics, Porius and Harris were being entertained by floating bands, dancing women and men, and the occasional soloist with a piano, harp, or one pretty girl dressed in white who sang so beautifully that Porius began to cry.

"Well, my friend, you do have a difficult task in the next three hundred and twenty-five years," Harris said, sipping his last sip of wine and looking in at the bottom of the empty goblet. "A ray awaits you so that you may return."

"Back to the cottage. My animals, friends, and forest need me."

"Yes—oh, and I forgot to mention, we love your French cooking, a very pleasant surprise from earth, for we have adopted many French dishes to be sure," Harris said, most pleased.

"I am fortunate to have two cooks, Parthenia and Grendle, who have gotten hold of some most efficacious dishes including coq au vin, my personal favorite. You must come and visit us at the cottage."

Harris led Porius out onto the vast balcony overlooking the village below while people massed in a large crowd, cheering loudly when Porius and Harris walked out toward the departing station and Porius returned to earth, his carriage a bubble of glass clear substance and liquid metals of gold, silver and rubies, emeralds, diamonds, sapphires, and other jewels decorating his carriage. Within moments, he returned to earth.

"They've told me about our going to Essex even though I did not like Mr. Coral. You'd agree to come with us, and I am afraid old Porius will not be pleased with the prospect, but I shall get great satisfaction, won't you, Leal?" Thomas asked Leal while eating a bit of toast, recently presented by Grendle to Leal, blushing as always, Leal in his tight-fitted black leather bands and boots.

"What will old Porius not be in agreement with?" Porius said as he entered the cottage.

"Welcome back, Porius. Leal was just stating that Mr. Coral in Essex is having most difficulty," Thomas said.

"Indeed," Porius protested, and his mind began whirling around to discover what Coral's grievance was.

Leal's eyes flashed with mild indignation. "Yes, Porius, Coral is a sort of farmer."

"I am well aware of Coral. He is the so-called wizard who attempted to bring to life the demons from some mystical legend to life, but instead in his clumsy way and not noticing had brough forth a dragon that was very difficult to remove. If I remember correctly, surprised he is still alive," Porius said, sipping a warm cup of tea. "Delightful, Grendle. Thank you."

"My pleasure, Lord Porius, and Parthenia is preparing a special luncheon, coq au vin," Grendle said, rushing back into the kitchen and assisting Parthenia to pluck a few chickens and prepare the meal.

"My favorite," Porius said with delight.

"But, Porius, what of Coral?" Thomas asked.

"Why don't you and Leal toddle off to assist Mr. Coral? I fear to see what mess he has conjured up this time."

"I am game," Leal said as he stood and added a leather open vest, sword, and dangling bag of water to his ensemble.

"Well, you must keep an eye on us through the pensive, surely," Thomas suggested to Porius as he brought the pensive before him, allowing it to float in midair before Porius and Porius lowering it to sit on the wooden table, which is carved with animals, plant life, and other carvings.

"What is the portentous expression? Ah yes, take care, you too, and be careful of the waving of Coral's wand. He is old and sometimes his belief in reality is obscured by the clouds in his head," Porius said as he walked Thomas and Leal to the front door, and out they went toward Essex by wooden tree branch, the deer, foxes, bluebirds, and Franklin all watching them prepare their wood, mount their transporting devices, and ascend into the fair sky, which showed no sign of rain and most agreeable temperature.

"I hope I am not hurting their feelings," mumbled Porius as he waved them goodbye, Thomas waving back as they climbed over the tree line toward Essex, Franklin following not too far behind their trail. Over lake and stream, village, and controlled bonfires. Over farmers toiling in the fields, rows of flower workers building churches, taverns, houses, and even a few working on the road toward Essex while Porius watched with delight through the pensive, showing him a clear vision of Leal and Thomas as they flew until they reached the small weather-worn Coral home, covered in ivy wildflowers and overgrown bushes, vines, and the like.

Leal bashed the ivy just to cut a path to the front door. "Coral, are you in there?" Leal shouted, cutting his way through the bramble.

"How does he get in and out of his home with all this overgrown garden?" Thomas asked.

Porius looked in and knew that Coral must have been practicing growing spells to have this much green fresh foliage covering his home.

Finally after thirty minutes of cutting a path, Thomas and Leal stood knocking with great force.

"Coral, are you in there?" Leal shouted again.

"Aye, I am good, Sir Leal?" came the voice from inside.

"Have you been practicing growing spells?" Thomas shouted through the slammed-tight large wooden door with diamond-shaped metal beading in four lines implemented across its walnut wood.

"This is a very nice door, I hate to smash it," Leal shouted.

"The window over to your right," Coral shouted back.

Leal looked at the window rather high up and placed a few large stones, climbed up, and pushed with all his might, trying to open, but alas was unlucky.

"It's all covered in growth, I will have to cut my way in," Leal said.

Porius smiled while eating a bit of cheese. "He has overgrown his home, silly old bugger." Porius smiled and then put the pensive out or sight. "They will manage, I've no doubt."

Cutting and wedging his body through the window, Leal finally broke through the thicket and stepped into the book-filled living room of Coral. Papers were everywhere, old books strewn about, mice running here and there, several large caterpillars, slugs, snails, frogs and toads lined the room. Covered from head to toe was Coral wearing a silken blue hat with gold bobble, both arms stretched out spread-eagle and tied to the walls with vines, bramble, and ivy.

"I cannot move, good sir Leal," said Coral.

"Hold still, you old fool, hold still," Leal said, cutting away the ivy that had wrapped around him like some alien blanket.

Just as Leal sent verbal abuses while trying to cut Coral free from the faster ever-growing weeds and ivy, he saw that Coral had his wand still clutched tight in his hand.

"Drop your wand, Mr. Coral, drop it!" Thomas shouted from the window, startling old Mr. Coral as he dropped his wand. Just as he dropped his wand the plants stopped growing and released Mr. Coral while Leal slashed and cut at the vines around his ankles.

"Thank you, my boys, thank yee." Old Coral dressed in silken robes, sandals, and long gray hair, beard, and hairy, knobby hands wiping his forehead. "Thank ye indeed." He pulled himself loose from the tightly bound ivy with Leal's assistance.

"Now you're free," Leal said, standing beside him and gazing around at the hundreds of bbos, potions, half-eaten meals, birds in cages. The bird's eyes rolled as they watched the circus pursue a smoothly executed participation of Leal as he gave Coral's newfound freedom.

"How long were you tied there, Mr. Coral?" Leal asked as Thomas came in the window to gaze at the room, every inch covered in books, bits of food, scattered mice, and even Franklin, who had perched himself on the windowsill and rolled his eyes.

"Ah, the raven. Franklin, is it?" Coral asked as he blushed at his newfound freedom. "Yes, I am an old fool."

"Well, I was only—" Leal said.

"No, no, no, you are correct, I was attempting to practice a growing spell to assist the farmlands, which were severely flooded this year in Essex. I am an old fool."

"I think it was a brilliant attempt," Thomas said, picking up Coral's wand and handing it to him while Leal picked up a book of spells.

"I have read this one," Leal said.

"Yes, that one is particularly good. Egyptian spells mainly, this particular spell I believe I am missing an entire incantation to stop the growing."

"Porius may know the rest," Thomas said in reassurance that old Mr. Coral was not an old fool after all.

"My dear Thomas, please ask Prorius," Coral said in excitement of the moment.

"Do you have a pensive?" Leal asked.

"Yes, it's over there, but it hasn't worked in years," said the defeated Coral.

"Let me see it," Thomas said.

"Here, have some ale from the local farm." Coral handed them both a bottle of local brew. "Old Peculiar."

"Very nice. Thank you," Leal said, popping open the brown bottle and enjoying its essence.

"Here we are, my old pensive," Coral said, showing the old silver pensive its silver stained after years of use and abuse.

"Well, we must clean it first. Give it to me, and I will go wash it in the nearby stream," Thomas said as he walked it outdoors, leaving Leal and old Coral to discuss the Egyptian spells Leal seemed so eager to remember.

"Farms you say? Flooded," Leal said. "My friend Walters has a farm not far from here, and he did not mention flooding this year."

"Aye, Walters was a good man," Coral said, knowing Walters should have died many years ago of old age as had Leal, Porius, and even Thomas would be well over three hundred. Thomas gazed his eyes at Leal, rushing indoors with the clean pensive, as together they concealed the fact of their flesh and form current existence and trying to avoid the questions.

"Hath ye gone into water after death as Porius suggests? I know I shall do the same, I would give anything to see the great Elysium," Coral said, clapping his hands and putting his wishes to rest.

"Yes, we have traveled by light as well," Leal said as Thomas rushed the cleaned pensive to try to stop the conversation, not knowing what Coral would do when he found out that he and Leal had long since passed from water to light and from flesh to flesh and form. The ability to become form from a ghostly origination is a rare gift as the number of humans who had taken this transformation can be counted on both hands.

"You have a long time to live still, Coral," Thomas said.

"Yes, a long time," Leal insisted.

"I am of ninety-six, and in four more years, I'll be one hundred, so surely not that long," Coral said skeptically. "Now here is my pensive spell. 'Rain from outside follow inside and bring us the contact we desire,'" Coral said, waving his wand over the unilluminated pensive, which just sat there lifeless.

"Allow me," Leal said, waving his wand over the silver plate as it filled with an unearthly milky-white fluid and within the picture of Porius gazing out at them.

"Greetings Coral, you are looking rather, well, troubled with the vines I see," Porius said, his figure bending in the waves.

"Oh, it worked. My dear Lord Porius, an honor, nay, a privilege to see you and thank ye for sending thy children to free me, such an old fool. Doth thee know the spell to stop growing?"

"Of course, just say, green to eat and eat of this green," Porius shouted back. "It will stop growing and will be unmovable by the coming storms."

"Yes, that is the incantation ending," Coral said, clapping his beard in his hands. "Green to eat and eat of this green." He wrote down the words. "I am writing it down because my memory is not what it used to be, my Lord Porius, not by a long shot."

"Regardless, you are looking rather well. Take Leal and Thomas to the fields and work the spells, sprinkle some lilac flowers. I see that you have dried lilac on the shelves," Porius said, his image fading.

"Thank ye, Porius, farewell," Coral said as he wandered out with wands and lilac. On hand to preserve what's left of the crops, the local Essex farms worked so hard to grow, one field to the next sight unseen as the crops regrew even stronger than before. By morning, all the farmers walked among the brilliantly regrown and healthy crops of wheat, corn, potatoes, vines, herbs, rape, and all the vegetables that make Essex great. Tears fell from farmers, and their wives and one farmer were amazed at the regrown wheat, saying only one word in whispered delight, "Porius," for he knew the damage previously done by the storms could only have been cured by magic.

Out in the fields, Coral said to Leal and Thomas, "I know a fairy named Aria who lives in those woods, and as far as I know, she is the only fairy left in these parts since, hmm, I am not sure. She is the only fairy I know or have had the pleasure of meeting."

"I have heard of Aria," Thomas said. "Very dangerous."

"Dangerous, why dangerous, good Thomas?"

"I think he means dangerous because I know Aria," Leal said while sprinkling the last bit of lilac and watching the field grow back before their eyes.

"Immense credit to Porius, these fields will yield many splendors," Coral said, heading back toward home. "How doth thou know Aria?"

"By good chance, I was instrumental in assisting with moving her realm to Elysium with Walters and Simon, and even Thomas has met good Aria. He said dangerous because we had a short fling, nothing very meaningful." Leal was stopped by Coral.

"Do you mean to say that you had, well, relations with a fairy?" Coral interrupted and positively lived. "You are beautiful, Leal, but how and why with a small—" Coral was stopped by Leal.

"At the time, I was transformed down to her size. It was the only way to meet other fairies. Plus, she was quite aggressive about it, but she does have wings so it was a bit odd."

"A bit odd, I bet," Coral said, laughing.

"Here she comes," Thomas said, pointing at a sparkling line of purple and gold embers, which trailed underneath her tiny feet. Upon her arrival, she landed on Leal's shoulder.

"Hello, sweet Leal," Aria said, standing on Leal's shoulder and looking down his front, back, and sides.

"My dearest Aria, so lovely to see you again," Leal said.

"I see that you have regained your normal size since last we met," Aria said. "Greetings and good tidings to you, Thomas, Coral. I thought you were responsible for the regrowth in the fields. All the farmers are delighted and praising the woodland wizards."

"Do they suspect me of tampering with the crops?" Coral said.

"Well, they know magic when the see it, and they won't tell the church. They don't want trouble. Let us say they will be glad to turn the other cheek if it helps the crops," Aria said, flying over to Coral's shoulder and landing upon it, wings flapping. Sparkles of purple and green lights sprinkled Coral's shoulder as she landed.

"High time I was getting home, but you men are headed south anyway, back to Kent no doubt," Coral said.

"Yes, we shall need to pull some wood, and we will be off," Leal said, Thomas pulling branches from the tree, which gave them gladly.

"Very clever trick, boys. Why don't we come back to my place first and have a drink?" Aria asked.

"Indeed, our pleasure," Thomas said, turning to Coral, "And you be careful of using spells when you don't have the whole potion or incantation, Coral."

"Yes, I surely will, Sir Thomas. Leal, give my regards to Porius. Aria, a pleasure as always," Coral said then turned and walked slowly back to his home, Franklin circling overhead, making sure no danger was imminent on his pathway to home.

"Follow Coral home, Franklin," Thomas said, waving his wand toward Franklin and a sharp ping was head from the sky. Franklin, getting the message, kept a watchful eye on Coral until he was safely home.

"Sorry, Franklin, oops," Thomas said while Leal and Aria giggled a bit then turned toward the forest. Inside, they saw the cave of fairies, which was covered by woven ivy and vines to make a large green man face above the wooden doorway. Aria tapped them, Thomas on the shoulder and then flapping over Leal, tapping his shoulder. Within moments, both men were down to about one foot three inches in height and everything else in proportion. Thomas and Leal buried under too much clothes as they came out naked from under the large clothes that fit their previous form. Wine was poured, and music played by two elves like trolls, one playing a harpsichord and the other a violin.

Later that evening while Thomas and Leal were drinking fairy wine and eating fairy bread and cheese, they all sang the ancient gallant song:

Whole together with peace and care
Feather of the highest fowl
Take thee medicine without a scowl
End of silence and end of pain
Clouds shalt hold source of too much rain
Whole together peace and care
Chancing the old ways, we shall dare
Fortunes for foe and friend
May we use them wisely
With song and dance we share
Whole together with peace and care,
My man and lady fare

Franklin waddled up to the doorstep and stuck his now large head comparatively to the form Leal and Thomas had recently taken. "Squawk,"

Franklin said and then popped his large head back outside and waited for Leal and Thomas as they sang and danced for at least another hour until once again and kissing Aria on the cheek, both men rose inside their clothes, pulled some wood to fly, and followed Franklin home.

Once back at the cabin, Leal stumbled off his wooden flying mechanism, laughing from the mixture of fairy wine and brandy, herbal smoke and mushrooms, and came giggling into the cottage.

"I see you visited Aria," Porius said, smoking a pipe inside the cottage and reclining on the large sofa by the fire dressed in his usual white embroidered gown laced with golden animal figures.

"We have indeed, Porius, and what a girl!" Leal said while Thomas brought him a large goblet of water.

"Here, drink this down, Leal," Thomas said to a totally drunk and high Leal.

"She shrank us this big," Leal said, his hands held a foot or so apart.

"I'm sure and enjoy your buzz. Aria's wine is full of surprises," Porius said as Thomas ran outside to vomit out in the edge of the forest.

"You will be eventually come down, but enjoy, enjoy," Porius said, watching Leal stumble to the back rooms laughing. Porius smiled, and finally Thomas came in all sweaty and washed.

"I think I shall turn in," Thomas said, running to his back room.

"I guess you better had," Porius said as the ghost of some illuminating body joined Porius on the couch. Leaves falling, rain spattering, moon glowing between the quickly moving clouds that dot the sky. Deer peered out as the last flickering stars faded upon early morning sunlight. Below the cottage grounds the bios merged—ant, slug, worm, and passerby. Down further underground below layer after layer, gray, white, and brown and black, starting at the exosphere, thermosphere, mesosphere, stratosphere, troposphere, and between the crust and upper mantle. Hidden among cavern, crevasse, tunnel, hollow cave, and hole. Creatures all in cover for the long wait to walk among the humans once more.

Mornings broke and sunsets faded to black with a mission here and a mission there, occasionally seeing all the friends of Porius when they make a visit to the cottage, Leal mostly staying on Elysium with Apollo while occasionally lending a hand to Athena and Walters in the safety of some under-siege civilization. Porius and Thomas spent the next twenty-odd years until 1750 shone like a beacon in all its glory. Or the fiftieth year of the eighteenth century was becoming a bit of a problem because Porius, even though he tried to merge religions together to get peace throughout the world, it was to no avail. Religions, people, races seemed to start getting farther apart. Puritans in America made war against Indians. January, a fire in Istanbul, killed thousands and tens of thousands of homes burning. Athena, Walters, Leal and Simon, Jewel and Frederick lent hands to rebuild, assist the sick, and bring food while Porius watched the raging fire from his trusty pensive safely in the cottage. Getting a bit too old to travel to far a distance, Porius resided mainly in the cottage, not knowing how many years his candle will burn. King George, also known as Augustus, was born and brought up in northern Germany, crowned king in 1727 and survivor of the Stuart Jacobite rebellion of 1727, a participant in the battle at Dettingen in 1743, Caroline of Ansbach, his wife occasionally visited the cottage, and with high regards for Porius, his spells and enchantments, assisting from Flanders to Dettingen and after floundering with the king of Prussia, civil disobedience, changes within court, parliament and the ongoing learning of what it means to be king are mostly daily struggles for George. March 7, 1750, came with calm and cool winds over London. Pope Prospero ruled the diocese and feverishly yearned to assist in admonition of the Librorum Prohibitorum, a list of forbidden books that contained most of the confiscated and stolen documents, spell books, malafactoriums, ancient learning and herbs, scientific discoveries of the ages. Pope Prospero knew that most books were burned or destroyed by raging Catholics in the past. This pope had a kinder and more scientific mind so he wanted to keep the ancient writings and secure something other than religion for the future. Some books of spells he privately locked all the vast documents in deep vaults under the Vatican and burned most, even though some monks took leave of their senses and palmed a few books, succumbing to torture and death. The heroic monks were sent into castles, large homes, places of worship, and all enemies of the church. Prospero the pope and most old-way folk, druid, pagan, African tribesmen, American Indian, Buddhist, and other non-Christians were killed and tortured by the church, especially if they hid something of value, something of learning.

Surrounded by legions of followers below in the crowds, aligned beside him the darkest priests, monks, ladies bound to the church, and a crowd in full agreement, the pope gave his speech with flags waving and clouds gathering black above the crowds.

"My good people of Italy, thy will was done many times before. We must end the raids, we must end the destruction of literature and science," Prospero loudly stated, and a hush came over the crowd.

"Good," said Porius, peering into the pensive from his safe haven in England.

"'Tis the time to desist and show mercy for others."

The pope was unlike other popes who would build up the crowd into a feverish pitch and eager in their minds to crush anyone who was not a follower of Jesus.

"They will listen to ye," Porius said as he witnessed the grand scene of Pope Benedict XIV Prospero Lambertini in his pensive. The fire crackled as night fell over England and the forest of the cottage.

Franklin flew overhead and finally came to rest upon the thatch of the cottage before hopping down to the cottage door and walked in.

"Ah, Franklin, have some fish," Porius said, pointing to a bit of raw fish in a pan upon the sill. Franklin hopped up and eats, "Squawk."

"The pope is pleading with his people to stop stealing all the old relics, Thomas," Porius said with delight.

"That is wonderful news. But are there many books still not destroyed over the last few hundred years, now they stop it, aye?" Thomas said, chewing a thick piece of wheat bread with apple jam spread thick.

"My dear Thomas, Harris will look at this as a triumph on our way to making a peaceful earth," Porius said, closing the pensive and with his wand levitating the silver pensive full of white milky substance and moving it until it rested upon a shelf.

"Brilliant, you have exactly three hundred years to make that happen," Thomas stated, knowing what a herculean task it shall be.

"When does our new student arrive?" Porius asked.

"Tomorrow he will arrive, and ye must be prepared," Thomas said. "For this is a special student."

"Aye, from Harris, know thee well."

"Name of Marcus, no last name," Thomas said.

"Yes, and I have met him, Thomas. He will be perfect and ripe for culture. He is traveling be a new form of light, a form I have not seen. He uses sound to travel and is attempting to break through six sound waves. By my calculations, England may have an earthquake tomorrow or to say, a moment shared by all when the place will rock and roll, pitch and twitch. The plates in the earth will slide a bit, walls may spit and bend, so be careful where you step tomorrow."

"An earthquake? I like the sound of that," Thomas said, interested in this discussion.

"Marcus is coming and will land, causing an earthquake."

Thomas said, "Who doth know of his arrival?"

"Well, that is a good question because of all his boasting, Marcus has expatiated to a few well-insignificant wizards from a few other places. Let's just say that Marcus packs a punch," Porius said, grabbing a bit of Thomas loaf.

"Marcus is a wonder. Mastered divination, spells, cunning, and trickery before he was seventeen. Now twenty-nine full to form and a rock-hard body that jealousy from Leal is imminent."

They both laughed.

"Can't wait to see him," Thomas said, sipping some ale.

"I met him in the silk factory. A factory you have never seen the like of. Vast in size and stature and completely clean running. No pollutants, no overworked employees, no ugly or obscene-looking factory. In fact, it's rather pleasant and home to several bees, rabbits, fowl, and other creatures. The entire echo systems are a work of combined thought and mastery of science. What we know now and will learn to know in future we must prevent, prevent, prevent," Porius said then gulped a huge goblet of ale. The goblet held the form of the dragon, its eyes sparkling in the fire reflection emerald green reflecting from the huge emerald eyes of the dragon.

"Marcus will assist us in spreading these ideas," Thomas said.

"Marcus will take us to a new age," Porius said with glee as he flicked his wand and out came the miniature floating band dressed in Spanish attire and playing a type of flamingo.

"Fetching," Thomas said, nodding to the floating band.

"We will learn so much and teach the earth to work without pollution," Porius said, stopping to think of Harris and Harris stating that "plastic, combustion, and coal are items you need to shy away from on earth."

To Porius, his memory in that air of concern for what he can achieve was against the rage of progress. Man fighting over man to build, invent, thrive, and make a bit of cash. Most probably that later being of more concern. "Hmm that, that of the one who builds using nature. For instance, because I am not sure how to explain this correctly, Thomas."

"I think I know without ye saying," Thomas replied.

"Yes, you can see it, the future. Large metal shafts piercing into the sky and billowing forth large black destructive nature-killing pollutants that will destroy the earth."

"No, Porius, you don't think it will come to that?" Thomas said with some concern.

"Oh yes, that is the only iceberg moment, for the horses now leave waste in so many areas that people are dying from the smell. Man will invent another communicative force with four wheels and end engine, you mark my words. And birth will not be controlled, which is actually the most dangerous thing of all. With no control, the earth will populate so much, and with use of plastics and wastable products, the millions and millions of humans will pollute the earth."

"Millions?"

"Yes, Thomas. Millions and millions," Porius said and blew out the candle.

The next morning of February 8, 1850, the earth shook all over London while the lord chancellor at Westminster hall and the courts of the kings bench fall about while the earth shakes.

"The edifice is going to collapse," the lord chancellor said, running for the exit of the large chamber. The Newcastle house and Duke of Newcastle and Gowen Knight saw furniture moving as the earth moved beneath their feet, lamplighters falling from ladders, the entire city of Westminster shook, rattled, and rolled back and forth and to and fro.

Marcus had arrived in silks of many splendid colors as he walked through Westminster before checking into a tavern for a whisky, something forbidden in his world. Fists full of money, Marcus walked through the crowded streets where everyone was in shock from the quake, some out on the street shaking heads, people talking and a few town criers proclaiming Armageddon. Marcus just rolled his eyes as he passed and flicked a few coins to beggars.

"Thank ye, ol' prince," one drunken fool said as he bit the coin, safely tucking it into his pocket and noticing people taking a shine to him for some unknown reason. The reason, though apparent, was of no concern to Marcus for his fighting skills far surpassed anybody to this primitive world. This jacobian ended eager Georgian families, powerful churches, busy taverns, and brothels in the west end where you can buy anything.

Londoners checking Marcus out in a tavern walked in and stepped up to the bar.

"My good man, your finest pint," Marcus said in perfect English.

"Aye, right on you, mate," the man behind the bar, portly and smiling, handed him a large imperial-size pint.

"Thank ye," Marcus said, handing him a gold coin.

"Aye, my lord, I don't have change for this size of coin."

"Keep it," Marcus said with delight.

"Thank ye, my generous lord. Anything else on the house?" he said, wiping a glass and helping another customer. An old man with a long beard and two younger women freshly painted behind him.

"I will pay you more for some information," Marcus said, tucking his leather satchel into his layers of silken delicate multicolored silk attire.

Other customers rushed up to the bar. Marcus stood there drinking on his own. More people came and went, men with men, women with men, men with women, some smelling of horse and some the fanciest perfumes of Paris, Rome, and Sicily. Marcus drank his third, and a couple of well-dressed full-on Londoners.

"My name is Curtis, and this is Jake," Curtis said, eyeing Marcus from head to toe and sending a piercing smile.

"Marcus, Curtis, Jake, the pleasure is all mine," Marcus said, slightly bowing.

"Well, the accent is good English, but where did you leave port?" Jake interjected, wearing period 1750 tight trousers, nicely pinned white stockings and well-crafted shoes, ruffled white shirts that both Curtis and Jake look like fancy men in a most easygoing way, giggly and milling about.

"I come from the north," Marcus said. "But do you know the way to Kent?"

"Sure, but I hope you have seen London," Curtis said, blushing.

"A drink?" Marcus said.

"Pleasure, let's get a table," Curtis said quickly and excitedly.

"Marcus is a Roman name, are you Italian?" Curtis said while he asked a guy to move so the three of them could sit together, and this other man just slowly moved to the back of the table, the barman bringing the man who now sat in the darkest corner of the tavern.

"Blitz, they call him," the barman said to Marcus, Curtis, and Jake, moving them into the table with drinks and eats of pigeon, pheasant, grapes and nuts, walnuts. Beers came and beers went.

"You have not had wines from France?" Curtis said to Marcus, and Marcus sat back, his thick silk outer vest opening, revealing muscular bulges against light blue or azure. A group of six women in loud conversation with bursts of laughter walked past.

"Hello, boys," one woman said.

"Women," Marcus said, sitting up and closing his vest.

"Yes, Marcus, this is London, there are a lot of women and men in London."

"Show me around," Marcus said.

"Well, this is Greek Street and farther are a few places to visit for late-night activities, and entertainment and the cat and the fiddle. Mayfair is just over there, nice homes. Several brothels down toward Westminster, very private. But I assure you that if you just turn up, they will allow you admittance, for that you can be sure," Curtis said as he stood, stretched, tucked himself here and there, Marcus and Jake doing the same.

"Time we walked a bit," Jake said and pointed out areas of interest, Curtis wisecracking between descriptions, Jake rolling his eyes.

"Marcus, you take that road, board that coach, and it will take you to Kent."

"I don't need transportation, I just need pointing," Marcus said as Curtis and Jake stared blankly in the middle of the street with small crowds of people occasionally walking past.

"Well, that way," Jake said and Curtis also pointed then turned back to look at Marcus.

"Are there any trees about?" Marcus said, smiling. "Oh, and how about another pint or two of ale?"

"I am all game for that, you Jake," Curtis said eager to spend more time with this non-Londoner and prince from some other world.

"This looks fine," Marcus said.

"The Wiltons," Curtis said as they went in and dined on one of the finest meals imaginable. Fish, duck, and lamb courses, three French desserts, two bottles of wines of France, followed by ice wine and the introduction of sultana to Marcus's vast dictionary of words.

"So this mysterious place from where you are from, Lord Marcus, am I to say is north, but can you express more detail on the place of your origin."

"Well, Kent is where I am bound," Marcus said mysteriously. "You have both been very kind and I am most pleased to have met you both. It would be a pleasure, nay an honor to be in your good company once again. This I grant you both," Marcus said after standing and paying in gold for the rich meal they had eaten and standing quite stumble after too much beer and wine; in fact, Marcus's vision seemed a touch impaired as was Curtis's and Jake's vision.

"Well, hang on, how're you going to get to Kent, walk?" Jake said as they all stood and walked out to the busy London street.

"I see a tree down the end of this path," Marcus said as it began to lightly rain. Marcus stood poised on the sky. "Let it rain."

"Oh, dear Marcus, we must be off in this rain. Come stay with us a night before your journey. Stay a week in fact," Curtis said as he wiped tears from his face in just meeting this chosen one, this man who rivaled all men in beauty and strength, dressed to the fashionably pleasing of all.

"Why a tree?" Curtis asked, running up to catch up with Marcus, Jake in tow. They arrived at the tree.

"Well, it's been nice, boys." Marcus shook Curtis's hand. "What is thy address?"

"You can just ask for me at the tavern where we met," Curtis said and batted his eye.

"I feel that you are leaving," Jake said, confused.

"Traveling by wood, someday you will learn," Marcus said, standing back to the tree.

"Traveling by wood, is wood a metaphor for something?" Jake said.

"Is anyone looking?" Marcus said.

"Looking, why looking, Marcus? Why would they be looking, and who cares? Yes, they are looking," Curtis said.

"You are acting very strange, Marcus," Jake said, standing closer to Marcus as Marcus edged backward toward the tree, both hands behind his back.

"Flying by wood," Marcus said with a wide grin from ear to ear. Marcus reached into his silks and pulled out spectacles with tinted glass over the eyes and put them on his head.

"Most peculiar pez," Jake said, now standing still as Marcus's back was flush with the tree. He reached behind, pulled the branch, straddled it, and a comfortable lip grew within moments. Curtis and Jake were stiff with fright unimaginative reality before them. This growth of wood and leave transformed before thee.

"Here my friends is the way to travel," Marcus said, holding the branch between his legs and searching for a star. He then wrapped his neck with a necklace, a medallion that within pointed or aimed toward a star.

"I shall see thee both again soon," Marcus said as he dashed off from the street, above the rooftops, and circled them. Two women witnessed the departure, screamed, and fell to the ground.

"Did you see that?" Curtis said, mouth open to Jake now arm in arm tightly.

"I surely did."

On his flying piece of wooden transportation device, Marcus soared above the buildings, above the construction over the Thames, boats, and into the clouds. Back at the cottage, Porius opened the front door and said to Franklin, "He is close, Franklin, show him the way." Franklin flew higher and higher, heading toward London, sensing Marcus and his trajectory toward the cottage.

Thomas came out into the yard with Porius. "Shall we begin?"

"Yes, indeed let's. Parthenia, start the meal. Grendle, prepare the desserts. Thomas, go to the village and bring the wine, beer, and some musicians. And anyone you feel adequate for a spectacular party," Porius said, filled with glee.

Porius took his wand and pointed to the air, floating pensive by his side hovering over the table.

"Walters, Athena, Leal, Simon and Apollo, Jewel and Frederick, come one and come all to meet our new member," Porius said, peering into the pensive.

"Athena, he comes and will be here within the hour—" Before he had finished his sentence, Athena and her two beautiful guards had appeared before him.

"Athena, Gloria, Alexandria, most pleased to see you," Porius said, dressed in his fancy white robes and golden sandals, Athena and her maidens in their usually Greek attire. Walters soon appeared, as the garden filled up with rainbows of light for each arrival. Leal and Apollo were dressed in the usual leathers and silk, muscles bulging like they had been exercising continuously for a month.

"My good lord Porius, a pleasure as always," Apollo said as he materialized several ancient musical instruments. "I thought I may provide some music for the event."

"Yes, good idea Apollo. We will give Marcus the finest greeting earthkind has to offer," Thomas said as he carried a few tables with Leal, Simon, and Walters.

"My good lord Porius, Marcus is coming to learn our magic?"

"And to teach us his magic." Porius, in agreement, pointed his wand toward the tree line. Deer, rabbit, fox, partridge, squirrel, peregrine play as a harpsichord began to play at the tree line made by Apollo.

"Nice bluebirds," Apollo said while his harpsichord was being played by a large African man wearing African garb and golden necklaces. Apollo had horn instruments and a small percussion section. Porius's floating band hovered above the ancient musicians, and they all played in tune.

"Bring forth thy friends from the underworld," Thomas said, pointing his wand toward the entrance by the garden fountain. Out popped Horan and several scantily dressed snakelike people, with Porius in agreement with their arrival.

Cherubs flew, their wings flapping quickly on the sides of their naked flabby young bodies as they brought material, some tinsel or dressings, flags of color.

The garden was filling up with magical creatures to meet Marcus, the visitor from the sixth green planet.

CHAPTER 26

The last few fairies including Aria sat watching the dancing ancient musicians, Porius greeting each one in turn—Walters, Simon, Leal, Athena and her maidens, several creatures from the underworld, including Horan who wore a beautifully decorated purple robe trimmed with golden lace. Several young men gathered around Leal and Apollo. Thomas arrived with a small crowd from the village including two beautiful young women from the village, Elizabeth with blond hair, shapely and shy, and Karen with hair of red and wearing an apron and gray frock, both of whom joined Grendle to help with the preparations. Cherubs circled and floated about the floating band in synch with even a visitor from the ancient city of Xinye in China appeared in red and white silks from the Orient. Porius was pleased to see them while the other guests greeted them and though unsure of each other due to language, heads nodding.

"Ping and Xoa, a pleasure you made it and welcome."

"We would not want to miss greeting this particular visitor," Ping said to Porius in Chinese, which Porius remarkably understood.

"Good, and here he comes. Look up," Porius said, pointing high above the trees. All eyes followed Franklin and Marcus, and they appeared like growing dots in the sky, becoming clearer and clearer, and the band played louder and louder with trumpets ablaze. As Marcus landed on the ground beside Porius, he tossed his wooden seat to a luck tree, which assimilated its plank into its being.

"Marcus, welcome to earth," Porius said while all bowed. Even Athena gave a dainty bow, and Franklin sipped a bit of water from the fountain then rested his weary feathery body upon the thatch of the cottage.

"My good people, I had no idea of such a gathering," Marcus said to the crowd, the band playing louder and louder. The fairies, a few elves, cherubs, dancing couples wearing golden-laced skirts and dainty dance shoes all together in laughter, song, and cheers could be heard laughing with the occasional shouts of "Marcus, welcome!"

Several fawns picking their way through leaves, perked up ears to hear his tale.

All of thee who hath come to welcome me, I bring you joy.

The tales Porius hath told to my kin have been recorded,

I aim to learn all your ways, traditions, histories, family problems and concerns.

Join me in celebrating this beautiful world called earth, earth and its amazing creatures.

Marcus touched the faun, and all stood silent to watch his graceful movements among the crowd. Walters bowed as he passed. "Welcome," Walters said as well as Leal, Simon, Thomas, and a small elf wearing only a straw hat who hid behind Thomas's leg.

"And who are thee?" Marcus said, bending down to greet this lonely-looking elf with green skin, large eyes, straw hat, and knobby knees.

"My name is Borin," the elf said, bowing.

"Athena, your beauty is even more than I can imagine and your two guards, Gloria and Alexandria," Marcus said, passing through the crowd, greeting each person, elf, fairy, as one small young male fairy sat upon Marcus's shoulder.

"My name is David," the young fairy whispered in Marcus's ear before flying off.

"Jewel and Frederick, I have heard of the good you have done."

"Thomas, great Thomas, keeper of grounds at the cottage which stands before me." Marcus stood at the doorstep and then turned back to the large crowd. "I am yours to command," he said and bowed to all, and the crowd's silence was broken by Athena.

"Welcome, my prince."

Even the water goblins came out to greet Marcus while piling squiggling fish at his feet before stumbling and darting back into the river. "Water goblins, this earth has it all."

"But where is your guardhouse?" Marcus asked Porius while the crowd danced, ate and sang, conversed, and shared stories of their separate ways. Even the ladies from the village had never seen such splendid and unusual creatures. Those from the underworld were wearing shaded glasses over their sensitive eyes, oils to protect their skins, while a banjo player started strumming an old folk tune from some pagan myth.

Leal whispered to Apollo, "Athena looks like she wants to have her way with Marcus."

"I could join her," Apollo said as they both giggled and sipped the ale provided in such abundance.

"Now listen, everyone, pay attention," Porius shouted, holding his wand high above a tall thin green milkweed growing by the fountain. Porius's pause was aesthetically perfect as all gazed in his direction including Marcus.

"Art thou performing magic?" Marcus said, running up toward Porius as all came closer, circling around and just leaving enough space between Porius and the milkweed stalk that stood about five feet tall.

"Hector, Lord of Butterflies, please bring these stacks to fill with caterpillars and bring to change into an overnight abundance of growth, caterpillars here I bequest of thee."

He waved his wand, and all held their breaths. Karen and Elizabeth had never witnessed any sort of real magic, except for the occasional card trick performed by Thomas or other traveling tricksters. Soon the fluttering silent sounds of thousands of batting wings filled the edge of the forest. Hence then from all sides pouring with colorful forces of nature came thousands of butterflies, one by one clinging onto the milkweed until the area was filled with butterflies. A dingy skipper, a few gatekeepers, heath fritillaries, and many other fritillaries, marble white and meadow brown, white admiral, small blues surrounded by orange tips as even the animals played with them as the guests all gaze upon them in wonder. Several small blues landed on a couple of deer scampering in the distance back in the meadow behind the cottage.

"Stand back and give them room," Porius said calmly as the gazing visitors stood in marvel at the thousands of butterflies, which apparently landed on the milkweed, laid their cocoon and flew off back to the forest, flickering in light and smiling faces watched each one come, lay a cocoon, and go off. But once this stalk was covered in cocoons, all the other butterflies gathered around other stalks, in the meadow, in the forest, and other parts of the garden.

"Now I understand why you enjoy milkweed so much," Simon said to Porius.

"Butterflies love milkweed. I believe Horan was first to point that out to me," Porius said to Simon while Horan, thrilled to hear the mention of his name, ran forward.

"Yes, yes, I have known about it for years," Horan said in his pompous tone. "Everyone should plant more milkweed if you want more butterflies."

The listening crowd was taking mental notes of Horan's and Porius's wise knowledge of butterflies.

"Didn't know they had milkweed within the underworld, Horan," Leal shouted out, laughing.

"Oh yes, yes we do. In fact, some of the best," Horan said, fading back into the crowd as taking turns watching the cocoons grow at an unusual rate. For tomorrow's opening will come soon enough and more festivities to come when a few more dances performed ballet around the water fountain to music played by two tiny string instruments musicians floating above the crowd at the control of Porius.

"Tomorrow morning, a new crop with several new breeds shall be born," Porius said, quite pleased with himself, knowing full well that even without his so-called spell, the butterflies were coming today. But keeping that to himself, Porius knew that it filled people's hearts and minds to know something magical was going on.

"Well done, Lord Porius, well done," Leal said, patting Porius on his backside.

Banjo music was playing, and an accordion-type instrument began playing by itself alongside.

"Porius, is that you?" Thomas said, looking at the floating accordion playing in rhythm with the banjo player who looked as if he just came from a bayou. The villagers laughed at the spectacle. Karen and Elizabeth waved their hands around the floating instrument in disbelief and giggling as they inched closer to Leal and Apollo, watching their every move and blushing.

"Ladies," Leal said, nodding.

Both giggled and asked them to dance as others joined—cherubs overhead, fairies floating in circles, elves, trolls. Horan, Athena, Porius, and Walters danced and sang the ancient songs of druid ancestors. Even the Chinese Ping and fellow attempted to dance in the western way, making all laugh and a few spill their ale.

"Daoism shall find you both a quiet place later on, but is this special for ye?" Thomas said to Ping.

Ping reacted in his best attempt at English. "My dear Thomas, Confucianism is going be replaced by some new ways," Ping said proudly.

"Porius doth through a good festival," Thomas said while Leal and Apollo knocked him about while dancing. And the music played for hours, Marcus greeting and listening, searching each person and creature's eyes for their inner thoughts, conditions, needs, and deepest desires. Until evening and beyond.

Later that night, Ping said to an elf, "From the words of Mauryan emperor Ashoka, my heart is with all of you."

"I believe I have heard of Ashoka, old-time emperor, way back," Thomas interjected. "Porius had us read him when I was a young student."

"Now will this Marcus be your student," Leal asked Porius.

"Oh yes, Leal, would you like to come and spend some time teaching him your battling skills?"

"My sword is always at your bequest, and nothing would give me more pleasure than to train Marcus," Leal said.

"I thought that would be the case," Porius said. "Though Marcus may have some insightful moves to even show you, Leal, oh great warrior."

"I am getting tired, Porius," Athena said late that night while the party died down, the music playing slower tunes, Leal and Apollo descending back to their secluded world upon Elysium. Athena finally took Walters, Simon, and her guards and boarded a golden chariot that vanished upon a ray of moonlight.

Twinkling stars shining high above the cottage grounds could be seen shapes and visions of departing creatures as the underworld swallowed back its inhabitants, Horan, and the other lizard-type people. Aria the fairy queen danced herself to sleep and floated upon a small white cloud which Porius's manufacturers sending her on her way. Several elves played about the garden snoring, the villagers dancing their way back to the main road. Stumbling, giggling, and laughing were heard from the distance. Thomas lay asleep with Parthenia at his feet on the grass until a cool wind came through and sent them inside to sleep a cool slumber. The night animals, owls picking up bits of food, and rats, mice, badgers, and moles came out for the takings while Porius showed Marcus to his waiting chamber then retired himself.

"Dream all who have been here this day, dream of a future where all men, creature, and spirit may live with each other in peace."

In the morning, the fields, gardens, and forests were filled with thousands of young butterflies, every color and some as if they had been etched from crystals the vibrant blue, black, yellow, red, amber, silver, and gold. Thomas, Porius, Marcus, and Parthenia bathed in the river, surrounded by hundreds of butterflies. One even landed on Thomas's nose. A bubble from the water goblin was close to Marcus as he felt the slither of a water goblin against his naked behind.

"Something just brushed me Porius," Marcus said startled.

"Most likely Harold the water goblin," Porius say head full of bubbles.

"Warm and slimy?" Marcus said with concern.

"Yes, that is Harold for sure," Porius smiles.

"There see at the edge," Marcus said pointing to the other side of the river.

"Indeed, hello Harold," Thomas said calmly.

"Welcome Marcus," Harold said and then before a blink of an eye he is gone quickly into the forest.

"I say, water goblins are fast," Marcus said.

"Aye, and they bring excellent fish," Parthenia said toweling off and walking back to the cottage, picking up a small pile of trout stacked neatly by Harold the water goblin.

"You know Porius, already I can report back to Harris that you are in tune with nature, I see now pollutants here," Marcus said.

"Yes, but it is the future and many other places upon the earth which tends to worry Harris's brow," Porius replied. "It is also man's intense passion for war which also concerns him, and I for that matter."

"All planets have the same problem, Porius," Thomas interjected.

"Fools all," Marcus said walking out of the river to towel off and stand to gaze at the forest. "There is this odd theory that most planets, in their evolutionary journey reach the same plateau."

Marcus putting on a pair of short pants and vest. "By the time a planet has evolved enough to travel outside the planet's atmosphere the same planet has already overpopulated, polluted and poisoned its very existence."

"Meaning that," Porius said also toweling off and slipping into clean white robes. "In time an evolution of species first then comes the evolution of learning, inventing and creating. This process is over thousands of years and while the learning is going on, so is the competition, which makes men and women green for the yearning of winning, being the best and earning the most money."

'And that is where all thy will stops, men's desire change from learning into a desire for wealth," Marcus said.

"It's a vicious circle," Thomas said, using the same towel as Marcus and Porius, which was already wet and then he just hung it on a branch to dry and put on his pantaloons.

"This is the curse of mankind. How are we supposed to make all men live together without competition, war, and territorial want?" Thomas stated.

"We have three hundred years to achieve this or Harris will have earth destroyed in the year 2050 and none will be the wiser or even know what is taking place.

"I shall help and together we will provide the learning, science, technologies, and peaceful ways," an optimistic Marcus said. "For from what I have seen of humans, we have hope."

"Yes, but these are all my friends, and those to whom follow these ways, not all humans are as calm and innocent, trust me," Porius said.

"Wait till you see Rome and hear of the many current wars and grievances from China, Africa, the Middle East, and even Europe and England," Thomas interjected.

"Yeah, we must not forget about America. I believe a bottle is about to be corked across the Atlantic, make no mistake of it," Porius said, walking back toward the cottage.

"That is why I am here, to teach you how my planet grew without any passion for war. Everyone has plenty, and let's not forget that on my planet, only every twentieth female born is allowed to give birth," Marcus said, following Porius and Thomas while thousands of butterflies circled, dove, fluttered, landing on nearly every branch within eye shot, wings moving slowly once landed.

"Oh, this is a very pretty one," Marcus said, gazing at a blue butterfly with black tips on the edge of its dainty wings.

"A small blue," Porius said. "Women will never go for that arrangement on this planet."

"So I gather, Porius, yes, it is a problem. With the population growth rate, how do you intend to deal with it?" Marcus said, concerned.

"It will be fraught with an impossible solution. All women would need to agree to letting only the twentieth born can give birth. To you and I, it seems like a normal way to save the planet from overpopulating. But to the races, countries, traditions, religions, and political views, it will be impossible to have this as a commonsense rule instead of a law," Porius replied as they all walked into the cottage and were presented with breakfast by Parthenia, Grendle away on other business.

"'Twill be most difficult," Thomas said, "and how will you even get the message out. No countries follow the same set of rules." Thomas finished, sitting at the table to eat breakfast.

Splashing in the river, the water goblins raced and played with a school of fish too young for eating coming into their advantage. Gurgling and panting, the goblins swiftly moved upstream followed by pigeons, crows, ravens by air, deer, fox, and other animals, which rushed alongside the river and crept at the edge of the cottage, all getting close to the cottage, sensing something in the air, mysterious, obsequious. Clouds filled the sky as rain began, lightning pierced the sky. Porius closed the shades of the window, ushering Thomas, Marcus, Parthenia, and Grendle to the main room. Holding his wand, he said, "Fools who plague us, fools of mischief who alter and convert old ways, reveal thy place."

"Really, Porius, that's the spell?" Marcus said, mildly disappointed.

"It's all in the doing. Patience, my boy, patience," Porius said, looking out the front door at the rain and the others standing behind him as something began to happen—animals queuing and looking skyward, small swift swirls of wind and dust, leaves and passion, within the mist as if by pensive Paris appeared in light and sound, rolling images of man sitting alone in a house with the street opposite on fire, shivering and alone. Porius stepped through the swirling light and appeared before the shivering man in Paris. Crowded streets of people running to and fro the building next door to him were on fire as figures of black hooded men wearing crosses pulled children from their homes, burning buildings and setting bonfires to scare the parishioners, packing their children on carts and the parents left screaming. The shivering man witnessed Porius as he appeared from the mist.

Multiple layer pauses for ascetic. Eye to eye contact always a remedy to misunderstandings.

Be calm and no heed to them my friend, calm thyself," Porius said.

"Are you not one of them?" the skinny, naked, shivering man said, sitting behind a potbellied stove. Marcus, Thomas, and all the animals watched the scene portrayed in light within the swirling mist of light, leaves, and circling dust, light rain falling through the mist, distorting the moving images of Porius in Paris.

"Transported to Paris, amazing," Marcus said Thomas agreeable and all tear-filled watch.

"Come with my fried, have you woken up feeling lost," Porius reaching his hand out to the stranger still shivering.

"They want me to carve out my eyes with this wooden spoon and swallow them until my eyes travel through my body or I shall burn in hell," The man now crying to Porius.

"It is not true for nothing they say is true, believe me, it is all lies," Porius reaching out his hand. Touch my hand and pay no attention to the outside events, look away and only think of peace," Porius said.

"Not true, but they told me I will die in hell unless I show them allegiance, and you say it's all not true?"

"None of it, my friend. Take my hand," Porius said, pleading as the man followed his instructions and Porius pulled him through light and leaves and fell on the garden grass, beside him the naked shivering man from Paris—another place, another language, and a new part of the family had arrived.

"My name is Frolan the Fourth," he said, covering his private parts while Thomas handed him a robe.

"House of Fraun from Paris." Porius thought his joy at meeting the greatest grandson of the French magical family, and he doesn't even know who he was or what power was within him.

"I have heard of Fraun, relatives of mine, I believe," Frolan IV said, still shivering and amazed at his new surroundings. "My son has been taken. Priest in black hooded cloak and dagger, shield, and whip have taken my boy, my darling boy, my darling Sam." Frolan was in despair as he dried his skin and dressed in the silks provided by Thomas.

"Men actually steal children?" Marcus asked with disgust in his voice.

"And ye shall be first to free him," Porius said, lowering the pensive.

"Is this magic?" Frolan asked, watching the floating silver plate, Porius ignoring the question.

"There he lies in cage and darkness with others. Look and reveal your son's current predicament," Porius said as the watery liquid within the pensive saw a group of young men in a cage, weeping, sulking, and tired of the struggle to resist. The wooden cage on wheels was bound for somewhere outside Paris to the north drawn by two horses, driver, and one large thug dressed in black robes and dangling a wooden cross. Occasionally whipping the sides of the cage, making the captives jump in fear as he laughed a gurgling laugh at the boys.

"I see, I can see my son! We must save him," Frolan said to Thomas, Marcus, and Porius.

"For we shall, and ye stay put with Porius and Thomas," Marcus said, eagerly wrapping his belt and sword around his waist.

"I believe you will need Simon or Leal to assist you and show you the way, for both know France well enough," Thomas said.

"Call them for me, Porius," Marcus said to Porius while Frolan sobbed, watching the excitement, engaged from every corner of the cottage. Parthenia came out in an apron and barefooted.

"Nice to meet you, Frolan. You're in good hands here, and I will make you a pleasant French meal, coq au vin, okay?"

"Merci, delighted I am sure," Frolan the Fourth said, wiping the tears from his eyes, watching Marcus as he rushed out to the edge of the forest and pulled the wood from a tall pine.

"Bring thee and seat thee for a journey," Marcus said, "I shall collect thy son, yes I shall free thy son Sam, dear Frolan, while you stay safe here with Porius."

Marcus checks his sword, sheath, and shoes. Since this wood becoming his means of transportation forming to fit his bodice.

A beautiful rainbow of light ascended upon the garden and within its glowing form of Leal, in only form and not flesh. Leal rushed up to Porius, Thomas, and Parthenia and his body somewhat see-through stood in his Grecian wardrobe of ankle sandals, leather shorts, and white-cape-type road held by golden clasp, long black hair waving over his shoulder, joining Marcus side by side materializing a wooden seat to ride upon, waving goodbye to Porius, Thomas, and the others.

High above the river, trees, animals moved swiftly above the forest as even the water goblins poked their heads up from the river and followed the two men flying south toward France on caressing and accommodating wood. Over hut and cabin, farm, and then only the white cliffs of Dover are seen behind them, over wave and ship, cod, squid and eel, rowboat ship, and even a large schooner, its occupants rushing to the bow to wave to Marcus and Leal as they passed, shouting, "Specter!" and pointing in sheer interest of this unworldly passers by witnesses survive for the magical conjurings and illusions. Nothing out of the ordinary for Leal and Marcus, Marcus learned to fly by wood as a child back on his home world and Leal an old hand, who actually preferred horses and being close to the ground. Though on this occasion, no time must be wasted for once the carriage holding, Leal pulled up close to Marcus in their southward direction from Kent to France.

"Calais is below. There are some rather nice folks in Calais." Leal pointed out to Marcus.

"Looks divine," Marcus said, swooping down to about ten feet from the ground to get a closer look. Passing the construction site of a church, two business-type buildings being meticulously crafted for a town hall or some other business brick and mortar.

"Come back up before someone notices," Leal said as they once again head for the clouds above and disappear at the bottom of a cloud, which sheltered them from view.

"Not that most mortal beings would ever look up and expect to see two men flying on wood," Leal said, still only inches from Marcus.

Passing schools, cottages and farmers plowing, planting, and pulling weeds passed ox, donkey, horse, and fowl and even flying close to a few very interested geese.

"Beautiful birds, Leal," Marcus said.

"Geese, and very tasty," Leal said as he circled a gray goose and leaving it in bewildered confusion.

"Mask my mind but look at that light," Marcus said while a large pool of light swirled in front of their flight path and they landed to rest and stare at the light.

"The sun is going down, but I believe this is my father," Marcus said, standing on a deer path surrounded by think bramble, conifer trees, elm, oak, and ivy.

"Harris?" Leal said as the winding light finally became the image of Harris, elongated and see-through as if a ghost was hovering about ten feet above their heads.

"Use the falcon which comes before you, my son, and save these children. Sam is important to the future of all mankind."

The large head of Harris echoed for anyone to hear within a mile or so; in fact, it was so loud that both Leal and Marcus covered their ears.

"The falcon, yes, Father," Marcus said as the swirling light, which once revealed Harris, faded into sunset. A falcon of gray, white, brown, and golden circled then and gave a squawk, which reminded Leal of Franklin.

"I think we had better follow the falcon," Leal said while fingering his ears and shaking his head.

"Your father knows how to make an appearance," Leal said, mounting his wooden seat, which cupped his buttocks tightly.

"He is quite the showman, I don't really like the fact that he is watching us, in fact," Marcus said, suspiciously feeling around his waist. "Oh, I see."

"A watcher medallion," Leal said, laughing.

"Yes, well at least I know now and can turn it off. Let's get after that falcon," Marcus said, and they both take flight over the treetops and after the wicked fast falcon, who kept squawking.

Back at the cottage, Porius was reading some manuscript aloud to Thomas. "A community feel more of a Highstreet than a hall the past couple of decades, it became a hum for South Americans who came to England, and Elephant Castle streamed with magical remedies and potions, drugs, and thoughts. Not to detail the story from the original figures, but this is to be taken down for restoration as the time prevails and witnesses survive for the magical conjurings and illusions." Porius laid down the manuscript.

"I believe there are hidden meanings within this story, Thomas." He sipped a goblet of wine.

"Have they found Sam yet?" Thomas said while Frolan peered endlessly watching their flight.

"I lost them for a while, but I now can see them again, ma parole."

"Yes, they should be close. I believe Harris is preparing a bird for them to follow, falcon most likely," Porius said smugly.

"Indeed, Monsieur Porius. Oh, my lord Porius, tell me more of my magical past," Frolan the Fourth said, gleaming into the pensive.

While Porius explained Frolan's past and his place in the future of all mankind, Leal and Marcus finally saw the white walls of the monastery while flying over with tremendous speed the slow and imagine the most likely place to keep slaves, the outer buildings. They landed searching the area without being seen, which is most easy for Leal since he was only form and could become invisible when needed, but will be unable to fight without flesh. Still, his frightening skills would be the best played card at this event.

"Listen," Marcus said, reaching out for Leal, but his hand just wiped through him. Leal stopped and then crept along the back of a building. The sounds of sobbing could be heard inside, and there were two teenage boys wearing ragged clothes and locked up in a large wooden cage. A man dressed in all black, greasy hair, and a large wooden cross was whipping the side of the cage with fierce aptitude.

"Quiet or I vill beat ye!" the man said as the two boys pushed toward the back of the cage and stopped crying.

Beyond in the back, a woman could be heard screaming. "Nice, oh nice," said a man in the back disrobing a young woman who was tied both feet and hands.

"No, s'il vous plait, no."

"That will be enough of that," Marcus said, rushing the rapist in action and pulling his sword. "You have raped your last victim," Marcus said as he plunged his sword deep into the back of the attacker who stood half dressed. "You elongated criminal, you disgusting maggot, you devil in black, die!" Marcus plunged again, and the man rolled to the flood in a swiftly mounting pool of blood, and he died with bubbling blood from his orifice that once shouted, "Nice, nice."

"Let's get you out of here," Marcus said as the other man came behind him, but Leal got between them and rushed toward the man, startled because of Leal's ghostlike figure. He slowed, amazed.

"Famtome a fantome, mon dieu," the man said, stopping to look back at Leal who went clean through his black vicious waste of space.

"Ye shalt not see another, and your god won't save you now," Marcus said. As the man turned back toward Marcus, Marcus plunged his already bloody sword through his attacker's leg then swiftly removed his sword and sliced toward his head, the blade going clean through his neck. His head rolled, eyes wide on the floor. "And there ye shall stay until the animals, insects, and farm animals devour thou every bit," Marcus said, bowing to Leal.

"Quick, free those boys and let's get them out of here," Leal said. Marcus broke open the cage with a large wooden pole that was lying around the back of the cage. "Better yet, you boys, grab the horses and let's take the lot."

"Qui etes vous? (Who are you?" one of the boys said as both boys ran to grab and harness the horses to the rolling cage.

"We are friends of your fathers, and we will take you to Paris, to a safe place, and bring him to you in a few days."

"My savior." The girl stood up, thankfully free and rubbing her wrists and feet.

"Put that oil on the burns, and I hope you don't mind wearing black," Leal said as he pointed to the oil and faded away.

"Leal, Leal," Marcus said, but Leal was gone. Form only lasts so long, and they all rode away after Marcus sliced a large piece of the unbloodied part of the cloak from the dead attacker and wrapped the young woman's body, and they departed. Marcus and the two boys and woman rode safely on the cart, two horses pulling and swiftly heading back for Paris along the forest road and into the dark moonless night sky.

"Take those two pieces of wood and place them safely in the back. We will get you safely back to Paris," Marcus said, trying to move the horses faster than they appeared ready.

"Look, Monsieur Marcus." Sam pointed back to two large priests racing toward them shouting with swords raised.

"I believe a storm is in order," Marcus said, pulling his wand, handing the reins to Sam. "Keep going." Marcus stepped back to the cage where the young woman shivered in the bouncing cage.

"My name is Lil," she said to Marcus.

"Pleasure, Lil, now don't mind the lightning but we need to stop these villains." He pointed toward the sky as clouds collided in fierce competition. "Correspond these demons with the light from the sky," Marcus chanted.

Within moments, the sky poured with hard rain. Gushing down in buckets all around them, the horses slowed and slipped in the mud. Thunder followed by many strikes of lighting. Some shafts of light just missed the cart cage, and then Marcus pointed his wand at the bewildered-looking fast-approaching priest on horseback. Nearly reaching the rolling cage on wheels, a flash of lightning hit the first square on the face and marked him from forehead to balls, leaving the mark of lightning veins directly down his body and knocking him off his horse blacked out in a puddle of mud and quickened rain. Then another bolt hit the other, knocking him off his horse and marking his back with lightning strikes.

"That will teach them and a little something to remember me by," Marcus said, quite pleased with himself and knowing the marks that lightning would leave upon his assailants.

———

383

"I knew there was magic. I always knew from stories my father told us," Lil said.

"Yes, and we must get you back to Paris," Marcus said.

"There is no one. Sam and James's parents were tortured and killed as were mine. They were all stonemasons and stonecutters. My father carved and formed all the grotesques, gargoyles, faces, and images in stone in many of the cathedrals including Notre Dame," Lil said, weeping.

"Yes, there is no one," Sam agreed.

"My father was also a mason," said James. "He was pagan and not a part of the Christian though he worked in every cathedral from Scotland to Paris and a few in Italy," James said as rain beat them all, and they drove further toward Paris.

"Then our first stop will be even more wonderful for all of ye," Marcus said, pulling the horse and cart. "Come to the edge of the woods." Marcus jumped out and whispered to the horses, "Wait for us here, my friends, and have some grass." Marcus took off the bridles so the horses could eat as he led Lil, Sam, and James into the edge of the woods.

"Behold, earth and stone reveal thy entrance," Marcus said somewhere between Paris and Orleans. "Open thy entrance and take thee."

Rock, sand, flower, earth, and vine moved away in syncopation; and within the earth opened a large crack, pressing the sides open and two adders retreated, rabbits, squirrel, and fowl parked themselves out of the way but watched Marcus as he opened the earth to reveal a cave, a hole with light shining from within.

"Welcome and enter," Marcus said as Leal reappeared from within.

"I have made ready your new world," Leal said, wearing his tight black shorts, black boots, and leather vest, waving the three young ones inside.

Sam, while gazing at the beautiful walls lit with crystals and unearthly glows of illuminous light which surrounds them, fell to his knees as the others follow suit.

"I knew it existed. I knew my father was not lying. I knew I knew," Sam said in French, and Marcus placed his hand on Sam as he rose.

"Welcome, Sam," a loud voice of Porius was heard echoing through the tunnel as the come to the edge of the warm spring water, "Bath and rejoice for I have your father wishing you well."

"Porius, the lord Porius whom I have heard tales of since youth?" Lil said, also standing to take in the glory of millions of sparkling lights, ivy, and the walk into the warm spring waters of the cave.

"And beyond the underworld," Leal said. Marcus gazed in amazement at the opening to the underworld. Horan came from far away with fairies, elves, dwarves, and other undetermined animal life as they all circled the pond in which Sam, Lil, and James bathed and were presented with clothes to match those of the Greek gods.

Athena, Walters, Simon, Porius, all welcoming through echoing voices. "We see you through our pensive and are wishing you well," Porius said as the others sang the welcome song to these youths.

Welcome ye forever free
Together now this place is to thee
Thy home, thy honor and grace await to keep thee warm
Peace of mind and honest of heart and spirit
Welcome ye forever free

"Your father is here in peace and will see thee soon," Porius said, his face now visible as a reflection in the pool in which they bathed. Smoke circled and surrounded his image. Sam, Lil, and James peering, eyes wide and gawking mouths. "You have been rescued, and a new life awaits you all," Porius said as he faded. Horan greeted them with several elven creatures wrapping their bodies in the finest-colored silks and jewels. Two dainty fairies wearing the Greek clothing so befitting them as a reflection of Athena and her maidens, cherubs circled in musical rhythms as singing and floating bands played their feet are fitted with golden sandals, such as Leal.

"I envy you all," Horan said while greeting Marcus, squeezing his hand in welcome and taking small squeezes with Marcus's muscular shoulders and giving short squeezes with his biceps, legs in handfuls. "A very nice physique," Horan said while turning his focus to the three young newly incorporated volunteers to protect the old ways. "The adventures that await you are more wonderous than you can imagine."

"We can imagine a lot," Sam said in deep admiration for the beautiful clothes they now wore, smiling at one another.

"You will be taught the herbal and magical ways of the past with Porius, Thomas, and Marcus, that is to say when Marcus is not out protecting someone or something from harm," Horan said as he turned toward the exit from whence the three came in and led by the ghost of Leal, Athena, and her maidens, the sky filling with magical creatures, hanging about on the outside of the cave and Sam turning to his interlocutor Horan with joy-filled eyes, Lil and James dressing as they came from the waters in finest silks and jewels, leather straps, and golden sandals led by many.

Trumpets blew in mighty syncopation; drums beat in rhythm while cherubs dropped rose petals circling above them.

"No more fear, starvation, or pressure from uncouth societies, your carriage awaits you," Horan said, leading them out of the cave as it motioned its rocks, stones, bushes, and trees covering the path. "Here your stories begin."

Outside the cave were all types of animals, fowl, and even an onlooking water goblin, elves, fairies, large lizard-like creatures wearing bow ties, spotted pigeons, and two unicorns. The carriage that once was a cage was now a brightly colored and exceptionally detailed golden and silver carriage, the steps declining to greet Sam's foot, James and Lil also stepping up into the blue padded silken seats. Marcus wiped his eyes at the spectacle, and the animals, creatures, cherubs, and elven folk sang.

Joyous day we bring you
Your lives begin a new
The glory of time awaits you
Your hearts heroic and true.

Lil was wiping rose petals from James, smiling and tearing up from the emotional event. Some villagers came wearing symbols unseen before by Sam, Lil, James, Horan waving them goodbye, and Leal departing with Athena and her maidens caught within the eyes of all as they ascended to Elysium.

"I shall drive the coach. All in," Marcus said proudly as he climbed up to the driver's seat and the old horse still grazing beyond. This horseless carriage was in no need of hoof or hair, reins, or harness for they floated upon a carriage made from trees rather like flying wood, only a different construction. Once climbed aboard and locked safely inside with Lil wearing the sheer tight-fitted golden silk and lace outfit presented by Horan and the fairies holding Lil's larger-than-average breasts and small waist, long legs as her long blond hair draped over her shoulder, and she pushed her back against the puffy blue silken material beneath her buttocks, James looked at her with love in his eyes as the carriage began to rise.

"Hang on, young ones, we're off!" Marcus shouted from the driver's seat. Sam was sticking his head out, and a flying fairy kissed him on the cheek, and he stuck his arms out, waving down to the crowd. Lil and James also waved and looked down as the coach got higher and higher, lifting toward the clouds. The crowd below were still waving as their figures got smaller and smaller until the foxes crawled into the forest. Horan evaporated, the fairies, elves, and dancing folk all dispersed with the animals into the forest until nothing is left below except a few villagers who walked slowly down the dirt road back to Paris. Soon when up in the clouds, James looked at Lil in her beautiful new outfit.

"I never knew how much I loved you," James said to Lil as he pecked her on the cheek then went back to his side of the carriage.

"My mind is set upon Marcus," Sam said, looking at the back of Marcus's leg through a slot in the carriage, his eyes filled with love for Marcus.

"I think he may fancy you as well," Lil said, smiling as the clouds came in with a cool wind.

"Paris, off to the left," Marcus shouted.

"I see the Sein, and I smell the city," Sam said, hanging his head out the window.

"Next stop, Kent," Marcus said.

"I have never been to England," James said, knowing Sam and Lil both went when they were six or seven with their father.

"Mon deu," Lil said, looking down. "It's very far down."

"Sans Blague, no kidding," James said as Lil removed his hand from her leg.

Soon the clouds covered their view, and after a while of floating among the white clouds and blue patches of sky that occasionally peaked through. A few high-flying birds flew alongside in odd curiosity.

"These gulls are flying high," James said as the gulls swooped down below them in playful circles.

"Calais," Marcus said like some leader of guided tours.

"Look, I think they see us," Sam said as a small group of bewildered people look up with hands over their eyes to block the sun.

"Wave," James said and they did.

"They are waving back," Lil said, still waving.

"I bet they will never forget seeing a floating carriage," Marcus shouted.

"I bet no one will ever believe them," James remarked, staring at Lil's breast as they bobbled in the sheer silken outfit that adores her every curvature of her body. Sam was still thinking of Leal and wondering if Marcus would be to his liking.

"I am looking forward to seeing my father," Sam said as they passed over the shore and out over the channel, the rough waves below, and fishing ships, and a foghorn let off from some distant port. More gulls passed by one after the other until they disappeared once more into the fog, then clouds, misty and dark.

Soon they lowered to the clear sky with clouds above and witnessed the oncoming white Dover cliffs.

"Dover!" Marcus yelled out. "I will swing by the castle," and they do barely miss its highest peak. Several men dressed in armor rushed along the battlement shouting and pointing in amazed wonder as they disappeared into another cloud and over forest, green, river, stream, fox, deer, faun and fowl. Until finally the set down in the garden of the cottage and a bit roughly, I might add, the carriage was falling apart as they landed into many pieces while Lil, Sam, James, and Marcus rolled on the grass and against bush and flower. "You call that a landing?" Sam said, laughing, the others still rolling.

"Well, it's not like I have ever driven a floating carriage before," Marcus said humorously, "but we made it, and that's all that counts."

Porius stepped out with Thomas behind him rushing to get out and greet the new students.

"Welcome Lil, James, and Sam," Porius said. "Welcome to the cottage."

Behind Porius stepped out Frolan. "My son safe at last."

"Father," Sam said, rushing toward his Frolan as they hugged.

"A feast is in order," Thomas said.

"Lil, James, and Sam," Porius said, "how was the trip?"

"We had a splendid time, and the coachman was marvelous," Sam said, still hugging his father.

"Thank ye, Sam," Marcus said as Thomas handed him a goblet of ale. "Nice to be back."

"A very successful trip," Thomas said. "Splendid clothing."

"Indeed, they were adjusted or fitted," Lil said, trying to keep English as the spoken word.

"And this silk is the world's finest," Thomas said.

"I have other clothes for you as well. You may wish to save these for special events, so dressy," Thomas said as he ran into the cottage and came out with new robes for all.

Marcus was standing with ale in hand and patting Porius on the shoulder. "Yes, it was a great success."

"My lord Porius, it is such an honor," Lil said.

"It is I that am honored for my dearest Lil. Your ancestors go back to the Venus of Brassempouy which goes back twenty-five thousand years ago and posed for the first statues on earth. Your face is not unlike that sculpture," Porius said as he studied her facial lines and mathematical balance which distinguishes beauty. "I shall teach you to use all the magic inside of you."

"I pledge to all of you, my dreams have come true," Lil said, bowing then resting on the outdoor table bench made of wood featuring carved animal. Lil thought she saw one small rabbit move but thought, "Maybe just a trick of the light."

Folks lost to the maundering evangelicals who swooped down on Lil's farm less than twenty-four hours ago.

"James," Porius said, patting him on the shoulder. "Your grandfather and I fished along the Sein, son of the Chantelperron family of France, good warrior and keeper of the old faith," Porius felt his muscles with both hands. You will be formidable."

"Mon englas nes pas si bon," James said, struggling with English.

"Not so good," She bowed to Porius and pledging his right hand over his heart in keeping the old ways sacred.

"C'est bon, it will do and I will teach you enough English," Porius said. "I see the way you look at Lil, is it a nuptial arrangement?"

"Not as yet, my lord," James replied in French, Lil coming to his side and grabbing James hand before Porius.

"But soon, Lord Porius and I hope ye shall perform the honors," Lil said, everyone looking on. Sam looked at Marcus trying hard in making sure Marcus did not catch his stare. For the insult to Marcus may go against his daily work and training with Marcus.

"Maybe someday when I know you better," Marcus said to Sam, winking. Sam's heart filled with hope and joy, and a large grin appeared upon his otherwise bewildered look after the event of the past twenty-four hours.

"We will have a grand day of if I assure you both, welcome."

"Has Parthenia made us a delightful feast, Porius?" Marcus asked, rubbing his stomach and licking his lips.

"A feast for a king," Thomas replied, running in to help with preparations for the greeting feast.

Deer, fox, pigeon, magpie, and squirrels ran, scampered, played, and grazed among them as the event came upon them. Mouths full, Porius kept on going on about past adventures. Even stories of Cadmus Upton not unsimilar to what Lil, James, and Sam had just been through. Lil was trying to keep from weeping with thought of her family's recent demise.

"We are your family now," Porius said while Frolan explained the last visit to England and the need for his return to France, his orchards being taken over by poachers, thieves, and villains.

"Protestants constantly fighting with Catholics and the rest of us caught in the middle, in fact most Parisians to whom I associate by drink, wine, and crops discussions are not particularly bothered by these religious fanatics," Frolan said, sipping his ale as the cottage filled up due to a quick heavy rain that began to pour over Kent.

"Agreed, in fact, Van de Venne's painting symbolizes the religious rivalry that is dividing Europe," Thomas said.

"I doubt all or you have seen this painting," Porius interjected. "People in boats cramming to stay alive are called catch, I believe."

"Lucky to have made it through," Lil said.

"Lil had a very close call. I was powerless to assist, if it wouldn't have been for Leal and Marcus, who knows!" James said as Sam joined them, his silks dripping wet.

"It's chucking down in buckets," Sam said as he remove his silken blue wrappings and asking Thomas for his robe, dresses, and Thomas began a tour of the cottage.

"Here is the water closet, which all of you may use. We have hot running water that flows in and out back into the fields," Thomas said, pointing at all the fixtures made for the flowing of water. "Here we have a hose for, well, you know and the waste here." He pointed to a stool connected by pipe. "The waste goes out into the crops and feeds the crops."

"Which is why our vegetables are more filled with goodness," Porius said standing at the back of the tour. Thomas was leading the three, Lil, Sam, and James through the rooms at the back of the water closet of which there are four.

"This is for the lady of the house, Lil," Thomas said, opening an oak door with carvings of monkeys and zebra. Inside the room was an African theme of jungle masks, wood carvings of animals, a few spears.

"Delightful, thank ye, Thomas," Lil said, walking around the room in total pleasure of her immaculately decorated African-themed bedchamber.

"Next James or Sam, maybe the blue room or the red one, you may choose amongst you."

"I shall take red," Sam said.

"Very well, I am blue," James said bother, peering into the rooms with satisfaction.

"Marcus is in the back room already set up, so we have a full house," Thomas said, pleased with his housekeeping and decorative skills in his meticulous preparations.

"Thomas, how did you know my interest in Africa?" Lil asked.

"My dear Lil, you know a good host always finds out about his guests and adding another layer of student. I took extra caution in learning about all of you long before meeting Frolan. You see, Porius has been watching you all off and on for quite some time."

"Oh, and not to spy, but just making sure that neither of you come too hard," Porius said, butting into the conversation.

"So that's how you know we were taken," Sam said, jumping into his bed to test the bounce. "Very nice," he said as he opened the wardrobe to reveal a few hanging clothes. "We have clothes."

"Oh yes, made by Marcus and some of the villagers, clothes for every occasion," Thomas said as Lil ran to her wardrobe and James checked out the blue room.

"I will leave you all to it. Please come to the main room around one hour and the feast will begin," Thomas said while Marcus was already chewing a large piece of game pie, washing it down with the finest ale.

Rain pouring down all around, beating down on the thatch, and even Franklin came in from the cold to perch in the nice dry windowsill of the cottage looking annoyed at his wetness.

"Hello, Franklin my friend," Marcus said. "Have some pie." He tossed a bit to Franklin who wasted no time in leaping at the opportunity and wolfing down the bit of pie, hopping round in circles until every morsel was taken down his feather neck. A small drip of rain in the blue bedchamber but nothing that worried James; he just placed a small wooden bucket, and Porius stuck his head into the blue room, "I meant to get that fixed,

James. Remind me to change the water occasionally. Sorry about that, James, my boy."

"It is truly no bother at all, Lord Porius, and thank you for everything," James said, taking off his wet clothes. "Which outfit should I wear?"

"I think the lederhosen and white silk shirt will be most fetching," Porius said, pointing out the lederhosen, which as he puts on makes him look like a true Swiss mountaineer.

"How's this?" James said, pleased with his fancy suspenders and short pantaloons, white silk shirt with lace around the wrists and puffy sleeves.

"Yes, most fetching indeed," Porius said and left James to enjoy his room. Then he poked his head into the red room.

"My dear Sam," Porius said, but when he opened the door to red room, Sam and Frolan were in discussion about the Catholics taking over Paris and what awaits them. Porius ejaculating into their conversation.

"It will be a long difficult time before the religious trials and wars shall end, but we are all in this together," Porius said.

"Merci Porius," Frolan said, his eyes teared up as he sat with Sam.

"I think the lederhosen may be good for you to wear this evening," Porius said, noticing Sam still in his robe.

"Right, lederhosen, that will cheer you up, Sam," Frolan said as he opened the wardrobe and handed the lederhosen to Sam.

"Thank you, Father, and thank you, Porius," Sam said as he ran over to Porius and hugged him tight. Then he ran back to dress.

"Together we shall survive and let's just hope we can salvage enough people to keep the old ways alive for the future." Porius closed the door and walked back through the water closet and bath area, past his chamber, Thomas's down the great hall, then arriving at the main room seeing Thomas and Marcus laughing as Franklin picked up another piece of pie.

"Don't feed him too much, Marcus, he won't be able to fly," Porius said jokingly as he entered the room. They all laughed as Parthenia brought out more grub.

"Plans, plans, plans, we have to make plans for all these upcoming events," Porius said, considering.

"Have you heard of the Chickasaw Nation in Louisiana?" Marcus asked.

"Yes, Sieur de Bienville, starting something called Alabama, I believe," Porius said.

"Indeed, there are many concerns and all quite long distances from Kent," Thomas said.

"Most of the settlers they command have already lost their will in humanity and joined the church. It will be difficult to regain their faith in nature," Porius said, his brow bent with concern.

"Marcus, uphill battles in the colonies is what it appears to me," Marcus said, reading the pages of news Porius handed him earlier.

"Yes, small groups in Europe are our best hope of success," Porius said. "As for the colonies, leaving to their own devices is the only way."

A long pause. "Religion has proven itself harmful to all, hundreds of Old World civilizations from the Mayans, druids, Aztec, African nations and tribes, American Indian, and countless others will fall. Torture and death will follow in their wake, as both James, Lil, and Sam have been witness to. Kasim's of thought will provoke them and their will is bent on one god, and this is where all the trouble will occur for without the knowledge and concern of yearning for scientific way, the race will become its own worst enemy. Overpopulating, poisoning earth's rivers and streams will materials soon to be made from industrial waste and a newer invention called plastic is coming. The old ways will try to prevent it."

Porius took a deep breath as he noticed around him several dwarves, elves, fairies, and other peculiar animals appear in flesh around them as the cottage filled with creatures. "These poor creatures are now hunted and slain until none shall remain in the eyes of man. Tyrants will rule nations with no care of thought for their future. Greed and avarice will prevail over the churchgoing dominions, and they shall believe they are right. Lil, James, Sam, and others shall promote and protect the old ways in hopes that someday in the far future, man will again see reason, but it is for us to attempt and guide them."

"This is a very tall order, Monsieur Porius," Sam interjected.

"You know it will be many centuries before the colonists begin to doubt the realism of their faiths?" Marcus said.

"Yes, and until then, we must keep parts of Europe free, our focus must be Rome, Paris, and London, Berlin, Geneva, and any other old ways houses. This will be our task with Lil, James, and Sam," Porius said as Grendle handed him a warm cup of mead.

"Pollution is another main concern where on this path no restrain will be made to keep birth control to stop the vast population. My thought of instead of draining the sea of all its minerals, give their body to the seas, rivers, oceans, and lakes. Minerals which each of us hold may replenish the waters, plants, corals, and species within them, which is where we and other species began, telling us from twenty-five thousand years ago that our care should be for the waters of the world, hence once our lives have spent each body, they may be placed into the waters within an hour or a day to replenish the earth and give a path to Elysium. The vast numbers will save the earth, but how to get a scientific point like this across to the blinded thoughts of man? That is the question among many others which we will have to endure. It will be long and difficult, and those of us who remain form and flesh will witness it all before us—battles, bloodshed, stupidity, pride in belief, scorn for the nonbelievers, homosexuals, freethinking and scientific minds will have long and arduous tasks. To have the constant thought of improvement and honesty when it comes to being a part of the earth is our main ally.

"We three have seen the darkness of men and religion," Lil said. "I pledge my allegiance to defend the old ways, here I become your student, Porius."

"I shall defend the trees and forests, rivers, and oceans," said James.

"je vous promouvoue l'honnetete, honesty," Sam concluded.

"Yes, oui, Sam. Honesty is the answer, but changing minds from what they are told or read will be difficult once they have been fed stories from their biblical text."

"Mead, my lord," Grendle said, wiping her hands on her apron.

"Thank ye, Grendle," a gracious Porius said, delighted with fresh mead.

"We will train the three on geography, mathematics, potions, herbs, animal care, and care for the villagers," Thomas said.

"I believe you do have a good method of gaining trust from villagers by treating and curing diseases they may come upon," Marcus said, pleased at Porius and Thomas's treatment of villagers. "Surely men will see the difference between actual remedies and cures to what I have read about called prayer, which truly has no actual cause or effect."

Laughing and joking, the creatures and animals faded into the night.

"We have a lot to teach you about earth and pious ways," Thomas said, pouring more mead for Marcus.

"They are one of our strongest allies. In fact, as soon as the medical profession gets up to snuff with remedies and care. I hope that most people will see it's all about facts and science and not an imaginary godlike being in the sky that will cure them of ills," Porius said. "But mortals are so impressionable and gullible."

"I never thought I would see the cottage," Sam said, bursting in with Lil, James, and Frolan.

"Yes," Lil, interrupting, said. "The long-imagined first meal at the famous cottage."

"Cooked by the world-famous cook Parthenia," Parthenia said, bursting in from the kitchen with a tray of hors d'oeuvres appetizers and bits of meat on sticks.

"That looks amazing," Marcus said as they all crammed around the large table carved with every known animal. James and Sam dressed in lederhosen; Porius in his best white robe; Frolan in purple silks; Lil in a white silk gown; Thomas in his fashionable pantaloon and waistcoat splendor of green, purple, and gold; Marcus in his leather pants and leather straps and suspenders, white silk sheer shirt and sitting right next to Sam and pressing his hand tightly on Sam's thigh, giving it a rough squeeze. "Wait till you taste Parthenia's cooking."

Outside, the rain beat down even harder, and even the deer decided to call it a night, making their beds, the owls swooping down on the occasional mouse, crows pulling up exposed worms, petals closing and falling, cracks of lightning and roaring thunder turning to night. Below the crust of the earth, the bios weaved between the layers of earth, avoiding the flowing and tunneling water from above, down deeper to the gleaming pools of the underworld. All here to rest and sleep, dreaming of adventures yet to come and the meaning of everything stays, steadying as we are all caught in the balance. The balance of nature both here and beyond from all the points of the six green planets, preserved, enhanced, loved, and nurtured for together they must all become one, one knowledgeable way of thinking that will always preserve life and never place a species to the edge of extinction.

CHAPTER 27

The Cottage Garden

Time seemed almost irrelevant one fine April morning in the garden, which surrounded the cottage, its flowers, vegetables, ivies, shrubberies, worms, mice, squirrels, deer, rabbits, chickens, turkeys, and other passersby grazes and played. Porius and Thomas were teaching Lil, James, and Sam all they could fit into each day's training. Today was like any other—farming chores in the morning, spells, magic, potions, and herbology in the afternoon and cooking in the evening. Today's particular spell consisted of something derived from magical tradition in its hope of turning someone invisible through the use of fern seeds, scraping the fern cells and seeds from the leaves, which in the modern uses St. John's day, but Porius taught them the old way, which also uses a cat's-eye gemstone, which Thomas hands to Lil.

"Now, say the incantation and make a wish of invisibility," Porius said to Lil as she held a cat's-eye stone in one hand and fern seeds in the other.

"Change thy form to clarity," Lil said with Sam and James standing back and looking on.

"You see," Porius said to Lil and pointing to her hand, which becomes clear, the skin evaporates then all bone and vein until gone.

"Only the stone remains," Lil said, amazed and looking down at the floating stone held by her invisible hand.

"My starts," James said.

"Brilliant in the extreme," said Sam.

"But what of the rest of me?" Lil said to Porius.

"Once you mast this portion, you will begin to realize the rest, but it will take practice," Porius said.

Lil held the stone tighter and dropped all the fern seeds in over her head, clasping tight to the stone in the other hand. "Take all of thee."

"No," Porius said, "you are not ready."

"Thomas, where has she gone," James said looking at the floating stone which began to move on its own and only Lil's clothes remain as her flesh and bone disappear from their sight.

"My dearest girl, it worked," Porius said, grinning and clapping his hands together. "Resum Appario." Porius flicked his wand at the empty gown that floated mysteriously before them as Lil reappeared cell by cell and hair by hair until once again filling her skirt, sandals, blouse, and as the veins filled quickly with blood, the running rivers gliding in slow motion over from elbow to hand, fingertip and thigh to toe, skin spreading and covering and then from neck to chin and cheek to brow. The process continued until Lil is reformed before them, only her hair was solid white.

"Lil, your hair is white," Sam said, pointing and laughing.

"Well, yes, that can sometimes happen," said Porius as he placed his wand back into his robes, set upon that built in pocket or holster, which has been home to the wand for several centuries though held or holstered in many different types of fabric.

"White as the clouds," Lil said, handing the stone to Thomas and holding her long once beautifully colored curls and grinning.

"It will grow back in time," Thomas said. "It happened to me the first time I tried that spell."

"I actually kind of like it," James said.

"I also like it, James," Sam said.

"Well, as long as it grows back," Lil said as she noticed the edge of the forest bushes moving.

"We have a visitor," Thomas said as they all turned toward the woods and outcome, Leal and Marcus dressed in full battle leathers, huffing and puffing.

"Soldiers, Porius, soldiers are close," Leal said as they run up, stepping over the rows of carrots and onions along the edges of the garden.

"Soldiers, aye," Porius said, pointing his wand toward the cottage, the doors widening and pensive coming from inside flying magically through the air.

"Reveal these soldiers," Porius said and the pensive revealed a battle over Bourbon-Habsburg in central Europe. "No Bourbon-Hapsburg is too far away. Reveal something closer," Porius said, but nothing appeared.

"Will they come here?" Sam said as he tightened his belt with sword.

"Not unless a soldier is pure of heart and mind, they may be able to see us," Porius said, hearing the hooves of horse and chatter of men.

"Quiet, everyone," Porius said, whispering. "Leal and Marcus, get some rest, have a meal, and tomorrow we will send you to follow them. I believe Rouen is in trouble. For according to my sources within the pensive, Rouen is home to a silver-tongue wizard named—"

"Phillip Jasper!" Leal answered with a smirk on his face as he removed his battle leathers, standing naked before them and walking into the water rooms at the back of the cottage.

"Yes, indeed, Leal. Phillip Jasper is correct."

"The last time Phillip created a problem was when he was practicing a toad spell and turned half the village into pink-spotted toads," Leal shouted from the back as he soaped down, washed his hair, and soon to be joined by Marcus also naked before them and rushing back to the water room. Lil blushed and took the clothes for washing.

"Yes, and remember how difficult it was turning the villagers back from toads?" Porius shouted back toward the room. A few moments later, Leal comes back dripping wet and drying his hair with hand towel, his muscular body dripping to dry on its own in front of the roaring fire.

"Nice to see you, Leal," James said, handing the naked Leal a large goblet of ale.

"My good James, thank yee," Leal said. He replied to Porius, "The tough part was not changing the villagers back from toads but catching them."

"Yes, I dare say, several were never found. Oh well, we can only hope they are enjoying their lives as toads."

"Phillip Jasper, that silly old fool, what is he up to now?" Thomas said. "Still living at Saint Maclou?"

"Yes, I believe a group of soldiers are heading there to most likely clean up some mess, created by Philip Jasper," Porius said, opening the front door and shouting for Franklin.

"Time for a journey by good raven," Thomas said, walking out as Franklin landed on his shoulder, picking seeds from Thomas's hand.

Once Marcus and Leal came out of the washroom and drank down a large goblet of ale, Lil, James, and Sam all walked with Marcus and Leal, still nude as the day they were born.

"No need to dress," Porius said out in the front garden. "Take a feather and stand in this circle," Porius said to the two men as he drew a circle in the dirt, pointing. Parthenia poked her head from the kitchen window, watching the white buttocks of Leal and Marcus as they were handed feathers and stepped into the circle.

"Take these feathers to thy skin and thy message from within, once at thy destination reveal again thy skin," Porius said to Leal, tapping him on the shoulder with his wand feather in hand.

"Very well," Porius said as he repeated the spell on Marcus as his naked body gleamed in the sunlight, fist clutching the feather.

"What will occur, Porius?" Leal asked patiently, legs still wet from his bathing.

But as soon as Leal spoke, feathers started to appear from his head, lips, eyelids, arms, torso, and slowly covering his entirety.

"Leal, you look like you're turning into a black bird," Lil said, giggling at the now-covered bodies of feathery men.

"Hmm, I hope this works," Porius said, Thomas shaking his head in disagreement.

"Porius, it's not like you to use an unpracticed spell," James shouted. Then Leal and Markus and all that was heard is a bit of bird squawking as their lips became beaks.

"Size of a raven," Porius said, quickly waving his wand fiercely at the two feathered men. "Sorry, I must have left out that part." Leal and Markus squawked rapidly as their bodies shrank down to the two largest and most muscular ravens ever seen.

"James, Lil, and Sam," Porius said, pointing at the two ravens now hopping about, hop up on the outdoor picnic table made of carefully carved wood. "Leal and Marcus are rather large-looking ravens, but they just have to fly top Rouen; once they land, they will find Jasper and protect him and his followers from the coming army."

"Squawking the pair of them, do they understand you?" Thomas said in disbelief even though he witnessed two men turn into ravens, but the ravens turned to Thomas, bowing their heads in agreement. "It appears they do."

"Le Vieux no. 3, once you land, Jasper will let you in, I promise," Porius said as the two ravens flew toward the channel, over the waves, boats, and Calais, then onward over forest, farm, field, and vineyard until circling over Rouen, they see the Le Vieux and land at the window of three. Outside the door was a plaque of wood carved PHILLIP JASPER in large print—Apothecary, Fortune Teller and Potions Master, in smaller print.

Pecking on the doors and windows repeatedly yet no one seems to answer, so the two ravens sit atop the roof waiting for Phillip Jasper's return. Couples walk by looking at the unusually large ravens and pointing them out to other passersby, children walk up close to the grey stonned three bedroom townhouse at the peculiar ravens sitting on top.

"Regaud grande Coupue!" (Look at those large ravens!), one child said.

"Now you kids go and play and leave those ravens alone," Phillip said as he arrived, seemingly from nowhere and wearing a silver and green cloak, red britches, and fancy pointed leather shoes.

Phillip opened the door and, looking quickly left then right, shouted up to the ravens, "Oh, come in and bonjour!" The ravens made a leap from the roof, a large swoop in the front door as Phillip Jasper slammed the door behind them, locking with a large bolted lock from the inside.

"Well, well, well, ye must be from Porius! My word," Jasper said, stepping back as two large and well-built muscular men stood naked both in a book of feathers.

"I'm Leal and this is Marcus. A pleasure to meet you, Phillip," Leal said, covering his private part and wiping off feathers with his other hand.

"Jimmy, come and clean up these feathers. Just leave a couple for their return," Phillip Jasper said. "Well, a fine couple of gents, what brings you here in such a peculiar and unexpected way?"

"We've heard that you may be in sone trouble and we—" Marcus said, interrupted by Jasper.

"I see word travels fast, oh my dear men," Jasper said, putting down a bag filled with cheeses, meat pies, and wine. Looking at the bag, he asked, "A meal first?"

"Indeed," said Leal sitting at the table and no longer covering his private parts. Both Marcus and Leal sat at the large table while Jimmy, a long blond-haired and thin as grassweed boy, swept up the feathers, one eye on the unusual naked intruders.

"Cloth of wind, cloth of wheat and wheel, dress thy bodies," Jasper said, nonchalantly pointing a wand at Leal and Marcus. Threads seemed to appear out of nowhere and line by line wrapped the men and moving both from their seated positions to float in the air sideways as the material wrapped every curve and muscle, Jimmy standing back and clapping his hands with laughter as he watched the forms become dresses and once again sit at the table.

"Wine?" Jasper said, pouring two large goblets of wine for Marcus and Leal. "How about we get Porius on the pensive?"

Jasper brought out a large pensive, and Porius already presented his reflection clear as day within.

"Jasper, I see you've met Leal and Marcus," Porius shouted out, echoing around the townhouse.

"Yes, my dear Porius, news travels quickly," Jasper said.

"We are thankful to be of assistance," Marcus said.

"Yes, yes, and thank you all, but how did you hear?"

"It appears your secret is not very well kept, you must have a trader in your midst because even the pope knows," Porius shouted back through the pensive, the words echoing around the room, objects bouncing on the shelves.

"The pope, oh dear, oh dear. Well, it's rather embarrassing, Porius, Marcus, and Leal. You see, it's like this. Last week, I was at the forest playing with a couple of deer, and it began to rain. Innocently, I tried to open the underworld only for a brief moment to shelter from the storm, and alas, I was . . . well—"

"You accidentally let something out, my dear Phillip Jasper? Leal and Marcus are there to help you put it back," Porius replied.

"And what is this creature, may I ask?" Leal said, gulping his wine.

"It's a large, well, troll-like creature," Jasper said. "Unfortunately, I am unable to find it."

"We'll find it and send it home," Marcus said.

"The pope has sent soldiers to take you in, Jasper. You must go to the country and hide your home," Porius said.

"Thank you kindly, Porius," Jasper said. "Jimmy, pack our bags, we are going on a little trip."

"Wishing you well, and please be careful with the magic love to Jimmy," Porius said, disappearing from the pensive.

"Joy has come to Rouen. Thank you, Leal, and thank you, Marcus," Jasper said, rushing to put things in a bag and headed out the door, knowing if the pope's men found him, they would torture him or, worse, burn him if magic was present. A large growl was heard from outside and screaming people, men shouting, crashes, more shouting.

"I think we found your beast," Leal said, jumping to his feet, rushing to the front door and stepping out into the street.

"Marcus, quick, let's grab this beast," Leal said, running out in front of the beast with a crowd of people running further on then stopping to watch Leal take on a ten-foot-high horned beast with scales like a dragon, red eyes, and large grabbing hands, but somehow awkward.

"Heal, you beast!" Leal yells and putting his hands up toward the beast. The beast stopped and, with a blank expression, wondered what this mortal will do to stop him and swung at Leal's head with his large fist. Leal ducked and kicked the beast in the stomach so hard that it doubled over.

"I don't think it knows what *heal* means, Leal," Marcus said as he leaped onto the back of the beast and hugged his neck.

"Get out of here, Jasper and Jimmy," Leal shouted, arms up facing the beast in the middle of the cobblestone street while Jasper and Jimmy, bags packed, ran out and quickly exited the scene. Behind the spectacle came a few soldiers who just stood and stared in disbelief. Marcus was on top of the neck, squeezing tighter and tighter, but the beast just get more angered and smashed two windows across the street as screams were heard from within.

"Stay inside," Leal said.

One young well-turned-out woman in the street pointing to Leal and whispering to her friend also turned-out and blushing, "Who is that beautiful man?"

"The beast is enraged and desperately attempting to reach back at Marcus who was still strangling his neck in an attempt to calm the beast."

"Heal!" Leal shouted once more at the top of his lungs, and the beast stood still and stiffened, slowed, and dropped his pace.

A large blank expression filled the creature's face and, seemingly hypnotized by Leal's stare, was motionless, and Marcus climbed down; now the beast appeared calm and in control by Leal's command.

"Follow me to the forest," Leal said, and the beast followed Leal and Marcus. They ran toward the forest, running block after block through the village of Rouen, cobblers, bakers, restaurant owners and laundry women, flower sellers, ironmongers, fishmongers, all watching and cheering as the beast ran after Leal and Marcus toward the forest. Finally, at the edge of the forest, Leal said his spell.

"Reveal thy gate to the underworld," Leal said clearly as the earth before him opened slowly before them, Marcus out of breath as his once-bound clothes set by Jasper's magic fell apart and left him standing naked. The floor opening full of dust and revealing a large hole, cave-like and primitive as the beast, hesitantly growled and slowly stepped into the cave as Leal waved his hands, his clothes also falling to the ground and disappearing into a pile of strings, buttons, and bows. Naked stood Leal and Marcus with feathers clutching in their fists.

"Take us home," Marcus said, and the feathers began to appear from head to toe and back to front as their once-muscular human forms became ravens once more. After closing the gaping hole that swallowed up the beast, they leaped, soring higher and higher until they fly over Rouen, crowds of people in conversations out in the streets, most likely discussing the previous unbelievable event. Flying over the forest and then the channel and more forest until they once again, hours later land back at the cottage, landing in the circles where once they had departed, feathers falling to the ground. Lil, James, and Sam ran out into the midnight sky, applauding as Porius stepped out. "Welcome back."

Beads of sweat and fountains of joy penetrated the surroundings, caterpillars crawling with beautiful colors adorning the leaded windows and the honeysuckle, ivies, and weeds.

"Thank you, Porius," Marcus said.

"Quite an adventure."

"Indeed," said.

"By tomorrow when the pope's men arrive in Rouen, there will be nothing to find and no Jasper either," James said, most pleased.

Sorcery blends with nature like the seed that grows into a living being or jewel that forms into star, caterpillar to butterfly, and the man-of-war, which is made up of many creatures whether above or below the sea. Religions may pressure these perpetuals changing natural beings, creatures, and forms of life, which never shall we explain fully unless we search, dream, study, practice, and participate in the changing ideas every day. Pollutants may come, but thy must be fraught with concern for the ever-nagging pollutants can be stopped, rematerialized, and made to blend with the earth and the control of every green, blue, and multicolored thing on the earth.

"Well done indeed," said Sam. They all walked indoors as Franklin slept quietly on the thatch of the cottage, only frogs, crickets, and the occasional to-wit to-woo from a pair of owls piercing the midnight sky.

"Tale of glory and friends from beyond," Porius said, waving his bejeweled wand over the garden under the moonlight, faun scurrying by quickly knowing when Porius was in the mood, something may all of a sudden pour from his wand and upset her delicate nature.

"Agriculture not only gives riches to a garden, but also the only riches we may call our own," Sam said from the doorway of the cottage wearing silks of blue and bouncing down from the porch next to Porius.

"Reveal," Porius said as a form began to come to life from his wand, first humanlike and then birdlike.

"Like Jethro Tull's seed drill make over the garden," Sam said while a small puff and the form disappeared over the garden.

"That shall protect thee," Porius said as he fell to the ground laughing, the smoke wisping out from his wand, rolling and sprinkling some ash-like substance over the garden.

"Fertilizer?" Sam asked.

"Indeed it is, Sam, and watch now a little rain," Porius said, Sam assisting him to his feet.

Rain fell over the garden as skunk, squirrel, fox, wood pigeon, bat, and turtle decorate the gardens amusingly.

Quick as lightning, the water goblins slushed their slippery nude bodies, sliming Sam as they passed, but too quick for Sam to touch. Porius and Sam watched the two water goblins deliver their cache of nightly fish, mushrooms, carrots, and two dead rabbits in a pile by the front door of the cottage.

"Oh yuck, I have been greased," Sam said, the others sticking their heads out laughing. Porius went in to get out of the rain.

"One of them likes you Sam," Lil said, giggling.

"I know, he is always sliming me, that Harold," Sam said, watching the water goblins run quickly back to the river, the sounds of their splashing heard in the distance. The rain got harder, the animals took shelter, and all was right in Kent this night.

The villages, still plagued by religious victimization, soldiers, factions whether Royalist, purists, pagan, Christian, or otherworldly, Buddhist, bickered and warred across the substantial miles that drew them apart; but they were getting closer together. Catholics, Church of England, being mixed in with old world ways as they sprout new recruits, capture hearts and minds, and bend to their will. Yes, Porius, LeL, Athena, and now Sam, Marcus, Lil, and James would soldier on to help the meek, those who suffer, or those with personalized persuasions of wealthy and of poor and those acquaintances and the leading lights of each previous century are bound to continue for freedom for all lies ahead.

These years of shadows as war approached for many either at sea, across England, France, America, Italy, China, Africa, and India. Shadows were growing longer, and a cataclysm that will test the mettle of all who were born or brought into the coming era. For in 1799, even Napoleon marched his armies through St. Bernard Pass in the Alps in midwinter to surprise the Austrians, who were besieging Genoa.

"Mind those windy branches, Mullin, and be quiet," said Barry, a small green-skinned elf who sat hiding in the bushes with Mullin.

"So that's Napoleon at the front. See him there?" Mullin exclaimed.

"Shh, they will hear you, you fool," Barry said as the marching soldiers went past on their way through St. Bernard Pass.

"Exciting, isn't it?" Mullin said.

"Shh," said Barry as he noticed a small young soldier whose uniform was far too large, his sword occasionally dragging along the dusty road, turning to walk toward the elves' hiding place. Quietly they lingered.

"Fernand, Reviet en Ligne" (Come back here), a large booming official voice shouted, and the inquisitive soldier only inches from the elves turned and went back to the line as the soldiers went on up the pass.

"We must report this to Porius," Mullin said as the two elves waited for cover of night then borrowing some wood from a generous pine tree, turned them into comfortable seats and flying back to Paris, the channel, and finally after a night in an elf-friendly tavern called the Hawk in Hastings, made their journey through the woods until Franklin spotted them on route and sent Marcus to greet them. This meeting in the woods found Marcus shaking hands with Barry and Mullin, two elves with green skin, wearing Scottish kilts and red with black checkered shirt, hats, and black buckled shoes made in a peculiar form to fit the large elvish feet; many times an elf's foot can be much larger than human even though elves are usually about three to four and a half feet in height. Marcus led them to meet Porius, listened to the miniature band's playing, feasted, rested, and enjoyed a few bottles of wine from Porius and Thomas's large wine cellar. These particular bottles were brewed over twenty years ago in Burgundy.

"Excellent wine, Porius," Mullin said. "But we mustn't keep you, just thought you should know."

"Yes, thank you, Barry and Mullin, for I fear we have not heard the last of the Napoleon, much more to come for I am sure of it."

Thomas found them comic and touching as if a division between worlds existed on earth with elves, trolls, underworld folks, fairies, water goblins, all separate from the basic human form, which spread across Germany, Italy, France, Japan, China, Russia, and America hiding everywhere.

Thomas led them out to make way for their safe haven in the elven woods of Kent.

Then opening an elegant green and light-speckled entrances into the forest surrounding the cottage and even when illuminated by night, a breathtaking explosion occurred as deer jumped, owls awakened, bats even flying from the sparks, there was no vast ball of light, just a quick burst and out. Molly the elf from Wales dropped her bags on the road as she poked her head here and there, frogs leaping from her feet, as a fox watched her searching.

"Someone's approaching," Porius said, walking through the garden toward the rustling bramble and verge so awkwardly moved about by Molly.

But at last Porius appeared to her, wearing his white-laced robes, adorned with jewels and a white lace hat that lay floppy on his head as his long white beard and silver braids were draped over his shoulder.

"Well, enchanted," Porius said, looking down on the elf, who wore old rags, a multicolored hat, and plain brown or earth-colored cloak, cane in hand and small bulging bag.

"Porius?" Moly said, her eyes filled with hope.

"Yes, Porius, and you seem to have the advantage of me, my dear," Porius said as he waved his wand and the trees and bramble released her to step softly into the garden.

"Porius, at last, I have come from America. my name is Molly." She wilted a bit.

"America, and in these desperate times," Porius said, face full of concern. "Let me take your bag."

"Thank ye," Molly said, handing the heavy bag to Porius as she waddled into the garden. Several elves appeared from the verge.

"You may have some relatives amongst us," Porius said as several elves appeared wearing much nicer clothes, jewels, silken lace, and golden chains that draped around each of the three.

"Other elven folk, my word."

"I am Molly from Virginia."

"So pleased to meet you, I am Samantha," one female elf said as she walked close to Molly and hugged her. "Porius, allow me to take Molly for a few moments and we will meet you later. I am sure you would like to freshen up, Molly," Samantha said very matter-of-factly, and with a snap of the fingers, they disappeared. Porius looked down at the bag in his hand, then within a flash, the bag also disappeared, leaving Porius only holding his wand and smiling, walking happily through the garden back to the cottage. There was deer playing and one rubbing its cheek against Porius as she passed, owls regained their sleeping haze, foxes went back to their scuttling about, and even toads were heard gulping their bubbling sounds.

"My word, but you have traveled far. Tea?" Thomas said as Molly nodded with pleasure.

"Thomas, your hospitality is always excellent, I imagine," Molly said as she seemed to change from a dark shade of green to add just a tint of red.

"Your skin seems a bit well," Thomas said over filling the cup as he witnessed her changing skin.

"Molly, you are quite the rainbow," Porius said.

"My colors change when I am comfortable," Molly said. "Sorry, it seems to be involuntary as I cannot control the change, but it will stop soon."

Parthenia came out from the kitchen gawking at Molly's changing colors. "I have heard of this occurrence but never seen it in person."

"And you are?" Molly said, smiling, her face changing from light green to purple, purple to orange, blue, pink, then settling finally on a light shade of green.

"Parthenia, my dear, I'm the cook. And I have some lovely game pie for thee," Parthenia said, shaking her head, and headed back into the kitchen with an obvious touch of the giggles.

"A bit like the aurora borealis," Porius said.

"And most probably just as rare to see," Thomas said, sitting and offering a scone to Molly.

"So glad I came to see you all," Molly said, gulping some wine and telling them the tales of her past. After a long, yet humorous tales of adventures, they all got a night's rest. After breakfast, the morning chores were started, and it's each to their own—gardening, chopping wood, and other tasks from Lil, James, Sam, Phillip Jasper even entering the garden as Franklin circled overhead. Molly showed a few spells she used to hide herself on board the ship as she crossed the Atlantic, went through crowded places.

"Now this spell will not make you invisible but will enhance the air around you so others do not see you. Well, it works on nonmagic folk.

"A pinch of salt, a few daisies, and a bottle wine or vinegar, then take a few bits of rosemary. Put the potion in a small leather satchel and let a few drops drip out every time you feel noticed. Oddly enough, the potion worked and kept folks form having any interest in your business. Just as if you are invisible," Molly said as Porius, Phillip, Lil, James, and Marcus listened and took notes.

"Good one, Molly," Thomas said. "If ever I need not to be seen, that is."

"My dear Molly, what road do you seek next?" Porius inquired.

"I'll be heading to Canterbury where I am meeting up with a couple of other cousins but wanted to make sure I visited the famous cottage."

"We are most pleased that you passed our way," Thomas said as the others went back to their chores. Lil and James headed for the water as they walked arm in arm along the river. Sam was picking fruit and then reading a large book given to him previously by Porius to study as he soon will become another brilliant wizard and protector of wildlife, old ways, and cottage garden.

"I will never understand the compulsory oath of loyalty Christians have to hunt down such a beautiful being as you Molly," Porius said, kissing her hand. Molly blushed blue and pink and blinked her long black eyelashes.

"The beauty in your eyelashes alone is enough to bewilder the simplest of man." Molly stared at Porius seriously as he waved his wand overhead and displayed a mood of deep concern, saying, "Molly, oh Molly, content to England and ye shall be protected," Porius said, handing her a goblet of wine.

"This wine shall give thee all the magic thy need to make well in England."

"Thank you of great Porius, my deed here is done, and I hand you the Matrious Stone," Molly said, holding out a stone that looks of basic sandstone. "From deep in the woods of Virginia, a magic stone."

Molly handed gently to Porius. As soon as Porius held the stone in his palm, it disappeared.

"It is seen and then gone, I have heard of such a stone," Porius said, setting the stone upon the table and, faltering not, ran to open the large multileathered Malifactorum book of spells. "You see," Porius said, shouting to the others.

"The Western stone shall come when called and then go, giving a call or pathway to the sixth green planet."

Porius calmly set down the book, walking back to the table where nothing was but wood.

"Come to thee," Porius said, and the stone appeared, some slight dust falling from its sandy and frail sides.

"Thank ye," Porius said and bowed to the stone as it once again disappeared.

"Quick, the dust," Porius said to Thomas who quickly sweeps the dust into Porius's hand.

"Pensive, come," Porius said as the pensive flew from its resting place among the books. Filling with water or a liquid substance resembling a milky water like song Swiss rivers and streams.

"Show thy message," Porius said as he sprinkled the dust into the pensive.

"Ah, an Indian tribe," Porius said as he held up his hand and shouted, "Come all!"

The pensive turned a shade of blue and purple, and within was wet remaining swirls the pooling waters, filled with images of trees, fences, farms, villages, and other worldly planets, out popped Athena, Walters, Simon, Leal, Marcus, Sam, Lil, and James, all pack into the cottage to watch the pensive and its swirling images until all present and wardrobes of the most wide a range of unprepared clothing.

"Reveal," Porius said.

Within the pensive were images of Indian villages, one by one being attacked by the colonies' Christian peoples, some so strong in their belief that they left England to persecute other nations, especially since the English were no so easily fooled. And destroy the Indian villages they did.

Porius turned to all and said, "A call to arms."

A brown and spotted duck waddled, by heading to the pond on the far side of the cottage eastern gardens trailing seven small ducklings, the females quacking as they trolled in search of seeds, worms, and other tasty morsels in their playful way. The hen duck looks back to the following ducklings, "Quack," which most likely means, "Stay in line."

Pigeons, sparrow, fox, squirrel, deer, goats, and other creatures went about their way in harmony, peace, and the safety surrounding the cottage.

The End
